# High Child

## Book Two in Red-Line: The Fletcher Family Saga
## J. T. Bishop

Eudoran Press LLC

**J. T. Bishop**

**P.O. Box 117021**

**Carrollton, TX  75011-7021**

**www.jtbishopauthor.com**

Updated Cover by J.T. Bishop

Author Photos by Mayza Clark Photography

Book Editing by Amie McCracken

**High Child/ J. T. Bishop**. -- 1st ed.

ISBN 978-0-692-91619-3

To my dad. You made me laugh, you made me cry, you showed me strength and you showed me weakness. Through all of life's twists and turns, you persevered. I learned so much from you. You were the very best, and you are missed.

# Other Books by J. T. Bishop

# Chapter One

ROYCE FLETCHER SAT CROSS-LEGGED, eyes closed, and unmoving on the hard ground. His hands rested on his knees, and his chest rose and fell with each deep, methodical breath. His mind silent, he listened intently to the sounds of the forest, letting each one lull him deeper into a trance-like state. Although he'd reached a point of deep meditation, his mind was alert, and he was aware of his surroundings.

The woods were quiet, save for the melodic whistle of a passing bird and the gentle whisper of the wind through the thick canopy of trees. Reaching out with his senses, he sought the animal he knew was near. Motionless, he reflected on his months of practice. His father had shown him this skill during his last visit three years earlier. Believing that his son would be as capable as he, he'd asked Royce to continue the exercise. And now, after many long months, weeks, days, and hours of focus and discipline, Royce prepared for the ultimate test. He didn't stop to think about the repercussions of failure. Thoughts like that would only hamper him and erode his ability to succeed.

Soft footfalls in the brush alerted him, but he kept still. He tuned in to the noise and listened as the movement through the brush grew louder. And then he heard the low chuff of the animal he waited for—the bear.

He'd surveyed these woods many times, and this animal visited this section of the forest frequently. Royce lived about two miles away, and he'd seen the brown bear more than once on his property. Soon after, he'd begun to track him. Although he didn't have his sister Eve's ability to speak with all manner of four-legged creatures, he still felt strangely connected to the beast. It was as if all the hours spent looking and studying him had somehow made the bear aware of him, too, and that he was just as curious about Royce as Royce was of him.

The footfalls grew closer. Royce maintained his relaxed stance and kept his eyes closed. Although his mind was acutely aware of the environment around him, he did not allow any unexpected disturbances to distract him. In order to succeed, he would need complete focus. His attention could not wander, or the bear would see him.

Seconds passed and Royce waited. The shuffling continued, as if the bear sensed a presence but could not determine its location. Then Royce heard shallow, heavy breaths. The bear was within feet of him, likely smelling the air to detect the unknown intruder's presence. Royce barely breathed, but reaching out with his mind, he dropped a barrier and cloaked himself further, intent on remaining completely invisible. It was too late to run now. There would be nowhere to go.

Royce remained completely still. Seconds passed. For a moment, there was no noise, but the air was thick. It felt as if the bear was somehow testing him, daring him to remain cloaked. Royce imagined the large beast. Black eyes, coarse fur, mighty paws, powerful haunches, and sharp claws emerged in his mind's eye. He pictured the bear listening, head cocked. Smelling a musty scent, Royce held his breath when heavy puffs of air brushed against his cheek.

The bear bellowed, and Royce almost broke. Another grunt and the exhalation tickled his nose. Then the air lightened briefly, before a heavy thump shook the ground and the atmosphere grew heavy again. Royce sensed that the animal, feeling Royce's presence, had raised up on his hind legs and sniffed, looking for what watched him—and then dropped back to all fours with a thud. He'd seen the bear do it before but from a safe distance.

This was the most dangerous part of the exercise. At any moment, the bear could walk right into him, exposing Royce and risking an attack. Feeling the animal loom closer, the only thing he could do was wait and pray the bear lost interest and returned to the forest.

# Chapter Two

SHERIFF RICK HENDERSON STOPPED his car at the side of the road. He took in the scene, flipped on his lights, and exited the vehicle. The second sheriff's car was parked up ahead and the fire truck and ambulance took up the small parking lot that sat at the foot of the trail leading to the Shady Point Park and campgrounds. Red and blue lights flickered from the other police car. Yellow crime scene tape ran across a section of heavy-trunked trees, and he walked toward it. His deputy, Aaron Carsons, a short, skinny man whose hat looked two sizes too big, saw him and headed over.

"What we got, Aaron?" asked the sheriff.

Aaron pushed his hat up and rifled through a notepad. "Hiker found a body down near an embankment of trees. Looks like she's been dead a couple of days."

The sheriff sighed. "Apparent cause of death?"

"Based on the initial look of the body, I'd say blunt force trauma to the head."

The sheriff was surprised. "Based on what?" he asked. There hadn't been a murder in this county in almost twelve years.

The deputy lowered his notebook. "Based on the fact that the side of her head is concave when it shouldn't be."

The sheriff grunted. "Could have fallen. Hit a rock."

They reached the yellow tape, and the sheriff ducked beneath it and the deputy followed. "No rocks to speak of, sir."

The sheriff observed the tarp on the ground. "You call the medical examiner?"

"Yeah." The deputy took a long breath and let it out. "They're sending a coroner's wagon. It's gonna be another thirty minutes though before they get here."

"I know," said the sheriff. The small town of Cranston sat on the outskirts of the city and was about an hour away from any major metropolis. Crimes like this usually required outside help. "What about forensics?"

"They're sending somebody to help with that."

"You get pictures?"

"Yes, sir."

"Talk to the hiker who found her?"

"Yes. I got his statement."

"You walk in the crime scene?"

"Just when I arrived to check the body."

"Anybody else?"

"The paramedics arrived before me. They were here."

"Okay. Find out who they are. Get their info."

"Right. Yes, sir."

"Was there any ID on her?"

The deputy continued to stand and stare at the tarp. His face was white and the sheriff felt fairly certain that his man was about to be sick. "Carsons?"

His deputy snapped out of his reverie. "Oh, no. Not that I could find."

The sheriff nodded. "Then go talk to the paramedics. Tell them this gal no longer needs their services."

The deputy shook his head and took another shaky breath. "Right. Okay." He glanced again at the tarp. "You think it really was a murder, sheriff?"

The sheriff removed his hat and scratched his head. "In my experience, Aaron, most people don't bash their own heads in."

The deputy shook his head, but stayed put, still staring. The sheriff put his hat back on. Careful not to disturb anything, and watching where he walked, he took two steps and squatted. He lifted the tarp. Seeing the victim, he could understand why his deputy was green. The victim was face down in the leaves, her blonde hair matted with blood and encrusted with dirt. The left side of her skull sported a deep crease. The sheriff observed the clothing and condition of the body, then dropped the tarp.

"Also..." said Aaron. "Did you notice?"

The sheriff looked at his deputy, feeling a little ill himself. "What?"

"She's missing a shoe."

"What was that?" asked the sheriff.

"She's wearing pink tennis shoes. But only one."

The sheriff thought about that. "Only one?"

"Yes. I can't find the other one."

The sheriff lifted the tarp again. "You checked around the crime scene?"

"In the immediate area. Yes. Nothing." He put his notepad in his pocket. "Not sure why it would be missing."

"Any number of reasons." The sheriff sighed. "Crap."

"Yep." The deputy scanned the dirt and thick brush that made up the forest floor.

"All right," said the sheriff, dropping the tarp. "Find some people." He stood and grabbed his phone. "Once the coroner and forensics leave, we've got some searching to do."

The deputy nodded. "Yes, sir."

Aaron walked away as the sheriff dialed a number and waited for the call to connect.

# Chapter Three

THE MAN AND WOMAN walked through the small store, looking at fishing rods and tackle boxes. The woman picked up a lure. She stared at it and shook it. The long, colorful plastic minnow with the three-pronged hook wiggled in the air.

"What is this for?" she asked. "It's so crude."

The man took it out of her hand. "I believe it's used for catching fish." He put the lure back on the shelf. "Would you please focus? We're here to watch."

The woman groaned in annoyance. "We've watched enough. We've been here for two days. Can't we get on with it?"

"Sarna," said the man. "Your impatience will undoubtedly result in failure with this assignment. We need to blend in, which is why we are here. If we're going to succeed, we need to learn of local customs and observe the actions of this society. If we can't do that, then we might as well go home."

She widened her eyes. "Listen to you," she said. "Learn of local customs? Observe the actions of this society? You sound like a robot. If you want us to blend in, then you better start sounding a little more natural. Use a curse word or something."

"I'm not going to do that unless it's necessary. Forcing it will just sound fake."

"At least stop talking like you're a machine." She sighed. "I don't know that it matters, though. We should just go home." She picked up a package of beef jerky and grimaced. "As far as I am concerned, we are already doomed to fail."

Jasper did not hide his annoyance. "Listen," he said, facing her. "You've done nothing but complain since we arrived. In fact, it almost resulted in our discovery at a most inopportune time. If we hadn't succeeded in alleviating the threat, then we would have failed before we even got started. You know why we're here and you agreed to come despite the risks. Why is it that now you choose to be so disagreeable?"

Sarna frowned. "I agreed because I know the importance of our mission, but what I do not agree with is this choice of action. I know you Jasper. You will act first and think later. I'm here to make sure you don't do something stupid."

Jasper kept his voice low. "You're here because you don't trust me?"

Sarna put the jerky back on the shelf. "No, I don't trust you. You have a personal stake in this. And I don't trust him, either. I doubt he'll help us anyway."

Jasper turned and walked into another aisle. Sarna followed. He picked up a package of Twinkies and pretended to study them. "We have not even engaged with him yet. You have no idea what he'll do."

Sarna yanked the Twinkies out of his hand. "He's half-human. He's from this planet. A planet that considers this junk," she held the Twinkies in his face, "food. How can you trust anyone who eats this and captures swimming creatures and eats them, capable of doing what we are about to ask of him?"

Jasper slapped at the Twinkies and pulled them from Sarna's hand. "Because of who he is. You and I both know what he is capable of. We wouldn't be here otherwise."

Sarna glared and opened her mouth to speak, when she suddenly smiled. "Oh, honey," she said, taking the Twinkies. "You know I can't eat these. I'm watching my waistline."

Jasper turned to see the woman who had been working the register approach them.

"Can I help you two?" she asked. She was an older woman with deep lines etched around her eyes and mouth. Her graying hair was pulled back in a bun. She had a white apron tied around her waist, and she wore no make-up.

Jasper smiled. "Oh, no, ma'am. Thank you. You are very kind. We're just looking around your nice store."

"You two going fishing? We have some nice cabins up on the lake."

"Fishing?" asked Sarna, dropping her grin. "Certainly not."

The woman raised an eyebrow. "Hunting then? It's duck season."

Sarna squeezed the Twinkies. The cellophane crinkled in her grip. Jasper answered first. "Um. No. We're just here to enjoy your lovely town."

The sales woman eyed Sarna, but then offered a grin to Jasper. "Couple of nature lovers, huh? Come up here to enjoy the woods, do some hiking?"

"Absolutely," said Jasper. He wrapped an arm around Sarna and pulled her close. She tensed, but did not pull away. "It seemed like a nice place for a little romantic getaway." Sarna remained still, but Jasper kept a smile on his face.

"Ah. That's sweet," said the woman. "Young love. How long you two been married?"

"Six months," said Jasper.

"We are not married," said Sarna, at the same time.

The woman eyed the both of them and her smile dropped. "Well," she said, stepping away, "Let me know if you need anything. I'll be up front." She turned and headed down the aisle, back toward the register.

Sarna pushed away from Jasper. "I don't like her."

"You don't like anyone and would you keep your voice down?" When Sarna grunted, Jasper walked up and whispered. "Can you at least try to act like you fit in here? The last thing I want to do is go home and explain how you ended this mission before it even started."

Her brow furrowed. "You would like that, wouldn't you?"

He rolled his eyes and sighed. "No, I wouldn't. I want this to succeed, but it's not going to if you're sabotaging us at every turn."

"I am not sabotaging anything. Did you feel her? She considers us outsiders. She doesn't like that we don't hunt or fish, and she sure as hell didn't approve of us being out of wedlock."

Jasper raised his eyebrows. "Sure as hell? Good use of the vernacular."

"I'm not simpleminded, Jasper. I can fit in here with the best of them. I'm just not a fan of the locals."

Jasper took the Twinkies from her and put them back on the shelf. "Who cares about the locals? That's not what we're here for. But we have to deal with them and that means getting along, so could you please just try to adjust your surly attitude long enough for us to see this through?"

She huffed and shrugged. "Fine. I'll be sweeter than that package of Twinkies."

He stared as if not believing her. "Thank you." He glanced toward the register where the sales woman watched them from behind the counter. "Now let's go buy something before she speaks to every customer in this store about the strange couple that visited her shop. That's all we need."

Sarna stared at the woman and when the woman's gaze did not leave hers, Sarna smiled and waved. The woman shook her head and went into a back room behind the counter.

"Great," said Jasper. "She's probably calling the local sheriff right now."

"Let her," said Sarna.

"Would you come on, we've got some shopping to do."

"What for? Why don't we just leave?"

"Because we've aroused suspicion, which is the last thing we need. Now we have to buy something, look normal."

Sarna snickered. "How about a package of condoms. Think that will go over well?"

Jasper didn't see the humor. Ignoring her, he walked toward the front entrance and picked up a metal basket. The bell on the entry jingled as a new customer entered the small store, just as the door behind the register the woman had disappeared behind opened. Sarna and Jasper stared in surprise when an immense man emerged from the back. His long black hair was tied back in a tangled ponytail, and Jasper surmised he easily tipped the scales at over three hundred pounds. His large belly hung over his waistband and folds of fat from his arms jiggled as he stood over the counter and leaned on it, staring at both of them. The older woman watched from behind the obese man.

"Uh," said Jasper, "how about we pick up a few things and get the hell out of here."

Sarna did not disagree. "Your use of the vernacular is improving," she said, picking up a package of toilet paper and throwing it in the basket.

Jasper grabbed some toothpaste. "Like you, I can use it when the situation requires."

Sarna added tissues, shampoo, and a package of trail mix to their items. Jasper found some shaving cream and bottled water. "I think that should do it. You ready?"

"Ready?" asked Sarna. "What, to face Mr. Happy over there?"

The large man still observed them. "Watch what you say," said Jasper, as he turned to head toward the counter.

"Always do," she said, following him.

Before they could reach the counter, though, the customer who had entered the store stepped in front of them. He was tall and lanky, stubble shadowed his jaw, and his honey-colored hair hung in his face. They stopped and watched as the man held something out to the giant behind the register.

The big man looked over the smaller one, who did not appear the least bit intimidated by the larger man's size. "What's that?" asked the hefty man with a sneer.

The lankier fellow snorted. "It's a picture." He raised the photo and brought it closer for the large man to see. "You seen her?"

The gray-haired woman moved closer and observed the photo. Her big employee glanced at the picture and then back at the man who held it. "You're not from around here. You a cop?"

"No, I'm not." The man waved the photo.

The woman shook her head.

"No. Never seen her," said the cashier.

"You sure?" asked the man. "Look close."

The fat man set his jaw. "I'm not blind."

"Don't know her," said the woman. "Who is she?"

The lanky man ignored her, turned away from the counter, and almost bumped into Jasper. He stopped and held the photo out again. "You seen her?" he asked Jasper.

Jasper looked at the photograph. It was of a young woman with long blonde hair. She was smiling as if she'd just been told a joke. Sarna moved up and looked at the picture.

Jasper shook his head. "I have not seen her."

"We're not from around here," added Sarna.

The man didn't say anything but brushed past them as if he was in a hurry, and the bell on the door jangled again as he left.

The store went quiet, and the enormous employee waited for Jasper and Sarna to approach. His sneer remained. Jasper stepped forward and placed his basket near the register. "Hello, sir. We'd like to get these items." He slid the basket toward the large man.

The man's greasy fingers scratched his puffy face. The older woman had stepped back and continued to watch from the doorway. Finally, after a few seconds of silence, the giant cashier picked up an item from the basket and began to ring it up. Sarna stayed quiet, and Jasper let go of a quiet, held breath.

"Where are you two staying?" asked the man. His voice was deep and gruff.

Sarna answered, using the story they had prepared. "We're not sure yet. We're on a road trip. We're just stopping wherever we find a place. We'll probably drive another hour or two. Hopefully find a place along the lake. We have camping gear, so we might just be in the tent tonight."

"It's beautiful up here," added Jasper.

"Secluded," said Sarna.

"Where are you two from?" asked the man. He rang up the final item.

"We're not from around here," said Sarna.

"City folk, right?" asked the man. He waited while Jasper pulled cash from his wallet to pay for their purchase.

"Right," said Jasper. "But we love to escape and get away for a while." He swiveled toward Sarna. "Right, honey?"

"Yes, dear." She smiled back at him. The man pulled out a bag and began to fill it with their items.

"We get a lot of your type up here," he said.

"What type is that?" asked Sarna, stepping closer. Jasper reached over and grasped her hand.

"City folk," he said.

"I'm sure you do," said Sarna. "Lots of hunting and fishing, right?"

The man added the toothpaste to the bag and slid it toward them. "Right."

"Well, we'll be on our way," said Jasper.

"Good," said the man. "Enjoy your drive. And your stay in the woods." He smiled at Sarna. "Watch out for hunters. Campers sometimes get in the way."

Sarna held his gaze. "Get in the way of what?"

Jasper picked up the bag and pulled on her hand. "Come on, dear," he said. "Let's go."

"Bullets," said the man, and the woman behind him chuckled. "Such a shame when that happens."

Sarna didn't speak but continued to hold eye contact with the immense man. Jasper tried to pull her toward the door. She let herself be pulled, but when they reached the door, she shot back. "Perhaps somebody should do you a favor and get in the way of you and those Twinkies. You're not looking too healthy there, countryman."

The man glowered. Jasper yanked hard on Sarna and dragged her out of the store. The bell rang, and the door closed behind them.

"Get in the car, Sarna," he said. "Now."

Sarna followed. She got in the passenger's seat, and Jasper threw the groceries in the back. Getting behind the wheel, he started the car and drove away.

# Chapter Four

THE AX SLICED THROUGH the air and hit the wood with a satisfying thunk. The short log split in two and each piece fell to the mossy, moist ground. Royce assessed the pile of remaining wood and set the ax down. He reached for a towel and wiped his brow and neck. He was shirtless, and the sweat ran down his muscled torso and back. Standing easily six-foot-five, Royce noted how his time in the sun had turned his skin a golden brown. He reached for his bottled water and took a drink. His strong arms and shoulders bunched and glistened in the sunlight. Even though it was a cool day, he'd been chopping wood for over an hour. The sunshine trickling through the trees and the exertion made him sweat. Catching sight of his reflection in a window of his house, he remembered his mother's description of him when he'd pulled weeds in her backyard the previous year. She'd said he'd looked like a Greek bronze statue twinkling after a light rain. Regarding himself, he didn't see the resemblance.

A polished black stone held by a leather cord hung around his neck, and it stuck to his sweaty skin. Reaching up, Royce touched the stone. Despite the warmth of his body, the smooth rock still felt cool to the touch. He set the water down and reached for another log when the sound of an automobile caught his attention. Looking toward the road, he saw a sheriff's car drive down his dirt and gravel driveway. It led up to Royce's small cabin, which sat on five acres in a wooded area near the lake. It was secluded and quiet, which is what he preferred. After all the dramatic events over the past six months, he preferred his time here. He figured it was safer, too.

As the car approached and stopped outside his cabin, Royce wiped his torso and arms with the towel, grabbed his shirt, which hung from a post, and pulled it on. Studying the car, he could see a lone figure in the back seat. He walked toward the vehicle and watched as the sheriff emerged from the driver's side.

"Rick," he said. He hadn't seen the sheriff in a few weeks. Royce rarely ventured into town for anything other than groceries.

The sheriff closed the car door. "Royce. How are ya?"

"Good. How are you?" He glanced in the back of the car and recognized the figure who slumped in the seat, looking away. "Is that RJ?"

The sheriff eyed the boy in his car. He sighed. "Yeah. That's him."

Royce felt frustration and worry drift off the sheriff. "What can I do for you?"

The sheriff rested his hands on his belt buckle and gripped it in a gesture of discomfort. "Listen, I'm in a bit of a bind and am wondering if you could do me a favor."

"A favor?" Royce noted the sullen figure in the back of the car. He suspected what the favor was.

"Yes. We found a body this morning up in the woods by Shady Point."

Royce furrowed his brow. "A body?" Crime was rare in this area.

"Yeah. Female. Found by a hiker. Her head bashed in. We're combing the woods, looking for clues and the weapon." He glanced back at the car. "RJ..." He tipped his head. "Well, his mom sent him up here to be with me. He graduated high school last spring, and he's been a handful ever since. Marion needed a break. Told her I'd take him for a while, keep him busy. He got here last week, but he's been quiet and moody. Yesterday, he got into an argument with Martha and Tiny down at the store. He threw a brick at the window and shattered it. I've spent a good part of the morning on the phone trying to smooth the waters. Tiny fixed the window, and I'm paying for it, and they agreed not to press charges, but I'm buried in work with this investigation, and I need someone to keep an eye on him."

Royce listened but kept his attention on the figure in the backseat. The boy's anger and embarrassment drifted off him like a kid who'd just had his pants pulled down in the middle of a playground.

The sheriff threw out his hands. "I know this is an imposition, but he hung out here a few days with you last summer and I know he enjoyed it, although he won't admit it. I thought..."

Royce thought back. Rick had needed to make an impromptu court appearance in the city and Royce had offered to watch RJ. "You want me to keep an eye on him?"

"Just until I can get my head above water with this investigation. It might be a few days though."

"You got his stuff?"

"His bag is in the back. Just to forewarn you, though, he's not happy about it."

Royce's expression didn't change. "I can see that."

"I think it's a cover, though. Secretly, I think he'd rather be out here with you than with me." He gestured toward the car. "He and I aren't exactly seeing eye to eye right now."

Royce nodded. "Bring him in."

The sheriff's faced relaxed. "Thanks. I owe you one."

"You owe me two," said Royce, holding out two fingers. He lowered his voice. "And personally, Tiny probably deserved getting his window broken."

The sheriff walked toward the car but glanced back at Royce. "Let's just keep that between you and me." He reached the back door and opened it. "Come on out, RJ."

RJ reluctantly slid out, small duffel bag in hand. He avoided eye contact with his dad and looked at Royce. "Hey."

"RJ," said Royce. "How've you been?" RJ had grown taller since Royce had last seen him. He'd thinned out and had a lithe frame. He wore baggy jeans, and a faded t-shirt.

"My dad sticking me with you?" he asked, saying the words with disdain.

"RJ..." said the sheriff.

"Your dad's working an investigation," said Royce. "You can hang out with me while he's busy. That all right with you?"

RJ's posture dropped. "Since when does anyone give a shit what I think?"

"RJ," said the sheriff. "It's just for a few days."

RJ glowered. "Screw you. You just want to dump me some place. Just like mom." He gripped his bag and walked away toward the house. "Fine with me. I'd rather be anywhere else. Even this dump." He strode into Royce's cabin and slammed the door.

The sheriff's face fell. "Hell," he said. "I'll go talk to him." He walked toward the cabin but Royce stopped him.

"Leave it," he said. "He's just angry."

"Royce if you'd rather not do this..." He shook his head. "I'll under-stand."

"He'll be fine. He's a teenager. I can handle it. Go find your murderer."

The sheriff began to answer when the distant sound of a slamming screen door interrupted him. It did not come from Royce's cabin and the two men swiveled to see where the noise had originated from.

Looking through the woods, Royce caught sight of a woman. His neigh-bor's cabin stood about a hundred yards from Royce's and, if viewed the right way, you could see glimpses of the porch and back of the house. Royce squinted. The woman stepped off the porch and into a thicket of trees, carrying a bucket. She had long blonde hair tied up in a ponytail, and she wore a long shapeless dress.

The sheriff watched. "Old man McDermott rented that place out again?" He narrowed his eyes. "You know her?"

Royce saw the woman look up. She peered through the tree trunks and saw the two men. Moving quickly, she darted back into the house. He heard her screen door slam shut.

"No. I don't know her," he said.

"Not too neighborly, is she?"

Royce shrugged.

"Anyway," said the sheriff, "about the murder. You seen anyone suspicious around town?"

"I haven't been into town recently."

"Anybody around your property?"

"No. Just me."

"Okay," said the sheriff. He gripped his belt buckle again and nodded toward the house. "Thanks for doing this."

"It's fine. I don't mind."

The sheriff nodded. "You call me if anything pops up. I can come get him if he gets to be too much."

Royce raised a brow. "You don't know me very well, do you?"

The sheriff chuckled. "Yeah, well, RJ can test any man."

Royce did not feel worried. "We'll see how I fare. If you come back and I've drowned him, then you'll know."

The sheriff chuckled, as if he didn't know whether Royce was serious or not. "I guess so." He walked back toward the car. "I'll call tomorrow and check in."

"That's fine," said Royce.

The sheriff frowned and then reached for his back pocket. He pulled out his wallet and took out some cash. "Here. This is for food and any expenses you incur." He handed the money out to Royce.

Royce raised his hand. "Keep it. Any food he eats, he'll work for."

The sheriff stood, holding the money, before nodding and putting it back in his wallet. He opened the car door. "All right. I'm all for that." He got in. "Thanks again."

"You're welcome."

The car door shut, and the sheriff backed out of the driveway and left. Royce turned back toward his house. Waiting a few seconds, he strode toward his front door and went inside.

· · · · ● · ● · · · ·

He heard the TV the moment he stepped through the door. RJ sat low on the couch with his feet on the coffee table. Royce caught a brief glimpse of space ships and laser blasts on the screen before he walked over and turned it off.

"Hey. I'm watching that."

"Get up kid. The only time the TV is on is for a major news event or a fishing show. You should know that."

RJ made no move to leave the sofa. "I want to watch TV."

Royce stepped closer and pulled RJ to his feet by the arm. RJ had grown over the past year, but he was no match for Royce's powerful physique.

"What are you doing?" RJ asked.

"You want dinner tonight? Then you better work up an appetite. Let's go." Royce pushed a reluctant RJ toward the back door. He opened it and stepped into the yard, bringing the teen with him. He pointed to the ax. "See that?"

"See what?"

"It's called an ax. You swing it, and it cuts wood."

RJ looked appalled. "You're not gonna make me do that, are you?"

Royce walked over to the ax and picked it up. He held it out to RJ. "It's pretty simple, really." He pointed to a stack of wood. "There are several more logs to cut."

RJ's mouth dropped open. "What the hell do I know about cutting wood?"

Royce was not deterred. "Nothing until you do it. It's the same with most things."

RJ continued to stand and stare. Royce could feel the boy's ambivalence, but also his curiosity. After a few quiet seconds passed, RJ sighed and took the ax from Royce. "What do I do?"

Royce picked up a log and set it on the stump. "Raise the ax and bring it down. Not too complicated." He began to pick up the wood he'd previously cut and add it to the stack a few yards from the house.

"What if I miss?" asked RJ.

"Then you pick it up and try again." Royce nodded toward a pair of gloves on the ground. "I'd wear those if I were you."

RJ spied the gloves. "Do you wear them?"

Royce dropped a log on the stack of firewood. "No."

"Then I don't either."

Royce looked back at the teen, who carefully raised the ax and stared at the log which sat upright on the stump.

"Suit yourself," said Royce.

RJ swung the ax down and completely missed the log.

# Chapter Five

SEVERAL HOURS LATER, Royce sat on his back porch and watched the stars through the trees. RJ had gone to bed an hour earlier, exhausted after a busy afternoon. The boy, who after several tries had finally sliced a log cleanly, had cut the remainder of the wood. After that, Royce had taken him to the trail that lead to the lake. Royce's acreage backed up to the water, but the trail was rough and overgrown. Royce had been working to clear out the brush, but it was tedious and slow going. He'd given RJ the proper tools and put him to work cutting back the vines and low-hanging branches, cautioning him to keep an eye out for poison ivy and snakes. While RJ worked, Royce headed over to the McDermott trail. The neighbor had asked Royce to help keep his own path maintained, and they'd come to a mutual agreement. If Royce helped out with the maintenance of the property, then the old man would agree not to rent out his cabin to any unruly guests. The last thing Royce wanted was a loud and obnoxious neighbor.

Now, after a busy afternoon, Royce was sitting on his porch, listening to the murmur of crickets. He thought back to a few hours earlier. He'd been cutting through some thick brush and had stopped to take a break and drink some water. Hot and sweaty, he'd reached for the cool stone around his neck, but it hadn't been there. The leather cord had broken. Not seeing the stone, he'd searched the ground and found the black rock underneath some leaves. He'd picked it up and laid it next to his tools. That's when he'd seen her. It was the same woman from earlier. Her long blonde hair was still in a ponytail, and she still wore the long shapeless dress. A floppy hat was on her head, and she walked through the woods, carrying the same bucket. She paused, picked leaves, and put them in her pail. She was not far from her cabin, but as she moved and studied the greenery, she stopped. Straightening, she turned and made eye contact with Royce. Royce barely had the chance to say "Hello," before she'd picked up her skirt and hurried back to the house, where from a distance, Royce saw her run up the porch and slam the door shut behind her.

Recalling the encounter, Royce took a sip of the beer he was drinking. He could still feel the woman's fear of him. He recalled the haunted look in her eyes, and he wondered what made her so afraid. After she'd disappeared into her cabin, RJ had found him soon after and finally admitted that he had blisters on his fingers and couldn't work anymore. Royce had brought him back to the cabin, bandaged his damaged hands, and fed him. After an hour of TV, the kid had succumbed to his fatigue, and Royce had directed him to the guest bedroom.

Studying the woods, Royce thought again about the woman who was staying only a hundred yards away, and wondered what her story was. He watched through the trees as the moon rose in the sky. He wondered if he should call old man McDermott when a flicker of unease made him shiver. He closed his eyes and opened up his senses, listening. The crickets continued to chirp and he could hear the trees sway in the wind, but he ignored the familiar sounds.

Sitting quietly, he knew he was being watched. He was familiar with the creatures that made the woods their home, but this was not an animal. His skin prickling, he sat up in his seat and put his beer down. After waiting a few seconds and seeing nothing, he stood and walked to the edge of the porch. It was dark, and the only illumination was from the moon. Its light danced on the ground as the trees shifted with the wind. Royce studied the darkness and crossed his arms, continuing to listen. Finally, he cocked his head and spoke out loud. "You might as well come out. I know you're here."

The crickets continued to chirp, but a low chuckle could be heard, and Royce looked to his left as a man stepped out of the woods and approached the house.

· · · · ● · ● · · · ·

"So when should we introduce ourselves?" asked Sarna. She sat in the passenger seat of the car.

Jasper stared out the window of the driver's side door toward the driveway of the house. They could see little. It was night, and the house sat farther back into the woods. The only reason they could see anything was because the moon and the front porch light partially illuminated the home. They'd been there an hour, parked across the road, but had seen no movement.

"Soon," said Jasper.

"How soon?"

Jasper sighed. "We can't just barge in there."

"Why not?" she asked. "Why are we waiting so long?"

Jasper threw a hand up. "You know why. This may take a while. We needed to acclimate anyway. Get comfortable here. Plus, it helps to watch. Study the area and him. It will help once we make contact."

Sarna shook her head. "We've acclimated enough." She rested her elbow on the car door. The window was open, and the breeze blew her hair. "You're stalling."

His head whipped toward her. "I'm not stalling."

"Yes. You are. You're nervous about meeting him, aren't you?"

He started to speak, but hesitated.

"He's no different from you. He's not better than you either."

"I didn't say he was."

"You didn't have to." When Jasper didn't reply, she asked, "What's holding you back?"

Jasper shrugged. "I'm not sure what we're going to say to him...what to tell him."

A squirrel ran across the dark driveway. Sarna tapped her fingers on the window frame. "I'd say let's start with the truth."

Jasper started the car and took a deep breath. "I doubt he'll believe us."

Sarna rested her head back. "Why wouldn't he? He's half-human. His father is from another planet. He has unusual abilities that no one else has. I'd say he'll be more open to us than you think. In fact, I wouldn't be surprised if he expected us."

"Maybe..." Jasper ran his hand through his hair. "But he won't know whether to trust us."

"He can sense us just as we can sense him. He'll know."

Jasper raised a hand. "So we tell him everything? Right up front?"

"Wasn't that the plan?"

Jasper stared through the windshield. "I'm having second thoughts."

"Then let's play it by ear," she said. "We'll see how it goes."

Jasper pointed a finger at her. "You let me take the lead, okay?"

Sarna widened her eyes. "What do you mean? You think I can't handle myself?"

Jasper raised an eyebrow. "I know you can't handle yourself. Especially after that scene at the store."

"That guy threatened us. He deserved it."

"He was no threat to us and you know it. You just didn't like him."

"No. I didn't. Or that crazy woman that was with him. This planet has some unstable people."

Jasper huffed. "Like ours doesn't? Why do you think we're here?"

Sarna didn't answer but looked out across the dark road. "You ready to go?" she asked. "Seen enough?"

Jasper put his hand on the wheel. "Yes. I've seen enough."

"Tomorrow then," she said. "We'll talk to him." She shifted in her seat. "And then we get the hell out of here and go home."

Jasper gripped the steering wheel. "Okay. Tomorrow." He put the car in drive. "And hopefully when we leave, he'll be with us."

# Chapter Six

THE QUIET MAN WALKED out of the woods and strode toward the porch. His easy gait and relaxed posture revealed his complete comfort with his surroundings, as if walking out of the dark woods at night was as normal as getting a glass of water before bed. Royce watched him approach. He took in the man's dark complexion and long, black hair. A necklace with a long gray and white feather hung from his neck. "What are you doing out here, Chief?" asked Royce.

The man got closer and Royce could make out his visitor's deep-set, dark eyes. The man smiled and the lines on his face creased deeper. "I could ask the same of you, Starman." He walked on to the porch and eyed Royce's beer. "You sharing?"

His friend sat down in one of the patio chairs. Shaking his head, Royce headed into his house and grabbed a beer. He returned to the porch, sat, and tossed the bottle. The man caught it and twisted the cap. "How you been, Gus?" asked Royce.

Gus took a swig and set the bottle on the side table. "Good. You?"

Royce rested a foot on the scarred wooden patio table. "Fine."

"I see you have company."

Royce was not surprised Gus knew about RJ. "His dad dropped him off for a few days." He didn't elaborate. "How long were you gone this time?"

Gus picked up his bottle. "About a month."

"That's longer than usual," said Royce.

"This one was different. Took a little time." Gus took another swig of his beer. "How's RJ?"

Royce nodded toward the house. "His dad asked me to keep an eye on him. Rick's working on an apparent murder investigation."

"I heard. Up near Shady Point."

"When did you get back from your walk?"

"This morning," said Gus. He studied his beer. "One of these days, maybe you'll join me."

Royce didn't answer, but considered his reply. He'd known Gus Longcreek for three years. He was a descendant of the Iroquois tribe and legendary in the area for being a master tracker and medicine healer. Raised by his grandfather, Gus knew how to live off the land. Naturally in tune with the animals and familiar with the various plants and vegetation of the forest, he took frequent trips or "walks" as he called them where he disappeared for days and weeks to "spend time with Mother Earth." Royce had met him after he'd bought his land and began to build his cabin. He'd been camping nearby and Gus had walked right up to his fire while Royce was roasting marshmallows. They'd begun talking and struck up an easy friendship. Despite Royce's attempts to reveal as little about himself as possible, Gus had known from the start that Royce was different. Said he'd seen it in one of his visions. Since then, he'd started to call Royce "Starman" and the name had stuck.

"Maybe one day," Royce finally answered. Although the thought of joining Gus on one of his walks intrigued him, Royce knew that keeping his secrets only became more difficult the more time he spent with the mystical man. "You see the bear?" asked Royce. He took another swallow of his beer.

"Not this time," said Gus. He held a flat stare. "But I know you did."

Royce choked on his drink and coughed. He had not told Gus of his experiments with the large animal that frequented the land around his property. "What do you mean?" he asked, wiping his mouth.

Gus chuckled. "Come on, Starman. You know what I mean." He raised his bottle. "I saw you in my vision."

Royce shot a glance at his friend. "Really. What kind of vision? Were you maybe smoking something at the time?"

Gus grinned. "Sometimes that's the best way to ensure a vision."

Royce made a half-smile. "I'm sure it is. But how accurate is it?"

"You saw the bear, didn't you?" He winked. "But he didn't see you?" Royce raised a brow. "You forget who you're dealing with, Starman."

Royce wasn't sure what to say. "Apparently so."

The two sat quietly before Gus finally spoke. "How'd you do it?"

"Do what?"

Gus put his drink down. "How did you hide from him? Disappear from his sight?"

Royce rubbed his fingers over the stubble on his jaw. He debated how much to say. "It's just something I'm practicing."

Gus's eyes widened. "Practicing? For what? You planning on joining the circus? What would you have done if he'd seen you?"

Royce shrugged. "I don't know." He picked at the label on his bottle. "Run?"

Gus said nothing. Royce changed the subject. "How'd you know about Shady Point?"

"What?" asked Gus.

"The murder?"

"Oh, that." He picked up his beer. "Saw Rick on my way in. He asked if I could help."

Royce was curious. "Help how?"

"They're looking for a shoe. They also want to see if I can track any movement through the woods."

"After the police have been through there?"

Gus shook his head. "Probably won't find much, but they think the murderer may have been at the Shady Point campsite earlier in the evening. He hopes I might find something there."

"Good luck. Teenagers love hanging out there at night. Especially out by the park."

"Don't need luck," said Gus, pointing outward. "Mother Earth will guide me."

"Well then, good luck to her." He took a final swig of his beer and put the bottle on the table. "She's gonna need it."

Gus laughed. "I won't argue with that." He eyed Royce's empty bottle on the table. "Do your trick."

Royce rolled his eyes. "No."

Gus put his own bottle down. "Come on, Starman. I want to see."

Royce tried to divert Gus's attention. "Why do you insist on calling me Starman?"

Gus eye's narrowed. "You know why."

Royce studied the trees. "I know. Another one of your visions." He sighed. "You should stop calling me that."

"Why?" asked Gus. He settled back in his seat. "Does it make you uncomfortable?"

"It's not something I talk about."

Gus's mouth turned up. "Don't worry. It's not something I plan to share."

"I don't even know why you believe it. It was just a vision."

Gus spoke with certainty. "I always trust my visions. And I know what I saw. You come from the stars." He raised a hand to the sky.

Royce sat up but didn't respond. He stared at his fingers. Gus continued. "I suppose that has something to do with how you hide from bears that are standing right in front of you." Royce fidgeted. "And how you do your trick." Gus raised an ankle and rested it on his knee. "Which I'm still waiting for, by the way."

Royce grunted and sat still. He didn't know how to feel about what Gus knew and how he knew it. In some ways, it scared him; in others, he felt relief. It felt good to share a secret that only his family knew. But he also realized the risks. Gus's foot bounced up and down, and Royce realized the man would only continue to pester him. He took a second to gather his thoughts and focused on the beer in front of him. A second passed and then his bottle slid across the table toward Gus without anyone touching it. Then Gus's bottle moved. It slid on its own toward Royce, did a reverse turn, and headed back toward Gus. When it hit the edge of the table, it lifted and traveled into the air, where Gus reached up and grabbed it.

Gus hooted and gripped the bottle in his hand, looking at it as if he'd never seen glass before. "Shit. That's awesome." He slapped his knee. "How do you do that, Starman?"

Royce tried not to squirm, but failed. "It's just something I learned a while back. Not that big a deal." He thought back on his Shift, three years earlier. Born to a human mother and Eudoran father, Royce and his sisters had all experienced a transformation, or Shift, as his father called it. It was an important transitional event for all Eudorans, similar to moving from adolescence to adulthood for humans, only at an accelerated pace. For Royce and his siblings, it was a crucial milestone. And because his father was a Red-Line, a unique species capable of unusual abilities, including energy manipulation and intuition, telepathy, telekinesis, and cloaking, Royce and his sisters had exhibited a mixture of these powers. But they'd all had a strength, and Royce's was moving objects with his mind. He was also practicing the skill of cloaking by hiding in plain sight of the bear. His abilities had revealed themselves shortly after his Shift, and his life had changed dramatically ever since. He wondered what Gus would think if he knew what Royce's sisters could do.

Gus took another swallow of his beer. "Can you turn water into wine?" he asked.

Royce finally cracked a smile. "I'm not that skilled. I'll leave that to a higher power."

Gus put his bottle back on the table. "Smart." He leaned back and stared out at the trees. Royce immediately felt his change in mood.

"What is it, Chief?" he asked. "Something on your mind?"

Gus was quiet and Royce waited. They both listened to the wind stir the leaves. "On this walk...I had another vision," Gus finally said.

"You told me. You saw me with the bear."

Gus shook his head. "Not that," he said. "Something else."

"What?" Royce tuned in to Gus's energy and felt the concern drift off the man. Since Gus rarely worried about anything, Royce perked up.

Gus shifted and held Royce's gaze. "You, my friend."

"Me, what?"

Gus studied his palms. "I saw death."

That made Royce straighten. "You saw what?"

"And there's a woman."

Royce didn't understand. He thought of his mother and sisters. "A woman? What woman?"

Gus's eyes drooped. "She will break your heart."

Royce didn't understand. He wasn't dating anyone, and considering who he was, he wondered if he ever would. "What the hell are you talking about, Chief? Other than my family, there are no women in my life."

Gus held his gaze. "Not yet."

Royce felt his body stiffen. "What are you saying?"

"I'm saying that there's trouble on the horizon. Someone's coming."

Royce thought back to the previous six months and felt his belly curl in fear. He gripped the chair. "Who?"

Gus was unfazed. "Two, maybe more. I can't be sure."

Royce thought of Eve and Gillian, his sisters. Their safety was his primary concern. "What do they want?"

"I don't know."

Royce's mind whirled. "When will they be here?"

Gus barely moved. "They're already here."

Royce sat for a moment, but then stood and stepped to his porch railing. He stared out at the trees and thought back to six months ago. His mind flashed to violent seas, flashing lightning, and a collapsing deck. "My family? Are they safe?"

Gus paused. "I didn't see them. Only you."

Royce gripped the rail. "Should I leave?"

Gus shook his head. "It's too late for that."

"Who are they? Do you know?"

Gus stood and went to stand next to Royce. "I didn't see that in my vision."

Royce didn't know what to think. "Damn it..." It was all he could think to say.

Gus spoke calmly. "But that might be the reason there's a car on the road, watching your house."

Royce whirled. "What? You mean now? Out front?" He didn't wait for an answer and jumped off the porch and ran toward the front of the cabin.

"Wait for me," said Gus, and he followed Royce into the woods.

Royce moved fast, but Gus kept up. Both men were comfortable in the woods and jogged easily past the side of the house and up onto the pebbled driveway. Royce picked up speed, and in a few long strides, he reached the side of the road with Gus right behind him. The street was quiet, and no cars were visible.

Despite his sprint, Royce's breathing had barely changed. "There's nobody here," he said.

Gus stood beside him. "Good observation."

Royce reached out with his senses to see if he could pick up on anything, but he could only feel the familiar sights and sounds of the quiet woods around him. He looked sharply at Gus. "Why didn't you tell me sooner?"

Gus shook his head in the dim light. "It makes no difference."

Royce attempted to calm himself. "What do you mean? They were here. If you'd said something before..."

Gus's expression remained unchanged. "It doesn't matter. They will return."

Royce's mind rushed. He didn't know what to think. Was he in danger? What about his sisters? Should he contact them? Gillian was living with her fiancé, and Eve had returned to the city. "The hell it doesn't matter." He strode off and headed back toward the house.

"Starman..."

Royce stopped. Gus stood unmoving. "You have a decision to make."

Royce nodded. "I know. I'm making it right now."

"That's not what I mean."

"I have to protect my family."

"Leaving won't help. You must face this," said Gus. "You cannot run from it."

"Run from what?" asked Royce. "What exactly am I running from?" He itched to race back to the house and start packing.

Gus didn't hesitate. "Your destiny, Starman. You have one and you must prepare for it."

# Chapter Seven

ROYCE PACED HIS LIVING room. He tried to ignore the angry wave of energy he felt from RJ, but as time passed, it became increasingly difficult. He tried to explain. "RJ..."

RJ didn't wait for an explanation. "Forget it. You don't want me around. Don't worry. I'm used to it." He picked at a thread on his overnight bag, which was packed and sitting on his lap.

Royce stood in front of him. "Stop playing the martyr. If that's what I thought, I would tell you. I'm happy to have you here, but something's come up and I have to leave. And you can't stay here by yourself."

RJ stared at him with wide eyes. "Why not? I'm eighteen. I'm old enough."

"That's not the point," said Royce.

"I have a car. I can take care of myself."

Royce raised an eyebrow. "A car? You have a car?"

RJ squinted his eyes. "Of course I do. How do you think I travel back and forth between my parents?"

"Where is it?"

RJ shrugged. "At my dad's."

"Why is it there? Why did your dad drive you here?"

RJ hesitated, but finally answered. "Because my dad took the keys."

Royce's brow furrowed. "So you don't have a car."

"I do."

"But not one you can presently drive?"

RJ looked away. "No."

"Why'd you lose the keys?"

RJ stared at the ground and sighed. "Because my dad's a pain in the ass."

"Yes," said Royce. "I'm sure it's your dad's fault. What did you do?"

RJ looked up in anger. "I went out to a party a few days ago. Came back late."

"How late?"

RJ stared at his fingers. "I'm eighteen, you know?"

"How late?" Royce asked again.

"Six a.m."

"How were you when you came home?"

RJ shot a hard gaze at Royce. "I was fine."

"How were you?" he asked again.

RJ moaned. "So maybe I'd smoked a little weed."

"And..."

"And had a few beers."

"Uh huh."

"But I'm eighteen. Old enough to go to war."

"And when you're fighting for your life, you can smoke all the weed and drink all the beer you want, but until then, you're breaking the law, and under your dad's jurisdiction."

"Screw him. He doesn't give a shit about me."

Royce could feel RJ's anger but also the hurt. "You need to understand something, RJ."

The boy's sullen look did not change. "Is this the part where you tell me I'm wrong? That dad really loves me. He just doesn't know how to show it?"

Royce rose up to his full height and rested his hands on his hips. "No. This is the part where I tell you to stop feeling sorry for yourself. You want respect? You want to be treated like a man? Then start acting like one. Decide what you want and go after it. You sitting in your parents' houses, wishing for a life you don't have, and blaming them for your problems, is not a way to live. The sooner you understand that, the better. You don't want your car keys taken from you? Then go out, get a job, pay your own way, and make your mark on the world. It's what every man does at some point. And the sooner you do it, the better."

The sound of a car coming down the driveway made him turn. He saw the sheriff's vehicle stop in the front of his house. He looked back at RJ, who stared at the floor. "And yes, your dad does love you, whether you know it or not. I'd give thanks every day that you have one. I'd have given my left arm to spend more time with my dad. So stop dwelling on your problems and count your blessings, kid. You got more than you realize."

The car door opened, and Rick stepped out. He wore his sheriff's uniform, and he put his hat on his head and walked toward the open entry.

RJ stood and held his bag. "Whatever," was all he said.

"If I could let you stay, I would, but it's not safe here. Besides, it's not a hiding place. You need to work things out with your dad."

RJ slung his bag over his shoulder as his dad approached. Royce turned to greet the sheriff. "Rick," he said.

"Royce," said the sheriff. He looked over at RJ. "He been okay?"

RJ rolled his eyes.

"He's been fine. Something came up though, and I've got to head out of town. I didn't think you'd want me to leave him here on his own."

RJ answered before his dad could. "I'd be fine, Dad. I could stay here. I'm old enough." He made brief eye contact with Royce before looking away.

Rick smiled. "I'm sure you'd like to be on your own. But I'd rather you come home." RJ's shoulders shrunk. "Besides, who am I going to go fishing with tomorrow if you're out here?"

RJ perked up. "Fishing? I thought you had to work."

"It's easing up a bit. I can find a few hours tomorrow to take the boat out on the lake if you're up for it."

RJ looked between Royce and his dad. "Sure. I guess so."

"Great. Why don't you head out to the car while I talk with Royce."

RJ stood for a second before heading out the door. He looked at Royce briefly before leaving, and Royce tipped his head at him. RJ made no reaction.

"Thanks for keeping an eye on him," said Rick. "I hope he wasn't too much trouble."

"No trouble at all," said Royce. "He'd be welcome to stay longer if I didn't have to go."

Rick noted the small suitcase on the floor. "Everything okay? Nothing bad, I hope."

Royce offered no details. "No. Nothing I can't handle. How's the investigation going?"

The sheriff shook his head. "Definitely a murder. Somebody swung something at a woman's head. Probably a rock. Plus, we're looking for a missing pink tennis shoe."

"Who would want to kill anyone out here?" asked Royce.

"Good question. She was probably out hiking. But how she ended up where she was or why she was killed is still unknown. There's no ID either, so we're still trying to figure out who she is."

"I hear Gus is helping."

"Yeah. He's coming out this afternoon. Gonna look around the area. Maybe he can find something."

"If there's anything to be found, Gus can find it."

Rick nodded. "I know that much." He looked back toward his car. RJ was sitting in the front seat. "I appreciate your help."

"He's a good kid," said Royce. "A little confused, but a good kid."

Rick put a hand on his hip. "He came home a few nights ago, drunk and high."

Royce rubbed his neck. "I had a few of those nights when I was his age."

"What did your dad do?" asked Rick.

Royce shrugged. "He wasn't around to say anything. But my mom made me pay the price."

"What'd she do?"

"She made me drink several glasses of whiskey. I puked for days."

Rick chuckled. "I guess that's one way to handle it."

"I haven't touched hard liquor since."

"I may consider that if it keeps up." Rick walked toward the open door. "You let me know when you get back. We'll have you up for dinner to say thank you."

"I'll do that," said Royce, wondering if he'd be able to accept that invitation.

"I'll make RJ cook."

"I thought you wanted to thank me."

Rick smiled. "I promise. We won't send you home ill...or make you drink any whiskey."

Royce offered a half-grin. "All right. I'll let you know when I'm back."

Rick tipped his hat. "See you, Royce. Take care."

"You too, Rick. Good luck with your investigation." Rick walked to his car, got in, and drove away. After offering a quick wave, Royce closed his front door and scanned the house. His packed bag was at his feet. His house was clean, and everything was put away. Royce listened to the quiet and wondered if he was doing the right thing. He thought back to his conversation with Gus the previous night. He didn't know anything about facing his destiny, but what he did know was that he had to ensure his family's safety. After what had happened six months ago, he didn't want to take a chance that someone might use him to get to his loved ones. He picked up his bag and reached out energetically, feeling for anything amiss. Gus said whoever was here would find him, and he didn't want to walk into an ambush. He didn't know who it was, but if it was someone from his father's neck of the woods, he knew he would have to be careful.

Feeling nothing awry, Royce walked out, shut the door, and locked it. He walked to his truck and threw his bag into the back seat. Before he slid behind the wheel, he reached for the stone around his neck. It always soothed him in stressful situations. Not feeling it, he cursed himself, remembering he'd set it aside after the cord had come loose the previous day. After being distracted by his neighbor walking through woods, he'd left it there. Royce grunted in frustration. The stone could not be left behind. His father had given it to him on his sixteenth birthday, and Royce always wore it. Not only was it calming and cool, but it always felt as if his father were with him when he touched it.

Without hesitating, he closed the car door and ran into the woods, remembering exactly where he'd put it. He'd been on the McDermott path leading down to the water. He'd set his things down on a tree stump. The stone should still be there. He jogged quickly through the brush. The day was warming, and the sun shone brightly through the trees, making him break out in a light sweat. He reached the edge of his property and stepped on to McDermott's land. There were no fences, but he knew where he was. Running farther into the woods, he reached the area where he'd been working. He saw the stump, but there was no stone. Cursing again, he dropped to his knees and felt through the dried leaves. Realizing he was rushing, he made himself relax, and instead of digging through the dirt, he closed his eyes and felt for the stone. It had a distinct feel, almost like diving into cool water on a hot day. Letting his senses guide him, he reached out with his hands and without opening his eyes, he searched a spot inches away from the stump. Within seconds, he felt the familiar smooth surface and opened his eyes. Breathing a sigh of relief, he slipped the rock into his pocket and began to stand when an ominous wave of energy dropped over him. It almost froze him in his tracks.

Moving slowly, he turned, and his breathing stopped. Standing only feet away from the stump was the bear. The distraction of looking for the stone had caused Royce to miss the animal's presence completely. The bear eyed him, as if to say, *I see you now*. It made a deep roar, reared up, and swiped its huge claws at Royce. Royce reared back, but not before the claws ripped at his shirt and chest. Rivulets of blood seeped out from his torn clothes, and Royce fell backward into the dirt. The bear dropped down on all fours and bellowed. Royce could almost hear the animal mock him. Royce stayed still, knowing that if he ran, the animal would give chase, and he doubted he would win a foot race with an angry bear. Royce forced himself to breathe, and he reached out, trying to use his own energy to calm the bear's, but it failed. Within seconds, the bear lunged forward and was on him.

Instinctively, Royce's arms came up for protection. He got his hands up underneath the animal's powerful jaws and pushed its huge head up and away. One well-placed bite would kill him. Despite Royce's strength, he was no match for the bear's brute force and tenacity. It would only be seconds before the beast had him by the throat. Summoning up a powerful dose of energy from his core, Royce sent a shockwave up and through his arms. Heat shot from his hands. The jolt hit the bear, and the animal jumped. Royce sent another intense wave of electric heat. The bear grunted, twitched, and then retreated. Breathing hard, Royce watched the bear shake his head and then study him, momentarily stunned and debating whether to renew his attack. Royce didn't move. Bleeding heavily from the wounds on his chest, he watched the bear roar at him, his huge mouth opening and his bare teeth dripping with saliva. The bear stomped the ground, eager to attack again but now with less vigor. Royce prepared in case the bear came again, but after a few terrifying seconds, the bear shook out his coat, turned, and walked back into the woods, apparently deciding he'd had enough for today.

Royce fell back hard onto the ground. Stunned from the attack, he'd been numb to the pain, but now the sharp sting from his chest wound turned into a fire and he moaned. He looked down at himself and saw the blood soak through his shirt and run down his torso. Leaves and dirt coated his clothes. He had to get help. Slowly, he pushed up to his knees. He took long, slow deep breaths, trying to stay calm. Shaking from adrenaline, he pushed up on the stump to support himself, but the soft dirt gave way and his foot slipped backward and disrupted the brush. His balance wavered, and he felt dizzy, but he righted himself and brought his foot back to stand. As he did, another sharp pain jabbed at his ankle. He fell hard onto the ground and gasped in shock to see the triangular head and thick body of a brown and gray snake, its fangs gripping hard to Royce's lower leg. Royce yelled almost as loud as the bear and scrambled back, kicking out. The snake, which Royce recognized as a water moccasin, let go and slithered back into the brush.

Royce stared in horror. Bleeding heavily and now bitten by a poisonous snake, his day had just gone from bad to disastrous.

·· • • • • • • • ·

Jasper drove the car down the rocky driveway and stopped in front of Royce's house. The two occupants saw Royce's truck in the driveway.

Sarna unbuckled her seatbelt and opened her door.

"Wait a minute," said Jasper.

"What for?" Sarna asked.

Jasper hesitated. He stared at the house.

Sarna sighed. "Jasper..." When Jasper didn't answer, she stepped out of the vehicle and closed the door.

"Sarna..."

Sarna ignored him and walked toward the front door. Jasper jumped out of the car and ran up behind her. "What are you doing?"

She knocked on the door. "What we should have done three days ago."

"We should talk first."

"There is nothing else to talk about." She knocked again. "Let's get this over with."

Jasper ran a nervous hand through his hair, but he gave up arguing and stood and waited as Sarna knocked again.

There was no answer. "Where is he?"

Jasper waited, but when no one came to the door, he stepped from behind Sarna and knocked. He turned the knob, but it was locked. "He's not home."

"His truck's here," said Sarna. She looked around. "Maybe he's out back." She stepped off the porch and walked to the side of the house.

"Wait a minute," said Jasper.

Sarna kept moving and Jasper caught up to her. He didn't say anything though.

They walked to the back of the cabin and saw the back porch, more trees, a pile of wood stacked neatly in a pile, and a small shed. Sarna stepped onto the porch and peered into the house. She saw a small living room and kitchen, but the house was quiet. Nobody was home.

"Anything?" asked Jasper.

"Nothing." She moaned. "Where is he?"

Jasper looked around the property. "Maybe he went on one of those walks in the woods?"

"You mean a hike?"

"Yes. Or maybe he went fishing."

Sarna's face fell. "You think he's killing fish?"

"Maybe."

She perused the woods. "Why would one of our kind eat an animal?"

Jasper raised an eyebrow. "He's not from Eudora. He's Earth born. I'm sure he eats animals."

"We should leave him here. He'll never fit in at home."

"After we've met him, you can make all the disparaging remarks you want, but until then, let's try not to assume the worst." He walked up to the back door, where he looked in through the glass. He put his hand on the knob.

"Me think the worst?" asked Sarna. "I'm not the one who's been avoiding this conversation for three days." She walked up next to Jasper and felt the wave of energy emit from him. "What are you doing?" She heard the audible click and watched Jasper open the door. "Are you breaking into his house?"

Jasper stepped inside. "He's obviously not here. I can't feel him. Can you?"

"No. Doesn't mean he's not around, though. Our senses only go so far, especially on this crazy planet."

"He could be gone for several hours. We might as well wait."

Shaking her head, she followed him inside. She saw a brown leather sofa, a small television, a tidy kitchen, and a square dining table. "For somebody who didn't want to walk up to the front door, you're suddenly very confident." She closed the door behind her.

Jasper looked around. Moving to the mantel, he studied the pictures there. One was of Royce with three women. They stood outside the cabin, arms interlaced, smiling. Another was of Royce and a Native-American man with long dark hair, holding a fish and fishing pole. Sarna frowned at the image. Jasper turned away, sat on the couch, and picked up the TV remote. Perusing it, he pushed the buttons.

"You're right," he said. "We've waited long enough. It's time to get this over with." After pressing a few more buttons with no results, he put the remote down. Sarna sat down beside him as Jasper stared at the TV. The TV flicked on immediately and a man appeared on screen, selling what appeared to be a set of knives.

Jasper sat back and crossed his arms. "It's time I met my half-brother."

• • • • • • • • • •

Royce stumbled through the woods. He'd broken off a sturdy vine and wrap it around his leg just below his knee to act as a tourniquet to prevent the spread of venom, but he knew it was only a temporary solution. Because of the location of the bite, he'd been unable to suck the poison from the wound. He needed medical help, but if he ended up in a hospital, he'd be vulnerable to whoever was looking for him. His family would also be notified, making them vulnerable, too.

Gus. If he could get to Gus, Gus could treat him at home. He doubted Gus would see it that way, but in Royce's present state of mind, it seemed a logical choice. Limping through the woods at a slow pace, Royce tried to ignore the ache in his chest. The blood flow had slowed, but it continued to run, and it soaked his tattered shirt and pants. His calf throbbed, and it felt like bugs were crawling up his leg—not over the skin but under it—and he made a considerable effort to not consider what that meant. Studying his surroundings, he realized he was still on McDermott's land and a good distance away from his own. If he'd had two good legs, he'd have been home by now, but under his present circumstances, he'd be lucky to get home before dark. He realized he didn't have that much time. Without medical attention, he'd be dead before dinner.

A wave of nausea hit him, and he fell hard on his hands and knees. His stomach lurched, and he vomited into a shrub. He gasped as the pain in his leg flared. He cleared his throat, spit into the leaves, and waited until the nausea eased. Sitting back on his heels, he laid his forehead in the dirt, panting. Sweat trickled down his back.

Knowing he didn't have the luxury of time, he made himself get back up on his feet, using a tree trunk for support. He blinked several times, trying to find his balance. After several seconds, he finally pushed off the trunk and started to walk again when another wave of dizziness hit. Vision blurring, he stumbled forward. His foot caught on an outstretched strip of root, and he tripped and collapsed to the forest floor. The ground rearing up at him was the last thing he saw before he lost consciousness.

# Chapter Eight

GUS WALKED ALONG THE trail leading up to the Shady Point campgrounds. He studied the winding path and surrounding forest, stopping periodically to observe the leaves and branches along the path.

Aaron, the sheriff's deputy, waited a few feet behind him and slowly followed Gus through the woods. The Native American was quiet, saying little since he'd arrived. Aaron had merely pointed him in the right direction and Gus had taken it from there. They'd been through the crime scene, where the woman's body had been found, up the trail to Shady Point Park, and now down into the campgrounds, where Aaron continued to watch Gus work. He didn't know exactly what the medicine man would find, since the police had searched the area twice, but he waited to find out.

Aaron checked his watch. They'd been out here for over two hours. His stomach growled. He wished the sheriff were here, but Rick had needed to pick up RJ and spend some time with him, so Aaron had agreed to meet Gus. Biting back a sigh, Aaron watched as Gus stopped again and dropped low to the ground. He traced his fingers through the fallen leaves and appeared to be studying the dirt, then he looked up. Aaron looked up, too, wondering what the man was seeing.

Aaron felt his impatience rise. "What is it?" he asked. "What do you see?" He continued to look up.

Gus rose from his squat. "The sun." He raised his hand to the sky. "It's a beautiful day, isn't it?"

Aaron felt a trickle of sweat roll down his neck. He could do with a little less sun. "Fabulous," he said. Gus grinned and continued down the trail.

Aaron looked at his watch again. The thought of eating a juicy cheeseburger at Minnie's made his mouth water. "You almost done, Gus?" Gus strolled down the path and Aaron heard him chuckle. "What?" asked Aaron. "You find something?"

Gus stopped. Aaron stopped too, and the two men eyed each other. Gus rested his hands on his hips. "I finished about an hour ago."

Aaron was confused. "Excuse me?"

Gus stood quietly. "I said I finished about an hour ago."

Aaron threw up his hands. "Then why have we been walking through these infernal woods all this time?"

Gus smiled. "Because it's a lovely day, like I said, and I was enjoying nature's gifts."

Aaron rolled his eyes. "Why didn't you say something?"

"Why didn't you ask?"

Aaron saw the twinkle in Gus's eyes and bit back a moan. Now he really wished the sheriff was here. If he were, Aaron would be enjoying that hamburger right now instead of contemplating leaving Gus in the woods right along where the woman's body had been found. He tried to show no impatience, but he couldn't help stomping around and past Gus.

"Watch where you're stepping," said Gus, and Aaron hopped back onto the trail.

"What?" he asked, staring at the ground. "Is there evidence?"

Gus walked up and stooped low. "You almost stepped on a dandelion." He reached down and brushed a finger on the round weed that sprang from the ground. Soft furry wisps dislodged from the circular head and blew into the wind. "Lovely, isn't it?" asked Gus.

Aaron swatted at a mosquito. He bit back an angry retort and almost turned to leave, but hesitated. He knew the sheriff would be angry if he were rude to Gus. He ignored Gus's question. "Did you find anything useful?" he asked. He watched Gus appreciate the weed. "Besides dande-lions?"

Gus straightened. He studied the surrounding woods. "Just that Mother Earth is a generous woman, but I already knew that."

Aaron sighed. "Good to know. Anything else?" He turned away. His suspicions that this would turn out to be a wild goose chase were con-firmed.

"Just that there was a party out here recently. Probably a group of four or five. And they're likely teenagers based on the joint I found and the discarded beer bottle in the shrubs up in the park. There are several sneaker prints in the dirt off the trail, too. If any of them were out late that night, I'd say they're worth talking to."

Aaron stared at him, saying nothing. How in the world did Gus know all of that after only an hour's walk? He continued to stand mute as Gus approached and passed him on the trail. "I'm hungry," said Gus. He glanced back at Aaron. "You up for a burger at Minnie's? I'm buying."

Aaron heard Gus chuckle as Gus walked away.

# Chapter Nine

ROYCE SHIVERED, BUT INTENSE heat rippled through him. He tried to stand, but something pushed him down. His leg throbbed, his chest ached, and he moaned in pain, but his cries went unanswered. Images formed in his head as his body fought the poison. They morphed one into another in a vicious cycle of fear and weakness—a snake, coiled and ready to strike, tongue flicking; RJ with the ax, striking the logs of wood; the bear rearing up and roaring, claws outstretched; Gus, with worried eyes, telling him he was in danger; and then a woman with long blonde hair watching him. Nothing made sense. The visions came fast and quick. Sometimes the snake would strike and bite him. Or the bear would swipe at Royce and its claws would rip into his flesh, making Royce cry out. Other times, he saw Gus standing over him, chanting and holding a feather. Then the woman would return and he felt the coolness of her approach. The heat in his body always eased when she was near.

He had no idea where he was. Was he still in the forest, slowly dying? During more lucid moments, he felt protected, as if someone was watching over him, but he couldn't form a coherent thought or escape the haze of heat and pain he was in. It felt like someone had thrown a heavy, hot blanket over him, and he had no idea how to get it off. He felt suffocated, and at times he fought to remove the cloth, desperate for air and release, until his limbs became heavy and then he couldn't move them at all. He wondered if this was death. Had he died? Was this the afterlife that awaited him? If so, it was not what he had envisioned. He had never seriously entertained thoughts of heaven or hell, but now he had to consider that he had somehow ended up in the latter. Why, he didn't know.

Another image in his head, but this time of his sisters. He saw Gillian and Eve at a distance in the woods. They saw him and waved, and he waved back. Beginning to walk toward them, he felt fear fire up in his belly and he yelled at them to run, but they didn't move. He picked up his pace. Something was wrong. He ran faster, shouting at them to get away. But they continued to stand and wave and then the bear attacked, taking his terrified sisters down to the ground. Cold terror plunged Royce into a dark abyss. He screamed and then he was in swirling water; the waves pushing him along the rough current. He couldn't surface. There was no air, and his lungs strained. He lunged upward, following the bubbles that escaped his mouth, desperate to break free of the surging liquid. He kicked hard with his legs and his arms pumped, and the surface loomed. He was close. With one more hard stretch, he reached out with his hand and felt someone grab it and pull him up. His head broke through the plane of water and he saw who gripped his palm. Galen. The man who had almost killed him six months ago. Galen's face broke into an evil smile and he cackled.

Royce reared back, voiced a muffled scream, and then his eyes opened. Everything was quiet and blurry. He blinked several times. Breathing hard, he tried to make sense of where he was. It was a low lit, small room, and he was in a warm bed. There was a blanket over him, and he was soaked in sweat. As his vision cleared, he could make out the surroundings. There was a window, a nightstand with a lamp and wide bowl sitting atop it, and a chair beside the bed. He turned his head and saw a small bathroom. The door to his room was open. He struggled to move his arms, but he couldn't. As the haze continued to clear, he realized his limbs were tied down. He fought to free himself, but the knots were tight and his efforts only made them tighter. Fear curled his stomach. Where was he?

"Starman. You back with us?"

Royce turned and saw Gus standing at the open door. Royce released an audible sigh of relief. "Gus?" His voice was weak and raspy.

Gus walked over and sat in a chair beside the bed. His tired, worried look reminded Royce of the face from his nightmares. "How do you feel?"

Royce wasn't sure how to answer. As his awareness improved, he could feel the aches and pains in his body. He swallowed and his throat stuck. "I'm thirsty." He moved his arms, but his bound wrists limited his movement. It was then he realized he was naked under the sheets. What the hell had happened to him?

Gus leaned over and undid the ropes on Royce's arm. "Sorry. We didn't have a choice. You were flailing and fighting us. You're a big man. We had to keep you from hurting yourself, and more importantly, from hurting us." He picked up a water glass with a straw and brought it up to Royce, who lifted his head and sucked deeply. The water felt cool and refreshing and Royce didn't think he'd ever tasted anything better.

After taking a long drink, Royce rested his head back. Gus set the water aside and undid the rest of Royce's restraints. Royce attempted to move and moaned with the effort. Everything hurt, especially his leg. The memories returned with a frightening thud. The bear. The snake. He shifted his leg and was gratified to still feel it attached to his body, although it buzzed with a low-grade heat from his foot to his thigh. His chest itched, and he fought the urge to scratch it.

He attempted to speak again. "How did I get here?" His voice sounded stronger. He looked around the room. "Where am I?" Gus's earlier answers finally pierced his muddled brain, and he asked the obvious. "And who is 'we'?"

Before Gus could answer, a woman walked into the room. She stopped when she realized Royce was awake. She wore a long, shapeless light blue dress and her long blonde hair was tied in a braid that hung down her back. Royce recognized her immediately. She was the woman who had rented the McDermott cabin. She was also the woman from his dreams. The one who had kept him cool as he blazed with fever. He stared at her, and she blushed from his intense gaze. A strange wave of heat engulfed him, but it wasn't from illness. Probably had more to do with the fact that he was naked beneath the sheets.

Gus finally answered the lingering question. "This is Alice." He looked back at her and then at Royce. "If it wasn't for her, you'd be dead, Starman, or at the very least in a hospital, where you should have been in the first place." He grunted his displeasure.

Royce finally broke eye contact with Alice and stared at Gus. "What exactly happened?" he asked. "The last thing I remember was collapsing in the woods."

Alice finally spoke. "I found you." Her voice was light and wispy, as if she were unsure whether she wanted to speak.

Despite his weakness, Royce could feel her timidity. "You did? How?"

Her hands gripped her dress in a show of nervousness. "I was out walking. I heard shuffling, moaning. I saw you on the ground."

Royce had no memory of the encounter. "How'd I get here?" He eyed the room. "I know you didn't carry me."

She made a small smile. She looked pretty when she smiled. "No. I didn't. You managed to walk with my help."

"I walked here?" How could he not remember that?

"You were in a lot of pain. You were bleeding. You were rambling about a snake bite. I brought you to my cabin, got you inside and into the bed." She hesitated for a moment. "I started to call for help, but you asked me not to. You said it was dangerous. Someone was looking for you."

Royce thought back, but his mind was blank. "I did?"

"Yes." She let go of her dress and her nervousness seemed to ease. She walked up next to Gus. "I have a medical background. You were very ill. I got you comfortable, tried to deal with the snakebite as best I could, cleaned your chest wounds, but I knew you needed more. When your leg started to swell, I was prepared to call an ambulance. But you begged me not to. You kept asking for Gus. Said Gus could help you."

Royce noted Gus's unreadable face. "Apparently you found him."

Alice nodded. "Luckily, he wasn't hard to find. I called the sheriff. Got a hold of the deputy. He gave me Gus's number." She put her hand on the back of Gus's chair. "I called and Gus showed up an hour later."

Gus's face was stony. "You should have called the ambulance."

"You could have called just as easily," Alice replied, in a show of strength. "You could have done it the moment you walked in."

"Hmph," Gus grunted, but made no other explanation.

"So why didn't you?" Royce couldn't help but ask.

Gus reached over and pulled Royce's blanket up to his chin. "There are some things, Starman, we may never know the answer to."

Royce fought the urge to yank the blanket back down. It felt like sweat was pouring out of him. "You obviously kept me alive."

"You're lucky I had a stocked medicine bag. I wouldn't have had the time to search for the proper ingredients. The ancestors were smiling on you," said Gus. He glanced up at Alice. "And Alice. She watched over you day and night." Gus's eyes met Royce's, and they held the stare. Royce remembered their conversation on the porch.

"Thank you, Alice," he said, glancing up at her. He saw her nervousness return when she looked at the floor. "I don't know what to say."

Her head bobbed up. "There's nothing to say. You needed help. I couldn't let you die in the woods."

"You could have called EMS, the police. Let them take care of me instead of you."

"I almost did, but…"

He waited for her to answer. "But what?"

"Something in your voice. You sounded desperate. I know how that feels." She went quiet again and looked out the window. Neither man spoke until Royce broke the quiet.

"How's my leg?" he asked, thinking it best to divert the subject for Alice's sake.

"Still there," said Gus. "I applied a poultice of ground leaves and roots to remove as much poison as I could. The rest you had to sweat out. We heated up the room to help with that. You also had a high fever and were delusional."

"How long have I been here?" asked Royce.

"Three days," said Alice.

"Your leg swelled and turned red," said Gus. "Alice was worried you would go into shock. We removed your clothes, kept you as comfortable as possible, helped you go to the bathroom, wiped you down to keep the fever low. We had to tie your hands and legs when your hallucinations became violent."

Royce was stunned at all they had done for him. "You helped me go to the bathroom?"

"Would you have rather soiled the bed?" asked Gus. "I suspect that would have been far more unpleasant."

Royce focused on a piece of dirt on the ceiling. "Point taken." He had no memory of any trips to the bathroom. He guessed that was a small blessing.

"How are you feeling now?" asked Alice.

Royce released a deep sigh. "Like I've been through the digestive track of that bear, and he left me in one of his droppings."

Gus chuckled. "That's what you get for hiding from him. You look like we found you in one of his droppings, too."

"Your fever's broken," said Alice. "Think you're strong enough to take a shower?"

Gus raised an eyebrow. "Would you like our help?"

Royce saw the twinkle in Gus's eye. "I think any more trips to the bathroom will be handled on my own, thanks." He scratched at his chest.

"Careful," said Alice. "I taped your chest wounds after I cleaned them. I didn't have access to a needle and thread. The injuries are healing, but go easy. We don't want them to reopen."

Royce thought about an earlier comment she'd made. "You said you have a medical background?"

She hesitated, but finally nodded.

"What is it?" asked Royce.

She crossed her arms. "It was a while ago...in another life."

Royce raised a brow. "Are you a doctor?"

She shook her head. "No." She paused, studying her shoes. "I was a trauma nurse."

"Really?" asked Royce and Gus at the same time.

"Yes. So don't be too embarrassed. I have some experience cutting off men's clothes. I've seen a lot worse. Believe me."

Royce pictured her removing his tattered shirt and pants from his body, and he warmed considerably. Based on the blush that colored her face, Royce knew she was thinking the same thing.

Gus cleared his throat. "Well, now that you're better, I'll be leaving."

Royce and Alice spoke. "Leaving?"

Gus's eyes lit up, and Royce knew exactly what he was thinking. "Yes. You don't need me anymore, Starman. The crisis has passed." He nodded toward the corner of the room. "I found your suitcase in the back of your car. You should have all you need."

"Are you saying I can go home?" asked Royce. His mind was racing. He knew he wasn't strong enough yet to take care of himself.

"I wouldn't advise it unless you've got someone to help you."

"Gus..." said Royce.

"Yes?" asked Gus, standing.

Alice spoke to Royce. "You can stay here," she said, looking composed despite her initial shock at Gus's impending departure.

Royce was surprised. "Alice, I can't ask you to do that."

"Why not? Like Gus said, the worst is passed. You just need to rest, eat, and build up your strength. I can help with that. Unless you'd be more comfortable at your place? I can help you over there, too."

Royce thought about his expected visitors. The ones Gus had warned him about. It was the last thing he wanted. To be found weak and vulnerable, and possibly putting Alice at risk as well. He couldn't do that to her.

"Alice," he said. "Do you mind if I have a word with Gus, please?"

She stood unmoving, but then nodded. "I'll step outside."

"Thank you," said Royce, and he watched her leave and close the door behind her. "What are you doing?" he asked Gus the moment the door shut.

"Just what I said. I'm going home."

"Gus. I can't stay here."

"Why not?" Gus pointed at the door. "She's pretty."

"Because..." Royce wasn't sure what to say.

Gus tilted his head. "Is it because of our conversation?"

Royce's vision momentarily blurred. He blinked, and Gus's face came back into view. "Is she the one?"

Gus narrowed his eyes. "One what?"

Royce didn't hold back a grunt. "The one who will break my heart?"

"Her?" asked Gus, nodding to the door.

Royce rolled his eyes. "No. Your mother. Of course her. You said I would meet a woman and she would break my heart."

Gus sat down in the chair. "I don't know. I didn't see what she looked like in my vision. It might be, but it might not be."

"Hell," said Royce, shutting his eyes. "You're a lot of help."

"Does it matter?"

Royce opened his eyes. "It would be nice to know."

Gus leaned down and put his elbows on his knees. "Listen, Starman. Maybe it is and maybe it isn't. What I do know is that you're not strong enough to be on your own. She's offered to help. Taking you anywhere else will only strain your system more. Unless you want to go back to your place, and judging by your desire to avoid home right now, I'd guess that's not an option. You have a warm bed, a place to shower, and a former trauma nurse who's offered to help. I'd say you're in good hands."

When Royce grimaced, he added. "Do I know if she'll break your heart? No. Does that mean you should avoid her just in case she might? No. Keep in mind, I did say I saw you with a broken heart, but I didn't say when. Could be years from now." Royce wiped a trickle of sweat from his neck. "Who knows?" Gus continued. "Maybe my vision was wrong. I may have just had too much peyote."

Royce furrowed his brow. "You said you saw trouble in my future. You said I'd meet a woman. And not twenty-four hours later, every one of those things has happened." He rubbed at his temples as a headache blossomed. "Have you ever been wrong?"

Gus stood from his seat. "There's a first time for everything."

"You could stay here."

Gus smiled. "No. This house is small. I need to sleep. In my own bed. She'll take care of you. Besides..." He turned to leave.

"Besides what?" asked Royce.

Gus put his hand on the doorknob. "You can't escape destiny, Royce." He stood quietly, as if reflecting on the events of the past seventy-two hours. "You tried it, my friend, and it failed. My suggestion is not to try it again. The ancestors don't like it."

Royce groaned under his breath. "You can tell the ancestors they made their point."

Gus chuckled. "They already know." He opened the door. "I'll call tomorrow to check on you." He stepped out of the room, and Royce heard him speak to Alice. "He's all yours."

· · · · ● · ● · · · ·

Royce sat at the small dining table. After Gus had left, Royce had summoned the energy to sit up and eventually stand. Alice had run the shower for him and he'd cleaned himself up before his energy completely evaporated. He'd put on a pair of pajama pants and collapsed back into bed, where he'd slept for the rest of the day. Finally waking, he'd sat up, thrown on a t-shirt, and walked on shaky legs into the front of the house. The light outside was waning, but a lamp lighted the room. He saw a small kitchen, dining table, and a set of stairs leading to a small loft area above. There was a sofa and TV in the living area, but no Alice.

They'd said little to each other after Gus left. She'd been almost professional with him as she'd prepared his shower, asking only if he'd needed anything. After falling back into bed, he'd smelled the clean scent of the sheets and realized that she'd changed them. Now, feeling a little lightheaded, he sat at the table and listened to his stomach rumble. He could smell something delicious. He hadn't had solid food in days, and his hunger had returned with a vengeance. If he'd had the strength, he would have walked into the kitchen to investigate, but he didn't trust his balance.

Footsteps caught his attention, and he heard a back door open. Alice appeared in the kitchen, holding what looked like green leaves in her hand. She stopped when she saw Royce.

"You're up," she said.

Royce noted she had changed but wore yet another shapeless dress. Apparently, that was the extent of her wardrobe. Her thick blonde braid hung down her back, and he envisioned it undone and her hair spilling over her shoulders. "Yes," he said. "Thought it might be a good idea to move around a bit." He looked at the greenery in her hand. "You like leaves?"

She glanced down. "It's mint. Thought I'd make some iced tea. You like tea?"

The thought of an ice-cold sweet tea almost made Royce pant. "That sounds like heaven right about now."

She smiled, and her eyes sparkled. "It'll just take a minute." She walked toward the sink and began to rinse the leaves. "You hungry?"

"Starving."

"I bet you are." She shook out the rinsed mint and put it on a paper towel. "I'm not much of a cook, but I made some spaghetti sauce. I just need to boil the noodles. You like spaghetti?"

Royce almost snorted. "Alice, at this point, I'd eat those leaves. And if you served me a boiled rat, I probably wouldn't turn it down."

She laughed, and Royce found himself wishing he could take her hair out of that braid. He cleared his throat and made himself think of something else. "How long you been out here?" He looked around the cabin. "You rent this place from Mr. McDermott?"

At the question, he noticed her immediate stillness. It passed quickly, though. "Not long," she said. She pulled out a pot and began to prepare the pasta. Royce could feel her nervousness and knew she was trying to hide it. "I just needed a place to stay for a little while." She filled the pot with water. "I saw an ad for a cabin rental. It seemed like the perfect place."

Royce tried to tune into her. He didn't want to invade her privacy, but he was curious. He knew she was telling him only what she had to. "You out here by yourself?"

She set the water-filled pot on the stove and turned up the heat. "Yes. Just me." She pulled out a smaller pot and began to fill it with water.

"How long you plan on staying?"

She lifted the lid off another pot on the stove and stirred what he presumed was the spaghetti sauce. "Not sure."

He wondered how far to push it. "You married?"

The lid fell out of her hand and clattered onto the counter, and she jumped at the noise. "Sorry." She wiped her fingers on her dress and picked up the cover. "It slipped out of my hand." She continued to stir, but did not answer his question.

"I apologize. I didn't mean to pry." He felt disappointment when he realized that the answer to his question was probably yes. She was married. He thought about what Gus had told him. Was Alice the woman who would break his heart? Watching her move through the kitchen, he felt his skin warm. He couldn't recall being this attracted to a woman so quickly.

She covered the pot again and rubbed her shoulders. "No. I'm sorry." There was a bag of pasta on the counter, and she opened it. "I'm just not used to talking about myself."

He noted her shape as she pulled plates from a cabinet. Her dress, in many ways almost made her more appealing. He wanted to know what was beneath it. "I get it. I'm not too forthcoming either."

She walked over and put a dish in front of him. "Are you married?"

Shaking his head, he answered. "No."

"Ever been close?"

Still shaking his head, he said, "No."

Her lips pursed. "Really?"

"Does that surprise you?"

"Yes, actually. It does." She walked back into the kitchen, threw the leaves into the smaller pot, and added some tea bags.

"Why?"

She glanced over at him. "Have you looked in the mirror? You're not hard to look at."

Her honesty surprised him and must have surprised her too, because she blushed. "I'm not?" He liked that she found him attractive.

Her eyebrows lifted. "Men like you rarely go very long without a woman on their arm."

He wondered about that. "I'm not like most men."

Their shared gaze held. Breaking the look, she searched the kitchen and found a colander. "Dinner will be ready soon."

His body tingling; he shifted in his seat. He tried to think of something else to say. "Do you have any kids?" Realizing too late that he was prying, he added, "Sorry. I'm asking too many questions."

She stirred the sauce and smiled. "No. It's fine. No. No kids. You?"

"No."

"You want them?"

That question surprised him. Now she was being direct. "Maybe one day."

"Me too," she replied.

He continued to watch as she prepared the meal. "Sorry. I'd offer to help, but I don't trust my legs right now."

She lowered the heat on the stove. "It's fine. You need to rest. I'm okay." She glanced at him. "You feeling better?"

He nodded. "Yes. Thanks. Glad to be out of that bed."

"I bet."

They kept the conversation light as the water boiled. She finished the spaghetti and brought everything to the table. When she placed an ice-filled glass of tea in front of him, he drank most of it in one swallow. It was delicious. She refilled his glass and gave him a full plate of pasta and meat sauce, which he tried not to inhale. As his hunger dissipated and his stomach filled, he found himself relaxing. He sat back in his seat and studied her from across the table. "Why are you helping me?"

She stopped mid-bite. She swallowed her food and wiped her mouth with her napkin. "What do you mean?"

"You don't know me. I'm a neighbor who got himself into trouble, who you found rambling and injured in the woods. You take a stranger into your house and proceed to care for him, wipe him down, take him to the bathroom, let him sleep in your bed, and feed him." He put his fork down. "Why? You should have called the cops."

She held her napkin. After a second passed, she put the napkin on her lap and took a sip of her drink. "You needed help."

"I know that. Doesn't mean you needed to do all that you did." She avoided his gaze. "Why?" he asked again.

She finally looked at him and shrugged. "I don't know. Guess I have a little Florence Nightingale in me."

She was trying hard not to answer, but he wouldn't let her off the hook. "Why aren't you still a trauma nurse?"

She picked up her iced tea and took a sip. When she put it down, she ran her fingers down the side of the glass. "It wasn't working out for me. It's a hard job. Long hours. Evenings and weekends. Holidays."

He spoke before he thought. "Bullshit," he said. She eyed him from across the table. "It's one thing if you don't want to tell me, but don't lie to me." She sat back and studied her plate. "You have a gift for caring for people. That's obvious."

She spoke quietly. "I loved being a nurse."

He felt her defenses weaken, and her posture eased. He didn't know why he was so curious. If he were smart, he'd finish his meal, go back to bed, and hopefully be strong enough to go home the next day. Then she'd go her way, and he'd go his. He had other pressing matters to deal with, anyway. But something compelled him to keep talking. For some reason, he wanted to know all about her. "So why'd you leave?" he asked.

She picked at her napkin. "I..."

He didn't interrupt, knowing that if he stayed quiet, she'd continue.

"I couldn't stay."

"Why not?"

She shifted nervously. "I was stupid."

"Stupid how?"

She glanced up at him, but then away. "I married the wrong man."

Not expecting to hear that, he felt the momentary regret that she was with someone else. "What does that have to do with you giving up nursing?"

She sighed deeply. "Because I left him."

Royce didn't know how to feel about that. "Sorry to hear it."

She quirked an eyebrow. "No, you're not." It was her turn to be bold. "You're not the only one who can sense bullshit."

He didn't argue with her. "What happened?"

She sat up, as if finally choosing to no longer feel afraid. "He was mean to me."

Royce stilled in his chair. "He was what?"

Her eyes glittered with either anger or sadness. Royce couldn't tell which. "He was mean. He hit me."

Royce made a visible effort not to react. "He hit you?" He picked up his iced tea glass and gripped it. He couldn't imagine anyone raising a hand to Alice.

"Yes." She pushed her plate back.

Royce sat in shocked silence. "How long were you with him?"

She stared off. "Four years."

He leaned forward. "He hit you for four years?"

"No, he didn't." She picked at a mark on the table. "At first, everything was wonderful. We were happy, young and in love. We married quickly, wanted to start a family, begin our lives together. But then..."

"Then what?"

She sighed and interlaced her hands. "We couldn't get pregnant. After months of trying, it turns out I can't have children. At least not the old-fashioned way."

Royce didn't react. "I'm sorry."

"I was devastated, of course, but we talked about adoption. He seemed happy, but then he lost his job. Was laid off." She paused. Royce said nothing and waited. "He couldn't find work. After a while, he would go out, but come home later and later. He was drinking and, I later learned, gambling." She went quiet, and Royce felt a jumble of emotions exude from her. "I tried to talk about it, but something had changed. He'd suddenly become so angry. It was then that I realized he blamed me."

"Blamed you for what?"

"For everything. No family, no job, no money. Things went downhill very fast. After seeing that side of him, I quickly gave thanks."

"Thanks? For what?"

She picked up her glass, but didn't drink from it. "For not having children with him. It was a blessing in disguise."

Royce nodded. "And that's when he became violent?"

She shifted uncomfortably. "Yes. When I told him I was leaving him, he..." She held her tea. "Well, he didn't approve." The tea in her glass quivered and Royce noticed her fingers shook. "I tried to leave several times. Finally, I went to a shelter for women, but he found me."

"Did you call the police?"

She laughed, and Royce shivered with the coldness in her tone. "A lot of good that did. I got a restraining order. Didn't help."

Royce was angry, but tried not to show it. "So that's why you're here?"

She leaned forward, put her elbows on the table, and looked directly at him. "I left my job about a year ago. He would come looking for me there. Caused too many problems. After the shelter didn't work, I packed my bags and left. Snuck out really. I sold my red convertible, which I loved, and bought an older brown sedan. Something that wouldn't attract attention. I've been on the move ever since. Don't stay in one place too long. I paid someone for fake IDs. Opened a bank account under a different name. Got rid of my credit cards. My own family doesn't know where I am."

Royce stared, dumbstruck. His mind could not grasp how this beautiful woman across from him was on the run from her own husband. "I..." His mind went blank. "I don't know what to say."

She nodded. "I know."

He shifted in his seat. "Is that why you didn't call the cops when you found me?"

Her face dropped. "Partly, maybe, yes." She looked away. "But if I'd believed your life was in jeopardy, I would have called. But mainly it was because of you."

"Me?"

"Yes." Her eyes softened. "You were pleading. Asking me not to call. You sounded so desperate. So afraid. It…" She met his gaze again. "I guess it reminded me of me. If I'd been in the same situation, I would have been in trouble if I'd gone to the hospital. Something about you made me think of me. So, I honored your request."

Was it true that they were in similar situations, but for different reasons? "How long do you plan to keep running?"

Her face fell, and it was the first time he saw her become emotional. "I don't know. As long as it takes, I guess." She crossed her arms and hugged herself.

Royce felt her mood shift into fear, and he hated it. "What's his name?"

She lifted her head and her eyes widened. "No."

"No, what?"

She stood. "This isn't the part where you swoop in with some misguided attempt to help me. You don't owe me anything." She picked up her plate and brought it to the sink.

"I just asked you his name."

She stopped and focused a hard glare at the sink. "You don't need to know."

"Alice, believe me, I'm in no shape to play Lone Ranger."

"It doesn't matter. I have to go anyway." She picked up the pot that had boiled the pasta and dumped the water into the sink. It sprayed up on her.

Royce sat forward. "You're leaving?"

She scrubbed the pot. "Yes. I've been here for too long. I can't stay."

He stood slowly. The food had helped improve his strength, and he was relieved when he felt no shakiness. He picked up his plate and silverware and brought them to the sink. "Alice…"

She continued to wash the plates even though she had a dishwasher. She didn't acknowledge him.

"Alice," he said more forcefully.

"What?" She wiped at a strand of hair that had fallen from her braid.

He leaned against the counter. "What's his name?"

The faucet ran, and she held the colander in her hand. "You're not going to do anything stupid, are you?"

There were soap suds on her cheek, and he resisted the urge to reach over and wipe them off. "I promise."

She sighed and stared, as if debating whether to answer. "Fine." She opened her mouth to speak, but she said nothing. He waited, but then she shook her head. "No. I'm not telling you."

"Alice..."

She pointed a scrub brush at him. "I don't want you involved. The last thing I need is you rushing in to save me, or worse, calling the sheriff. No. I have enough man problems. I don't need more. I can take care of myself."

Royce started to say something, but his vision briefly spun and he gripped at the counter. She dropped the brush and bolstered him when his legs buckled. He leaned forward and took a deep breath.

"Easy," she said. "Tighten the muscles in your legs. It will force the blood up."

He did what she said, and the dizzy spell eased. He slowly straightened, but she continued to hold on to him. Even though she was petite, she was stronger than she looked. He couldn't help but feel another tingle move through him at her touch. "Sorry," he said. It surprised him how quickly his fatigue had returned.

"Can you make it back to the bed?" she asked.

He nodded. "Yes. I think so." He pushed off from the counter, and she let go of him.

"Go lay down. I'll bring you some more tea if you want it."

He hated leaving the conversation. He wanted to know who her idiot husband was, but he could also tell she had closed up and didn't want to say anymore. He started to walk away, but stopped. He had to ask her one more question. "You'll still be here, won't you?"

She wiped the suds off her cheek. "What do you mean?"

He debated being honest. "When I wake up. You'll still be here?"

Her gaze held his, and for a moment he considered ignoring all his fears, pulling her close, and kissing her until all thoughts of her husband were forgotten. But then the haze cleared, and he didn't move.

She nodded. "Yes. Don't worry." She reached out and took his fingers and held them in her own. Chills ran up his arm, and he felt regret when she let him go. "I'll still be here." She nodded toward the bedroom. "Go get some rest."

# Chapter Ten

SARNA STOOD BEHIND JASPER and swatted at a bug that kept buzzing by her head. A cold breeze blew, and she shivered. "We can't stay any longer. We're almost out of supplies."

Jasper rose from his squat and stretched. "We can't leave until we've spoken to him."

Sarna wrapped her blanket tighter around her. A leaf fell in her hair. She sighed heavily and brushed it away. "In case you haven't realized, he's not home. He's gone. We don't know where he is."

Jasper turned and walked past her and returned to the tent. "His car is here. He'll be back."

Sarna stomped toward him. "You idiot. We don't know when he'll be back. It could be days. We've run out of money; we're staying outside; it's freezing out here; and all we've got for food is trail mix."

"It's not that cold."

She couldn't believe her ears. "Damn it Jasper. It's over. We've lost our shot. Maybe he got wind of us and somehow knew we were coming. I don't know. But we can't continue like this."

"We've got plenty of water, and the trail mix will last us a little longer."

Sarna tried to rein in her anger. She knew it was only making Jasper dig in his heels. He sat down on a log, and she joined him. "Listen, Jasper." She kept her voice calm and soft. "I know this is disappointing. We have a lot at stake here. But it was a long shot at best."

Jasper whipped his head toward her. "A lot at stake? You know what awaits us when we return? Without him..."

"You don't know what will happen when we return. For all you know, things may be better."

"Come on. You know that's not going to happen. We were lucky to get out of there in the first place."

"And you don't know if we'd succeeded that it would have made things better."

"They can't be much worse."

"Yes, they can." She looked around at their crude shelter and the trees around them. "We could stay out here another night."

Jasper picked up a stick and poked at the ground. "We can't afford to stay anywhere, and we can't stay at his place without risk of discovery. That's the whole point of having the tent."

Her calm evaporated, and she stood. "We were already in his home. We should have just stayed there. We are not campers. You and I know nothing about surviving on this planet."

He grimaced at her. "We know plenty about survival."

"That's not what I mean." She walked back to their surveillance spot and pulled back the branches. Royce's quiet house could be seen in the distance. "What are we going to do? Keep watching? For how much longer?" She let go of the tree and raised her hand. "What do we know about living like this?"

Jasper stood. "I'm not asking you to live like this. I'm asking for a few more days." He threw out his hands. "How hard can it be?"

She stared in disbelief when he ducked into the tent and left her standing there. The wind blew her hair and chill bumps popped out over her skin. Anger and disbelief coursed through her, and she took a step forward, ready to scream, but then stopped. She cocked her head as she considered her options. Kill Jasper and return to the ship? But another choice came to mind. Without thinking, she threw off her blanket and headed into the trees. She didn't look back. She pushed through some dense foliage and then saw her destination clearly. The house. After a few seconds, she heard Jasper's yell from behind her.

"Where are you going?"

She kept walking. Before long, she could hear his footsteps as he jogged up behind her. "Sarna, answer me."

"You want to wait?" She finally said. "Fine. Let's wait." She kept moving.

He tried to keep up. "Wait where?"

She pointed. "There's a perfectly good empty house right in front of us. I'm waiting there."

He grabbed at her elbow, but she yanked out of his grasp. "No. We can't stay there. We risk discovery."

She threw up her hands. "Discovery by whom? We've been watching this house. No one has been here. You want to wait? Well, I'm not staying another second unless I'm warm and fed. I'm sure he has some food."

Jasper raced to keep up with her. "We can't eat his food."

"Why not?"

He didn't answer, and she figured he didn't know why not. She kept walking and neared the house.

"Please," said Jasper, in a last attempt to stop her.

She whirled on him. "I'll give you forty-eight hours. If he's not here by then, we leave. Until then, I am not sleeping in that tent again. So you have a choice." She crossed her arms in front of her.

"What if someone stops by or sees us? How do we explain ourselves?"

She shook her head. "How hard can it be? Think. You're a long-lost relative. I'm a friend. We're traveling salesmen. We had car trouble, and we needed a place to stay. We're homeless people. I don't care. Pick something." She turned and continued toward the house. She walked up to the entry, opened it, and walked in, slamming the door shut behind her.

Standing in the quiet house, she rubbed her arms, glad to be out of the cold. A few seconds passed, and she turned and poked her head outside. Jasper still stood in the driveway, his expression as cold as the tent.

"You coming?" she asked.

Jasper stared back in resignation. "I really hate you sometimes," he said under his breath. Shaking his head, he turned back toward the tent. "I'll get our stuff."

Smiling, she closed the door.

·········

Royce awoke with a start. Blinking and breathing hard, he looked around the room, trying to remember where he was. He saw the lamp and nightstand and then he remembered. Alice. He was staying in McDermott's cabin with Alice. Sweat trickled down his chest, and he sat up in bed. He'd been dreaming again. The bear had returned, but he couldn't remember much else. His foggy mind tried to retrace the hazy images, but they faded too quickly. All he retained was the fear, which was slowly dissipating. Royce kicked off the covers. He wore only his pajama pants. The T-shirt he'd worn earlier was thrown over the chair in the room, but he was too hot to put it on. His throat was dry. He stood on shaky legs and was pleased when he felt no dizziness. He felt stronger and was confident he would be able to return home later that morning. He might still be a little weak, but he was certainly capable enough to care for himself.

He took slow steps out of the room. He didn't want to wake Alice. He figured she was sleeping in the small loft area and a small surge of guilt ate at him that he had taken her bed. He felt relief that he was well enough now that he could give it back to her, but then realized she would not need it. She would also be gone by the end of the day.

He bit back a frustrated sigh and walked into the kitchen. His mind raced. There had to be a way to help her. But how? He had his own issues to deal with. He couldn't stay. But he didn't want her to leave. He opened a cabinet and found a glass. Considering his options, he flicked on the faucet and filled his cup.

"Can't sleep?"

Startled, he jumped. The glass slipped and fell from his hand. Instinctively, he reached for it, but it hit the hard surface and broke into shards, one of which sliced his finger. The blood welled up from his skin, and he winced. The cut wasn't deep, but it stung. He cursed and held it under the running water.

"Here, let me see." Alice came over from her seat on the couch. She wore another shapeless dress, but this time he saw it was a nightgown. It was sleeveless, and Royce noticed the contours of her shoulders. Despite his injury, he imagined how smooth they would be to touch.

She took his hand. "You scared me," he said, his heart thumping.

He thought he heard her laugh. "Sorry," she said. "I didn't mean to." Turning his palm, she examined the cut.

"It's fine," he said, trying to pull away. "It's not deep."

She grabbed a paper towel, wrapped it around his finger, and applied pressure. "I don't think you need stitches."

Royce almost laughed himself. "Stitches? No. I've had worse cuts from my ax."

Her eyes widened. "Ax?" She took a step back, but still held his finger. "What do you need an ax for? Something I should know?"

He froze a flat stare on his face. "Yes." He paused as she stared at him. "There is. I hate to tell you this, but...I...chop...firewood."

Her shoulders dropped, and he couldn't help but smile. "Feel better?"

"I suppose," she said. "Any other serious weapons you use I should know about?"

"Just my charming personality."

She giggled, and his insides flipped. It was the first time he'd heard and seen her happy. She took off the paper towel and studied his finger. "I think a Band-Aid is all you need. I'll get one." She let go and leaned down to open the cabinet beneath the sink.

"What are you doing up?" he asked. He searched the kitchen and found a clock. "It's four a.m."

She straightened, and he saw she held a small box. She opened it and pulled out a bandage. "I couldn't sleep."

He didn't say anything as he let her treat his finger. It was then that he noticed that her hair was out of the braid. Long, thick blonde tresses fell over her shoulders and without thinking, he reached over and took hold of a lock. It curled around his finger.

She stilled immediately. "What are you doing?"

He dropped his hand. "Sorry. Your hair…"

She ran her hand through it, and he could sense that she was self-conscious about his appraisal. "What about it?"

"It's out of the braid."

She put the box down and pushed her hair back. "Yes. It is. So?"

"It's beautiful. You should leave it down more often."

She swallowed. "Yeah, well, male attention is not what I need right now." She shut off the sink and began to pick up the shards of glass.

"Hey…" he said softly.

Finding a trashcan, she dumped the shards into it. She returned to the sink and flipped it back on to remove any remaining slivers of glass.

"Hey," he said again.

She flipped off the faucet and looked at him. The room was dimly lit and her face seemed luminescent in the light. "Hey, what?" she said.

He wasn't sure what he wanted to say until he opened his mouth and said it. "Don't leave."

She took a step back. "Royce…"

"Running away doesn't solve anything. You have to figure this out."

Her jaw dropped. "Figure it out? Figure what out? I've got a crazy person following me who will probably kill me when he finds me, and he will find me. Just what exactly am I supposed to figure out?"

Royce had to admit, his suggestion didn't make sense, but he couldn't give up and just let her walk away.

"There's always a way out."

"Oh. I see. You want to be my savior, is that it? I helped you, so you have to help me. Right? Like I said, you don't owe me anything."

"Listen..."

"No. I won't. I have to leave. As soon as you're well, I'm gone."

She backed away, but Royce took her by the arm. "Alice..." She pulled back, but he held on. "Alice wait..."

"No." She flailed, but he wouldn't let go. He couldn't let her disappear and never see her again, knowing that her crazy husband was after her.

"Alice." His voice boomed, and she froze, and then he realized what he'd done. He'd scared her. He instantly let her go, and she backed away. He held out his hand. "I'm sorry. I didn't mean to frighten you."

She was breathing hard, but she stood in place. After a few seconds, she collected herself. A strand of hair fell in her face, and she pushed it away. "Royce...I know what you want."

He stilled at her words, but didn't answer.

She paused, but finally whispered. "I want it too."

His whole body reacted. It took everything he had not to move toward her.

She shook her head. "But that can't happen. Whatever it is between us has to die here. I can't start anything with you. I can't involve you in my problems. You and I...we're just bad timing." She stood resolutely, and he didn't say a word. "I'm sorry," she said. "If things were different, then maybe we..."

Tears sprang into her eyes, and she set her jaw. He wanted to say something, but his mind went blank. All he could think about was taking her in his arms. After a few seconds passed, she spoke quietly. "I think you're strong enough now to go home. I'm going to go pack."

They stood staring at one another, and when he didn't speak, she finally moved. When she took a step toward the stairs, he broke out of his trance. It wasn't words they needed. It was something else.

Acting before he could stop himself, he reached out and slipped a hand around her waist and pulled her against him. Her curved body pressed against his, and he stifled a groan.

She barely had the chance to say his name in protest when he slid his free hand into her hair and brought his lips down and covered hers with his own. There was a brief stillness in her, but when she didn't pull away, he slanted his mouth over hers and kissed her, pulling her hard against him.

He heard her intake of breath and before he knew what was happening, she responded. Returning the kiss, she opened her mouth and delicately probed with her tongue. She trailed her hands up his shoulders and wrapped her arms around him. Her reaction made all his doubts vanish. His tongue met hers. He lowered his hand from her waist, cupped her buttocks, and pushed her hips against him. They kissed deeply, letting their mouths express all the pent-up raw emotion they felt. She pressed her body into him, and her breathing picked up its pace. Feeling more energy than he had in days, he lifted her off her feet and carried her to the dining table. Her hands trailed down his back as he continued to stroke her tongue with his own. He laid her down on the table as she pulled at her nightgown. Her legs came up and wrapped around his waist. Dragging his lips away from hers, he slid them down her cheek, and kissed and nuzzled her neck, letting his tongue and teeth flick against her warm skin. Breathing hard, her head fell back and her hands gripped his shoulders. Her nails dug into his skin. While kissing the sensitive skin just below her ear, he dropped his hands down to her hips and ran his fingers over the fabric of her soft nightgown, feeling her curves. As their hands explored, he brought his lips back to hers and captured them again, letting his mouth express his voracious need for her. Her reaction conveyed her equal desire for him. Moaning, she rocked against him.

She caressed his bare chest and back, and he slid a hand up her waist and torso and squeezed her breast. She arched against him. Their desire rapidly escalating, he reached low and found the edge of her gown and pulled it up. His fingers wound their way underneath, and he lifted the fabric higher and stroked her thighs. Trying to catch her breath, she groaned.

"Royce..." she said, but he barely heard her. He let his hands stroke higher and discovered she wore no underwear. The silkiness of her skin and the way she trembled at his touch made him feel like he was on a speeding locomotive. His whole body was ablaze, but no longer from fever. All he wanted was to feel like this forever. Feeling her hands slide down his abdomen and then move lower, he sucked in a raspy breath when he felt her slide down his pajama pants and she pulled him closer with her legs, urging him forward. Breathing fast and eager for release, Royce gave her exactly what they needed and desperately desired—a much needed respite from the fear of the unknown.

•••••••••

Hours later, as soft sunlight filtered through the windows, Alice snuggled into Royce's shoulder. They were in bed and had not slept since their encounter in the kitchen, preferring to enjoy each other's bodies instead.

Royce stroked her shoulder. They had spoken little, but now, as the day began, he couldn't help but think of their current situation. He voiced his worries. "You're still planning to leave, aren't you?"

He couldn't see her face, but he heard her sigh. "Can we talk about something else?" Her fingers grazed his skin.

"What else do you want to talk about?"

"Let's talk about you." She played with the hair on his chest. "Why don't you want to go back?"

He wasn't sure how to answer. She wasn't the only one with secrets. "I'm expecting someone..."

She shifted her head to look at him. "Who?"

He stared at the ceiling. "Someone I'd rather not meet."

"Why not?"

Her question was not surprising. "Because I think it's someone who doesn't have my best interests at heart, or my family's."

"Your family?"

"Yes."

"You said you weren't married."

He smiled at her. "I'm not. It's my mom and sisters. Sisters, mostly."

"Sisters?"

He nodded. "Yes. Gillian and Eve."

She rested her jaw on his chest. "Why would anyone want to hurt you and your family?"

He sighed and wondered how much to reveal. "My sisters and I, well, we can attract the wrong attention."

Her fingers traced his ribs. "Why?" she asked. "Did you annoy the wrong person with that charming personality of yours?"

He couldn't help but chuckle. "Something like that."

"Where are your sisters? Do they know you're in trouble?"

He tensed at her question. Was he in trouble? Were they in danger? All of his actions had been based solely on Gus's vision. Had he been wrong to react so quickly? In his heart, he knew the answer was no. Gus had told him a woman would appear in his life, and here he was, lying in bed with Alice. He was vulnerable right now, and he knew it. Gus had said there would be trouble. Was he putting Gillian and Eve at risk because he couldn't leave the arms of a beautiful lady? The thought made him quiver with unease. What was he doing?

"You okay?" Her question brought him back to the present. "Where'd you go?"

He studied her blue eyes and fought the urge to lean down and kiss her. If he did, then he knew he'd spend the rest of the day in her arms, trouble or no trouble. He reached to touch a locket that hung from her neck and rested between her breasts. It was the only thing she wore. It was silver and square-shaped and had two intersecting hearts etched on its surface.

"This is pretty," he said. He felt the cool surface warmed only from her skin. "You always wear it?"

She touched it too. "Yes," she said. "It was a gift from my father. It's precious to me. I wear it all the time."

Royce thought of the black polished rock that sat on the nightstand beside the bed. It was the gift his father had given him. Apparently, Alice had found it in his pocket when she'd cut his clothes off. "Really?"

"Yes. He gave it to me when I left home." She held the locket when Royce let it go.

"Where's your dad now?"

She was quiet for a moment. "He died. Heart attack."

He felt the emotion swell in her. "I'm sorry."

She let go of the locket and returned her hand to his chest. "It's okay. At least I had several years with him. A lot of people don't get that."

Royce thought of his own father. "Yeah."

She was quiet and snuggled into him. "You sound like someone who knows what I'm talking about."

"Maybe," he said.

"Your dad still alive?"

"Yes, he is. But I...we...rarely saw him growing up."

"He and your mom were together?"

"Yes. Still are, in fact."

"They are? Then why don't you see him?"

Royce considered how to answer. "His job. He travels."

"Even now?" She caressed his sternum.

He thought about his dad and wondered where he was. "I haven't seen him in three years."

"Three years? Where is he?"

He stroked her cheek. "Your guess is as good as mine."

"When's he coming back?"

He smiled, but with sadness. "I don't know."

Reaching up, she cupped his cheek and rubbed her thumb along his skin. "Do you want to talk about this?"

He shook his head. "Not really, no."

She made an impish smile. "Then what would you like to talk about?"

Her eyes sparkled, and he felt his body flare with heat. He kicked at the covers and they dropped off the bed. He let his eyes rove over her naked body. He loved that she didn't act self-conscious. "How about we do something else?"

She rewarded him when she raised her torso, slid a leg over him, and then sat astride him. She ran her hands over his chest, and she moved her hips against him. "I've never been big on conversation," she answered. She let her eyes travel over him as well.

Throwing all thoughts of danger aside, Royce lifted his upper body, pulled her against him, and kissed her hard. She wrapped herself around him, matching his ardor, and before he could think about what could or should happen next, he found himself completely vanquished by her.

· · · · •· • · · ·

A noise woke him. The first thing he became aware of was the sound of crickets. The window was cracked open and the melodic whirring drifted into the room. Widening his eyes, he saw it was dark and night had fallen.

As his mind shook off his sleep, Royce remembered the previous day with Alice. They'd made love throughout the afternoon, pausing only for food and water to keep up their strength. He'd said nothing else to her about her husband, and she'd said nothing else about his visitors. Gus had called the cabin and Royce had informed him he was better and in Alice's capable hands. The Native American had chuckled, but Royce had told his friend nothing more. He'd wanted to keep his time with Alice to himself. The two of them were enjoying their secluded world, focusing only on each other. It was an experience neither had been able to enjoy before. And now that they had it, they reveled in it, soaking up as much pleasure as they could. They talked only about small things—the food they loved, the places they'd visited, where they'd grown up, their most embarrassing moments. And they'd made each other laugh. He remembered her giggle when he'd tickled her and his body had immediately responded, wanting her again.

He sat up in bed, and realizing she wasn't beside him, he reached out energetically for her, expecting her to be in the kitchen or bathroom. When he felt nothing, he jumped out of the bed. He strode into the kitchen and called for her. Looking up into the loft, he saw nothing. Running back into the bedroom, he opened her closet. Her clothes were gone. It was then that it hit him. Alice had left. She was gone.

Shocked, Royce walked slowly back into the front room. The quiet unnerved him, and her absence stunned him. He had not expected her to leave without saying goodbye. Feeling a heavy weight in his chest, he slunk down and sat on the first stair leading to the loft. Resting his head in his hands, Royce wondered what he could have done differently.

He should have considered that she might do this. She would have expected him to argue and his reluctance to let her leave after their time together.

"Damn it," Royce muttered. His chest ached, but not from his wound. Groaning and feeling miserable, he realized that Gus had been right. A woman had broken his heart.

# Chapter Eleven

SARNA STRODE THROUGH THE kitchen. It was a mess. She'd attempted to cook a meal of beans and rice, but having no idea what she was doing, she'd quickly abandoned the attempt after almost burning the house down. The food choices in the home had appalled her. There was meat in the freezer, unborn eggs in the refrigerator, and cow's milk that was souring. She had almost gagged at the smell. She and Jasper had finally settled on dry cereal and apples. It was the only thing she could find to eat that had not been derived from anything with legs. Looking around the kitchen, she peered at a clock on the wall. If they could just get through this day, then they could go home and leave this awful planet. And if she was lucky, maybe she could convince Jasper to leave sooner rather than later.

She glanced at the wristband she wore. It was black and narrow, with a thin band that widened into a small square box on the underside of her wrist. Clicking a small button on its side, the box slid open to reveal several small white pills. She took one out, closed the box, filled a glass with water, and swallowed it.

Jasper emerged from the back bedroom, wearing a large blue robe. His hair was askew and his eyes were puffy. "What time is it?" he asked, yawning.

Sarna put the glass in the sink along with the other piled dishes. "It's early." She took in his disheveled appearance. "You look terrible. Did you sleep?"

He gave her an annoyed stare. "No. I kept hearing things, thinking he'd come home. I barely closed my eyes."

"Hmm," she answered. She straightened the clean shirt she wore. She'd been up for an hour and had already had breakfast. She'd eaten the last apple. "I slept fine."

Jasper glared. "Of course you did."

She didn't let his mood upset her. "Being in a warm bed instead of a cold tent does wonders for the body."

"Especially when you take the bigger bed and warmer room."

She shrugged. "I offered it to you."

Jasper walked past her and into the kitchen. "I'd rather lack comfort than put up with your constant complaining."

She dropped her jaw. "Constant complaining?"

He opened the refrigerator and pulled out the eggs, and put them on the counter. "Yes. It's been a highlight of this trip."

She noticed the eggs. "I didn't want to sleep in that tent another night. It was cold."

"And it was uncomfortable. And you don't like this place. And you don't like the food. And the people, nor how I choose to do things."

"I don't have a problem with how you do things." She eyed him as he took three eggs out of the carton. "You're not going to eat those, are you?"

He groaned. "Yes, as a matter of fact, I am. I'm hungry. I need food." He closed the carton and put it back in the fridge.

"Eat some cereal."

"I don't want cereal."

She walked to the pantry and opened it. "There's got to be something in here you can eat." Her eyes searched the shelves. "Here..." She reached for a jar and pulled it out. "You can eat this." She put the jar on the counter.

He looked at it. "That's mustard."

"So?"

"I am not eating mustard."

"Why not?"

"Because I don't want mustard. I want eggs."

"But those are living creatures."

"They are not. They are eggs. If you warm them up, they will not hatch."

She rolled her eyes. "You know what I mean."

"Yes," he said with frustration. "Unfortunately, I do." He found an untouched pan and put it on the stove. "Now, how do I use this?"

"Jasper, I'm serious."

Jasper erupted. He picked up the pan and slammed it on the counter, making Sarna jump. "Stop telling me what to do. If I want to have eggs, I will." He fumbled with the knobs, successfully turning one on. A small blue flame flickered to life.

Sarna watched him try to unsuccessfully crack an egg. The yolk spilled on the counter. "What is the matter with you?"

He tried to crack a second egg, but he punched a hole in the surface and the egg white dripped into his hands. "What is the matter with me?" He wiped his hands on a nearby dishtowel, grabbed a third egg and threw it into the warming skillet. It cracked and broke. "I'll tell you what the matter with me is." He left the broken egg where it was. "We're about to leave this planet after having completely failed in our mission. The one person we had to talk to, who might be able to help us, has vanished, and I'm stuck with a spoiled, difficult, and uncooperative partner." He threw out his hands. "And now I have to go home and face my grim future, which likely involves a cell of some sort. And the only thing I have to show for it is bug bites."

She started to speak, angry that he was blaming her for their troubles. He raised a finger at her, though, and she held back. "And don't you say one word. You wanted to know what the matter was, and I told you. Now please, just give me one moment of peace and let me eat some damn food."

She didn't respond, and he gave a relieved sigh and returned his attention to the broken egg.

Seeing Jasper's mood, Sarna realized that now was not the time to talk to him about leaving early. She turned away but stopped and froze. Standing in the front doorway, watching her and Jasper, was a man. She knew immediately who it was.

Recovering from his outburst, Jasper had completely missed the entrance of the person who'd been his sole object of attention for the last several days.

Sarna barely spoke above a whisper. "Jasper."

Jasper slammed his hand on the counter's surface. "What, Sarna?" He looked over, and she tipped her head toward the door. His face scrunched. "What is your problem?"

"I believe I am her problem," said the man. Jasper startled and almost knocked the skillet off the stove. His jaw dropped.

Sarna stood, eyes wide. Standing in the doorway, eyes glittering like blocks of ice, was Royce Fletcher.

· · · · ● · ● · · ·

Royce stared at the intruders, but caught sight of his reflection in a mirror hanging on his wall. His face was haggard, his hair was sticking up, and his eyes held a haunted look. He dropped his duffel bag to the floor and almost groaned at the exertion.

He had not slept since he'd woken and found Alice gone. He'd spent the early morning debating what to do next. Go look for her or deal with his own problems? Undecided, he'd called his sister, Eve. Last time he'd spoken to her, she'd returned to her small apartment in the city and was working as a lounge singer in a swanky uptown bar. She hadn't been home though, and he'd left her a voicemail. He at least needed to ensure she was safe. He'd called Gillian next and discovered she was on vacation overseas with her fiancé. Because of the time difference, he'd woken her. He apologized and told her he would call later, but he felt better knowing she was out of the country and would be harder to find if anyone came looking for her.

After finally summoning the strength to move off Alice's couch, he'd made himself useful. Trying to stay busy, he'd washed and dried the sheets, cleaned the house, and gathered his things. As he was about to leave, he'd realized that his stone was lying on the nightstand. That's when he'd seen the small envelope with his name written on it. He slid the rock into his pocket, opened the note, and read it.

*Royce,*

*I'm sorry. I know you will be upset that I left. I know you want to help, but you can't. This is something I must handle, and I don't want to get you involved.*

*I wish things could be different for us. I hope you find the answers you seek and an end to your own troubles.*

*Perhaps if we both figure it out, we can find our way back to each other one day.*

*Thank you for our time together. You made me feel like the most beautiful woman in the world.*

*Alice*

Royce crumpled the note in his hand. After taking the entire morning to pull himself together, Alice's words only served to drag him back down into despair. Anger coursed through him. He was mad at the whole damn mess. Mad that he'd met her. Mad that he'd fallen for her. Mad that she'd left. And mad that he had to deal with whoever it was that was looking for him, instead of searching for Alice.

He'd yanked up his overnight bag and thrown it over his shoulder, stomped out of the cabin, and slammed the door shut. Trying not to think about her, he trudged through the woods back to his home. His leg throbbed, his body ached, and his lack of sleep only added to his irritation. A dull pain in the back of his skull signaled the beginning of a headache.

As he neared his house, the only thing on his mind was images of Alice, warm and willing in her bed, despite his attempts to do the opposite.

Walking out of the woods, he made no attempt to conceal his presence or worry about whether the rest of Gus's vision would come to fruition. But when he reached the front entry, he stopped short. The door was closed, but Royce knew someone was in his house. He sensed their presence the moment he hit the threshold and probably would have noticed it sooner if he hadn't been so preoccupied. Standing there, he could have easily turned, gotten into his car, and driven away. But at that moment, the anger grew, and he found himself itching for a fight. If someone wanted to get to him, then so be it. If he went down, then he'd do plenty of his own damage before he succumbed. He opened the door and walked in.

Standing in his foyer, he saw a man and a woman in his kitchen arguing. The woman had dark, almost black hair, a trim figure and pale skin, which went paler when she saw him. The man was tall, had honey-colored hair and a lean muscular build. Looking at him, Royce almost did a double-take. The stranger looked very much like his father. Royce shut down the chatter in his head. He'd learned that in situations like these, it was best to remain calm but prepare for the worst.

"Either of you two want to tell me who you are and why the hell you're in my house?" The two stared without saying a word. It was as if Royce had walked through the pearly gates after being sent to hell. Considering his mood, he felt like he was in hell. "I'll try again," he said, his voice gravelly. "Tell me who you are."

The woman spoke first. "Um." She paused. "We're here to see you."

"Really?" he answered. He crossed his arms. "Why?"

The man spoke next. "We...we've..." He held Royce's skillet in his hand.

Royce sneered at him. "You mind putting that down?"

The man knitted his brow, but then, realizing what Royce meant, laid the pan down on the burner. Realizing the burner was hot, he turned it off.

The woman stood rooted to her spot. "We need to talk to you."

"Ever consider picking up the phone?" asked Royce.

The man, whose name was Jasper if Royce had heard right, answered. "Uh, well, that would be difficult."

Royce's irritation pricked at him. "You don't know how to dial a number?"

The woman, who Jasper had called Sarna, perked up. "You don't have to be rude."

Royce almost laughed. "Rude?" He took a few steps into the room. Sarna startled but didn't move away. "I come back to my house to find two strangers in my kitchen." He eyed the mess in the house. "The plates are dirty, my bed is slept in, and you..." He stared at Jasper. "...are wearing my robe." Jasper peered down at himself. Royce stepped closer to Sarna. "And I'm rude?" He worked to control his voice.

Sarna looked up with a flat stare. "You're a hard man to find."

Royce held her gaze. "Maybe because I don't want to be found."

She didn't back down. "Looks like you failed."

"Sarna," said Jasper.

The urge to grab the woman by the hair and drag her out of the house occurred to Royce, but he stifled it. It had become obvious that these two did not pose the danger he had anticipated. He didn't know what they wanted, but he didn't sense a serious threat. Regardless, he didn't trust them, and he wanted them out of his home.

The itch to pick a fight grew. "Failed?" he asked. He cocked up an eyebrow. "I suspect you and your boyfriend's failure will far surpass mine. Now get out."

Sarna's eyes went from dark blue to violet. "We're not leaving."

"The hell you're not."

The room was silent until Jasper cleared his throat. "Royce, please listen."

Royce startled. "You know my name?"

"Of course we know your name," said Sarna, her own voice on edge. "You may be stupid, but we are not."

Her insult almost amused him. "I'm not convinced of that," he said and was rewarded when Sarna set her jaw. He spoke to Jasper. "Since you seem to be the level-headed one, why don't you try and tell me what you want before I take you and your girlfriend here and toss you both out."

"Level-headed?" Sarna sputtered and pointed at Jasper. "And I am not his girlfriend."

Royce couldn't help himself. "Lucky man." He realized then that if Sarna had been holding the pan, she would have clocked him with it.

"I know this is a shock to you," said Jasper.

"A small one," said Royce.

"We don't you mean you any harm."

"Speak for yourself," answered Sarna.

Jasper glowered at her. "Shut up, Sarna."

"Good idea, Sarna," Royce added.

Sarna's face turned red. "This is a waste of time. This man is nothing like we thought. He's thoughtless, ill-tempered, and obviously lacks common sense. Any hope that he might help was foolish on our part. He's right. We should leave."

"At last, we agree," replied Royce. He almost smiled when she fired another glare at him. Baiting her was improving his mood.

"Wait," said Jasper. "We've come all this way. We can't leave. Not yet."

"Yes, we can," said Sarna, walking toward the door.

"No, you can't," said Royce. He raised a brow at Jasper, whose eyes widened. "You're still wearing my robe. And I'd like it back." He held up a hand. "Let's assume you're wearing something beneath it."

Jasper's face dropped, and Royce grunted. "Never mind," answered Royce. "Robe's all yours. So feel free to follow your lady friend's advice." He shot out a thumb. "There's the door."

"My name is Sarna."

"Good for you," said Royce.

Jasper responded. "My name is Jasper."

"Great," said Royce. "Now that we all know each other, get out."

Jasper didn't move. "Jasper Fiss."

Royce frowned. "You don't seem to understand. I don't care."

Jasper continued. "Son of Carson Fiss."

"Give him my regards."

"Otherwise known as Carson Fletcher."

Royce froze. The name sent shockwaves through him. His mind raced as he considered the implications of Jasper's revelation. He darted his eyes between Jasper and Sarna.

"Your father," said Jasper. "And mine."

# Chapter Twelve

ROYCE WASN'T SURE WHAT to say. He stood like a block of wood from his firewood stack. He finally spoke. "What did you say?"

Jasper stood just as still. "I'm your half-brother."

Royce narrowed his eyes. He considered calling Jasper a liar, but his resemblance to Royce's dad stopped him. The man was telling the truth.

The woman stayed quiet, and Royce was thankful. He needed a second to think.

"What are you doing here?"

Jasper's shoulders relaxed. "I came to see you."

"Came from where?"

"Eudora."

Royce knew the name. "Eudora?"

"Yes. It's where we're from. Where our father is from."

"How?"

"How what?"

"How'd you get here?" Royce imagined space ships hovering in the sky.

"By ship. How else would we get here?"

Sarna chuckled.

"Where's your ship now?" Royce asked. A brief image of a craft sitting in his backyard appeared in his head, and he almost turned to look.

"Hidden. Away from here. Don't worry. It won't be found."

Although Royce knew his father had traveled between planets, his dad had rarely spoken of it. His father preferred to keep his earthly home life separate from his origins.

Royce regarded Sarna. "And who are you? Another member of the family?"

She huffed. "No, I'm not. Thankfully."

"She came to help me," said Jasper.

"Help you what?" asked Royce. "Annoy me?"

Sarna narrowed her eyes.

"Not really," said Jasper, "but she seems to be doing it, anyway."

"She's got a knack for it," answered Royce.

Sarna snapped back. "It's easy to annoy people I find extremely unpleasant."

Royce ignored her and spoke to Jasper. "So now that you've made the introductions, what do you want?"

Sarna answered. "Like I said. We want to talk to you."

"About what?"

Jasper and Sarna didn't answer. Royce eyed the skillet and heard his stomach grumble. It had been a long morning. Despite his desire to remove these people from his home, he had to admit he was curious. "You plan on eating something?"

"No, he wasn't," said Sarna.

"Eggs," answered Jasper. "Haven't got the hang of it, though."

Royce's stomach growled again. "You traveled from another planet to talk to me?"

"We did," said Jasper.

"Anybody else with you?"

"No. Just the two of us."

"Anyone else know you're here?"

Jasper shook his head. "No. We did this on our own. No one knows we're here."

"Not even Dad?"

Jasper shrugged. "He may have an inkling, but we didn't discuss it. Better for him not to know."

"And after you talk to me, then what?"

"We go home," said Sarna. "The sooner, the better."

Royce frowned. "You want to talk to anyone else?"

"Like who?" asked Jasper.

Royce debated whether to answer.

Sarna spoke first. "We didn't come to speak to your sisters. Gillian and Eve are safe, if that's what you're worried about."

Royce was surprised that Sarna knew their names. He shot her a worried glance.

"Yes," she said. "We know about all of you."

Royce didn't like that. "Who knows about all of us?"

"Dad told me," said Jasper. "I told Sarna. No one else knows."

Another name came to Royce's mind, along with an image of white waves slamming against a rickety pier. "What about Galen? He knew."

Sarna sucked in a breath and took a step forward. Jasper's face went pale. "Galen?" he asked. "What do you know about Galen?"

Royce set his jaw. "Just that he tried to kill me and my sisters."

Sarna gripped the kitchen counter. "When?"

"About six months ago."

"What happened?" asked Jasper.

"He almost succeeded. But we got to him first."

"You what?" asked Sarna.

"Is he dead?" asked Jasper.

"If burning alive counts as dead, then yes, he's dead."

Sarna expelled the air she'd been holding. "Dolan said he was doing research."

"Now we know what kind," said Jasper. "And why he's been gone so long."

"I wouldn't expect him anytime soon," said Royce.

"This will be a problem," said Jasper.

"What problem?" asked Sarna. "The man was evil. He deserved what he got."

"We agree again," said Royce.

"That's not the issue," said Jasper. "He was a political nightmare, but if it's discovered…"

"Who's going to discover anything?" asked Sarna. "The only people that know are the three of us."

"And Gillian and Eve," added Royce.

"And unless one of us says anything, then what's the issue?" she asked.

Jasper stayed quiet.

"I don't suppose one of you could enlighten me as to what this is all about?" asked Royce.

Jasper seemed to debate his answer. He looked at Sarna as if to gain some confirmation, and she nodded. He spoke to Royce. "We came to ask you to come back with us. To come to Eudora."

"You want me to what?"

Sarna sighed. "He wants you to return with us to our planet."

Royce dropped his jaw. "Why would I do that?"

"Well," said Sarna, "for one thing, you could experience a planet that appreciates all living creatures."

"Stop it, Sarna," replied Jasper.

"I appreciate all living creatures," answered Royce.

"Not if you eat them, you don't."

Royce studied her. "I get it. You don't eat meat on Eudora, is that it?

"Absolutely not," said Sarna.

Royce faced her squarely. "You're one of those radical vegan people?"

Her shoulders rose. "If a vegan means I care for all living beings and don't want to see them used as fuel for other beings, then yes."

"What about animals that eat meat? You have a problem with them, too?" Royce asked.

"Can we focus on the real reason we're here?" asked Jasper.

"You know what I mean," said Sarna.

"I know exactly what you mean," said Royce. "You mean if you don't do it, then no one else should either." She started to object, but he kept talking. "Listen, you're here as a visitor. Maybe everybody eats non-beings where you're from and that's fine. But don't come down here and tell me what I can and can't eat. I appreciate all living creatures, especially if it's a juicy steak."

Her face turned beet red. He didn't know why he was having this conversation. He didn't know her and didn't care what she thought about him, but for some reason, he felt the need to argue with her. Apparently, she felt the same way about him.

"Anyway..." said Jasper. "Can we get back to the point?"

"What is the point?" asked Royce. "What were we talking about?"

"You. Coming back to Eudora with us."

"Oh." Royce shook his head. "I'll make it easy on you. No."

"No?" asked Jasper.

"Fine," said Sarna. "You heard him, Jasper. Let's go."

"But don't you want to know why?" asked Jasper.

"You're probably going to tell me, aren't you?"

"Yes, I am."

"Fine. Talk fast, though. I've got things to do."

Sarna spoke. "Forget it." She threw up a hand. "This was a waste of time. He's not interested. He would never fit in. They'd kill him on sight."

"That's exactly why we need him," said Jasper.

"Need me for what?" asked Royce.

"To save our planet."

"From what? The tree and animal huggers?"

Sarna glared at him.

Jasper made no reaction other than to rest his hands on the counter. "No," he continued. "From ourselves."

Royce turned from Sarna, deciding to give Jasper a moment to explain before he kicked him out. The thought of a long, hot shower beckoned him. "What do you mean?"

"We are on the verge of a complete overthrow of our Council. Our father is the only one standing between the old regime and a new one. One that will reclaim a life where all people are respected and valued. Where we could all come and go as we pleased. Before the Dark Reds took over. They separated the Red-Lines from the Gray-Lines. Forbade us from leaving our own planet. Stopped us from our explorations. Because it risked Red-Line contamination with other species. But that's changing. Our people are restless. Sarna and I are members of those willing to reclaim the open ways. To be as we once were. But there is a crucial moment coming. One that could change everything."

Royce tried to keep up. "And what's that?"

"A change in power. Our father must hand over the reins."

"What reins?" asked Royce.

Jasper's eyes widened. "You don't know?"

"Know what?"

Jasper sighed. "Our father is the leader of the High Council."

"What is the High Council?"

"Much like your president and his cabinet."

Royce began to understand. "You mean—"

"Yes." Jasper nodded. "Dad is a powerful man."

Royce had no idea. "Then it sounds like you don't need me."

Jasper leaned against the counter. "That's not true. Dad can only do so much. If he were to show leniency to any members of our group, even me, it would be considered treason. He would be removed from the High Council in disgrace and replaced. Likely by someone far more easily swayed by the dark ones."

"So how do I fit into this?" asked Royce.

"Because you are first born. You're the High Child."

"I'm what?"

"First born," said Sarna. "You are the High Leader's first-born child. We call it the High Child."

Royce squinted. "What does that mean?"

"Basically," said Jasper, "it means you're next in line to the throne," said Jasper.

Royce didn't move or speak. He couldn't believe what he was hearing. He was next in line to be some sort of High Council leader? The High Child? It sounded like a teenager on a drug binge. He looked at the kitchen counter and the skillet with the broken egg. His mind raced, and his stomach growled again. He needed time to think. Reaching up, he scratched his head. "Animal or no animal," he said to Sarna. "I think it's time to scramble up some eggs."

# Chapter Thirteen

AN HOUR LATER, ROYCE pushed back his plate. After the revelation from Jasper that he was some sort of Eudoran leader, he'd chased Jasper and Sarna out of the kitchen. He'd taken a quick hot shower to clear his head, then proceeded to make some breakfast. If he was going to have this unexpected conversation, he needed some energy. He made Jasper clean up as well and told Sarna to go pick some mint outside. Not that he wanted any, but he needed them out of his space. He required some quiet, and arguing about his food choices or his leadership obligations was not helping.

He'd made bacon and eggs for him and Jasper. After digging through his pantry, he'd found some peanut butter. Since the bread in his freezer had milk and eggs, he used some healthy crackers Eve had brought on her last visit and slathered some peanut butter and jelly on them for Sarna. He'd hoped she didn't have anything against nuts. She'd frowned when she'd sat at the table but said nothing as he and Jasper finished their meal and she ate her crackers.

Once they'd eaten, he sat back in his seat and eyed his guests. "So," he said. "Now that I'm feeling a little more human..." Seeing their faces, he explained. "It's just an expression." They didn't seem any less confused. "Never mind," he said, waving his hand. "How about you just explain this Eudoran situation to me."

Jasper put his napkin on the table. He'd wiped his plate clean. "We want you to return with us to assume your role as leader of the High Council," said Sarna.

Royce chuckled.

"What's funny?" asked Jasper.

Royce shook his head. "That you honestly think that I could show up on Eudora and assume the highest position you have to offer."

"They won't have a choice," said Jasper. "They have to give it to you."

"Because I'm High Child."

"Yes," said Sarna.

"I suspect they could find a way around that if they wanted to."

"This is not like your world here on Earth," said Sarna. "Where the wealthiest or best-looking wins. This is a ritual that has been followed for centuries on our planet. Your father was first born, as was his mother before him. It was her father who changed everything for us. He ushered in a new regime. One that created our closed world. We suspect he was easily influenced by the Dark Reds. They convinced him that the new ways were dangerous. That our exploration of other worlds invited intruders and the contamination of our species."

"Contamination?" asked Royce.

"Yes." Sarna put down her empty coffee cup. Royce had made them all coffee and apparently she was a fan of the brew. "Back then, Gray-Lines existed on many worlds, and were procreating there, raising families and choosing to remain on their host planet. Red-Lines also traveled and visited other planets, but they always made Eudora their home base. They never mated outside of their line, and their families were raised on Eudora. But that changed when it was discovered that a member of the High Council had fathered a child outside of the Line. One that lived on another planet. This particular Red-Line asked to leave Eudora and make his home elsewhere because he wanted to marry and live on another planet."

"And I take it this was frowned upon?" asked Royce.

"Yes," said Jasper. "It was." He pushed his plate back. "Now we suspect he was not the only Red to mate with others and probably not the first to have children with someone other than a Red, but like all other secrets, as long as you didn't talk about it, it was as if it never happened."

"Until someone brought it out into the open," Royce said.

"Yes," said Sarna. "They couldn't keep it under wraps after that. If they allowed him to do as he wished, it opened the door for all others to do the same. It brought into question our lineage. Our descendants. Our abilities. If this open stance were allowed to continue, then could we still be called Red-Lines?"

"The Council argued over what was best," Jasper said. "What they didn't realize was that there was a faction of Reds who were intent on eradicating any possibility of diluting the line. To the point of eradicating the Grays as well. They saw the Grays and open Reds as a threat. The Grays were proponents of openness. They were even beginning to question the Reds' need to remain in leadership positions. That alone made this faction of what we call the Dark Reds believe that the Grays were dangerous and needed to be eliminated."

Sarna continued. "This faction had already been working behind the scenes to find ways to eliminate the Grays silently, with little knowledge of their plan reaching the High Council. Ivtar, the High Leader at that time, and your great grandfather was unfortunately easily swayed by the Dark Reds. He denied the councilman, who'd asked for permission to leave Eudora and mate outside the line. The councilman protested and was eventually imprisoned. Other Reds suspected what was happening and the implications of it, but before they could do anything, the Dark Reds had convinced Ivtar to cease all travel. Basically, exploration was ended. The Council ordered all contact with Grays outside the planet to discontinue. Reds were no longer allowed to leave. And Grays remaining on Eudora were forced to stay, many losing status and eventually becoming subservient to the Reds. Our world changed overnight. We went from an open, sharing community to a closed world, where only the approved could come and go. Studies and research of other worlds stopped. Schools closed. All activities were questioned, and Gray sympathizers were under constant supervision."

Royce listened to the story. "It seems as if Earth is not the only planet that deals with tyrants and dictators."

"No," said Jasper. "No one is immune to fear."

"So, how do I exist then?" asked Royce. "How is my family here? If you're not allowed to leave the planet?"

"Certain Reds could still leave," said Jasper. "Your father, as High Child, gained approval from our grandmother. Before he assumed his role as High Leader, he asked to travel. He wanted to explore before he assumed his leadership role. His mother granted him permission."

"And who is Galen?" asked Royce.

Sarna clasped her fingers. "He is...was...your uncle. The younger brother of Carson."

"And such, not in line to the throne?" asked Royce.

"No," answered Jasper.

"So," said Royce, leaning in. "My father, Carson, broke every rule in the book by meeting my mother and having me and my sisters. But somehow, he kept his secret and assumed his expected role. At the same time though, he had another family. One on Eudora. Is that correct?"

"Yes," said Sarna.

Royce pointed at Jasper. "Then as far as everyone on Eudora is concerned, aren't you High Child?"

"No," said Jasper. "I have an older sister."

"Roma," said Sarna. "She's next in line. At least as far as she knows."

"So why not let her have it?" asked Royce. "Why me?"

Jasper and Sarna stayed quiet, but Jasper finally spoke. "Because she is much like Galen. She very much wants to keep conditions as they are. In fact..." His eyes widened.

"What?" asked Sarna. "What are you thinking?"

"Galen..." said Jasper.

"What about him?" asked Royce.

Sarna sucked in a breath. "You think she sent him to find Royce and his family?"

"But I didn't think she knew," answered Jasper.

"Galen. Would he have told her?" asked Sarna.

"But how did he know?" asked Jasper. He tapped his fingers on the table. "Our father. He must have said something. Or Galen overheard something. Dad told me, but I don't think he would have told Roma. He knows her too well. And he knows the risks if his Earth family is discovered." He sighed. "If Galen told Roma, though...and she thought her reign was in jeopardy..." He met Royce's gaze. "She plans to take Dad's place, and eventually she will. Unless..."

Royce understood. "Unless I show up and steal her thunder."

"Yes," Sarna said. "You're the only one who can stop this." She fiddled with her empty coffee cup.

Royce wasn't sure what to think. How was he supposed to respond to his newfound half-brother? Jasper expected him to become leader of a High Council of a planet he'd never been to and knew nothing about, other than their low tolerance for meat eating. He said the first thing that came to mind. "You want some more coffee?" He lifted his empty cup. "I know I could use some."

Sarna raised hers, too. "Please," she said.

"You?" he asked Jasper.

"Yes, thanks."

Royce picked up Jasper's mug and brought all three to the kitchen counter. He realized the pitcher was empty, so he began to make a new batch.

"The coffee is good," said Sarna.

"So's the bacon. I'd love some more of that."

"Jasper..." said Sarna.

"I'm serious. Eudorans would love it."

"No, they wouldn't," Sarna said.

Royce filled the machine with water. "Everybody loves bacon."

"I don't," said Sarna.

"You didn't try it," said Jasper.

"Nor will I. And you are not bringing any of it with you to Eudora."

"Why not?"

"Because we do not eat bacon."

"No. You don't eat bacon."

"And neither do Eudorans."

Jasper shrugged. "I'm a Eudoran."

"You know what I mean."

"What do you mean?" asked Royce. He flipped on the coffee and listened as it began to brew.

"I mean, we are what you call vegans. We don't eat meat."

"You don't now," Royce answered.

"What?"

"You're asking me to assume the role of the High Leader. If that happens, and I open up the planet, what happens when I start eating bacon at the royal breakfast table?"

"Wh...what?" Sarna stammered. "You wouldn't."

Royce leaned against the kitchen counter. "You need to think about what you're asking. You want openness? You want to explore? You want to oust those who want to maintain your closed world? Then you better prepare for some changes. Because the world outside your own is very different. There are different customs, beliefs, rituals, and yes, eating habits on a myriad of other planets. We see it on Earth all the time. And we don't even visit other planets. I have been raised to judge none of that. So, if you expect me to lead, then you better get used to bacon on the table."

Sarna sat rigid in her seat.

Jasper pushed back from the table and stood. "So you'll do it?"

The coffee percolated, and the smell filled the kitchen. Royce picked up his mug. "Absolutely not."

# Chapter Fourteen

"WHY NOT?"

Sarna stood too. "Yes. Why not?"

The coffee continued to drip. "Because. My home is here."

"Your home can be anywhere you make it," said Jasper.

"I choose to make it here."

"But why?" asked Jasper.

Royce raised his brow. "Why? Because I was raised here. I have a family here."

"Your sisters?" asked Sarna.

"Yes. And my mother."

"Don't you understand?" asked Jasper. "By staying, you put them at risk."

Royce watched the coffee level rise. "And how do I do that?"

"Galen came after you," Sarna said. "We can only assume there will be others."

Royce crossed his arms. "Not if they don't know about us."

Jasper threw out his hand. "If Galen knew, then we have to assume he's not the only one."

Royce stared at the floor. "You want to know what I think?"

"What?" asked Sarna.

"I think my—our father told him."

Jasper shook his head. "Why would he do that?"

"Because they're brothers. They're family. It's the same reason Dad told you. He confided in you. He needed someone he could trust."

"But he couldn't trust Galen."

"How do you know? We have no way of knowing what our father was thinking or when or why he may have told his brother. It may have been years ago. Maybe that's what turned Galen against him. Maybe they were close before then."

"But if that's true," said Sarna, "then Galen could have told others."

"Maybe," said Royce. "But probably not."

"Why wouldn't he?" asked Jasper.

"Because that would mean that others would know that Roma was not next in line. He wouldn't want that. As you say, if the High Child assumes power regardless of their background, then it's the last thing he'd want to share. Which is why he came after me and my sisters. To get rid of us."

"You can't know that for sure," Jasper said.

"And you can't know for sure that he told someone. You can't be sure of anything." He picked up a mug and filled it from the pot.

"We can be sure that if Roma takes power," said Sarna, "that all hope of change on our planet is lost." She took the mug from Royce.

Royce nodded. "So tell Dad to hold onto the reins. Who says he has to step down?"

Jasper and Sarna exchanged a look. "You think if it was that easy we would have traveled the distance we did to find you?" asked Jasper.

Royce cocked his head. "So why isn't it easy?" He grabbed Jasper's cup and filled it.

"Because Dad must step down," said Jasper.

"Why?" asked Royce.

Jasper took the coffee and hesitated. "Because...because he's..."

"Because he's reached the end of his reign," Sarna answered. "A High Leader can only lead until such time that the Council deems he must step down. A unanimous decision will end his rule. The Council is suspicious of your father's leniency toward those who desire change. They already know of Jasper's allegiance to our cause. He's already been imprisoned once."

"Imprisoned? For what?"

"For voicing his opinion," said Sarna. "For arguing with the Council."

"It wasn't for long," said Jasper, sitting down.

"You were beaten," said Sarna.

"I recovered," said Jasper.

"You were lucky. Others were not."

"Only because I was the High Leader's child."

"I doubt you'll be that lucky again."

"Wait a minute," said Royce. "Dad had you imprisoned?"

"No, not our father," said Jasper. "He didn't realize what had happened. He was away at the time." He blew the hot liquid and took a sip.

"Galen. That bastard punished Jasper."

Royce raised a brow and felt a kernel of anger in his belly. "And what happened when Dad found out?"

"By the time he did," said Jasper, "the crisis had passed. He was angry, though."

"Angry?" asked Sarna. "Word is he and Galen came to blows."

"We assume," said Jasper.

"I remember. It wasn't long after my sister Shifted. About three years ago. Galen was not seen in public for almost two months. The rumor was his face was a mess."

Royce felt his face pale. "When?"

"When what?" asked Sarna. She drank from her cup.

"How many years ago was this?"

Sarna paused. "I think it was three." She knitted her brow. "Why?"

"What is it?" asked Jasper.

The machine beeped and Royce filled his own cup with the brew. "You said Dad was away?" asked Royce.

"Yes. He was traveling."

Royce sat at the table. "He was visiting us. He was here. It's the last time I saw him." He picked up a spoon and added some sugar from a bowl on the table.

Jasper's eyes widened. "Really?"

"Yes. He came because we were..." He swirled his coffee and looked at Sarna. "What you called it. Shifting."

Sarna leaned forward. "You were? You and your sisters?"

"Yes."

Her eyes furrowed. "Why so late?" she asked. "You should have Shifted much sooner."

"They're half-human, Sarna. Don't forget. That's probably why."

Royce frowned. "I had no idea I was such a late bloomer."

"How long did he stay?" Sarna asked. She looked almost sad. "Was he able to explain things? About your Shift?"

"Not long," said Royce. "But long enough to see us through it. It took a while to adjust, though."

"I'm sure it did," Jasper said. "It's traumatic enough when it happens on Eudora."

"So what can you do?" Sarna asked.

"What can I do?" Royce asked.

"Yes," she said. "What are your strengths?"

"Dad has an array of abilities," said Jasper. "Most of us do. But everyone always has a strength."

Royce thought about it. He stared at the table. Suddenly, the empty dining chairs slid up against the table. They hit the edge with a bang.

Jasper nodded. "Impressive," he said. "But how do you do with the small stuff?" His gaze moved to the kitchen cabinets. One of them opened and Royce watched as a stack of plates lifted from their perch, hovered, drifted out of the cabinet, and then slowly dropped to rest softly on the counter.

Royce lifted an eyebrow but didn't say a word. But he focused on the same stack of plates. The top one lifted and floated to the sink, where the faucet turned on. The dish hovered and dipped below the nozzle. Water splashed over the plate. The sink turned off, and the dripping dish floated to the drainer, where it dropped gently to stand upright to dry.

Jasper nodded. "You take after dad."

"You both do," said Sarna.

"What's your strength?" Royce asked Sarna. "Other than your need to tell people what to do?"

"That's definitely one of her better abilities," Jasper said.

Sarna set her jaw. "I don't tell people what to do. I simply express my opinion."

Jasper snorted. "That's an understatement."

Sarna ignored him. "Besides that, I am intuitive and empathic. I am very sensitive and read people easily." She looked at the sink. "I can move things, too, if I need to, but not as well as you."

"That's true," said Jasper. "Don't ask her to move any plates if you want them in one piece."

Royce pointed. "You're like Gillian. My sister. She can do the same. She can read people like a book."

"Don't lie to Sarna," said Jasper. He cocked his head toward her. "She'll catch you every time." He drank again from his mug.

Royce saw them exchange a look. "How do you two know each other?" He waved a hand at Sarna. "I know who Jasper is and why he's here. But what's your involvement? Why'd you travel across the galaxy to come see me?"

She shifted uncomfortably. "Well," she said. "I didn't want Jasper to come alone."

"I told you that you didn't have to come," said Jasper.

"You needed help." Jasper started to interrupt, but she held up her hand. "You did. This is a hard enough journey as it is, and no one should do it alone." She sighed and tapped on the tabletop. "I've been close with his family since childhood. Roma and I were best friends growing up. Jasper is like my big brother."

"And what happened? I take it you're not friends anymore."

"As we got older, it became apparent that our loyalties differed. It wasn't an issue until our Shifts occurred. Roma went through it first. Then Jasper. Then me. Afterwards, Roma was different. She'd become closer to Galen, as Jasper did with his father. I sided with Jasper. It wasn't long before our friendship suffered. Now we barely speak." She stared off.

"And there was Ander," said Jasper.

Sarna looked back. "Jasper..."

"No. He should know."

"Who's Ander?" asked Royce. He stood and picked up the dirty plates from the table.

"Her brother."

Royce glanced at Sarna, who bit her bottom lip. Her eyes glistened.

"He and Sarna were very close. Sarna is vocal, but Ander was a walking bullhorn. He didn't back down from a fight, and he argued constantly for change. He would lead uprisings and gather as many as he could to the cause. He was imprisoned many times."

Sarna let out a deep breath and wiped at her eye. "Until..."

"Until his last incarceration. He didn't make it out."

"Why not?" asked Royce. He put the plates in the sink and ran the water.

Jasper's shoulders fell. "He was killed in his cell. No one knew by who. The murderer was never found. Or at least never identified."

Sarna cleared her throat, blinked, and straightened. "It devastated my family. We were a tight-knit group. But Ander...well, I think he always knew."

"Knew what?" asked Royce. He rinsed the plates and left them to soak.

She let go of a deep breath. "That his death would spawn a movement. That it would spur our people to action."

"And it has," said Jasper. "We are at a tipping point. I have never seen so much pressure on the Council to make changes. But they are pushing back. Very soon, the vote will come. And they will oust our father. But if we can be ready...if you are there, and you take power, there will be no choice. You, a half-human, half Red-Line, will lead the High Council. And there's nothing they can do to stop it."

Royce returned to the table. "Can't they just vote to oust me? Like Dad?"

"No. A new leader must be given three years before a first vote is taken."

"So, you are in an important position," said Sarna. "You can be my brother's voice."

Royce stared at the two of them. The hope in their eyes made him wonder. Where exactly did he belong? He thought of Gus's words. *You have a destiny.* But what did that mean? He thought of his mother. And Gillian and Eve. What would become of them if he left? And what about Alice? Now that he knew he didn't have to run from his visitors, he could find and help her.

He bolstered himself and leaned against his chair. "I'm not your brother, Sarna." Her eyes widened. "And I know nothing about your cause, Jasper." Jasper's face fell. "This is your fight. Not mine."

"How can you say that?" asked Jasper. He sat back. "We're talking about our father. How is this not your fight?"

Royce could sense Jasper's budding anger. "Our father?" he asked. "You're the one that had a father. Not me."

Jasper's face furrowed. "What are you talking about?"

Royce recalled the past, and for the first time, allowed his long-held frustrations to rise. "I saw the man, at most, every three to five years. I remember him vaguely from childhood. I love him, but he wasn't there for my birthday parties. He didn't advise me when I had my first date. He didn't watch me play football. I know little about him. My mother was left to take care of us. She did all the work. She was the one who missed him, who pined for him. She raised us. She helped us with our homework, stood up for us when we got into trouble, taught us wrong from right. She soothed our hurts and thrilled in our accomplishments. If I'm loyal to anyone, it's her."

"You're mad because he wasn't there to help you with your schoolwork?" Sarna asked.

Royce felt his waning headache return. He gripped the back of his chair. "Don't be absurd. Use those intuitive gifts of yours. I'm mad because he wasn't there, period." Royce walked to the counter, picked up the plates and put them back in the cabinet. The rush of anger he was feeling surprised him. He'd never talked to his sisters about his mixed emotions regarding their father. But now that he'd finally expressed his disappointment, he found it difficult to hold back.

"You want to spend more time with him?" asked Jasper. He threw out his hands. "Do it now. Come with us."

Royce turned. "No. If he needs my help, let him come and ask me. Not send an errand boy."

Jasper set his jaw and his cheeks turned red. "An errand boy? He doesn't even know I'm here."

"You're sure about that?" asked Royce. Something warned him to shut up, but his mouth didn't listen. "How do you know he's not just using you?"

Jasper straightened. "Using me?"

"He's not doing that," Sarna said.

"Why not?" Royce stepped closer. "The man's on the verge of losing power. He needs help. So he drops all his worries on you. Tells his son all his woes. And just happens to mention his other family on planet Earth. What a coincidence."

Jasper spoke in a low tone. "That is not what he's doing."

Royce turned stony and leaned forward. In his heart, he knew what he was saying wasn't fair, but his pent-up emotions spurred him forward. "Isn't it? Looks like he's manipulating you, like you're manipulating me."

Jasper stood, eyes wide. "Manipulating you?"

"Jasper..." said Sarna. She raised a hand in warning.

"Shut up, Sarna." He slammed his chair into the table. "Who do you think you are?"

Royce didn't move and his gaze didn't waver, despite the tide of fury he felt from his half-brother.

"You think I came all this way because my daddy can't take care of himself? He's the strongest man I know. He's lasted longer in his position than any other man should have. He's braver than you and I combined." He stood in front of Royce, flushed with anger, and pointed. "You think I like coming here and asking you this? Asking a man I don't know, who my father sired in secret, who knows nothing about Eudora, to come and take a position that I wish I could take. Would take in a heartbeat if it was offered. And I have to give it to a spoiled, angry, unappreciative, and incapable fool?"

Sarna spoke quietly. "Jasper...stop."

"Fool?" asked Royce. "You're the one who came here on a wild goose chase." Jasper's eyes flared. "Who's the fool now?"

The tension in the room ignited, and a wave of heat flared from Jasper's body. Jasper's mug flew off the table and shattered against a wall, spraying it with dark liquid.

"Dad told me about you," said Jasper. His voice was deep, and his energy churned. "He told me what a good person you were. How you were strong but kind. That you always wanted to make everything right."

Royce didn't know what to say, so he didn't respond.

"I had no idea my father was such a poor judge of character."

Royce's own heat flared. "Maybe if he'd stuck around long enough, he would have known me better." He gritted his teeth. "Dad made a choice.

Just like I am right now. He made the choice to leave us, to start a new family, and take power. He left us to fend for ourselves. So don't talk to me about choices. He's courageous? How about sticking up for the family you got, instead of ducking us because he didn't have the guts to admit we existed? Sounds like Ander had true courage. Not Dad. You grew up with a man who had a secret. One he never told until it suited his purpose. And now you want me to do what he couldn't?"

Royce realized his hands were curled into fists and he tried to relax them. "No. I'm not leaving." He held Jasper's fiery gaze. "That's my answer. Now get out of my house."

"Royce," said Sarna softly. "Please..."

Royce kept staring at Jasper. "And take her with you."

Jasper didn't speak, but his body language was obvious. He was shaking with fury. Royce braced himself just in case any dishware from the sink came flying at him.

"You're my brother," Jasper finally managed to say. "I thought..."

"You thought what?" asked Royce. "That we'd bond?" He regretted the words as soon as he said them, but couldn't bring himself to take them back.

Jasper's jaw worked. "I hate you."

The words and the energy that came with them hit Royce in his mid-section, and he sucked in a breath. A war of contrary thoughts banged through his mind about what he was doing—alienating himself even further from the family he never knew. It was not what he wanted, but he couldn't break through the haze of disappointment and simmering fury. He decided the best thing he could do was to send them home. Then he could return to his routine life. Or as routine as possible, considering who he was. Maybe find Alice. Discover some normalcy.

"You should go now. Your space ship is waiting."

Seeing Jasper's face, Royce knew then that he would likely never see his father, or brother, again. He felt a momentary flutter of pain in his heart.

Jasper stood unmoving, like the still plate in the drainer. Sarna stayed quiet. Suddenly, the entire table lifted and the remaining cups, silverware, and the sugar bowl crashed to the ground and shattered. Sugar and Sarna's mug skittered across the floor, along with the splash of coffee. The table fell sideways, and the chairs slammed into the walls and toppled to the floor. Jasper, eyes hard and nostrils flaring, glared at Royce.

At the same time, the front door flew open. All three of them, so distracted by their argument, had missed the impending arrival. RJ ran into the house, sweaty and disheveled.

"RJ?" asked Royce. He disengaged from Jasper and approached the sheriff's son, who was breathing hard as if he'd sprinted there. Broken shards of the sugar bowl crunched beneath his feet. "What is it?"

RJ tried to catch his breath. "Thank God. You're here. I need to talk to you."

Royce gestured toward Jasper and Sarna. "I'm in the middle of something here."

RJ yelled at him. "This is important. I'm in trouble." He paid no attention to Royce's guests.

Royce stepped over a broken mug. "Where's your dad? He's the one you should talk to."

"I can't. Not about this." He walked over and tugged on Royce's arm. "I have to show you."

"RJ..."

"Hurry. Please. I need your help."

Royce groaned and reluctantly left Sarna and Jasper in the house. He followed RJ out to the front driveway where he saw a beat up, two-door, blue sedan that had seen better days. "Is this your car?" asked Royce.

"Yes," said RJ. He pulled Royce to the back of the automobile and stopped.

Royce looked back toward the house. Sarna and Jasper were still inside. "What, RJ? I need to get back."

"This," said RJ, and he pulled a key from his pocket and opened the trunk. It creaked open and Royce peered inside. "Look at that." RJ pointed.

"It's a tackle box." He leaned in and opened it. "Oreos? In your tackle box? That won't catch many fish."

RJ groaned. "Not that. *That.*" He pointed behind the box.

Royce saw the object. "It's a shoe. So what?"

"It's not just a shoe." He moaned some more and shifted uncomfortably. "Look at it. It's a pink tennis shoe. It's the missing shoe from my dad's murder scene."

Royce remembered the conversation with Rick. The murder victim had been missing a shoe. He looked closer. It was indeed pink and there was a flower on the toe. A flicker of unease coursed through Royce. He glanced back at RJ, who looked like he'd just been asked to kill a family member. "What did you do?"

RJ's eyes widened. "What did I do? I didn't do anything."

Royce straightened. "Why is this here?"

RJ shook his head. "That's just it. I don't know."

Royce glanced back at the shoe. "When's the last time you were in your trunk?"

"Uh," RJ ran a hand through his hair. "I don't know. A few weeks ago. I had a flat."

"What about the tackle box? Didn't you just go fishing?"

"We used Dad's."

Royce scanned the rest of the space. He saw a tire iron and jack across from the pink tennis shoe, but nothing else. His stomach dropped. Could it really be the missing shoe? "This doesn't belong to someone else?" He peered back at the teenager. "A girlfriend?"

"No."

Royce scrutinized the shoe again.

"What is it?" asked RJ. "What are you looking at?"

Royce ignored RJ. He pulled back. "Close the trunk."

RJ's face froze. He was as pale as Sarna. "Oh, hell. I'm in trouble, aren't I?"

Royce stared at the boy whose eyes shone as if he was about to cry. He opened up every one of his senses. "Tell me the truth. Do you know anything about that woman's death?"

RJ shook his head in a whipping motion. "No. I swear. I don't know anything about that shoe or why it's there. Or anything about the dead lady in the woods."

Royce studied him, feeling for any deception, but he couldn't find any. "Close it."

RJ remained frozen in place before he finally nodded and closed the trunk.

"Jasper...wait."

Royce turned at the sound of Sarna's voice and saw Jasper striding toward him with a backpack slung over his shoulder. His posture was rigid, and he didn't acknowledge Royce as he neared.

Sarna ran after him. "Where are you going?"

"To the ship. This trip is over."

"Wait..." said Sarna.

He whirled on her. "There is nothing to wait for. You heard him."

"I need to get my things..."

"No. I'm going on my own."

"What?" Both Sarna and Royce spoke at the same time.

Jasper scowled. "I'm not leaving you, but I'm going to prep the ship. We can't leave till tonight anyway, when it's dark."

Royce glanced at RJ, who thankfully seemed to be caught up enough in his own fears and was paying little attention to the drama unfolding in Royce's front yard. "Jasper..." he started to say.

Jasper shot him a furious look. "Forget it. You've had your say."

"It will just take me a few minutes," Sarna said.

"I need a break, Sarna," said Jasper loudly, and Sarna stood still. "I need some space and I need some quiet. I can't take you, your opinions, and your justifications right now."

Sarna started to speak, but he held up a hand. "Just let me go and prep the ship. After it's dark, you can join me and we're gone." He glanced at Royce. "The sooner, the better."

"But how will I get there?" asked Sarna.

"I'll take you," said Royce. He eyed RJ again and wondered how in the hell he'd ended up with two Eudoran visitors and a kid who was a likely murder suspect all on his front lawn at the same time. He shook his head and sighed. "Just tell me where and when."

Jasper's jaw jutted out, but he spoke to Sarna. "I'll be in touch as soon as I'm ready. You know where to go?" She nodded. "Good. I'm out of here." He whirled away and stomped off, never looking back.

Royce considered stopping him, but he knew it was fruitless. He watched his half-brother walk up the driveway and turn down the road, and knew all chances of ever forging a relationship with his Eudoran family were lost to him.

"Royce." Royce heard RJ, but didn't acknowledge him. His headache was in full swing now. "Royce. What do I do?" RJ was wringing his hands.

Sarna walked up at the same time. "I hope you know what you've done." Her face fell, but her cheeks were still flush with anger. She pointed toward the road. "You broke his heart."

Royce looked between RJ and Sarna, groaned, and rubbed his temples. He thought of Alice and wondered where she was. If he'd been smart, he would have disappeared with her.

He groaned. "I didn't mean to."

"Didn't mean to what?" asked RJ. "What the hell is going on here?" He looked at Sarna. "Who are you?"

Sarna acknowledged him. "Who are you?"

RJ's voice pitched high. "I'm about to be accused of murder. You think I could get some help here?" He couldn't stop squirming.

"Murder?" asked Sarna. She squinted at Royce. "You keep interesting company." She crossed her arms. "So, how do I convince you to change your mind?"

Royce huffed. He wasn't sure how much more he could take. "Okay, you two. Inside. Both of you." He grabbed RJ by the collar of his shirt and dragged him forward. He left Sarna standing by RJ's car. "We have a lot to talk about."

# Chapter Fifteen

ONCE INSIDE, HE PICKED up the dinner table and set it upright. RJ paid little attention to the mess. After righting the chairs, Royce ushered RJ into one and sat next to him. "Okay," he said. "Tell me what's going on."

"What is going on?" Sarna asked. She rested her hands on the table. "We have a crisis on our hands. Don't you understand?"

Royce grumbled. "Sarna, I've given you and Jasper my answer. Now I have to talk to RJ. Why don't you go pack?"

RJ hugged himself. "What am I going to do? What do I tell dad?" His eyes were round and shiny.

"Pack?" asked Sarna. "Is that all you have to say?"

Royce slapped his palm on the table and it shook. "Listen. I don't have the time or the desire to argue with you. Right now, RJ needs some help. You're not the only one in the room with problems."

That seemed to get her attention. She straightened. "What's wrong with him?"

RJ's head shot up. "What's wrong with me?" He shot a worried look at Royce. "Who is this lady?" He looked Sarna up and down. "Is she why you had to leave?"

Royce rested his head in a hand. "It's a long story, RJ. But that's not your concern right now."

"Is she your girlfriend?"

Sarna laughed, and Royce grimaced. "God, no. She is not."

"He should be so lucky," added Sarna.

Royce offered her a raised brow. He spoke to RJ. "Just tell me about the shoe."

RJ put his elbows on the table and bounced his knee. "I don't know anything about the shoe. I just went out to my car this morning. Dad's battery died and I looked to see if I had jumper cables. I opened the trunk and there it was."

"You didn't tell your dad?"

RJ shook his head emphatically. "No. I can't."

"But if you didn't do anything..."

"He's the sheriff. He'll have to take me in."

"What exactly is going on here?" asked Sarna.

RJ moaned and lowered his forehead to the table.

Royce watched the pitiful teenager, but he addressed Sarna. "This is not your problem. I'll deal with it."

"Deal with what? What does this have to do with a shoe?"

RJ gripped his head with his hands.

"Sarna," said Royce. "I think it's better if you stayed out of this. You're leaving tonight, anyway."

"Stay out of what?" Her face reflected her curiosity. "He feels very agitated."

"You could say that," said RJ to the table.

"Sarna..."

"Just tell me. It's not like I've got anything else to do until tonight."

Royce studied her worried face. Her dark, almond-shaped eyes looked back and for a moment, he caught himself admiring them. He shook his head though and shifted his attention back to RJ, whose forehead was still on his table. "RJ. You care if I tell her?"

RJ's head rocked back and forth. "She's not the cops, is she?"

"No. Far from it. But from what I know about her, she's going to drive us nuts until we tell her. And I don't have the strength for it."

RJ sighed and raised his head. "Fine."

Sarna sat down at the table and Royce informed her of the murdered woman in the woods and her missing pink tennis shoe. And how that missing shoe was now in RJ's trunk. The same trunk that belonged to the son of the sheriff leading the investigation.

When he finished, Sarna didn't speak. After a few moments, she rested her hand on RJ's forearm. "Look at me," she said.

RJ lifted his drooping head. He had deflated after his initial outburst. "What?" he asked. "You think I'm a killer?"

Sarna's expression did not change. "You tell me." She cocked her head. "Are you?"

Tears filled RJ's eyes. "No," he said quietly. "I'm not. I swear."

Sarna nodded. "He's telling the truth."

Royce hesitated. He trusted his own instincts, but he suspected Sarna's gifts, if she was anything like his sister Gillian, were far more reliable.

"Okay," he said, patting RJ's arm. "So let's talk about the night you came home drunk and high. Isn't that the same night this woman died?"

RJ squinted, but then his eyes widened. "Is it?" He stared off. "Yeah. Maybe it was. They found her a couple of days later. That was the day dad brought me over here." He groaned again.

"What happened that night?" asked Royce.

RJ sat straight. "Nothing."

"Who were you with?"

"Just some friends from high school. We went up to Shady Point about midnight. Thought we'd watch for meteors. We had some beer. A couple of girls met up with us. They had some weed. We smoked it. I ended up with Mary Lou over by the campgrounds. We made out for a while, but then I passed out. I woke up early. Nobody was there. I found my car and drove home."

"Did you see anyone else?"

"No. No one."

"Anything suspicious? Strange noises? A strange feeling?"

RJ shook his head. "No. But I was half out of it."

"Shady Point? Where is that?" Sarna asked.

"Not far from here," Royce said. "Down at the base of Hikerman's Hill. You pass it when you come into town. It's a popular place for hiking and camping at certain times of the year."

"And what night was this?" she asked.

Royce thought about it. "Five days ago." It felt like weeks.

"Meteors?" Sarna asked. "You go out in the woods to look at meteors?"

"Good point," said Royce.

"We didn't see shit," RJ said.

"Trees tend to block the view."

RJ shrugged. "It sounded like fun. Plus, the alcohol helped."

"I'm sure it did."

"Interesting," Sarna said.

"Why?" asked Royce.

She started to speak, but paused. "Can I talk to you for a second?"

Royce pursed his lips. "Something on your mind?"

She inclined her head toward the teenager who was picking at the table, lost in his own thoughts.

"Uh, RJ," said Royce, getting the message. "Give us a second. Okay?"

"Sure. Whatever." He rested his forehead in his hands.

Royce stood, and he and Sarna walked into Royce's bedroom and closed the door. "What is it?" asked Royce.

She spoke softly. "That's the night Jasper and I arrived."

"Arrived?"

She narrowed her eyes at him like he'd been kicked in the head. "Yes. You know. From..." She raised her hand and pointed upward.

"So. What does that have to do with anything?"

"That description you gave. Of Shady Point? Where the woman's body was found?"

"Yes. What about it?

"That's near where we landed."

"You landed your ship at Shady Point?"

"Well, not in the middle of it, but close."

"Why there?"

"You'd have to ask Jasper. He's the pilot."

"But how? How were you not seen? How is the ship not visible?"

"Don't worry about that. We have technology that prevents the craft from being detected."

"You landed in a popular place. Why didn't you just put her down in the center of town?"

"Funny," she said.

"I don't think so."

"You're missing the point."

"What is the point?"

"We were there the same night. As RJ. As the murder."

Royce stared at her as if she'd just said she'd descended from an ancient race of frogs. "What are you trying to tell me? Did you kill her?"

She frowned. "Don't be stupid. I know it's hard. But try."

He sighed. "Enlighten me."

"I don't know much about flying, but I do know that before we landed, we did a thorough check of the area. We don't land if we suspect we might be detected."

Royce snorted. "Looks like your equipment could use some maintenance."

"We didn't detect any issues at the time we landed." She cocked her head. "Your friend must have already passed out by then. But..."

"But what?"

"If Jasper did a sweep of the area prior to or after, we might have caught something."

Royce considered what she was saying. "You mean you might know who did this?"

She nodded. "Maybe. The ship scans the perimeter around the landing site. It keeps track of movements. If we can look at the sweep from that night, it might show what happened."

"You mean if someone was being murdered, it wouldn't have alerted you?"

"It's a ship. It's doesn't have a mind of its own."

"I thought you guys had advanced technologies."

"You watch too many science fiction movies."

Royce put his hands in his pockets. "You think we can get a look at this footage?"

"Maybe. There's just one problem."

He chuckled. "Just one?"

"You pissed off the one man who could show it to you."

He rubbed his temples. "Jasper."

"Yes. Jasper."

Royce nodded. "Okay."

"Okay?" She crossed her arms. "What does that mean?"

"This is what we're going to do."

"What?" She leaned in and her closeness almost made him pull back. Instead, he found himself leaning in as well.

"We're going to talk to Jasper."

That made her pull back. "And how do you plan to do that?"

"Tonight. I have to drop you off, right? We'll ask him to take a look for us. See what we see."

"What makes you think he'll do it?"

He straightened. "Because I asked him to."

"That may not carry much weight right now."

"I'm his brother. He'll do it." She raised a brow. "Plus. I'll have you with me."

"Me?"

"Yes. Don't you plan on leaving tonight?"

She huffed. "The moment I can."

"Then you can help me convince him."

"Why would I do that?"

"Because I felt you in there." He realized how that sounded. "I felt your energy," he clarified.

"You what?"

"With RJ. You feel sympathy for him."

"Maybe I do. But I have no stake in this."

"Neither do I," said Royce. "But it doesn't change the fact that if RJ didn't do it, then somebody's gone to some trouble to make it look like he has. And that's a person I'd like to find." She stood and stared. "And I suspect," he added. "That there's something else about this that's got you intrigued."

"Something else?"

"It was hard to miss."

She hesitated. "What?"

"Your brother."

Visibly tensing, she said, "What about him?"

"RJ. He reminds you of him."

She opened her mouth to speak, but no words formed. Her eyes softened. "You're more intuitive than you let on."

"I have my moments."

They stood quietly in the bedroom. The longer they stood there, the more he became aware of her nearness and the fact that they were alone together, and she wasn't all that undesirable. In fact, with her shiny black hair, dark brown eyes, and alabaster skin, he realized she was rather striking. Surprised by the direction of his imagination, especially after Alice, he immediately cloaked his thoughts. He knew she would be able to pick up on them with ease.

"So? You'll help me convince him?"

She paused, and he had the distinct feeling that her perusal of him was leading her imagination to run in a similar direction. The minute he felt it though, it evaporated. She cleared her throat. "Fine. I'll help you. On one condition."

Royce pointed at her. "I'm not leaving with you."

"Just think about it. That's all I'm asking."

"Sarna..."

"That's all I want."

He set his jaw. "And if my answer is still no?"

She hesitated and glanced toward the closed door. "Don't worry. I won't take out my frustrations with you on your friend. I'll still help him out."

"Great." He scanned the room. "By the way..."

She followed his gaze. "What?"

"Before we go, you mind picking up a bit?" He motioned toward clothes in a pile on the floor. "You're a slob."

He escaped the room before she threw something at him.

# Chapter Sixteen

ROYCE SHUT THE DOOR to his shed and slid the bolt closed. It didn't have a padlock because, living where he did, he had not seen the need for one.

"You sure this is a good idea?" asked Sarna. The moon had ascended, and its light reflected in her eyes.

Royce pushed on the shed door for good measure. "No. I'm not."

"The sheriff finds you with that shoe, and you're in trouble."

Royce had taken the shoe from RJ's trunk, put it in a plastic bag, and buried it in his shed. He'd sent RJ home, telling him to stay quiet and remain calm. "I know, but it can't stay in RJ's car."

A breeze blew, and Sarna brushed a hair away from her face. "You could have. You could have picked up the phone and explained everything to his dad."

Royce recalled RJ's terrified face. He thought of Gus and Alice and how they could have called an ambulance. "I know, but that puts Rick in a tough place. I guess I took pity on the kid."

Sarna nodded. "Let's go inside. Jasper should be in touch soon."

Royce followed her into the house. Yawning, he walked into the kitchen and put on some coffee to brew. The night wasn't over yet. Sarna sat on the couch. She'd packed her bag, and it was sitting by the front door.

Flipping on the machine, Royce listened to it percolate and rubbed his face. Fatigue and the events of the day made him feel as if he had weights tied to his body. It occurred to him the level he'd gone to help RJ, and he hoped he and the kid didn't end up in jail.

"Stop worrying," said Sarna.

Royce popped his head up. "What?"

"You're worried. About what you've done. To help him."

He nodded. "It's hard not to. We don't know who did this. If the killer's a drifter, we'll likely never know the truth."

"But what if they're not?"

"If they're not...if they're someone in town, then all they have to do is pick up the phone. Call the sheriff. Lead him to RJ."

"But that won't matter," said Sarna. "There's nothing in RJ's trunk."

"Not now. But the first thing they'll do is talk to RJ."

Sarna stood and walked to the kitchen counter. "You think he'd tell them he came here?"

"It's his dad. I can't ask him to lie to his father."

"What if they did come here? What would you do?"

"I'm hoping it doesn't come to that." He crossed his arms. "I'm hoping your ship's computer caught the killer in the act. Then we can get the police involved, find this guy, and end this charade."

She nodded. "Don't get your hopes up. This is a long shot at best. But if we do find something, how do you plan on revealing the evidence? You can't exactly hand the sheriff a video of the crime without explaining where it came from."

Royce stretched his neck and stifled a yawn. Despite all that had happened that day, he knew if he went vertical, he'd be asleep within seconds. "We'll...or I'll deal with that when the time comes."

"You know there's an easy solution to this."

He frowned at her, knowing what she wanted. "I'm not leaving with you."

She cocked her head. "You sure? We can dump all the evidence. You fly away. And there's nothing to tie RJ to the crime. It's a win for everyone."

"Except me."

Her eyebrows furrowed. "What are you so afraid of?"

The question caught him off guard. "Afraid?" He reached for two coffee cups in the drainer.

"Aside from the fact that you're leaving your home and family. I get that. It's not easy. But I sense there's more going on here."

He studied her and knew she was reading him. He thought about cloaking his thoughts, but didn't see the point. "More? Of course there's more. You two want me to lead a High Council on another planet. What makes you think I know anything about leading anyone?"

"Because of who you are. You're the High Child."

He put the cups down on the counter. "Big deal. There've been plenty of sons who've messed up what their fathers did before them."

"Is that what you're afraid of? Screwing up?"

He studied her. It was dark outside and the only light in the house was from a lamp in the living room. It softly lit her face. "No. I'm more worried about being shot on sight the moment I show myself." While the coffee still dripped, he walked out of the kitchen, opened the back door, and went outside on the porch. The soft breeze blew against his face and he took a deep breath. He secretly hoped Sarna would not follow him, but then she spoke from behind him.

"That won't happen."

He sighed. "How do you know that? Roma is not going to give up power so easily."

Sarna started to answer, but stopped when there was a shuffling noise. It was not the sound of the wind or the murmur of crickets. "What's that?"

Royce cocked his head. The shuffling became scraping and then he heard a low, deep huff.

Sarna came up next to him. "What?"

"Shhh." He held up a hand.

She stilled, and he pointed. "Look. Beyond the trees."

Squinting, she stared. "I don't see..." There was movement, and she sucked in a breath. "It's a bear."

The large animal, nose low to the ground, encroached on the house, seemingly oblivious to Royce and Sarna.

Sarna gripped the porch rail. "Shouldn't we go inside?"

"Watch." It was not the same bear Royce had hid from earlier. This one was smaller and its fur, from what Royce could see, looked darker. The bear lumbered into the trees that bordered Royce's backyard, and Sarna visibly tensed.

"Royce..."

"Wait."

The bear stopped at a thick tree and pawed at the ground. Its large claws pulled up leaves and scattered dirt until it found what it was looking for. Its mouth gripped an object, and the bear sat back on its haunches and began to eat.

"Is that an apple?" asked Sarna.

"Yes. Bears love 'em." The bear finished the treat and looked for more. "It's not uncommon for them to come around at night for a snack." He wondered where his bear was.

They watched for a minute as the bear ate. "That's amazing," said Sarna. "He's beautiful."

"It's probably a she. She's smaller."

"She's making me hungry. You got any apples left?"

He smiled. "You're welcome to go grab one. I'm sure she'll share."

"I bet you'd like that."

He chuckled.

After a few minutes, the bear had its fill and ambled back into the night. Sarna leaned against the rail. "I can see why you like this place."

The sounds of the forest returned to normal. "It's peaceful."

"You can find peace on Eudora, too, you know."

He shut his eyes. "Can't we talk about something else?" He looked at his watch. "Shouldn't Jasper be ready by now?"

He startled when his phone rang. He picked it up and read the display. Sheriff Rick was calling. A chill ran down his back.

"Who is it?"

Royce hesitated. "RJ's dad."

They glanced at each other for a moment before Royce raised the phone and answered the call. "Hello?"

Listening, Royce was relieved when Rick failed to mention RJ. But as the sheriff continued to speak, Royce's blood ran cold. Sarna saw his expression and certainly felt his reaction.

"What is it?" she asked, stepping closer. "What's wrong?"

Royce answered the sheriff's questions blankly, barely able to think. "I don't know," he said into the phone. "Yes. I'm on my way." He hung up, feeling numb.

Sarna looked paler, too. "No." She shook her head. "It's Jasper, isn't it?"

Royce swallowed. "Yes."

He felt sure her stricken face matched his own. "Is he alive?"

Feeling the guilt build, Royce slipped the phone into his pocket. "Yes, barely. He's in the hospital."

Sarna's jaw dropped. "Hospital? What happened?"

"A patrol found him in the woods. Near where the first victim was found. Someone tried to cave his head in with a rock."

She covered her mouth with her hand. "What? How did they know to contact you?

"They found a picture of me in his pocket."

"Jasper." She looked lost, as if she'd been told she could never go home.

"Come on. Let's go." He moved to find his keys. "We're heading to the hospital."

# Chapter Seventeen

THEY DROVE INTO THE city and arrived at the hospital about an hour after hearing from the sheriff. Royce walked into the emergency room with Sarna right behind him. He approached a nurse behind a counter, but was stopped by a voice from behind.

"Royce?"

Royce turned to see the sheriff. He wore his standard uniform and held his hat. His belt buckle reflected the fluorescent light in the room.

"Rick?" asked Royce. "How is he?"

Sarna stood beside Royce and waited for the sheriff to answer. Rick glanced at Sarna before answering. "He's still with the doctors. I haven't heard anything else." He turned his hat in circles in his hands.

"How can you not know anything?" Sarna asked. "Where is he? I want to see him."

Royce placed a gentle hand on her arm. "We have to wait. Let the doctors evaluate him."

Sarna pulled away. "Evaluate him? What are they going to do to him? They might hurt him." She looked past the sheriff down the hallway. "Where is he?"

The sheriff watched her, and Royce knew the man's mind was swirling with questions. "This is Sarna, Rick. She's a friend of Jasper's. The man who's injured."

Rick nodded and tipped his head toward Sarna. Sarna barely acknowledged him. "You mind if I ask how you know the victim? Why was your picture in his pocket?"

Royce anticipated Rick's questions. He figured the truth was the best way to respond. "He's my brother."

Rick's eyes widened. "Your brother?"

Royce nodded. "That's why I had to leave suddenly last week." He glanced at Sarna, who looked like a caged antelope anxious for escape. "I didn't even know he existed."

"That's why he had your picture?"

"Yes."

"I can't wait here," said Sarna, who moved around the sheriff. "I have to see him."

The sheriff extended an arm to stop her progress. "Hold up, ma'am."

Sarna stopped. "This is silly."

"Sarna," said Royce. "We have to wait."

"What are we waiting for? He's being treated, isn't he? What's taking so long?"

Rick glanced at Royce with curious eyes.

"They'll have to do tests," said Royce. "It takes time to evaluate a head injury." He waited and hoped she understood.

She threw out her hands. "Why don't you just scan him?"

Royce inwardly cringed, and the sheriff's face furrowed. "It's not like that."

"Scan him?" asked Rick. "You mean like an MRI?"

Sarna raised an eyebrow. "What is that? Will that heal him?"

"That's exactly what she means," said Royce, stepping in. He shot a warning glare at Sarna, sending a clear signal with his thoughts. Hoping she got the message, he turned back toward Rick. "So what happened to him? Do you know?"

The question successfully distracted Rick from Sarna's strange be-havior. "Just what I told you on the phone. We've had officers walk through that area of the woods, keeping an eye out. One of them found your brother. He was unconscious and bleeding. It looked like he'd been hit with a rock."

"But why him?" Sarna asked.

Rick shrugged. "I was hoping one of you could tell me that. Any idea why someone would want to harm him?"

"No," Royce said.

"What was he doing in those woods?" asked the sheriff.

Royce kept his face passive, but he looked at Sarna, warning her again with his eyes to stay quiet, but she answered anyway.

"They had a fight."

Rick's face furrowed. "Who?"

She cocked her head at Royce. "Him and Jasper."

Royce shook his head but didn't speak.

"About what?"

Sarna glanced at Royce, and Royce could almost hear her voice in his head. "Over their father." She sighed. "They have differing opinions about the man."

"And where do you fit in? How do you know the victim?"

Sarna was unfazed by his questions. "His name is Jasper. I've known him since we were kids. He wanted to reach out to his half-brother Royce, but was afraid to do it. I told him I'd help him."

The sheriff nodded, seemingly satisfied. "But why the woods?"

"The woods?" asked Royce.

"Why'd he go there? Specifically to Shady Point?"

Royce looked at Sarna.

She answered immediately. "We stopped there briefly on our way here. Jasper likes the woods. It would be like him to go there to let off some steam."

The sheriff rubbed his neck. "Hmm." He crossed his arms. "Unfortunately, he picked the wrong spot."

"You think that this has something to do with the murdered woman?" Royce asked.

Rick scratched his jaw. "I don't know. But it's highly coincidental that we now have two victims attacked in the same place."

"So he was found where the woman was killed?" asked Sarna, her eyes pointed.

"You know about that?"

"It's hard to keep that quiet in a small town," answered Royce.

Still holding his hat, the sheriff put his hands on his hips. "How long have you and your brother been in town?"

Royce knew that if Rick kept asking questions, that at some point, their answers would become trickier. He opened his mouth to answer, but was interrupted.

"Sheriff?"

They all three looked to see a doctor enter the room. He wore green scrubs, which looked relatively clean, although they were wrinkled. He stopped and rested a palm on the counter of the nurse's station.

"Doctor?" asked Royce, who walked closer.

Sarna immediately spoke. "Are you treating Jasper? How is he? Where is he? I need to see him."

The doctor almost stepped back at Sarna's approach. "Jasper?" he asked. "Are you a relative?"

"That's his name, doctor," said Rick. "Jasper…" He looked at Royce.

"Jasper Fiss," said Royce. He realized then that if the sheriff did any sort of background check, that he'd only become more suspicious when he found nothing. "He's my half-brother."

"Please let me see him," Sarna said. "Where is he?"

The doctor shook his head. "He's got a serious head injury. He's unconscious. His brain is swelling and we're monitoring it closely. If it gets worse, he'll need surgery."

"Surgery?" asked Sarna. "No. You can't do that."

"Sarna..." said Royce.

"His brain is pressing against his skull," said the doctor. "If it doesn't stop, we'll need to relieve the pressure. Otherwise, it will lead to serious and potentially permanent complications. At a minimum, this sort of trauma can result in motor and speech impairment and memory loss if not treated quickly, and at worse coma or death if not treated properly. We're keeping a close eye on him."

"There have to be other ways besides surgery," said Sarna, her eyes pleading. "You'll kill him."

"On the contrary, ma'am. We're trying to save him."

"What's the prognosis?" asked Rick.

The doctor grimaced and stretched his back. His red eyes revealed his fatigue. "Right now, we've moved him into the ICU. He's on a ventilator to help him breathe. We'll monitor him and hope the swelling doesn't worsen. If he's lucky and doesn't decline, he should come around in a day or two and then we'll know more. If he doesn't improve and the swelling progresses, we'll do surgery to relieve the pressure."

"Royce..." Sarna walked up and took his hand. The gesture surprised him. "We can't let that happen. Trust me. We have to get him out of here."

The doctor watched their exchange. "I know we're not a big hospital, ma'am. But we have everything we need here to treat him. We'll do everything we can to avoid surgery. But believe me, if we do it, it will be to keep him alive."

Royce realized Sarna's concerns had nothing to do with the hospital they were in. He didn't understand it, but based on what he felt from her, he knew there were other issues to consider. He squeezed her hand in reassurance and tried to communicate empathically with her. "We'll figure it out, Sarna. Let's hope it doesn't come to that, but if it does, we'll decide what to do then."

Her upturned face revealed a rare vulnerability which he knew did not come lightly. He nodded at her, and he felt her squeeze his hand in return.

Royce noted how the sheriff studied them and realized how it looked. He figured at some point the sheriff would have more questions, but he'd have to deal with that later. "Can we see him?" he asked the doctor.

The doctor nodded. "Head up to the ICU on the fourth floor. Once they get him settled, you should be able to visit for a few minutes."

"A few minutes?" asked Sarna. "That's it?"

The doctor waved a hand. "The ICU has various restrictions. Just talk to the nurses upstairs. They'll let you know the rules."

"Rules?" asked Sarna. "Why are there rules? He needs us by his side. It's important."

"Talk to the nurses. They'll tell you what to do."

"But—"

"Sarna," said Royce. "Don't worry. We'll see him."

"We'll need his clothes," said Rick.

"Clothes? What for?" Sarna asked.

"This is a police investigation," said the sheriff. "If he put up a fight, there might be DNA evidence."

"I think the nurse bagged them," replied the doctor. "They probably brought them up to the ICU. I'll make sure you get them."

"Thanks," said Rick.

"We have to go upstairs," Sarna said. She pulled on Royce's arm. "Now."

"Okay. You need anything else from us, Rick?" He didn't want to look like he was hiding anything.

Rick shook his head. His eyes looked as heavy with fatigue as the doctor's. "I'll catch up to you. Go check on your brother."

Royce nodded. "Thanks, Rick. You know where to find us."

"I'll tell RJ you're back in town. He'll be glad to hear it."

Royce wasn't sure how to respond, but the way Sarna kept pulling on him made it hard to give a lengthy answer. "Yeah. He's welcome to visit anytime."

Following Sarna, he turned and headed toward the elevator.

· · · · **·** · **·** · · ·

Upstairs, after speaking to a nurse and being told to wait, Royce sat next to an anxious Sarna and asked the question plaguing him. "Will the doctors find anything suspicious about Jasper?"

Sarna stared at the door to the ICU as if expecting Jasper to walk through it any moment. "Like what?"

He lowered his voice. "Like he's from another planet?"

"You've been to the doctor before. Have they found anything strange about you?"

Royce thought back to the number of times his mother had taken him to the ER for a myriad of injuries. "No."

"Well, unless they plan to do some sort of in depth DNA testing on him, then no, they won't find anything."

Royce nodded, pleased that there was one less thing to worry about. He sat in a chair and Sarna paced the room quietly while they waited forty-five minutes.

Finally, a nurse arrived and ushered them behind two big, white, sliding doors. They passed a sprawling counter, with three nurses behind it, all looking busy. One held a pen and studied a chart, and another typed on a keyboard in front of a computer screen. Their vantage point allowed them easy access to any area on the floor. Royce followed the nurse, who ushered them into a room that contained numerous machines, most of which made a beeping or whooshing sound. Jasper lay in the middle of it all, amongst a sea of tubes and wires. He was covered by a blanket and looked small in the bed. A breathing tube protruded from his mouth and a ventilator pumped oxygen in slow rhythmic pulses. His eyes looked sunken, and his skin had a gray tinge.

Sarna approached the bed and gripped the handrail. Royce stood next to her. It was hard to see the man who had just been eating at his table and arguing with him, now looking so weak and vulnerable.

"This is barbaric," whispered Sarna.

"What?"

"What are they doing to him?" She waved at the equipment. "What is all this?"

"They're keeping him alive," said Royce.

"They're killing him."

"He has a head injury. He'll die without treatment."

She shook her head. "You don't understand." She turned away from the bed.

"Understand what?" She began to open cabinets and drawers. "What are you doing?"

"His things. I need to find them."

"The sheriff wants them."

"I don't care about the sheriff." She slammed the drawers shut and opened a small closet. There was a bag hanging from a hangar. "Here..." She grabbed the bag and took it down.

"What are you doing?"

She dug through the bag, ignoring the clothes. "Here it is." She pulled out a watch.

"What do you need his watch for?" He pointed at the wall. "There's a clock right there."

"I don't care about the time." She turned the watch over and pushed a concealed button. Royce was surprised when the back opened to reveal a tiny opening. Inside were several small white pills. She popped two out and closed the container. She put the watch in her pocket. "Help me," she said.

"Help you what?"

She walked up to Jasper and grabbed his jaw.

"What are you doing?"

"I have to get these in his mouth."

"He's unconscious."

"It doesn't matter. They'll dissolve, and he'll absorb them."

"Do you know what you're doing?"

She froze and shot a worried stare at Royce. "He's a Red-Line, Royce. Our sensitivities make us more susceptible. This planet is not good for either of us. These pills help us acclimate. Without them, neither of us will last long." She rubbed Jasper's arm. "But with an injury like this..." She squeezed his wrist. "I don't know if there's enough pills to get him through."

"But they're treating him..."

"With earthly means. It's very traumatic to our systems. At some point, it will become too much. He'll start to deteriorate."

She continued to hold the pills, waiting for him. He realized the implications of what she said. Jasper might not survive. He walked up to the bed. "What do you need me to do?"

"Help me hold his mouth open. It's harder with the tube. But the pills are small. I can get them in."

Royce did as she asked. He held Jasper's jaw while she adjusted the tape and dropped the pills into Jasper's mouth. He let go and stepped back. "What next?"

"We have to figure out how to get him out of here."

Royce couldn't help but chuckle. "What are you talking about?"

Sarna waved her hands. "Look at all this. It's awful. It's breaking him down bit by bit. And he'll never make it through a surgery."

Royce eyed the watch she wore. "Do you take these pills too?"

"Of course. Once a day. We won't last long in this environment without them."

"How many do you have?"

She eyed Jasper with worry. "We brought enough, but not for something like this. He'll need much more."

"How would you treat him on Eudora?"

She pointed at the machines. "Certainly not with any of this. We have people who are medical empaths. They can sense injuries and illness and make diagnoses."

Royce blinked. He tried to imagine what she meant. "Wait. They just wave their hands and they're healed?"

"It's possible, yes. Depending on the injury."

"And who is doing all this healing?"

"There are Red-Lines who have the ability. It's rare, but it does occur. They can evaluate the problem and often heal it on the spot."

"Really?"

"Yes." Her eyes widened, and she gripped the handrail on Jasper's bed. "Your sisters."

He raised an eyebrow. "What about them?"

"Do they have it?"

"Have what?"

She huffed. "The gift. The ability to heal?"

He thought of Gillian and Eve. Although they had some unique gifts, healing was not one of them. "No. They don't." A memory flashed in his mind. "I think Eve healed a dog once."

Sarna shook her head. "It's not the same. Animal healers are different. We need someone more advanced."

Royce pulled up Jasper's blanket. "We're on Earth, Sarna."

"Then we have no other choice. I have to get him out of here and back on the ship. I have to take him home."

He wasn't sure how to respond. "How do you propose we do that? Look at him. We can't move him. And the moment we do, the medical staff will know. Sheriff Rick will arrest us before we get out of the lobby."

Her eyes glistened with unshed tears. "We don't have a choice. I can't let him die. I've already lost a brother. I can't lose him too."

Her fear was palpable, and he identified with it. He knew how he'd feel if his sisters were in jeopardy. He'd do whatever it took to keep them alive. "There has to be another way." He sighed and pushed Jasper's IV stand a few inches back. The room felt small with all the machines. "Why don't we wait? See if he responds to the pills."

"Because every day he will get weaker with all this stuff attached to him and the medication they'll give him. It will slowly kill him. The pills will only slow his inevitable decline. So unless you've got access to some secret Red-Line you've been hiding who has the healing ability, we've got to get him out of here. Tonight. I've got to fly him home." She wrung her hands and bit her lip.

Royce tried to imagine them wheeling Jasper down the corridor past the nurse's station. "I thought you didn't know how to fly."

"I know enough to start up the ship. After that, it's all up to auto pilot. Not ideal, but it will have to do."

His mind reeling, Royce opened his mouth to speak, but no sound emerged. How in the hell did she think they were going to disengage Jasper from all these machines, sneak him out of the hospital, get him to a spaceship in the woods, and fly him out, without being discovered? "Sarna..."

"What?" She stood unmoving in the room, leaving little room for discussion. It reminded him of his sisters' responses when he'd told them one year he was considering spending Christmas in the woods camping, instead of at home. He'd quickly changed his mind.

"There's absolutely no way..." A thought occurred to him and he froze.

"What is it?"

The idea grew.

"Royce?"

The memory flickered and blossomed. Royce recalled what his father had confided to him during his last visit. He'd told Royce of another group of Eudorans that lived on Earth. A community of Gray-Lines. Only a few hours away. Galen had also mentioned the group before almost killing Royce.

Royce had been curious but had never investigated the community. For some reason, he'd felt uncertain knowing there were others like him. He could not envision what he would say if he came into contact with them. But after what happened with Galen, he'd decided it was worth the trip to see for himself. His father had told him where they lived.

He didn't plan to introduce himself, but if others like him and his sisters existed on Earth, then maybe Royce could eventually summon the nerve to meet them and he could get some answers to some long overdue questions. Based on what his father had told him, there were no Red-Lines among them. But Galen had suggested otherwise, making Royce believe there was more to their story.

Following his instincts and using his energetic gifts, he'd driven about three hours, taken some back roads, and feeling pulled to a certain location, he'd wound up outside a one-story house on a small wooded lot. Something or someone in the house had drawn him, as if Royce was a magnet and the source a huge refrigerator.

He'd parked on the street, far enough away to not look suspicious, but close enough to see the home through the trees. He didn't know what the appeal was of that particular house, but something about it felt comfortable to him.

After waiting an hour, he'd finally seen a woman, with a baby in her arms, emerge from the home. She walked outside to get the mail. She looked tall, had shoulder-length brown hair, and a lithe frame. Her child looked to be around six to eight months. While she retrieved her mail, a man also emerged from the front door, carrying another child approximately the same age. The man was slightly taller, with dark wavy hair and a lean, muscular build. The child he held was crying.

The woman closed the mailbox and turned toward the man, who Royce presumed was her husband. They talked, and the man pointed to the child's hand. They switched children, and the woman took the wailing child's hand in hers. There was a brief pause. Within seconds, the child quieted and stopped crying. The woman smiled, kissed the baby's fingers, and they all walked back toward the house. They looked like a happy family, and Royce couldn't help but feel somewhat envious of the couple. He'd opened up his senses and could feel the mutual love and affection between them.

As he watched, a flare of electric current zipped through him when the woman stopped as she reached the porch. Her husband went inside, but she turned and stared toward the street. Still holding her baby, her eyes scanned the area before stopping on his car. He froze when he realized she'd sensed him. Despite the distance, they made eye contact. Feeling exposed, he started the car and pulled away, but before leaving, he saw a message clearly in his mind's eye—it was a name and a phone number. He'd left the scene and never looked back.

"Royce," said Sarna. "What is it?"

Royce shook his head at the memory. At that moment, what he'd seen the woman do, what he'd sensed from her, and how she'd reacted to him, suddenly all made sense.

"Royce..."

He whipped his head toward Sarna. "A Red-Line who heals..."

"What?"

The name and phone number flashed in his head. The woman had known exactly what she was doing. She'd sensed him and had tried to communicate with him. He dropped his jaw. "I think I know one."

# Chapter Eighteen

SARNA STARED BACK AT him as if he'd just told her that they would be having steak for dinner. "What do you mean?"

"I mean," he said, "I know a Red-Line."

She squinted her eyes. "Where? Here?"

"Yes," he answered.

She furrowed her brow. "Are you okay?"

"I'm fine."

"How could there possibly be a Red-Line here? On Earth? Besides you and your sisters?"

"The same way it's possible that we're here is the same way it's possible that she's here."

She hesitated. "Are you saying that someone else traveled from Eudora and had children with a human?"

"It happened to me. Why not with her?"

Her eyes widened. "It's not your father, is it?"

He grunted. "No, of course not. I'm not exactly sure how she got here. I'm just making assumptions. What I do know is that my father told me about a community of Gray-Lines that live here. Galen mentioned it too."

"Galen?" she asked. "How would he know about it?"

"Well, if Dad knew, then why wouldn't Galen? Galen told us that after he killed me and my sisters, he planned one more stop before he left Earth. He said there was another Red he would have to remove because of mixed lineage."

"Mixed?"

"Yes. Half-human, half-Eudoran."

She shook her head. "There's a whole community of Gray-Lines here?"

"Yes. After Galen's death, I got curious and traveled up there. I watched a woman." He thought back. "She had a child. The child was crying as if she'd been hurt. The woman took her, and the child stopped crying." The memory made him shiver as the pieces connected. "I think the woman healed her."

Sarna's knuckles turned white as she gripped the handrail. "You think, or you know?"

Royce wasn't sure how to answer. It was hard to say. But based on what he'd seen and felt that day, he felt fairly confident that he was right. "She spoke to me. In my head."

Sarna drew in a breath. "Telepathically?"

"Yes."

"She has to be a Red-Line. What did she say?"

"She gave me her name and phone number."

Sarna's mouth dropped open. "Well, what are you waiting for?"

Just then, a nurse popped her head into the room. "Sorry," she said. "Visitation in the ICU is fifteen minutes every hour."

"That's it?" asked Sarna. She glanced at Jasper. "But I don't want to leave him."

"I'm sorry," said the nurse. "We limit visitation for patients with brain trauma. You can visit fifteen minutes every hour."

"Come on," said Royce. "We'll stay in the waiting room. We'll come back in an hour."

"You won't do anything to him, will you?" Sarna asked the nurse.

The nurse pursed her lips. "Nothing harmful." She walked to the closet and picked up the bag of Jasper's clothes. "The sheriff has asked for his belongings."

"That's fine," Royce said. "Come on, Sarna."

"But this is silly. Why can't we stay?"

"Hospital rules," said the nurse.

"But he needs our help..." said Sarna.

"Don't worry," said the nurse. "He's getting excellent care."

Royce took her elbow. "Come on. We have a phone call to make."

Her head shot up, and she nodded. She reached down and took Jasper's hand and squeezed it. "Don't worry Jasper. We're going to get you some help. Just hang in there."

The nurse waited as Sarna and Royce walked out. They returned to the ICU waiting area. The bland colors of the walls and furniture matched their somber mood.

Royce pulled out his cell phone and held it. He hesitated.

"What's wrong?" asked Sarna.

He sat down in a chair. "What exactly am I supposed to say?"

Sarna sat next to him. "How about the truth?"

He rubbed his thumb over his cell. "What if I'm wrong?"

"Do you think you're wrong?"

He took a second, but then shook his head. "No. I don't think I am."

"Then make the call."

Royce recalled the number the woman had delivered to him. The numbers were etched into his thoughts like a scar on his skin. Taking a deep breath, he dialed the number and brought the phone to his ear. He could feel himself begin to sweat.

It rang three times before he heard the audible click of the phone being answered. There was a brief silence, and Royce held his breath. Then a woman's voice, soft but serious. "I was wondering when you would call."

· · · · ·· · · · ·

Sarah Ramsey held the phone to her ear. The moment it rang, a shiver ran down her spine and she knew who it was. Sitting at her breakfast table, the memory flashed in her mind of the day she'd sensed the man in a car on her street. She'd been outside, holding her son Ethan when her husband, John, had emerged from the house holding Rosie. Her blonde hair shone in the sun, but her tear-stained face was clouded with pain. Sarah could feel her distress, and John told her how her finger had been caught in a door. He'd looked and felt almost more upset than Rosie. Sarah had given Ethan to John and took her daughter. Holding the child's hand, Sarah had summoned the healing energy she'd harnessed since her Shift had occurred almost two years earlier. Rosie's tears stopped.  Sarah kissed her daughter's fingers, and they returned to the house. But before entering, Sarah had stopped and turned on the porch. Something had felt different, as if a long-lost relative had arrived. Someone with similar energy to her own. There was a momentary twist of fear as she recalled the last time she'd encountered someone who was like her. But that lasted only a second.

She'd scanned the street, eyeing each car, and she'd seen him. He was sitting behind the wheel of a red pickup parked beneath a large leafy tree. He pressed back against the seat the moment she saw him, as if the shadows would conceal him. Tuning in telepathically, Sarah sensed he meant no harm; he was only curious.

Curious herself, she probed further, and was shocked when she recognized why he felt so familiar. Her jaw dropping, she realized he was a Red-Line, like her. She stared and knew he felt her surprise. He'd started up the car, but before he could leave, she'd quickly sent him a message. A way to contact her. She wondered if that was the best thing to do. She didn't know him, and her husband would probably not appreciate his wife sending out her name and number to a strange man. But the man's curiosity, as well as his conflict, had convinced her. She'd watched him drive away.

Now, months later, the familiar sensation had returned. The man in the car was calling. John was in the other room, putting the twins down for their nap. Sarah stared at the phone as it rang, and she answered. Hesitating, she listened on the phone and waited for the stranger to respond. Tuning in, she felt no threat, but could still feel his conflict. How the two of them existed was a question he likely wanted an answer to. So did she.

"Hello?" she asked after there was no answer to her initial response. "You there?"

"Yes. I'm here," he finally said. His voice was just above a whisper.

Sarah bounced her knee. "What's your name?"

He cleared his throat. "Royce. Royce Fletcher."

"I'm Sarah Ramsey."

"You're the woman on the porch?"

"You're the man in the car?"

She heard a shaky breath. "Sorry about that."

"Don't worry about it. How'd you find me?"

There was a pause. "That's a long story."

She nodded her head in understanding. "I'm sure you're curious about me."

"Yes. Very."

She paused and considered her next move. "Would you like to meet?" He was quiet, but Sarah could hear a distinct female voice in the background. "Is someone else with you?"

He sighed into the phone. "Yes." He paused. "Don't worry. She's like us."

Sarah sat up in her seat. "Really?" She thought of her history with other Red-Lines. "Someone you trust?"

Another shaky sigh. "Yes. I trust them."

"Them?" she asked. This story was getting stranger by the second. "What exactly is going on?"

She knew he could feel her wariness. "I'll explain everything," he said. "You have nothing to fear. But I'll be honest. We need your help."

His concern drifted through the phone. "What do you need?"

Her husband, John Ramsey, came into the room. His dark hair was ruffled, his shirt was wrinkled and there was dried food on his collar, but he always looked good to her. "Kiddos are down," he said. She nodded at him.

The man on the phone hesitated, but finally asked, "Correct me if I'm wrong, but that day, in your front yard, you healed your child. Yes?"

The question surprised her. Apparently, this man was quite capable. "Yes, I did."

"Who's on the phone?" asked John. He sat beside her and flicked the food off his shirt.

"My friend," said the man, "the one who's here with me now. She has another friend with her. They're visiting."

A tingle ran down her spine. "Visiting? From where?" She held her breath and looked at John. His eyebrows knitted together.

"You know where."

Sarah reached out and took John's hand. His look turned worried. "What is it?"

Sarah wasn't sure what to say. "How is that possible?"

"Listen," said the man. "I know this is crazy. I think it's crazy. But, in a nutshell, they came to see me. There's two of them. But one of them is injured, and we're in the hospital. He won't survive his treatment. Without help, he'll die."

Understanding dawned, and Sarah eyed her husband. "You want me to come there?"

There was a pause. "Can you? I promise. I'll explain everything when you're here."

John quirked up an eyebrow at her. "What the hell is going on?"

She spoke into the phone. "Tell me where you are."

# Chapter Nineteen

SARNA AND ROYCE, WEARY after a long day, walked back in to Royce's house. After speaking with Sarah, they'd stayed at the hospital, sitting with Jasper when they could and giving him additional pills until visiting hours had ended at eight o'clock. Sarah would not arrive until the next morning, and they planned to meet her at the hospital.

On the way home, they'd stopped for a bite to eat and made it back to Royce's cabin at ten o'clock. Exhausted, they sat at the dining table.

Royce eyed Sarna's tired features. "You take my room tonight. I'll sleep in the guest bedroom."

"Hmm?" asked Sarna. Her far off stare shifted toward him.

"You're tired. You should go to bed. It's a big day tomorrow."

She nodded and studied him. "You look tired too."

Royce thought about his day. He'd woken up this morning to find Alice gone, only to return home to find two strangers in his house who were from another planet. One was his half-brother and the other a woman who seemed to enjoy irritating him. They'd argued and his brother had walked off and got his head bashed in and was now in a hospital bed—his only hope a female Red-Line who Royce knew nothing about, but who apparently had the power to heal. All of this after being attacked by a bear and a snake only a few days before, along with helping RJ hide a murdered woman's shoe.

"Tired?" he asked. "I don't know how I'm still standing." He rubbed a hand over his pounding head.

"I bet," she said. "You should pack tomorrow. After you've had some rest."

He lifted his weary brows. "Pack? For what?"

She pursed her lips. "For when we leave."

He squinted. "The hospital?"

She shook her head. "No. The Earth."

"But I'm not leaving the Earth."

She shifted toward him. "But I thought..."

"You thought what?"

She straightened. "I thought you'd reconsidered."

"Since when?"

"Since we talked."

"Talked? About what?"

"I told you that you had nothing to worry about. You would be safe."

"That's great. But that doesn't mean I changed my mind."

She stood. "Even after what happened to Jasper?"

Royce considered himself level-headed, but his fatigue was wearing him down. "What does that have to do with anything?"

She walked into the kitchen and crossed her arms. "This planet is so toxic. How do you stand it here? Don't you want to go someplace else?"

Royce rose out of his seat. "Yes. Like your planet sounds so welcoming. I suspect I'm more likely to get slaughtered than greeted with open arms."

"To kill a High Child is treason. Anyone stupid enough to do that won't live long."

"If you find them."

She raised a brow. "Are you kidding? We are intuitive, empathic, and telepathic. You can't keep that kind of secret where we come from."

"Thoughts can be cloaked."

"It's hard to stay cloaked all the time and with everyone. It's not a permanent shield. And with the kind of scrutiny that crime would garner, it would only be a matter of time."

"So, you're saying I'd be safe?"

"From death? Probably."

"And I should take your word for it? That makes me feel so much better."

She clenched her jaw. "You are so stubborn."

"You are so aggravating."

"I'm not aggravating. I'm passionate. I tell you what I think."

Royce figured Sarna was tired too, which was only fueling her own irritation, but he didn't care. He squared his shoulders. "Believe me. I know. I could deal with a little less of what you think."

Her mouth dropped open. "You need to hear it, whether you like it or not." She pointed at him. "And what I think is that you're scared. Scared to fail. Scared you won't measure up to your father."

Royce's frustration inched higher. "Listen. I've had a long day. I've listened to your and Jasper's pitch about how great it would be to be a supreme leader. I've put up with your disparaging remarks about this planet. About what we eat and how abhorrent we all are. But what I'm really sick of is how you seem to think you know everything about my relationship with my dad. My feelings about my father are between the two of us, and they are none of your business."

"And what I'm sick of is your incessant need to stick your head in the sand. We have a real crisis here."

He stepped around the table. "If anyone's head belongs in the sand, it's yours. At least that way you wouldn't be able to talk."

Her face flushed. "You're so ignorant about what's at stake here."

He narrowed his eyes and his muscles strained further. "I'm ignorant? You're the one living in some sort of fairy tale. You think if I do what you want, that it will change everything. That your world will become exactly as you want it. It doesn't work that way. Bringing me back changes nothing. There will still be conflict. Maybe even war. And it sure as hell won't bring your brother back."

Her face went from red to white and she stilled. "My brother had more integrity in his palm than you have in your whole body. He was a better man than you will ever be." She shook her head. "Maybe that's why your father visited so rarely. He knew you could never be the man to take his place."

It was Royce's turn to turn pale. He opened his mouth to speak, but shut it, knowing whatever he said would only be cruel and unnecessary. Breathing hard, he willed himself to stay calm. He took a measured, deep breath and stepped back. "I think we've both said enough." He pushed a dining chair out of the way and slammed it into the table. Sarna jumped at the noise. "I'm going to bed." He walked toward the guest room, wishing he could punch something.

"Royce..."

"Good night." Without looking back, he flipped off the kitchen lights, entered the guest room, and shut the door, leaving her in darkness.

· · · · ·•· · · · ·

The next morning, Royce made coffee, and they sipped in silence, neither mentioning their argument. Royce preferred it that way. Thoughts of hospital bills and potential questions about Jasper's background had kept him awake and his head felt like it was full of sand. Soon after, the sheriff called and told Royce he would be coming to the hospital to speak with him about Jasper. Royce had no idea how he was going to handle Rick's questions without raising more suspicions about his guests. His only hope was to answer what he could and then escort Jasper and Sarna to their ship as quickly as possible before Rick could delve any deeper into their background. Once Royce did that, he could figure out how to deal with the hospital bill.

Arriving back at the hospital after a quiet car ride, he and Sarna stood quietly in the waiting room. Visiting hours began at nine a.m., but they'd arrived early. Sarah was due to arrive at any minute, and Royce paced the room, checking his watch. He didn't know if he was more nervous about meeting Sarah or talking to Rick about Jasper.

Sarna stood with her hands in her pockets. She kept looking at the clock. "She should be here soon."

He studied the floor. "Yes."

Restless, she bit her lip and spoke softly. "Listen. About last night...what I said..."

He waved at her. "Forget about it. It was a long day. We both said things we shouldn't have."

She took her hands out of her pockets and wrung her hands. "I'm sorry. I was tired and upset."

Her eyes were wide with uncertainty, and he sighed, feeling his anger dissipate. "Me too."

Her shoulders came down, and she nodded. He found himself staring at her, wanting to say more and wishing he could, when the elevator dinged. Turning at the sound, they watched the doors open and a woman step out into the waiting area. Royce recognized her immediately. It was the same woman he'd seen from his car. She wore slim khaki pants and a loose-fitting red blouse. A man stepped off with her. It was the man who had joined Sarah on the lawn. He wore relaxed jeans and a navy shirt. His wavy hair looked longer, and he brushed it back with his fingers.

Standing in the hallway, they looked around, and Sarah saw Royce. She stared, and the man behind her turned. Seeing Royce, he looked him up and down. Sarah eyed Sarna as well. Nobody spoke. Sarna walked over to stand beside Royce as the couple approached with tentative steps.

Now all together, they hesitated in uncertain silence, as if they were walking into a stranger's house unannounced. Royce cleared his throat and spoke first. "You're Sarah?"

She nodded and took the elbow of the man beside her. "Yes. You're Royce?"

"Yes." He gestured toward Sarna. "This is Sarna."

Sarah nodded. "And this is my husband, John Ramsey."

They shook hands. Another moment of awkward silence ensued until John looked up at Royce. "I hope you're not one of the little ones."

It helped to break the ice and Royce smiled. "No."

John smiled back. "I feel like I should call you Thor."

Royce made a knowing grunt. "Growing up, I made my sisters call me Batman."

John pursed his lips. "I like Batman. He's got that whole brooding thing going on. I always preferred Captain America, though. Give me a shield any day."

Royce tilted his head. "True, but Batman's got the Batmobile."

John's brow shot up. "Good point."

"And the Bat Cave."

"I'm not a big fan of the dark, or of bats, but I see the appeal."

"I don't know," said Sarah, taking her husband's hand. "I've always been partial to Superman." She eyed her husband. "I like his cape."

John's lip quirked. "And you'd make a fantastic Wonder Woman," he replied with a wink.

Royce noted the faint blush on Sarah's cheeks. Royce's insides warmed, and he realized he was picking up on the powerful connection between the couple. A flicker of envy flared, but then quickly disappeared.

"Excuse me," said Sarna, interrupting. "But just who exactly is this captain and bat person?"

They all stared at her.

"She would be the Black Widow," said Royce.

"What?" asked Sarna, frowning.

"She really is from another planet, isn't she?" asked John.

"She is," said Royce.

A short woman with silver hair up in a bun and a purse on her wrist walked by. She glanced at the group as she crossed the room to sit next to an elderly gentleman.

"Um...perhaps we should move this conversation to the corner of the room. There are some seats." Royce gestured behind Sarah, and the group moved away from the other older couple and sat.

"So," said Sarah, leaning forward and speaking in a low voice, "tell me what's going on."

Sarna didn't hesitate. "Jasper is injured. Someone on this crazy planet almost killed him, and if we don't get him out of here, he is going to die."

"Whoa," said Royce, holding up a hand. "Hold up. One step at a time."

"One step at a time?" asked Sarna, in disbelief. "What other steps are there?"

"Plenty," said John Ramsey, leaning in. He spoke to Royce. "Like before we get to your friend Jasper, how about you tell me how you found my wife? And where you," he pointed toward Sarna, "and your friend here, come from."

Sarah put her hand on her husband's forearm, and he took her hand in his. Sarna eyed the interaction, and Royce wondered if she could feel the same connection from the couple as he'd felt. Sarna spoke to John. "Are you a Gray-Line?"

"I am," answered John. He paused, his eyes narrowing. "Is that a problem?"

Sarna shook her head. "No. No. Not at all. It's just that..."

"Just what?" asked Sarah.

Sarna held up a hand. "Nothing. It's just not something I've seen."

"You've never seen a Gray-Line?" asked John. "Based on where you're from, I would expect you've bumped into a few."

"No. That's not what I mean."

"What do you mean?" asked Sarah.

"I'm sorry, it's just that…" She gestured toward their hands. "You two together. It's not allowed where I…we come from. Hasn't been for as long as I can remember. Maybe never."

"Not allowed?" asked Sarah. "What's not allowed?"

"A Gray-Line and a Red-Line. As a couple."

John squeezed Sarah's fingers. "Call us rule-breakers." He eyed Sarah. "Things are a little different here."

"Believe me," said Sarna. "I know."

"Anyway," said Royce, "getting back to your original question about how I found you."

"Yes?" asked Sarah.

"My father told me about you."

"Me?" asked Sarah.

"Not you specifically." He shook his head. "Let me start at the beginning."

"Please do," said John.

Royce leaned forward and clasped his hands. "My father came to this planet many years ago. He met my mother. They had triplets. Me and my sisters—Eve and Gillian." He continued with the background information, telling her about his father, his past, Galen, Jasper and Roma, how he'd found Sarah, and his role as the High Child.

After hearing Royce's story, John whistled and nodded toward his wife. "I thought your story was complicated."

Sarah sat forward, eyes wide. "So, let me see if I understand. You and your sisters have a father from," she stopped and looked toward a man sitting nearby, "Italy."

"Italy?" Sarna asked.

"Just go with it," John said.

"And he met your American mother and had three children, all half-Italian. All who are, shall we say, master chefs?"

Royce nodded at her.

"And your uncle Galen is peeved because your father didn't marry an Italian woman?"

"He went outside the family," said John, scratching his neck and speaking in a mock Vito Corleone accent.

They all stared at him.

"Are you okay?" asked Sarna.

His face fell. "Sorry."

"Pretty good imitation," said Royce.

"I thought so," said John.

"Anyway," Sarah said, shaking her head, "back in Italy, your father married someone else and had two other master chefs. Now, he's about to lose his job as the owner of the restaurant, and his eldest daughter from his second family wants to run it. But she's not the true owner." She pointed at Royce. "You are."

Royce nodded. "That's it."

"What about your uncle? What happened when he found you?" asked Sarah.

Royce considered how to answer. "There was a confrontation. It didn't go well. It was then that he mentioned to us that he knew about your community."

"He did?" asked John. "Why? As far as we know, there's been no communication between us and Italy in over seventy years. What's the sudden interest?"

Royce pointed at Sarah. "You. He knew about you. Said there was another mixed Red-Line that needed to be eliminated. Said after he took care of me and my sisters, he was going to take care of one last job. I assume that meant you."

John's face turned stony. "Son-of-a..." He glanced at Sarah. "How would he know?"

Royce shook his head, along with Sarna. "We don't know."

Sarna answered. "I can only assume he went looking for his brother's family. Probably watched your people for a while, wondering if you could be harboring them. He didn't find Royce and his sisters, but he probably discovered Sarah the same way Royce did."

Sarah's forehead creased. "But how didn't I feel him the way I felt Royce?"

"A powerful Red-Line can cloak themselves. He would be hard to read, even for you."

Sarah nodded, her face looking pale. She looked at her husband, who squeezed her hand in reassurance. "What happened with him?" she asked. "Did he leave America?"

"Not the way he expected to." Royce stared at his hands and thought back to flashes of lightning and a ball of fire. "He won't be making any return flights to Italy."

Sarah and John stayed quiet. "You do what you have to do to protect your own," said John, eyeing Sarah.

"Exactly my thoughts," said Royce.

"Your sisters are okay?" Sarah asked.

"Yes. They're fine."

"Good," said Sarah. "I'd like to meet them."

Royce shook off his memories. "They'd like that."

"So you and Jasper came to see Royce?" asked John to Sarna.

"Yes. We want him to come back to Italy with us. The restaurant is in disarray. It needs a great master chef. Roma is not that person. She would only wreak more havoc in the kitchen. Royce could change all that."

"What about the Italians?" asked Sarah. "How would they feel about a half-Italian in charge?"

Sarna went quiet for a moment. "My country..." she stopped to think. "It has been closed off for many years. It used to be open. Scientific exploration and travel were the norm. But there were those who felt there were too many chefs in the kitchen. And many of them were beginning to fool around with the wait staff."

John sat up. "Hey..."

"Sorry," said Sarna. "Just a matter of speech. Because of that, though, a faction of master chefs broke off and took over. They changed everything about the way it was run. No more wait staff in the kitchen. And no more contact outside of Italy."

"That must have been when the accident happened," Sarah said.

"What accident?" asked Royce.

"Many years ago," she said, "when we were still in touch with the Italians, an...Italian plane...went down. Our contact with Italy ended afterwards."

"That probably has something to do with why the plane crashed," said Sarna.

"We believe so," said Sarah.

John studied Royce, who squirmed in his seat. "I take it you're unsure about your role as master-chef?"

Royce snickered. "I'm not interested in cooking."

"He and Jasper argued about it. Jasper left. We were going to go home that night. But next thing we know, we got a phone call. Jasper had been hurt."

"Hurt how?" Sarah asked.

Royce rubbed his neck. "Someone hit him over the head with a rock. He's in the ICU and hasn't regained consciousness."

"Why would someone do that?" asked Sarah. Her eyes widened. "It's not another chef, is it?"

"No, it's not that," said Royce. "We had a murder in the woods a few days ago. Jasper was in the same area when he was attacked. The sheriff thinks it's somehow related."

"What for?" asked John. "Who would go after Jasper?"

"I don't know," Royce said. "Maybe he saw or heard something he shouldn't have. He was just in the wrong place at the wrong time."

"They've got him attached to machines and tubes," said Sarna, her eyes round. "They might take him into surgery. We...Italian chefs...can't handle that. Our bodies are very sensitive, especially when we leave Italy. This environment is toxic to us. We take," she paused, searching for the word, "medication, pills, to help us adjust...but it's not designed for this level of trauma. And we don't have enough with us, anyway. So I've either got to get him out of here now and get him back to Italy. Or..."

"He'll never make it home," said John.

Sarna nodded, her eyes shiny. "That's why we called."

"You need another master chef to help you out," said John.

"One who can cook the main meal," said Royce.

Sarah reached over and took Sarna's hand. "Where is he?"

Royce checked his watch. "It's past nine o'clock. We should be able to see him now." He glanced at Sarna. "You take her back. I'll stay with John."

Sarna and Sarah stood just as the elevator dinged. The doors opened and the sheriff stepped off.

"Hell..." said Royce, grimacing.

"What?" asked John.

"That's the sheriff. He has questions about Jasper. Questions I have no idea how I'm answer."

The sheriff walked into the waiting area, but before he could speak, his phone rang. He picked it up and read his caller ID. He put up a finger and addressed Royce, who'd waved hello. "Hey, Royce. Give me a sec. I have to take this." He picked up the call and walked away.

John stood. "Sarah, you and Sarna tend to Jasper." He glanced at Royce. "Can the sheriff go back there with them?"

"No," said Royce. "Only two visitors at a time."

"Good."

"John?" asked Sarah. "What are you thinking?"

"Just go with Sarna, honey, but pay attention to my signals."

Sarah nodded and followed Sarna back into the ICU.

John watched his wife walk away and spoke to Royce. "What did you tell the sheriff about Jasper?"

"Not much," said Royce. He thought back. "Just that he's my half-brother that I didn't know existed until now."

"Did you give him Jasper's full name?"

"Yes."

"What is it?"

"Jasper Fiss."

"Fiss? F-I-S-S?"

"Yes." John reached for his phone.

"What are you doing?" asked Royce.

John dialed a number and put the phone to his ear. "When he gets off the phone, stall him."

"Stall him?" asked Royce.

"Yes...try not to talk about Jasper." He listened as someone answered. "Hello? Declan?" He turned away as he spoke into the phone.

# Chapter Twenty

SARNA WALKED INTO JASPER'S room. Royce had called earlier that morning and had learned that Jasper's condition had not changed overnight, and based on how he looked, Sarna decided that was true. If anything, his pallor was worse. Shadows had deepened under his eyes, and his cheeks appeared sunken.

Sarna approached the bed. "Jasper?" She took his hand. "Can you hear me?"

Sarah walked to the other side. She studied Jasper without touching him. "You said you've been giving him something. Pills?"

Sarna nodded.

"How many does he take?"

"One a day if he's well. I gave him four yesterday."

"Let's give him two now."

Sarna raised her wrist and turned it to reveal the backside of her watch. She pushed a button and a small compartment opened. She'd added Jasper's supply of pills to her own. She shook out two and closed the compartment. Sarah helped her drop the pills into Jasper's mouth despite the respirator tube.

"They'll dissolve?" asked Sarah.

"Yes."

A nurse walked in and both women stepped aside to let her check Jasper's vitals. She studied a computer screen beside the bed and noted something on a tablet she carried.

"How is he?" asked Sarna.

The nurse glanced at her. "He's hanging in there."

"Any sign he's coming around?"

"No. But I just came on duty. His vitals are okay though."

Sarna nodded. The nurse looked at Sarah. "Just fifteen minutes for visiting."

"Yes. Okay," said Sarna as the nurse left the room.

"Just fifteen minutes?" asked Sarah.

"That's it," said Sarna.

Sarah looked up at the ceiling and around the room. It was separated by walls, but there was no door and the nurse's station sat just outside. The only thing that would afford them privacy was a curtain. It hung loosely beside the bed, but when pulled closed, it would surround Jasper's bedside.

"Pull that around him," said Sarah, motioning to the curtain.

Sarna nodded. She pulled on the curtain and dragged it around the bed, giving them some privacy with Jasper.

"You keep watch," said Sarah. "I'd rather not have the nurses walk in during this. You let me know if someone's coming."

"I will." Sarna stood at the edge of the curtain where she could watch Sarah and the entrance to the room at the same time. "It's all clear."

"Good." Sarah shook out her hands and let out a deep breath. "Here goes." Placing her hands on Jasper's chest, she closed her eyes. Sarna watched with interest. While she'd heard of the healing talents of various Red-Lines, she'd never seen the process up close.

"So," said Sarah softly. She took another breath and let it out. "Tell me about yourself."

"What?" asked Sarna.

Sarah opened her eyes, but continued to look at her fingers. She widened her hands on Jasper's chest and let out another deep breath. "I know about Royce. Tell me about you."

Sarna raised an eyebrow. "Don't you need to concentrate?"

"I am concentrating. I'm reading him. But I can still talk."

Sarna opened her mouth, but found she didn't know what to say. "Um, well..."

"How do you know Jasper?" asked Sarah. She moved her hands to Jasper's shoulders and moved to the head of the bed. She took another deep breath and closed her eyes again.

"We're childhood friends. We grew up together."

"Why did you come with him?"

"To help him. I didn't want him to come alone."

Sarah didn't respond, but she moved her hands up to Jasper's head and held them there. "And now that you're here," she asked after another breath, "are you glad you came?"

"What do you mean?"

"You came all this way, told Royce who he is, but he seems to prefer to stay. What do you think about that?"

Sarna observed the nurse's station. No one was watching or seemed interested in the closed curtain. She thought of her argument with Royce the previous night. "I'm frustrated. I've tried to get him to understand, but he won't listen." She paused. "We argued last night. I said things..." She shook her head. "I was angry. So was he." She stared at Jasper as Sarah worked on him. "He should come back with us. I know that in my heart. His path is to return to Eud–to Italy, not live out his life here. He has a role to fulfill."

Sarah's eyes remained closed, and she was quiet. She moved her hands to the sides of Jasper's head. "Have you told him how you feel?"

The question surprised Sarna. "Of course. I told him he was being stubborn. He's just scared."

Sarah remained quiet. "No," she finally said. "I mean, have you told Royce how you feel about him?"

Sarna dropped her jaw. She wasn't sure she heard right. "How I feel? About him? What do you mean?" Her heart thumped.

The corner of Sarah's mouth curved upward slightly, but then dropped back. She took another deep breath and released it. "You should tell him."

Sarna stood rooted to her spot. "There...there's nothing to tell," she stammered.

Sarah dropped her hands and moved back to Jasper's side. She placed her palms back on his chest. She watched Jasper. "You're sure about that?"

"What are you implying?"

Sarah finally looked at Sarna. "You came all this way for a man you don't know, to ask him to do something you knew he likely wouldn't do, at great risk for you and potentially your family." She held Sarna's gaze. Sarna felt her heartbeat pick up its pace.

"I did it for Jasper."

Sarah didn't reply, but focused back on her hands. Closing her eyes, she went still. Sarna didn't interrupt as Sarah stayed quiet. A few minutes passed before Sarah took another deep breath, released it, and straightened. Her hands fell to her side. "That's it."

Sarna furrowed her brow. "That's it?" She studied Jasper. "But nothing's changed."

"He needs rest. His body will catch up. He should come around soon."

Sarna walked to the side of the bed. "You're sure?"

Sarah nodded. "Yes. He'll be good as new." She pushed the curtain back. "You will need to be patient, though."

"Patient? Why?"

"Things move slowly here. He will recover, but they will want to keep him overnight for observation. Maybe two."

"Keep him?" asked Sarna. "You mean in the hospital?"

"Yes."

"But why? You said he'll be fine."

"But they don't know that. They'll want to be sure."

"But we need to go home."

"What for?"

Sarna hesitated. "Because...as you say, Royce has made up his mind. Besides, after this..." She gestured at Jasper.

Sarah adjusted Jasper's blankets. "Perhaps you should change your perspective."

Sarna rubbed her temples. She couldn't seem to gather her thoughts. "This is crazy."

Sarah stepped away from the bed. "Think about it. Jasper's injury has afforded you the time to spend with Royce."

Sarna laughed and crossed her arms. "Why would I want to spend time with Royce? He's been nothing but difficult." Sarah grinned. Sarna found it irritating. "Why are you looking at me like that?"

"A family member of mine has a saying."

"What's that?"

"What you resist, persists."

Sarna bit her lip and looked away. "I don't know what you're talking about." Sarah continued to watch her though, and Sarna felt uncomfortable, as if Sarah was reading her mind.

Sarah rested a hand on the bed and cocked her head. "I think perhaps that Royce is not the only one who's scared."

Sarna looked sideways at Sarah. She took her own deep breath. "Well, not that what you're saying is true, but it doesn't matter, anyway. He cares for someone else."

Sarah's eyebrows rose. "Does he?"

"Yes. I felt it from him yesterday."

Sarah paused. "Funny. The only thing he was thinking about when I stepped off that elevator was you."

Sarna sat lightly at the foot of Jasper's bed. "We'd argued. That's all it was."

"No. I know anger. And it wasn't that." She eyed Sarna. "At all."

Sarna set her jaw. Surely Sarah had misinterpreted Royce's feelings, but for a moment, her cheeks flushed.

Sarah noticed and smiled softly.

"What?" asked Sarna.

"That's exactly how I felt."

"What?" Sarna fanned her face as warmth flooded through her. "When?"

"When I met my husband."

Sarna froze and started to argue, when the nurse walked in. "Your fifteen minutes are up. You'll have to step out for now."

Sarah and Sarna held eye contact. "Time to go," said Sarah. She stepped from the room and looked back at Sarna, who still sat on the edge of the bed. "You ready? Royce is waiting."

· · · · ● · ● · · ·

In the waiting area, the sheriff talked on the phone as Royce paced. He kept an eye on the sheriff and Ramsey, who was also on the phone. He wondered who would end their conversation first.

*Stall?* He thought to himself. How was he supposed to do that? And what was Ramsey up to, anyway? He thought about Jasper and wondered how Sarah was doing. He checked his watch. She only had fifteen minutes. Hopefully that was enough time for Sarah to do her thing and Sarna wasn't pestering her.

He listened as the sheriff spoke. It sounded as if he was wrapping up his conversation. Royce looked around the room. How was he going to keep Rick from asking about Jasper? The sheriff hung up. Royce glanced at Ramsey, who held up a finger. Royce figured that meant that Ramsey needed more time. He groaned to himself.

"Hi, Royce," said Rick, walking closer. "Sorry about that."

"No problem, Rick. How's it going? How was your day yesterday?" Royce tried not to grimace at his rambling.

The sheriff paused. "Busy. All this nonsense has kept me on my toes. How's Jasper doing?"

"Not much change. They're keeping an eye on him, waiting to see if he'll come out of it on his own. He's stable."

The sheriff nodded. "That's good to hear. Once he regains consciousness, I'll need to talk with him."

Royce bobbed his head. "Of course. I'm sure he'll be happy to speak with you."

The sheriff reached into his pocket and pulled out a small pad of paper. "Speaking of Jasper, I have a few questions."

Royce scrambled to think. "How's RJ doing? He should come by. We'll go fishing." Royce could feel the sweat break out under his arms. If Ramsey didn't finish up soon, his shirt was going to be soaked.

The sheriff raised an eyebrow. "Uh...sure. He'd like that. He's doing fine. Actually, he's been quiet since yesterday. Barely been out of his room, which is unusual, but he hasn't been any trouble."

"That's great." Royce reached up and touched the cool stone that hung from his neck. He'd replaced the cord that had broken in the woods. As his body heated, the stone continued to retain its cooler feel. But Royce's temperature spike was far outpacing the stone. He glanced at Ramsey, who was still on the phone.

The elevator dinged.

"So," said the sheriff. "I need to get some more information on Jasper. So does the hospital. I need a home address and any next of kin information you have on him."

Royce focused in on the elevator. He heard the doors open. Mentally, he sent out a wave of energy. It traveled toward the elevator, and Royce heard and felt the doors close before the occupant could disembark.

Royce glanced at Ramsey, who continued his conversation.

"Royce?" asked the sheriff.

The doors opened again and Royce refocused his energy and held them shut. Suddenly, an alarm sounded.

The sheriff turned, as did everyone in the waiting area. Pounding could be heard from the elevator.

The sheriff trotted toward the noise. The elevator door was cracked, but would not open farther. The pounding came again. "Help," said a woman's voice. "The door won't open."

"Hold on, ma'am," said Rick. He tried to pull on the doors, but they didn't budge. "We'll get you out." He glanced back at Royce, who'd walked over with the sheriff. "Help me out."

"Oh, sure," said Royce. He maintained his mental focus on the elevator while he grasped the metal door at the edge. He and the sheriff both pulled. The door didn't move. An alarm continued to blare. The passenger continued to complain.

"Ma'am?" asked Rick.

"Help! I can't get out!"

"Ma'am, don't worry. Are you holding the alarm button?"

"Yes! Please help me."

"Ma'am. We know you need help. You can stop sounding the alarm."

The alarm blared for a few more seconds before it stopped. Fingers with red painted nails wiggled through the crack between the elevator door and the wall. "Don't leave me," said the woman inside.

"I'm calling for help right now," said the sheriff. "Just stay calm." He raised his cell phone.

"You gentleman need help?"

Royce looked to see Ramsey, now off the phone, standing in the corridor.

"It's stuck," said the sheriff. "I'm calling for..." The elevator door slid open. A middle-aged woman in a formfitting dress with bleached-blonde hair and heavy make-up stood inside. She held her chest, and a purse hung from her elbow.

"Oh, thank god," she said, stepping out of the elevator. She eyed the sheriff. "Thank you. I appreciate your help."

"No problem, ma'am," said Rick. "Glad you're out."

"That's the last thing I needed today, to be stuck in an elevator." She smoothed her hair.

"Nobody wants that," answered the sheriff. His eyes traveled over her. "Glad you're okay."

Royce glanced at Ramsey, who nodded at him.

"Well," said the woman, eyeing all three men. "Thank you again." She gave the sheriff a second look. "Especially you."

The sheriff gripped his belt. "Ma'am?"

She smiled at him. "I always did like a man in uniform." Offering the sheriff a sly smile, she stepped away and walked down a hallway, her hips swaying in her slim skirt.

Rick swallowed, and Royce noted how the sheriff watched her as she disappeared from sight. "You're welcome," said the sheriff.

"Nice lady," said Royce.

The sheriff didn't answer, but continued to stare down the hall. Finally, he turned. "What?"

"You must be Sheriff Rick," said Ramsey, with his hand outstretched. "Royce told me about you."

The sheriff noticed Ramsey and glanced down at Ramsey's hand before extending his own. "Yes. I am. And you are?"

"I'm John Ramsey. My wife and I are here to see Jasper."

"Really?" asked the sheriff. "That's nice." He looked at Royce. "About those questions…"

"That's right," said Royce. "You were starting to ask them before the interruption."

The sheriff glanced at the elevator doors. "Strange. We should notify maintenance about that."

"Yes. Probably a good idea."

The sheriff spoke to Ramsey. "How do you know Jasper?"

Ramsey was unruffled. "We've been friends for a while. He recently stayed with me and my wife for about a week."

"Stayed with you?"

"Yes," said Ramsey. "Jasper doesn't stay in one place for very long. We had an extra room we rented out occasionally. He used it."

"I've had a hard time learning anything about him," said the sheriff. "There was no ID in his belongings. I don't have an address or a date of birth." He glanced at Royce. "I was hoping you might have some more information."

Royce shook his head. "Unfortunately, I just met him myself. We never got around to exchanging addresses."

"I can give you his mother's phone number," said Ramsey. "She should be able to fill you in on the details."

"His mother?" asked the sheriff. "You have her number?"

"I do." Ramsey pulled out his cell phone. "We got to know him during his stay. Nice guy. But he can be hard to get in touch with. He always checks in with his mom, though. Said if we need to reach him, we could leave her a message and he'd call us back."

"Is she aware of his injury?" asked Rick.

Ramsey accessed a number on his phone. "Here it is," he said. He showed the phone to the sheriff, who noted the number. "And yes, she knows. Sarna called her. Apparently, Jasper left our number with his mom when he stayed with us, and she still had it. She told us what happened. His mother lives nearby and has some health issues. She was unable to make the trip. So Sarah and I agreed to drive down and find out what's going on."

"Sarah?"

"Yes. My wife. She and Sarna are in with Jasper now."

Rick nodded. "And Sarna is the woman I met yesterday?"

"Yes. She is," said Royce. "She and Jasper were camping together. She came with him to meet me."

"I see. She called Jasper's mom?" Rick asked Ramsey.

"She did."

"Okay." Rick checked the number he'd written down. He glanced at Royce. "I'm still curious about how he's your brother."

"You and me both, sheriff," said Royce. "Apparently, my dad had a few secrets."

"And Sarna. Is she staying with you while Jasper's in the hospital?"

"Yes, she is."

"I should talk to her, too."

"Of course. She's rather worried about Jasper."

The sheriff nodded. "I could tell. Still, she might have some information…"

Royce picked up on something more than curiosity from the sheriff. "What is it? Is there something else?"

The sheriff paused. "It's probably nothing."

"What's probably nothing?"

"We've had two people attacked in the same area. One died. The other is in the hospital."

"Yes?" asked Royce.

The sheriff eyed Ramsey, as if gauging his trustworthiness. "Did you know his shoe was missing?"

"Shoe?" asked Royce. "Who's shoe?"

"Jasper's."

"Jasper is missing a shoe?"

"Unless you took it out of his bag of belongings."

Royce thought back to Sarna rifling through Jasper's things to find his watch. "I didn't take anything out of the bag."

"The doctor says he doesn't recall anything about a shoe. The ambulance drivers don't either."

"A shoe?" asked Ramsey.

"Yes," said the sheriff. "The first victim was missing a shoe, too. It still hasn't been found."

"Are you saying that whoever did this to Jasper took his shoe?" asked Royce.

The sheriff crossed his arms and sighed. "Which makes it likely that the person who did this to Jasper is the person who killed the first victim."

Royce squinted. "So there's a madman running through the woods? One with a shoe fetish?"

The sheriff pressed down on his belt buckle and the leather groaned. "I hate to say it, but it appears that way. And Jasper may be able to identify him."

Royce's jaw dropped. He hadn't considered that the sheriff may need Jasper to help with a murder investigation. He suppressed a groan. "Sheriff..."

"There was a man in town a few days ago," Rick continued. "He was asking questions. Showing the picture of a pretty blonde woman. Asking if anyone had seen her. Tiny told me he'd come into his store on the day we'd found our first victim. Tiny said there were two other people in the store too. They match the description of Jasper and Sarna. They said they weren't from around here but were driving through. They planned on camping."

Royce shook his head and tried to wrap his head around what the sheriff was saying. He thought of Alice and felt a flicker of worry. A man was showing a picture around town of a blonde woman? Was it Alice's husband? Had Alice's ex talked to Sarna and Jasper? He wasn't sure what to say. "Sarna and Jasper were in Tiny's store?" he asked.

"Yes. Five days ago."

"Five days?" Royce did a quick calculation in his head. He wondered where the sheriff was going with his questions.

"You left four days ago? Right? The day I picked up RJ from your place?" asked the sheriff.

Royce glanced at Ramsey whose eyes narrowed as if to say *sorry, can't help you with this one.*

"Yes," said Royce. "My mother had called. She had just learned about Jasper as well. She was upset. I came back yesterday morning, which is when I met Jasper." He didn't know why he didn't tell the sheriff about Alice. She was long gone by now. And if her ex was still in town looking for her, it was unlikely he would find her.

"If Jasper and Sarna bumped into our potential bad guy at the store, then they met up with you and now Jasper ends up getting assaulted. That feels too coincidental to me."

Royce furrowed his brow. "You think the man in the store, asking about a woman, is the killer? But by then, your victim was already dead. Why show her picture around town?"

"I don't know," said the sheriff. "Alibi maybe? When I find him, I'll ask him." Rick made a few notes on his pad of paper. "I'm wondering if Sarna might have more information."

A voice sounded from behind them. "About what?"

Royce turned to see Sarna and Sarah walking out of the ICU.

Sarna walked up to the group. "How can I be of help?"

Sarah and Ramsey exchanged a knowing look. Then Royce heard Sarah's voice in his head. "Don't worry." It took a monumental effort from Royce not to react.

"Hello, ma'am."

"Hello, sheriff. Just call me Sarna."

"Sarna Lambert," said Ramsey. He eyed Sarna, who stared at him before looking back at the sheriff.

"Yes. Sarna Lambert."

The sheriff wrote in his notebook. "Can I ask why Jasper doesn't have an ID?"

"They were stolen," said Sarna, looking calm.

"Stolen?"

"Yes. Jasper and I were camping. We were waiting for Royce to return home. We met a drifter. He ate briefly with us and he left. The next morning, we woke and found that Jasper's credit card and ID were gone. The drifter must have returned when we'd slept and taken them."

"He took your money?" asked the sheriff.

"Luckily, we kept our cash in a separate place. He didn't take that."

"Can you describe him?"

Sarna appeared to think. "Tall. Lanky. Growing a beard. Dirty blonde hair."

"Did you get a name?"

"Said it was Larry."

"Last name?"

"Didn't get one."

The sheriff rubbed his neck. "Had you seen him before?"

"Yes, actually."

The sheriff cocked his head. "Really? Where?"

"When Jasper and I got to town, we stopped at a store for some supplies. He was there."

The sheriff made eye contact with Royce, who didn't say a word. "You met him in the store?"

"Not really. He was asking about someone. A woman."

"Did he have a picture?"

"Yes. He did. It was a blonde woman. Pretty."

"And you didn't think that was odd?"

"What? That he was showing a picture around town?"

"Yes."

"Maybe a little. But at the time, we had other things on our minds. He didn't stick around. But when he showed up at our campsite, we recognized him."

"What was he doing there?"

Sarna paused. "Let's see. He said he'd run out of money. Needed a place to sleep."

"Did you ask him about the woman?"

Sarna nodded. "We did. He said it was his sister. Said she'd gone missing."

"Did he tell you her name?"

"No."

"You weren't worried about a stranger staying with you?"

Sarna shrugged. "That's Jasper for you. He's a drifter himself. And he'll take in any stray. Especially one with a sob story. It's one of his best, or worst, traits. Depending on how you look at it."

"And you haven't seen this man since?"

"No."

"Did you report the crime?"

"No. The next day, we met Royce. And well, you know what happened after that."

"Yes," said Rick, flipping his notebook closed. "I guess I do."

"Anything else?" asked Sarna.

Rick nodded toward the ICU. "How's Jasper?"

Sarna sighed. Royce noticed her face looked less harried than it had earlier. "He's better. I wouldn't be surprised if he woke up soon."

"I'd like to talk to him if he does."

"Of course," said Sarna. "Once the doctors give the okay."

Royce listened to the conversation with surprise. Sarna was handling herself like a pro.

"There's another thing," said Rick. He glanced at Royce. "I'd like you both to be careful."

"Careful?" asked Royce. "What for?"

"This man, whoever he is, may still be around. And if Jasper, or Sarna, can identify him..."

Royce felt a shudder run through him. His protective instincts were kicking in. Even though he'd just met and barely knew Sarna and Jasper, he still felt responsible for them. "You think he might come after them?"

"More than likely, he's long gone. I've asked the hospital to increase security and I've brought some more men on duty, but we have limited resources. So just keep an eye out."

Sarna and Royce made eye contact. "I'm sure you're right, sheriff," said Royce. "This man is long gone."

"I hope so. By the way..." The sheriff pointed at Sarna.

"Yes?"

"Do you have Jasper's shoe?"

"Shoe? No. You have his things."

"He's missing a shoe."

"I'm quite sure he was wearing two when he left," said Sarna.

The sheriff shook his head. "I figured." Sliding his notebook into a shirt pocket, he tipped his head toward Sarah and Ramsey. "Nice to meet you. Sorry it had to be like this."

"No problem, sheriff," said Ramsey, shaking the sheriff's hand.

"You think Jasper's mother can get in touch with the hospital?" asked Rick. "They need some information about him."

"She's probably talking to them as we speak," said John, glancing at Royce.

Royce quirked up his brow. He didn't know who this John Ramsey was, but apparently, he had some clout.

"Great," said Rick. "Thanks, Royce. Sarna. I'll be in touch."

"No problem, sheriff," said Royce.

"You'll stay in town?" Rick asked Sarna.

"While Jasper is in the hospital, yes, I will."

"Okay. I just need to be able to reach you."

"That shouldn't be a problem," said Sarna.

"Thanks, Rick," said Royce. "Let us know if you learn anything."

"Will do." Rick turned and headed for the elevators and hit the button. A few seconds later, the doors opened. The sheriff stepped forward, but then stopped. "Actually, I think I'll take the stairs." He walked down the hallway the woman with the slim skirt had taken a few minutes before.

"Uh, Rick," said Royce. He stuck out a thumb. "The stairs are that way."

The sheriff rested his hands on his belt. "I know." He headed down the hall, but looked back. "I'll get there, eventually."

John smiled. "Good luck, sheriff."

Rick waved a hand, turned a corner, and disappeared from sight.

Royce expelled a long-held breath. Running a hand through his hair, he turned toward the group. "Let's not do that ever again."

"Agreed," said John. "Nice job with the elevator doors."

"Nice touch with the mother," said Royce. "I assume that number calls someone?"

"Sure does," said Ramsey. "Someone who will be happy to fill in any details about Jasper." He eyed Sarna. "You'll need to call her soon. Give her some details about Jasper for when the sheriff calls."

"I can do that," Sarna said.

"This woman will let us know if Rick gets in touch?" asked Royce. "We'll have to fill in Jasper before he speaks with the sheriff."

"I gave her your number. She'll call you after she talks with Rick," said Ramsey.

Royce nodded and spoke to Sarna. "How'd you come up with that story?"

"What story?" she asked.

"About the drifter?"

"It wasn't a story. A man did stop by our campsite. That was all true. The only thing that wasn't was the stuff about him taking our money and IDs. But the sheriff didn't have to know that."

Royce thought of Alice. Had this been her ex? Had he found Alice? "This is the same man from the store? Who showed you a picture?"

"Yes. Same man. But it wasn't his sister."

Royce cringed. "You're sure?"

She tipped her head. "You know I am."

"Who was it?"

"I don't know. I didn't ask."

"It was a great way to explain the missing IDs," said John. "It was smart to blame it on a stranger."

Royce's worry for Alice was tempered by the fact that regardless of who the man was, there was nothing he could do about it now. "How's Jasper?" he asked. "Everything go okay?"

"He's going to be fine," Sarah said. "He needs to rest, but he should come around soon."

"Is it true that if he wakes, he won't get to leave until tomorrow?" asked Sarna.

"At the very least. It may take longer than that," Royce said.

"Why can't we get him out of here today?"

"We can't without creating more suspicion. Which is not what we need right now."

"But the longer we stay, the more questions we'll have to answer," Sarna said.

"I think you've bought yourself some time," said Sarah. "I think the sheriff will leave you alone for now. You should be able to wrap things up before you leave." She and Sarna held a shared gaze.

"Well," said Royce, "I can't thank you enough for doing this. I'm sure my phone call was a bit of a shock."

"A small one," said Sarah. "But a welcome one."

"Do you know what you're going to do?" asked John.

"About what?" asked Royce.

"You're the Supreme High...something or other. Are you gonna take the gig?"

Royce didn't answer, but he caught Sarna's look. Her upturned face looked vulnerable in the light of the corridor. It was how she had looked earlier, when she'd apologized for what she had said last night. For a brief second that morning, her shield had come down, and he'd seen and felt her soft side. Something had flickered within him, but the elevator had opened and Sarah had stepped out, ending the moment.

"No," he said. "I can't go." He waited for the anticipated outburst from Sarna, but none came. She looked away.

"I can imagine it's not an easy decision to make," said Sarah.

"No, it's not."

"Since you're staying," said John. "You have an open invitation at our place. Come by anytime. We have several people who would be interested in meeting you. Your sisters too."

"Thank you," said Royce. "I appreciate that."

"And you," Sarah said to Sarna.

"Yes?" asked Sarna. Her face still held a forlorn look.

"I don't know what's in store for you, but please be careful. You and Jasper, both."

"We will. And don't worry. You and your community? Your secret is safe with me."

John raised a brow. "What would they do if they knew about our group?"

Sarna shrugged. "Probably nothing. I'm sure there are pockets of Grays on various plan–" She looked around. "Uh, countries, that have survived. I doubt they care. Grays on Eudor–sorry, Italy, are mostly in subservient roles."

"Subservient?" asked John. He set his shoulders. "Not a role I'd handle well."

"Should anything change though," said Sarah, "and if Italy should open its borders and welcome us with open arms, then we are open to traveling. There are some of us who would like to see Italy."

"It's a beautiful country," said Sarna. She glanced at Royce. "I think you and John would love it."

There was a moment of quiet before John spoke. "You ready, babe?" he asked Sarah. "I'm sure if Leroy had hair, he'd be pulling it out by now."

Sarah smiled. "Leroy? He's great with the kids."

"As long as they're sleeping."

The four exchanged handshakes and hugs, and Sarah and John hit the elevator button.

"Let us know how it goes," said John. "If you need anything, ask."

"I will," Royce said. "Thanks."

The elevator dinged, and the doors opened. Sarna remained quiet as Sarah and John stepped inside.

Royce and Sarna stood together, waiting for the doors to close. Before they did, Sarah spoke. "There's a saying my husband has," she said. "I think you both might benefit from it."

"What is it?" asked Sarna.

John eyed his wife and then looked back. "Trust destiny," he said.

"Trust destiny?" Royce asked.

John smiled. "I know it sounds irritating as hell, but damned if it isn't true." The doors began to close. "See ya," he said, as he and Sarah disappeared from view.

# Chapter Twenty-One

EIGHT HOURS LATER, Royce and Sarna sat in Jasper's room. He'd shown no change since Sarah had left.

Sarna stood and walked to his bedside. "Why doesn't he wake up?"

Royce stretched his back. The long hours in the hospital sitting on hard chairs were taking their toll. "She said he needed to rest. Be patient. He'll come around."

She leaned over. "Jasper, can you hear me?" Getting no response, she crossed her arms and huffed. "He always likes to take his time. Drives me crazy."

Royce rubbed his shoulders and studied his brother lying in the bed. "Tell me something."

She looked back. "What?"

"Since we have time to kill," he shifted in his seat, "let me know about Jasper. What was it like growing up with him?"

She leaned a hip against Jasper's bed. "You really want to know?"

He nodded. "I do."

Pausing, she seemed to think about it, before walking over and sitting next to him. "Okay. Well, let's see, growing up, he was a lot of fun. We all were. He, Roma, and I were always hanging out."

"What about your brother? Where was he?"

"He was older. Had his own friends. Didn't want to hang out with the little sister."

"That's a brother for you."

"I guess so." She sat back. "Anyway, the three of us were almost never home. We liked to explore and be outside. There are numerous trails and outdoor spaces on our pl–where we're from."

"Similar to here."

An alarm buzzed in another room, but adapted to the sounds, they barely heard it. "Yes, but from what I've seen, most of your children stay inside."

He thought back to his own childhood. "It wasn't always like that. Me and my sisters played outside all the time."

"You did?"

"Yes. I think that's why I like the cabin. I like being away from everything and being able to walk out my door and into the woods."

She looked off. "It's similar to my home." She turned and rested her elbow on the back of the chair. "There's a waterfall not far away. Whenever I can, I walk there, sit and listen. It's one of my favorite things to do."

Royce smiled. "I like to go camping. There's nothing like just you and the trees. I like to sit and listen to the wind."

She cocked her head. "Are you telling me we have something in common?"

He chuckled. "Miracles do happen." A few moments passed in quiet. "When did things change?" he asked.

"You mean with me and Roma?"

"Yes. Obviously, you two had a falling out. How did Jasper handle it?"

Raking her fingers through her hair, she rested her head in her hand. "As we got older, it became obvious we saw things differently. My brother became more vocal. It was hard to ignore what was happening around us."

"What was happening?"

"As kids, we played with other children, some of them Grays. We never thought anything of it. But, after we Shifted, that changed. We weren't able to stay friends. We were expected to keep our distance."

"Why?"

"Obvious reasons. Much like your teenagers, it's a period of exploration. Temptations and attractions can cause problems, especially with the supposed wrong group of people."

"I see your point." He grunted. "I find this so hard to believe. Your society sounds like something out of our past. We've persecuted many people throughout our history."

"Sadly, it seems it's a common trait, no matter where you're from."

He nodded. "At least we're progressing."

Sarna raised a brow. "Are you? You treat everyone the same, regardless of differences?"

Royce grunted. "I said we're progressing, but we're not perfect."

"Neither are we. It seems we have a long way to go."

Royce scratched his jaw. He hadn't shaved that morning and felt the stubble. "Getting back to your brother—he became more active?"

"Yes, he did. He was attracting attention. I, of course, sided with him. So did Jasper. Roma did not. After a while, it became apparent why. She was the High Child. The role was important to her. Jasper and I tried to talk to her about all the things she could change in our society, all the good she could do, but she looked at us like we were Grays sitting at the Grand Council meeting. She didn't want to be a change maker. She liked the status quo."

"Power can do that."

She sighed. "It wasn't long after that when Jasper told me about you. He was shocked of course. It took him a while to assimilate that his father had another family."

Royce snorted. "I know the feeling."

"He and his...your father, are very close. They are similar in that they are passionate and loyal. Once they commit to something, they rarely look back. Once Jasper adjusted to the news, then an idea began to grow."

Royce straightened. "Oust Roma and introduce me to the family."

"Yes. It's a good idea."

"Sarna..."

A nurse walked in. "Visiting time is up. You'll have to..." Her attention was drawn to the bed.

Royce and Sarna followed her gaze. Jasper's eyes were open and blinking. Sarna jumped out of her seat. "Jasper?"

Royce joined her beside the bed. Jasper blinked again. "Jasper? It's Royce. Can you hear me?"

Sarna touched his hand. "Jasper. It's okay. You're in a hospital."

The nurse punched a button beside the bed. "You need to clear the room."

"But why?" asked Sarna. "He's awake."

"I need to call the doctor. We'll evaluate him and keep you posted."

Sarna gripped the handrail. "Keep us posted? But we're right here."

"Fifteen minutes are up anyway," said the nurse. "You can wait outside the ICU."

"We're familiar with that," said Royce, dreading the thought of sitting in another uncomfortable chair. Jasper blinked again and then closed his eyes. "Let's go, Sarna. He needs to rest. Let the doctor check him, and we'll be back in an hour."

"But—"

"It's okay. Let the nurse do her job." He patted Jasper's arm. "We'll be back, Jasper."

• • • • • • • • • •

An hour later, after an anxious Sarna paced a trench in the waiting room and Royce envisioned nightmare scenarios in which Jasper woke and told everyone he was from another planet, they were allowed back into the room.

Entering, they were happy that Jasper was resting comfortably and his breathing tube had been removed. Approaching the bed, they were amazed by how much better he looked. The deep, dark circles beneath his eyes were almost gone and his pale cheeks had more color.

Sarna touched the bed rail and his eyes opened. "Jasper?" She took his hand.

His eyes were alert, and he blinked. He cleared his throat. "Sarna? His voice was rough and weak, but he was talking.

"Yes. It's me. How are you?"

"Where am I?" His eyes traveled around the room. "Where is this place?"

Royce leaned in, looking from side to side. "It's a secret room. They've discovered who you are and they're doing secret experiments on you."

Sarna's jaw dropped, and Jasper's eyes widened.

Royce chuckled. "Just kidding."

Sarna slapped him on the arm. "What is the matter with you?"

Royce threw out a hand. "It's a joke." He looked at Jasper's paler face. "Don't you two joke where you're from?"

"Not with people who almost died," said Sarna. She shook her head at him.

Jasper frowned, but his eyes still looked doubtful. "Very funny."

"He's kidding, Jasper. Just ignore him."

Jasper's face dropped, as if his memories had returned. "No problem there." He tried to move in the bed, but moaned. "Where am I really?"

They explained what had happened to him. Other than walking through the woods, he had no memory of the incident, which Royce assumed was normal. They told him about Sarah and the sheriff and filled him in on what to say if he was questioned. Jasper understood and seemed unfazed by all that had occurred. All he wanted to do was leave.

"You have to wait until the doctor clears you," said Royce.

Jasper yawned. "You have too many rules." He blinked.

Royce waited as a nurse walked by the room. "You don't want to attract attention. Just do as they say and then you and Sarna can leave and never look back."

Jasper made eye contact with Sarna. "That's the plan." He shut his eyes. "The sooner the better."

Sarna's shoulders drooped. "I've been trying to convince him, Jasper. He still says no."

"It doesn't matter. Just leave it."

She sat on the side of the bed. "It does matter."

"He's right," said Royce. "Just leave it."

Sarna looked between the two of them. "You two are just alike. Both stubborn as booloos."

"As what?" Royce asked.

Jasper opened his eyes and stared at the ceiling. "It's an animal on Eudora."

"Oh, you mean like a mule."

"Yes," said Jasper. "Close enough." He put a hand on his belly. "I'm hungry."

Just then, the doctor arrived. "Well, here's the miracle patient." He stepped up to the bed. "I'm Dr. Trask."

Jasper shook his hand. "When can I leave?"

The doctor grinned. "How about we see how you do overnight first. I'd like to do some additional tests too. Make sure that brain of yours is still intact. You took a hard hit."

"I'm fine, Dr. Trask. Look, I can stand and everything." Jasper had started to push the sheets back and lift his torso, when he put a hand to his head and moaned.

The doctor gently pushed him back. "I think we need a bit more recovery time. How about you rest a bit?"

"Doctor. I promise. I'm fine." Jasper settled back into the bed, and Sarna pulled the sheets up.

"You're better. But not healed." He studied a computer and punched a few buttons on a keyboard. "We'll schedule the tests for first thing tomorrow. Then we'll talk more after the tests."

"Tomorrow? Why not now?"

The doctor raised a brow. "It's late and our technicians are going home. Besides, you need sleep..."

"I've slept enough."

The doctor rested his hand on the side of the bed. "How about this. I move you to a private room. That way your guests can visit more often. And I'll allow some chicken noodle soup and some Jell-O for you tonight. How does that sound?"

"Chicken?" asked Sarna. "No. How about something else?"

"Sounds delicious," said Royce and was rewarded with a frown from Sarna.

Jasper sighed. "I'll take it." He yawned.

"Okay," said the doctor. "I'll see about getting you moved and fed." He looked at Royce and Sarna. "Do you two have any questions?"

"Yes," said Sarna. "Why do you serve chicken—"

Royce took Sarna's elbow. "Actually, we're fine doctor." He directed Sarna toward the door. "Jasper, you rest up. We'll be back tomorrow."

"Royce," said Sarna, as she let herself be led, "it is a legitimate question."

He kept going. "Good night Jasper. Thanks doc."

"You're welcome."

Jasper settled back into his pillow. "First thing tomorrow, Sarna. Make sure you're ready."

All Sarna could do was wave as she and Royce left the room.

· · · · · · · · · ·

Walking in the door after stopping for a quick dinner on the way home, Royce threw his keys on the counter and rubbed his face. It had been another long day, but now it felt like he could see a dusky haze at the end of the tunnel. He walked into the kitchen and flipped on the light.

"Hey, Starman."

Royce jumped and whirled. He relaxed when he saw Gus rise from the couch. He raised a hand to his heart. "Gus. You scared the hell out of me."

The Native American smiled. "You're usually more sensitive than that."

Royce's shoulders dropped. "It's been a hell of a couple of days."

Sarna walked into the house. "I don't see anything out there."

Royce sighed. "I said you wouldn't. It's dark. You should look tomorrow."

Seeing Gus, she stopped, but kept speaking. "I know. But you never know. Maybe Jasper's shoe is nearby."

Royce grunted. "I don't know why you're looking. His shoe is not out there. He didn't walk away with one shoe on." He noticed Sarna's stare. "I'm sorry. Sarna, this is Gus. Gus, this is Sarna."

Gus walked up. "How do you do?"

Sarna took his hand. "Fine. Thank you."

"Why are you hiding in my house, Gus?" asked Royce. "And where is your truck?"

"It's a nice night. I walked."

"Do you usually visit this late?" asked Sarna.

"Sarna..." said Royce.

"My friend here," Gus gestured to Royce, "usually keeps late hours." He paused, but smiled. "And is usually alone."

Sarna's face reddened, which surprised Royce. "I'm leaving tomorrow."

Gus grinned. "I didn't know you were staying."

Royce rested a weary arm on the counter and groaned inwardly. "A lot has happened since I've seen you, Gus."

Gus tipped his head. "I can see that."

Sarna squirmed under Gus's scrutiny. "I'll let you two catch up. I'm going to take a shower."

"Okay," said Royce. She walked into his bedroom and closed the door. Gus looked at him and lifted an eyebrow. "It's not what you think," said Royce. He poured himself a glass of water and sat down at the dining table.

Gus chuckled. "I leave you snake bit with one woman and I come back to find you coming home late with another. You're a busy guy."

Royce rubbed his temples. "You have no idea."

Gus was quiet, but his eyes were curious. "She's different?" he asked.

Royce chuckled. "That's one way to describe her."

Gus came over and sat at the table with Royce. "But she's like you?"

"What do you mean?"

"I think you know." He pointed up. "Is she from the stars?"

Royce gripped his water. "Why would you think that?"

Gus smiled. "You seem to think you can hide things from me. If I can sense your origins, why couldn't I sense hers?"

Royce clasped his fingers. "The less you know, the better, Gus." He stared at his hands.

"What does she want? Why is she here?"

Royce debated how to answer. "She came here with a friend." He scratched at his stubble. "My half-brother, Jasper. Remember your vision? They're my two visitors."

Gus sat back in his seat. He crossed his arms. "You have been busy."

"Yes. It's been an interesting week."

Gus nodded. "They want you to leave with them?"

Royce straightened. "How do you know that?"

"Why else would they be here? It's a long way to go for a family visit."

Royce went quiet. "I'm not going anywhere."

Gus raised a brow and glanced around the house. "Where is your brother?"

Royce snorted and waved a hand. "He's in the hospital. Unbelievably, it seems he ran into the person who killed that woman in the woods. Jasper was hit in the head. He's okay, but it was touch and go at first. Sarna's been a mess. She's upset with me. She wants to leave, but she can't. Jasper's upset too. We argued." Royce shook his head when he realized he was rambling.

"Sarna..." Gus poked a thumb toward Royce's closed bedroom door. "She's staying in your room?"

Royce nodded. "I'm staying in the guest room."

"Where's Alice?"

The mention of Alice's name pulled Royce out of his reverie. He couldn't believe that he'd been with her only forty-eight hours ago. "She's gone. We spent..." He tried to think of what to say. "I thought..." He cleared his throat. "I don't know, Gus. She and I had a moment. We shared a night together. But she's got some problems she's got to figure out. She didn't want me involved. When I woke up the other morning, she was gone. And I have no idea where."

"I see," said Gus. His face showed little reaction. "I'm sorry."

"You and me both. I might have gone to find her, but I came home to find my unexpected family waiting for me."

Gus studied him. "Your half-brother. The one in the hospital. You two have the same father?"

Royce didn't see the point of continuing to hide anything from Gus. The man was almost as sensitive as his sister. "Yes. We do."

"And where is your father?"

Royce hesitated, but glanced upward.

"I see."

"You asked."

"I know." He rested his forearms on the table. "When will Jasper leave the hospital?"

"Sarna hopes tomorrow. But you know how hospitals are. It may not be until the next day."

"And then they will leave?"

"Yes."

"So you have some time?"

Royce shot a pointed look at Gus. "Time for what?"

"Time to think."

Royce shifted in his seat. His conversation with Gus several nights earlier replayed in his mind. "I know what you're thinking. I remember what you told me." He held out a hand. "There would be a woman. She would break my heart. I would have visitors and face my destiny. Well," He flicked his finger in the air, "check, check, check." He released a deep breath. "But I know what I'm doing, and I'm not going anywhere." He dropped his hand back to the table. "Whatever my destiny is, I'm sure it does not require me leaving the planet. I would hope for that much." It was the first time he'd audibly vocalized his origins to anyone, but at that point, he didn't care how it sounded.

Gus studied him but said nothing.

Royce moaned. "What? What is it?"

"Nothing."

Gus maintained his relaxed composure, and Royce found it irritating. He pointed at his friend. "No. I know that look. It's definitely something."

Gus interlaced his hands. "Only that I want you to make this decision with a clear head. You've been through a lot these last few days. This visit and this choice is unexpected. Jasper's injury, while unfortunate, has afforded you exactly what you need. Time."

"I don't need any time." He shifted again and stared at a potted plant on his counter.

Gus continued. "Regardless, you have it, so you should use it. At least you can get to know Sarna better. Since you will likely never see her again after she leaves."

Royce flicked his eyes toward Gus. "Stop that."

The side of Gus's mouth turned up. "Stop what?"

"Sarna and I are not together. She and I argue more than anything else. We don't like each other."

Gus nodded, his expression still serene. "That's too bad."

Royce tapped his finger on the table. "Is there a reason you stopped by? Other than to check on me?"

"Actually, yes. It's a good thing too."

Royce furrowed his brow. "What?"

Gus reached into his jacket pocket. "I brought you something. Now I know why."

"What do you mean?"

Gus pulled out a small gray pouch. He put it on the table. "I had a dream. I saw you may need this."

Royce eyed the pouch. "What is that?"

"Spirit powder. My grandfather's own special recipe."

"Spirit powder?" Royce reached over and picked up the pouch.

"I use it on my walks. It can help cut through confusion. Help to clear the mind."

Royce sighed and dropped the pouch. "I don't need any peyote, Gus."

Gus laughed softly. "Don't worry, Starman. Nothing like that. But it will help you maintain calm, despite whatever you may be facing. Perhaps it will help you make your decision."

"I've made my decision."

Gus shrugged. "Then use it to help with Sarna. Perhaps you'll argue less."

Royce narrowed his eyes. He picked up the pouch again. "How do I use it?"

"Very simple. Take a pinch in your fingers, and rub it on your skin. It's a powder. You can inhale it as well. It has a delicate scent. But be careful with ingesting it."

"So, don't put it in my tea?"

Gus shrugged. "You can, but stay close to home. Once it kicks in, it's a strong purging agent. I might take a small amount before a walk to cleanse the body. But it's not necessary in your case."

Royce held the pouch. He was normally not someone who would use a Spirit powder, but he knew Gus. And if Gus made, used, and trusted it, then he knew it had merit. "How does it help with sleeping?"

"It can't hurt."

Royce nodded. "Thanks. I'll try it."

"Good." He stood. "I'll leave then, so you can spend some time with Sarna."

"Gus..."

Gus held up his hands. "It may be her last night here."

Royce stood. "I'm okay with that."

Gus walked to the door, but stopped before leaving. His eyes held a contemplative look. "Be sure of what you say, Starman. Don't let your feelings for Alice cloud your judgment of Sarna. Perhaps you should consider that Alice was only a stepping stone."

Royce wasn't sure how to respond. He opened his mouth but didn't speak.

Gus patted Royce on the arm. "Use these next twenty-four hours wisely, my friend." Smiling, he turned and left.

# Chapter Twenty-Two

ROYCE THREW ON A pair of sweatpants and a T-shirt. He'd taken a long hot shower and rubbed some of Gus's Spirit powder on his chest and arms. He didn't know how much was too much, but considering his circumstances, he figured he could use an extra dose.

He stepped outside the bedroom and into the living area. The lamp was on, but the room was empty. He hadn't seen Sarna since she'd gone to take her own shower. A wooden squeak made him turn, and he saw her silhouette on the porch. She was sitting in the wooden rocker. Royce grabbed two bottled waters from the fridge and went outside to join her. Stepping through the door, he felt the cool air against his skin.

"Here," he said, handing her the water. She took it and continued to rock, but stayed quiet. "I figured you'd be sound asleep by now." He leaned against the porch rail, unscrewed his water, and took a sip.

A breeze blew her hair, and she brushed it away. "Your friend, Gus, was right. It's a pleasant night. Figured I'd sit outside for a bit." She rocked gently. "It might be the last time I get to do it on your lovely planet."

He cocked an eyebrow. "I thought you'd had enough of this lovely planet."

She rested her head against the chair. "It's growing on me."

"Meat lovers and all?"

She made a face. "Don't push it."

He smiled and looked out over his property. The frogs were croaking, and the crickets were singing. The trees swayed in the wind as moonlight peeked through the trees. It was indeed a lovely night.

"Your friend Gus seemed nice."

He drank his water. "He is."

"He seems different from the others I've met."

"He is."

She paused. "Does he know about me and Jasper?"

He noticed she was wearing his bathrobe. "You sense that from him?"

"I do."

"You're right. He knows."

She had no reaction. "Does he have an opinion?"

"About what?"

"About you. What you should do?"

He tensed. "Does it matter?"

She shrugged. "Just curious." She stared out at the trees.

"I'm sure he does," he said, "but he's kept it to himself. It's what friends do."

She shot a stony glare at him. "I would think good friends would offer their advice if they cared."

Her rigid posture and furrowed brow conveyed her steely determination to again attempt to change his mind. His normal reaction would have been to argue and annoy her, but Gus's Spirit powder appeared to be kicking in. So instead of telling her to mind her own business, he walked over, pulled up another chair, and sat across from her. Her eyes rounded as he did so.

"Listen to me," he said, leaning forward. "I know what you want and why you want it. You're upset. You came a long way. Jasper's been hurt, and you've had a difficult trip. You have a lot riding on my decision, and you want me to help solve all your planet's problems." He hung his head. "I wish I could be what you wanted. I wish I could give you the answer you seek. But Sarna," he looked up at her, "you've been here one week. You don't know me or anything about my life. I'm not staying here to annoy you. I'm staying here because it's where I belong."

He waited for her outburst, but none came. She simply stared with an expression that told him she had something to say, but wasn't sure how to say it. Suddenly, she stood, walked to the railing and studied the trees. A few seconds passed, and she looked back. "Come here," she said.

Her strange mood surprised him. "What?"

"Just come here."

He stood slowly and walked up next to her.

"I do know you."

He shook his head. "I'm confused. I can appreciate the fact that we've been stuck together since you got here, and that you don't like me personally..."

"Would you shut up?" She nibbled her lip. "I know you better than you think I do." She sucked in a breath and let it out. Shaking her hands, she raised them, palms out, as if she were giving him two high fives. "Put up your hands."

Royce looked at her as if she'd just told him she wanted to climb a tree. "What for?"

She rolled her eyes at him. "Would you just do it? Before I change my mind?"

Unsure, but curious, he did as she asked. He raised his hands, palms out. Sarna pressed her palms against his and interlaced her fingers with his own. He felt her skin warm beneath his fingers. "What are you doing?"

"This is a connection exercise. It's called Shakti on my planet."

"Shak-what?"

She scrunched her face. "It doesn't matter what it's called. All that matters is what it does. As Red-Lines, we can connect on higher levels beyond the five senses. All you have to do is open up."

"Open up? What are you going to do? Read my mind?"

"That is completely up to you. You can give as much or as little as you wish. This is mainly about communication without words. Sometimes, it's much more effective. Words can get in the way."

He frowned at her. "What do I have to do?"

"Look at me. Open up your senses and connect. I'll do the same with you. Just search for the connection."

He fidgeted. "There's no phone number?"

Sarna stared back. "If you take this seriously, you'll have a direct line."

Her tone and look turned serious, and he felt the energy shift around him. She was staring right at him, and he looked back. Her dark eyes softened, and warmth spread through his hands and onto his forearms. Small chills coursed through him. As the swirling energy picked up pace, he felt like he was sitting in a whirlpool. He didn't know what this exercise was, but he was liking it. Feeling himself calm, he relaxed his shoulders and face. Everything seemed to slow down, and the longer he looked at her, the more serene he felt. The whirlpool became a warm tub. His heart rate slowed and his mind went clear and still. And then came the unexpected—he felt her. Not physically, but energetically. The heat continued up his forearms and moved into his chest. The energy she exuded was peaceful and soothing, like he'd just walked onto a white sand beach. And although his body warmed, her essence had a cooling effect. She felt soft and sweet, as if tasting ice cream for the first time. He closed his eyes, just as she closed hers; eyesight was no longer necessary.

Her presence was magnetic. Without thinking, in his mind, he stepped forward and their energies merged. His strong and sturdy; hers confident and secure. The power of the connection caused him to take a deep breath. The feeling was indescribable. Adjusting to the sensations, he knew exactly what she'd meant. If he'd allowed her to, she could see everything about him. Every thought, feeling, word, and deed. He continued to breathe deeply, trying to control the overwhelming response of connecting with her. He heard her take a breath, and the warmth in his torso moved into his belly. His head felt like he was submerged in syrup. They remained that way as they adapted to each other's presence. Once he felt himself settle down, he felt a shift in her. Suddenly, he could see her back on Eudora. Numerous flashes of insight rushed at him, and he tried to follow them. He saw her laughing with a group of friends, arguing with a man, running and hiding from an unknown assailant, holding an older woman's hand, crying over a coffin, talking with Jasper and two others in a dark place, speaking with Royce's father, weeping in seclusion, and staring at a picture she held of a man. Her emotions became his. He felt everything—joy, hope, and excitement mixed with grief, fear, and doubt. As he tried to assimilate everything, the picture she held caught his eye. It was faded, but he could make out the face in the photo. He sucked in a breath when he recognized himself. He was the man in the picture.

The awareness surprised him, and he almost pulled back. But in the same second, he felt her fear of his judgment and he stopped himself. He realized how much she had shared with him and how vulnerable she was, and in return, before he could stop himself, he opened up and let her in. His mind reflected on his past. His sisters and how they grew up. His father's visits, and Royce's ambivalence toward him. How much he missed him. His love for his mother. All of these things came easily. But then he found himself showing her his isolation, his worries for his family and his doubt about his future. His revelations surprised him. As she read him, the heat continued to spread through his body. It ran down his legs and everything felt like he was on a tropical island with no shade. Connecting with her was peaceful, but also exciting. Suddenly, other thoughts entered his mind. Thoughts of what he and Sarna could do together. Instantly, he felt her shut down and pull back, but not before he'd read the same thoughts from her. He wasn't the only one on the tropical island.

He opened his eyes as she opened hers. Hands still interlaced, they stared at each other. The heat coming off him was intense, and he knew she felt the same. He couldn't stop looking at her.

Neither of them moved. Visions of pulling her into his arms swam in his head. Feeling a desire for her he could not deny, Royce stepped closer. She took an unsure step toward him, but a nearby bird cawed loudly. She stopped. Something shifted in her, and she pulled her hands from his.

Her face flushed. "It's been a long day. We should get some sleep." She swallowed and took a shaky breath. "We'll talk more in the morning."

Before he could say anything, she stepped away and walked back into the house, leaving him alone on the porch.

· · · · ●· ●· · · ·

Royce leaned on the porch rail, staring out at the dark night. He'd been there an hour, still reeling from the experience with Sarna. After she'd left, he'd needed time to catch his breath. The feeling and emotion of connecting with her still swirled inside him. He had so many questions. Why and how did she have his picture? What had she been talking to his father about? He felt confident the coffin she wept over was her brother's and the woman whose hand she held was her mother's.

Royce hung his head. He didn't know how that exercise was supposed to have helped him because now he felt more confused than ever. He looked up again and studied the woods behind his cabin. The woodpile was neatly stacked and the small picnic table nearby was clean. It was where he normally stacked his tools while working. He heard the shed door bang as the wind blew it.

Royce frowned as his thoughts shifted from Sarna to the shed. It was on the side of the house, but he always closed the door after putting away his tools and camping equipment. But the last time he'd opened it was when he'd hidden the shoe. He knew he'd latched it then. The door should not be moving with the wind.

Listening as the door banged again, he stepped off the porch and walked around to the side of the house. The small shed stood quietly beside his home, lighted only by the moon. A breeze blew, and the door swayed. It was open.

He recalled putting the pink tennis shoe in the shed and carefully concealing it. Something cold washed over him. Looking around, he reached out with his senses to feel for anyone's presence, but saw and felt nothing. The only sound was the breeze blowing through the trees. He walked over to the shed and swung the door all the way open. There was a flashlight on a shelf, and he picked it up and flicked it on. He swung it around the small shed. Nothing looked disturbed. His tools were all where they should have been, and nothing appeared out of place. He moved to the back of the shed, moved some items, and pulled up a board in the floor. The plastic bag containing the pink shoe remained right where he'd left it—in the small hole in the ground under his camping gear.

Royce dropped the board back in place and snapped off the flashlight. Images of a scared RJ pacing in his home flashed in his brain. He remembered their plan to check the ship's camera and made a mental note to talk to Jasper about it before he and Sarna left. He exited the shed, closed the door, and studied the latch. It was a simple bolt that slid shut. Nothing that required a key or combination. He'd considered adding a padlock after what happened with RJ, but figured that would look more suspicious. Royce slid the bolt closed again, and it clicked into place. He thought back to when he'd put the shoe here. Had he forgotten to bolt it? Had someone else come into the shed after him? It was possible Sarna could have looked inside if she'd been curious. Royce sensed for any presence that might have been nearby, but again felt nothing. He shook his head and decided that tomorrow, he'd better find another place to hide the shoe.

He left the area and returned to the back of the house. Concerns about the shoe drifted away as thoughts of Sarna and their encounter returned. Right now, she was in his bed, sleeping. He imagined her lying there, eyes closed, her body... Grimacing, he stopped himself as his body heated again. Sighing, he walked back toward the porch stairs. He needed to go to sleep, but he knew he would only toss and turn while images of her plagued him.

Taking the porch steps two at a time, he reached the top and stopped short. Standing outside the back door, watching him, was Sarna.

# Chapter Twenty-Three

ROYCE FROZE. HE HAD absolutely no idea what to say and apparently neither did she. Her hair was tousled, she still wore his robe, and she looked as conflicted as he was.

His heart began to pound and sweat popped out on his skin. He didn't know what the intention of that connection exercise had been, but it had definitely flicked some sort of switch inside him. Just looking at her made him feel like a bolt of lightning had hit him in the chest.

She took an unsteady breath, and he wondered if she felt the same.

Finally speaking, she said, "Just listen."

Royce nodded his head. His throat was stuck together, anyway.

Her eyes reflected the porch light. "Repeat after me," she said, raising a hand. "We are not Binding."

He spoke despite his closed throat. "What? We're not what?"

"We are not Binding. Say it."

Royce recalled the word. His father had mentioned it during his last visit. And then it had come up again when Gilli, his sister, had met her fiancé. He knew what it meant. When a female Red-Line took a mate, it was called a Binding.

He said it. "We are not Binding."

She let out a deep breath. "Good. Say it again."

Royce recalled Bindings were initiated by the female and involved a prolonged period of sexual activity. He swallowed. "We are not Binding."

She stepped forward. "This is not a Binding," she said. "Just a moment of distraction. That's it. Nothing more."

He nodded and took a step. "That's right. Simple and harmless. No Binding involved." His heart was thumping so hard, he didn't know how she couldn't hear it. Maybe she did.

"That's right," she said, sounding breathless. "No Binding. No Binding at all." She walked right into his arms, and he bent lower. Their lips met. She wrapped herself around him, and he lifted her and slanted his lips over hers. The effect was instantaneous. Everything flared and sparked and he felt like a box of fireworks suddenly all lighted inside him at once. She kissed him back and moaned into his mouth, and he groaned deeply. Holding her, he felt her legs lock around him. He slid his hands into her hair and kissed her hard. The energy between them was ramping up so fast he could barely breathe. He heard her own hurried breath as her tongue probed his mouth. He carried her to the side of the house and pushed her against it as the kiss continued. He moved his lips over hers as she raked her fingers up his shoulders.

She pulled away and spoke against his mouth. "We are not Binding."

"No," he said in a breathless whisper. "This is not a Binding."

Her lips slid back over his, and he ran his hands down her back, cupped her buttocks, and pulled her against him. The high-pitched moan that came from her almost overwhelmed him, and he fought to stay in control. Her mouth and body moving against him were like nothing he'd ever felt.

He reached out, found the edge of the door, and swung it open. He wrapped his arms around her and carried her into the kitchen. They continued to kiss as he stumbled on a rug and almost fell, but he found his footing and managed his way through the dark into his bedroom.

He pushed her against the back wall and let go of her. Her legs slid down and he yanked on the belt of her robe and pulled it open. She wore one of his white T-shirts. She let the robe drop, and he grabbed at the shirt and pulled it off of her. There was nothing on beneath it.

He spoke a muffled curse and pulled her back into his arms. They kissed deeply as Royce let his hands roam over her body, making the noises that escaped her sound like purring. The feel of her skin against his fingers was intoxicating, and she moved against him, trying to get closer.

He pulled back and removed his shirt as she grabbed the waistband of his sweatpants and pulled them down. He kicked them off and yanked her back. Her skin against his created a furnace around them. He felt her hands explore his chest and then move downward. They were breathing hard as he slid his lips to her neck and trailed kisses behind her ear and down to her shoulder. Her head fell back, and her fingernails dug into his skin.

Eager for her, he picked her up and brought her to the bed. He let her fall against it. He followed and hovered over her, trying to catch his breath. She looked up at him, her eyes glistening in the light. Staring down at her, he couldn't believe how beautiful she was. How had he not noticed before?

She lifted a hand and let her fingers trail down his chest. The sensation was electric. He lowered himself slowly and grazed his lips over hers. The kiss was soft and patient, but he sensed the powerful force behind it, and he wanted to savor every part of it. Their breath intermingling, she raised her head to deepen the kiss, but he pulled back, letting the energy build.

Forcing himself to slow down, he leaned sideways against her and rested his head in his palm. He raised his other hand and trailed his fingers down her body, taking his time at her most delicate areas. Her soft skin was exquisite. She moaned and her body writhed as he thrilled at his ability to pleasure her.

He bit his lip as she moved her own hand over him, starting at his chest and slowly moving lower. Groaning and unable to hold back, he shifted his weight and loomed over her. She arched against him, and he lowered himself against her, bracing himself on his elbows.

Their lips met, but before he let the kiss deepen, he spoke against her lips through a heavy breath. "Tell me you want me."

Her eyes lit up. She wriggled her hips against his, and he almost screamed at the sensation.

"I want you, Royce Fletcher," she said. Her voice was deep and a soft whine escaped her as he moved against her. "But," she said, as she closed her eyes and clenched her jaw as he continued to grind against her, "we are not Binding." She spoke so low, he almost didn't hear her.

"No," he said, feeling her fingers grip his back. "Absolutely not." His body aching, Royce lowered his head and met her lips once more in a fierce kiss.

·········

The phone rang. Its melodic tone traveled through the house and reached the bedroom. Royce cracked an eye open. Sunlight filtered through the curtains. He had no idea what time it was. The ringing stopped, and Royce lifted his head. Blinking his eyes, he looked around. He was naked in his bed, but he was alone. He sat up. "Sarna?"

"Right here," she said, walking back into his room. She carried two cups of coffee and his phone under her arm. She wore his bathrobe. Royce admired her in the soft light. Her hair was askew and her eyes puffy, but she looked just as beautiful as she had the previous night.

Sarna handed him a cup and put his phone by the bed. "It was Jasper. He's waiting for them to do their tests."

"What time is it?"

"Ten o'clock."

He eyed her robe and remembered what she looked like without it. "What time did we finally go to sleep?"

She blushed. "I don't know. Five, maybe six." She put her coffee down on the nightstand and sat next to him on the bed. She opened the drawer and took out her watch. Turning it over, she revealed the small compartment with the tiny white pills. She took one out, closed the watch, and put it back in the drawer.

"You take that every day?" asked Royce.

"Yes." She popped the pill in her mouth, picked up her coffee, and took a sip.

"What happens if you don't take it?"

She stared at his bare chest. "Our bodies would break down. We'd become weaker, become susceptible to illness. If we stayed, we'd eventually succumb."

"You can stop taking it once you leave?"

"Eventually, yes. Depends, though, on how sensitive you are and how quickly you readjust."

"You have enough after what happened to Jasper?"

Her eyes traveled downward and lingered on his lower body, although the sheet covered him. "As long as we don't stay much longer."

"Would I need to take something to survive on Eudora?"

Her eyes didn't stray. "No. You might have a few adjustment issues, but a healer could help with that. Once you were there for a while, you'd acclimate."

She took another sip, and Royce took a gulp of his own coffee. The thought of her leaving made him feel heavy, but he tried not to think about it. He just wanted to enjoy being with her. At the moment, the heat of her gaze, along with the coffee, was making him warm considerably. He let go of a deep breath. "What are you thinking?"

Her gaze traveled back up his belly and chest and she stared at him, picking up on the energy he was giving off. She moved her hand to his knee. "How long do these tests normally take?"

"Once they start them? I don't know. An hour, maybe two." He put his coffee cup down on the side table.

She put her own cup down. "Well, I suppose we have a little time."

"We sure do," said Royce, feeling his body react.

Sarna stood and dropped her robe. Naked, she slid into the sheets and moved over Royce, straddling him. He moaned as she slid her hands over his chest. "Feel like a little more non-Binding?"

Still sitting up, he wrapped his arms around her waist. Her head came down, and she kissed him.

"Yes," he said over her lips. "Let's non-Bind."

Smiling, she pushed him back against the sheets.

· · · ● · ● · ● · · ·

A few hours later, Sarna snuggled into Royce's chest. His arm wrapped around her; he pulled her close. She trailed her fingers over his skin, and he savored the sensation of having her beside him. How he had gone from disliking this woman forty-eight hours ago to now having her in his bed, he had no idea.

She touched the pink raised marks on his chest. "What happened here?" she asked.

He glanced down. His injuries were healing quickly. He'd realized after his Shift that being a Red-Line had its advantages. "Just a run in with an angry animal."

"An angry, big animal." She placed her palm over the marks. "Don't tell me. You pissed him off, didn't you?"

"I may have played a small part."

"No doubt."

"I chased him off, though. We're on good terms now."

"Good. I hope so." She sighed contentedly. "Now I know about your apparent issues with the animal kingdom, but what about your family?

What's it like growing up Red-Lines when everyone else around you is human?"

Royce ran his hand down her arm. "Not that difficult, really. It's not like we act or look different. We were just normal kids. Except for dad being gone all the time."

"How did you explain that?"

Royce thought back and smiled. "I used to tell other kids he was a secret agent. That he worked for the government. And that if I told them what he did, I'd have to kill them."

"Did they buy it?"

"No. I don't think so. My mom just told people he was in the military. Seemed to work."

"What about your sisters? What was it like for them?"

Royce shrugged. "Same as it was for me, I suspect. We just dealt with it. Heck, plenty of families have no dad at all. At least we saw ours occasionally." He paused. "It was mainly after we Shifted that life became difficult."

"Why?"

"Because things changed. Our abilities revealed themselves. Then we had to adjust to that. We had to be more careful about not revealing ourselves."

He felt her nod against him. "I didn't think about that," she said. "I remember after my Shift, I felt overwhelmed. I was feeling, sensing, and hearing things I'd never felt before. I had no idea how to control it."

"Exactly," said Royce. "I couldn't walk through a room without breaking a plate or a light bulb. Mom basically tied a broom to my hand and told me to clean up after myself."

"What about your sisters? What can they do?"

Royce pictured Eve in his head. "We all seemed to get different gifts. Eve can talk to all things non-human. Animals, plants, the Earth. After her Shift, she wouldn't come out of her room. Said there were too many voices in her head. She couldn't hear anything else. Took her a while to figure out how to handle it."

"That's a unique gift," said Sarna. "Not many others I know can do that. And if they do, it's usually limited to one thing. They can talk to animals, but that's it."

"Eve's strength is animals. But if you tell her what frequency, she can usually pick it up."

"What about your other sister?"

"Gillian," said Royce. He thought of how he almost lost her six months earlier. "She's like you. She's highly empathic. She can sense feelings and emotions. You can't lie to her."

"Hmm," Sarna said. "I know what that's like."

"Gilli had a hard time after her Shift. She and Eve are different. Eve retreated for a while, but she's highly social, and eventually she found a way to cope. For her, being around others was her way of dealing with it. But Gilli was the opposite. She's more introverted. Suddenly, having all that chatter in her head was very debilitating. She withdrew. Said it was too hard to be around people. She didn't like knowing when friends were lying to her or her family, or what people were really thinking."

"I can sympathize. It's very hard."

"After a while, we finally coaxed her out. Told her she had to find a way to cope with it. Plus, we had other issues to consider by then."

He felt her move against him. "What issues?"

"Dad told us that because of who we were, now that we'd Shifted, we'd have to separate."

"What?" asked Sarna, lifting her head. "Why?"

"Because the three of us together were very powerful. We emitted a signal that would be easy to track for anyone who might come looking for us." Royce remembered that day with discomfort. "We were shocked. Up until that point, we'd spent almost every day together. But now, according to Dad, we would need to leave home. We couldn't stay together anymore."

She sighed against him. "I guess that's true. You're triplets. All Red-Lines. All with exceptional gifts. I suspect you would give off a signal that any sensitive Red-Line could find if they came looking." She snuggled back into his neck. "He must have worried that one day his secret would come out."

"He must have. He told us to keep our distance from each other. We could visit on occasion, but not too often. I suppose, in retrospect, it was inevitable. I think Eve was ready to venture out, anyway. She wanted to make her mark on the world. Move to a big city. Meet lots of people. Date lots of men. Experience everything she could."

"Sounds like she is adventurous."

"She flourished. Did exactly what she set out to do. She's fiercely independent. You want someone to tell you the truth? Ask Eve."

"And Gillian?"

"It was much harder for her. Getting out of the house was painful. No matter what she did to silence the voices, she could still hear them. She did move out, but kept to herself, made few friends, and rarely strayed far from her home. We were worried about her."

"What changed?"

"She decided she'd use her gift for good. Instead of tuning in to all the negativity, she taught herself to pay attention to all the positive. Then something interesting happened."

"What?"

"She began to hear people's calls for help. It was like a public broadcast. Some stood out more than others. She found these people. She'd meet them, get to know them, and try to help them. Since she couldn't be around her family, she learned how to fill the void."

"Smart."

"We didn't like it at first. She'd disappear, not tell us what she was doing. We made her promise to stay in touch and let us know where she was. We quickly learned she can be just as stubborn as Eve. And just as brave.

Helping others breathed new life into her. Despite our objections, it was the best thing that ever happened to her."

"Funny how that happens, isn't it? Our greatest challenges become our greatest gifts."

"Yeah. I agree."

She played with his chest hair. "What about you? What happened when you left?"

"I'm sort of a cross between Eve and Gillian. Before the Shift, I was like Eve—pretty active. Sports, girls, fast cars, music. Afterward, things changed. I was more like Gilli. But I found that I liked my space. I can be solitary and not feel lonely. I found a piece of land, built a house, and I've been here since. I like it."

"But..."

"But? What 'but'?"

"I sense it. There's something else you're not mentioning."

He paused. "Not really. I guess what you're feeling is that I'm restless."

She lifted her head. "Why?"

"Because," He considered how to answer. "I can't help but wonder...what's next?" He waited for Sarna's expected response—for him to leave with her, but to her credit, she didn't say what he expected.

"That's understandable. At some point, everyone asks that question." She paused, wrapped her arm around him, and hugged him. "Tell me about Gus. What's his story?"

He chuckled. "Gus? He's my best friend. I met him not long after I moved here. I was out camping, and he just walked into my campsite, sat down, and started talking. Said he'd seen me in a vision. Knew we would be friends. And knew I was different."

"A vision?"

"Yes. Gus is Native-American, a descendent of the Iroquois tribe. He's a well-known healer and tracker. I think he's just as gifted as me and my sisters."

She laughed. "You sure he's not a Red-Line?"

He rested his jaw against her forehead. "Pretty sure."

"And he knows who you are?"

"I think he's getting the picture. He knows I can move objects. Says I come from the stars. It's why he calls me Starman. Knows I can hide too. He sees it in his visions."

"You can hide?"

"Well, I'm not great at it. Dad told me about it. He called it cloaking. Said he developed the skill over time. Most people can cloak their minds, but few can cloak their physical body."

She looked up. "He's right. It's not easy. You have to muster a lot of control for a long time. You can do that?"

"I had to sit and quiet my mind for long periods. It was gradual. But I managed to hide from a bear."

"A bear?" She pushed up. "Are you crazy?"

"It seemed like a good idea at the time."

"Did it work?"

"Walked right by me."

"And he didn't see you?"

He thought back. "He sniffed the air and pawed the ground. Chuffed a bit. I think he sensed me, but just couldn't place where I was."

She stared at him open-mouthed, then looked at his chest. "Don't tell me." She pointed at his injuries. "Did your bear do this?"

The bear's roar echoed in his mind. "I wasn't cloaked then. He snuck up on me."

"Uh-huh. Suddenly I don't feel so sorry for you."

"He was just expressing his frustrations."

She dropped her head back down to his chest. "You're lucky."

He touched his wounds. "You're right. I suppose I am."

"Next time, try cloaking yourself around a squirrel."

He smiled. "Good idea. I'll consider that."

She picked up the stone around his neck and held it. "I'd appreciate it." She picked up his necklace. "Where'd you get this?"

He eyed the dark rock. "Dad gave it to me. I wear it all the time."

"You know what this is, don't you?"

"It's a stone. That's all I can tell you."

"It's from Eudora. It's an Elgith Stone."

"It's a what?"

"An Elgith Stone. It's sacred."

"Really? What, does it have special powers?"

She nodded against him. "Yes, actually. It's a healing stone and is supposed to protect the wearer." She rubbed her thumb over it. "Have you noticed that it's always cool to the touch?"

He touched it. "Yes, I have. Feels great on a hot day."

"This rock is protected on Eudora. If you were found wearing it, it would be confiscated."

"Confiscated? What for?"

She dropped the stone and put her hand on his chest. "There's a story behind it."

"What's that?"

"Well," she said, snuggling back into him, "many years ago, there was a mythical, wealthy king who had a son named Elgith. The son was spoiled, but the king could not refuse him and granted his every desire. When the son grew up, he found and married the most beautiful woman he could find, who, in turn, married him for his wealth. They lived for years enjoying his money and parading her beauty."

"Nice guy," said Royce.

She sighed and continued. "Eventually, though, the king died. Those on the Council elected a new king and the son, who had few friends on the Council, saw all his riches stripped from him. He and his wife had nothing. His wife, now poor, left him. She knew her beauty would win her another rich man. Elgith was despondent. He'd lost everything, save for one thing.

The Council had allowed him to keep the land his father had given him. It was beautiful, with majestic trees and a shimmering lake. But when Elgith returned to the land, he'd found that over the years, the land had fallen into neglect. The trees were small and bare, and the lake had dried up. Elgith put all his time and effort into his property. The trees grew mighty again, and the grass became thick and green, but the lake would not fill. There had not been enough rain. As the years passed, Elgith focused on other matters. His land bore beautiful fruit, which he sold at the marketplace. And it was during one of those visits that he saw her."

Royce ran his fingers through Sarna's hair. "Who?"

"The wife who had left him. He was shocked to see her. She came to his stand and bought his fruit, and he learned she had married a wealthy man, but her beauty had faded. She did not love her husband and knew that he took other lovers. Over the years, she'd come to hate him, and all the wealth in the world had not brought her happiness."

"I hope this story has a happy ending," said Royce.

"Let me finish. After their meeting, Elgith continued to meet with her at the market. Over time, they fell in love. She eventually left her husband, asking for nothing, and remarried Elgith. They lived many happy years together on his property."

"How does the stone fit into this?"

"Would you shush? I'm almost done." She played with the stone again. "One day, Elgith's wife became ill, and she died not long after. Elgith was devastated. His tears began and did not stop. Years of grief caused his tears to fall continuously, until, as the legend goes, the lake filled with his tears."

"This is not a happy ending."

"I know."

"What happened then?"

"Elgith died from grief."

Royce snorted. "What kind of story is this?"

"The story goes that after his death, his land was retaken by the Council. As the years passed, the lake began to lose water again until it was empty, but what was left behind was this stone. The Elgith Stone."

"Really?"

"Yes. Soon, they began to mine and sell the stone. Those who wore it spoke of how it made them feel. How they healed from injuries and illness. How it had protected them from disaster and prevented poor decisions. They believed that Elgith's tears had mixed with the elements to create and give the stone special powers. The stone was mined from the empty lake until there was almost none left. It was at that point that the political climate had changed. The Council deemed it a sacred stone and thus protected it. All those who owned it were to return it to the quarry from where it came."

"So technically, Dad broke the law?"

"Technically, yes. But he is the High Leader, so he has some leeway. But no. It's not supposed to be privately owned. Of course, many people still have it, they just keep it hidden. But if it were to be found, it would be confiscated and returned to the quarry."

"A healing stone, huh?" Royce touched it. Had the rock helped him recover from his snake bite and kept him from collapsing from exhaustion the day he'd returned from Alice's and met Jasper and Sarna?

"I think he gave this to you for a reason."

Royce shifted to his side and faced her. "What's that?"

She put a hand on his cheek. "You're the rightful heir. You should have it. He wanted to be sure you were protected and safe."

Royce thought back on their connection the night before. "Can I ask you something?"

She rested her head on her hand. "Yes."

"During our connection last night. I saw things."

"What did you see?"

He recalled his vision. "Why did you have my picture? And what did you talk about with my dad?"

She went still and sighed. "Your father gave me your picture." Her eyes shifted as she thought back. "He'd told Jasper about you and your sisters. Jasper told me. Your father found out and wanted to talk to me. I agreed."

Royce furrowed his brow. "What did he say?"

She paused. "He explained to me why he had another family. How he had left you all behind and visited infrequently. It was to keep you safe, but he was wracked with guilt. He pulled out a picture. It was of you. He told me about you...how strong you were. How proud he was of you. That you were all the things he wished he could be. Brave, smart, kind, and compassionate. He wishes he'd told you that."

Royce didn't know what to say. His father had rarely expressed emotions with him.

"Even though Jasper kept it a secret, your father knew Jasper was going to try to reach out to you, against his wishes. He doesn't want you or your sisters to get caught up in his issues. He wants you left alone. But at the same time, he knows the situation on Eudora. The next leader is critical to the path he wants for our planet, and he knows Roma is the wrong choice."

"He never talked to me about this."

"I know." She rested her hand over his. "He felt it was too much of a burden to put on your shoulders. He knew it wasn't fair to ask of you, so he didn't."

"But Jasper could."

"Yes. Your father asked me to go with Jasper. Jasper is a good man, but he is impulsive and acts before he thinks. Your father was afraid he'd get himself into trouble, or worse, create a wedge between you and your other family."

"I can see that."

"So I agreed."

"But why you?" asked Royce. "No offense, but Sarna, you're just as impulsive and even more opinionated."

Sarna squeezed his hand. "I asked to go."

Royce raised an eyebrow. "Why?"

She paused. "Because of the picture."

"The picture? Am I that attractive?"

She smiled. "You are. But not in how you mean."

He rubbed his fingers along her forearm. "I'm confused."

"I saw the picture...and I felt something. I didn't understand it. It felt like a pull." She held his gaze. "I couldn't stop staring at it. There was something about you I can't explain. I felt..." She blushed. "I knew I had to meet you." She grazed her thumb over his fingers. "I didn't understand and I still don't, but I believe you and I have a purpose, Royce. I don't know what it is, but it's there. I knew it then, and I know it now."

Her eyes glistened, and Royce felt a constriction in his chest that he didn't even realize existed. An energetic pulse rushed through him. Her words soothed him, and he understood what she meant. There was a reason they had come together. He took her fingers in his own. "Listen."

"What?" A tear escaped and ran down her cheek, and she wiped it away. "Sorry. I don't know why I'm so emotional."

Royce sensed her turmoil but felt his own uncoil. Feeling a knowing sensation settle over him, he made a decision. "Hey."

She swiped at her face again. "What?"

He let go of her hand and stroked her jaw. "I'm not promising anything, and I need to talk to my family, but..."

"But what?" Her eyes widened.

"I will consider leaving with you."

Her mouth fell open. Fresh tears flowed down her cheeks.

He shifted forward and kissed her cheeks. "Stop crying. Everything's okay."

"I just...I didn't know..."

He wiped at a tear. "Didn't know what?"

She sniffed. "Nothing."

He caressed her cheek. "No. Tell me."

"What I would do if...if I never saw you again." Another tear spilled from her eye, and she sniffed.

His heart melted at her words, and he kissed her gently. He was worried and doubtful, but also excited and eager. It was a strange sensation, but it felt like all the craziness in his life was beginning to make sense. "One step at a time, okay? This is going to be hard for me. So be patient. Please."

She blinked through watery eyes. "I will. I promise."

He chuckled. "Sure you will."

Leaning forward, she kissed him. She wrapped around him and hugged him, and he hugged her back. Snuggling into his neck, she spoke into his ear. "We should probably go check up on Jasper. He's probably wondering where we are." She trailed her fingers down his lower back.

Her hot breath tickled his skin, and he dragged his lips up her jawline and nipped at her earlobe. "Probably." He felt her respond instantly to his touch.

Her knee came up, and her hand dropped lower. She wrapped her leg around him and moaned as Royce teased her with his tongue. She pulled her head back and grazed her lips over his, her gaze saying everything. Royce tried to breathe. "A few more minutes won't kill him," she said as her hand slipped between them.

Royce's heart almost thumped out of his chest. "My thoughts exactly," he said, and he captured her mouth with his own.

# Chapter Twenty-Four

THE ELEVATOR DINGED, AND Royce and Sarna stepped out into the hospital corridor. Nestled in their private world, they'd never made it to the hospital the previous day. They'd called, but the doctor was still waiting for Jasper's test results, so there were no plans to release him. Enjoying their privacy, they'd stayed home, telling Jasper they'd be there first thing the next day.

They'd called that morning and learned that Jasper had been moved into a private room, allowing them easy access. Holding hands outside his door, they knocked and stepped inside. Jasper was sitting back in bed, his frown revealing his irritation.

"Where have you been?" He sat up. "I sat here all day yesterday. The only person I talked to who didn't work here was the sheriff, who asked me all these questions. And then when he left, I waited for my tests, which they didn't do until the afternoon, and I still don't know the results. I keep telling these people I'm fine, but they don't believe me. And when they finally did the tests, they put me in with all these machines. I've never seen anything so antiquated." He threw his hand out. "And where were you two yesterday? I thought you were coming to get me. I was bored and—" He eyed their hand-holding. He looked up and his eyes darted between the two of them. "Oh, no." He sat back against the pillows, his eyes staring blankly. "Never mind."

Sarna squeezed Royce's hand. "Royce and I..."

Jasper narrowed his eyes. "I think I know."

Royce tried to help. "Sorry about yesterday. How was the talk with the sheriff?"

Jasper pulled on the covers. "Fine. I told him what you said."

"He seem suspicious?"

"No." He set his jaw.

"We planned to come by," said Royce, "but since it didn't look like you would be leaving the hospital until today, we," he looked at Sarna, "took the time to get to know each other." He raised their clasped hands. "We sort of bonded while you recovered."

Sarna sucked in a breath.

Realizing his mistake, he shook his head. "Bonded," he clarified. "Not Binded."

Sarna shook her head too. "Definitely not Binded."

Jasper's eyes widened, and the sheet he held bunched in his hand. "What are you doing? We're about to leave, and you Bind with him? Are you serious? I thought you didn't like him."

She pointed a finger. "We did not Bind. Besides, Royce is...reconsidering."

Jasper's jaw dropped. "What?"

"I am," said Royce. He felt a flutter of anxiety bubble up. "I can't promise anything. But I've agreed to talk with my family, and then I'll decide."

Jasper threw his covers off and slid his legs to the side of the bed. He wore only a hospital gown and his IV hung from his arm. "Then let's get out of here."

"Whoa," said Royce. "You need to be cleared before you can leave."

"What for?" asked Jasper. "What are they going to do? Search for me? Good luck to them." He tried to stand, but his IV pulled at his wrist. He held up his arm. "And what is all this stuff?"

"That's why you have to wait. They need to take all that stuff out of you."

"I can do it myself," said Jasper, reaching for the clear tube.

Just then, the door opened, and Dr. Trask stepped in. "How's my patient?"

Jasper stopped pulling at the needle in his arm. "Finally. Doctor, when can I get out of here?"

The doctor walked to the computer monitor in the room and typed. A screen pulled up with columns and data. He studied the screen. "Your tests came back fine. I have to admit, I'm amazed at how quickly you've healed. That's unusual in a head trauma case."

"I feel great. I just want to go home."

Dr. Trask glanced at Sarna and Royce. "Are you family?"

Royce opened his mouth to answer, but Sarna spoke first. "Yes."

The doctor looked at Jasper. "Normally, considering your injury, I'd recommend staying another night for observation."

"Doctor, please," said Jasper. "What do I have to do? I'll run around this building if you ask me to. I'm okay."

The doctor paused, then spoke to Sarna and Royce. "Can you two assure me he'll get plenty of rest this next week? No strenuous activity? No travel?"

Royce bit the inside of his lip, and Sarna answered, "Absolutely."

The doctor sighed. "All right. I'll sign the release papers. Give the nurses a little time to prep everything." He held up a finger. "But if you experience any dizziness, fatigue, or nausea, you come back in. Understand?"

"I understand. Thanks, doctor."

"And I want you to make an appointment with your primary care physician."

Jasper looked at Royce.

"He will, doctor," said Royce.

"All right," said the doctor. "The nurse will be in soon." He headed to the door. "You take it easy."

"I will," said Jasper as Dr. Trask left. "We have a lot to do." He rested back on the bed, his energy calmer now that he knew he was going home. "We should leave tonight." His gaze met Royce's, and Royce knew what he was thinking.

Royce squeezed Sarna's hand. A wave of sadness washed over him, and he sighed. "I have a phone call to make." Her eyes softened and her fingers tightened around his. She nodded.

Royce let go of her, glanced at Jasper, who was quiet, and left the room.

· · • • • · • • · ·

Lillian Fletcher dug into the soft dirt with her trowel. Digging deep enough, she pushed the soil aside and reached for the small plant beside her. She picked it up, placed it in the ground, and swiped the loose earth back into the hole. Patting the soil, she made sure the new plant was securely in place.

Sitting back on her heels, a trickle of sweat ran down her neck. It was a hot day, and she removed her floppy hat and wiped her face with a handkerchief. Reaching for her water bottle, her cell phone rang. She picked it up and read the display. It was her son, Royce.

Smiling, she stood. She picked up her water and answered the call. "Royce, honey. How are you?" She walked to her covered patio and sat down, dabbing the sweat on her neck.

"Hey, Mom."

She checked her watch. "What's wrong?"

He chuckled. "What do you mean?"

"You're a creature of habit. You always call me in the evening after dinner. I've never known you to call me on a Sunday at noon. I know you. You're usually puttering around outside."

"Like you?"

"Exactly."

"What are you planting?"

"Never mind that." She sipped her water. "What's going on?"

There was a quiet pause. "Mom, I need to ask you something. Something that's hard for me to ask."

She sat forward in her seat. Something in his tone made her put her water down. She fiddled with her handkerchief. A flicker of worry flared in her belly. "You know, don't you?"

"Mom?"

"About his other family." She heard his intake of breath.

"You know about that?" he asked.

She'd known this day would come, and she thought she would be prepared, but now she wasn't so sure. "Of course I do. He told me."

"When?"

"A long time ago." He didn't respond. "Do your sisters know?"

"Yes."

"When did you find out?"

"Six months ago. Remember when we told you about Galen?"

A cold shiver ran through her. She recalled her children telling her about her brother-in-law's visit, but she knew they hadn't told her everything. "He said something?"

"Yes." He paused. "We wanted to ask you, but..."

"I know. You weren't sure if I knew or not."

"No."

Another pause and she knew he wasn't sure what to say. "Your father told me years ago. I was understandably upset, but over the years, I came to terms with it. I understood that a man in his position has certain expectations. He couldn't tell his Council he was in love with someone else."

"Yes, he could have."

She rubbed her head. "Royce, there is no point in dredging up the past."

"You knew who he was?"

"The High Leader? Yes. I accepted it and all that came with it. So should you."

"He chose to stay home and leave you here to raise a family, while he raised another one with someone else. I have a problem with that."

She sighed. "Would you rather I left him and married someone else? Would you have preferred a step-father? A man who could never know of your origins?" Her son was silent. "I loved your father, Royce. I knew the situation. I didn't like it. Neither did he."

"He had two children with her."

"I know. Roma and Jasper." She heard him breathe. "He's your father, Royce. He had choices to make and other people to consider. I can't imagine how difficult it was for him."

"To leave everything for the one you love?" There was a pause. "Yes. I can imagine."

"If he hadn't been the High Child, things would have been different."

"You know about the High Child?"

"Yes, of course. He told me everything. He said if he left the role, then Galen would take power as next in line. He knew how detrimental that would be to his people." She cocked her head. "How do you know about the High Child?"

There was no response.

"Royce?"

"Jasper is here."

She stilled. "Your brother? He's here?" Her mind flew in a million directions.

"Yes."

"Is your father okay?"

"As far as I know."

She fanned herself. "Jasper came alone?"

"No. He came with someone else. A woman named Sarna."

"Who is Sarna?"

"A friend of the family. Dad asked her to come."

Lillian shut her eyes as she tried to digest the news. The pieces clicked together, and she realized the implications of this visit. A chill ran through her.

"Mom?"

"They came for you, didn't they?" She bit her lip. She pressed a hand to her mouth, but took a deep breath and collected herself.

"Mom...listen..."

Carson had told her this moment might come, but she wasn't sure she could handle it. There was no way to prepare for losing your son. "Is it time for you to go?"

Silence, and then he murmured. "Jasper tells me I'm the High Child."

She bit back a sob but pulled it together. She knew how important this moment was. "I know."

"They say it's time for Dad to step down." She nodded but didn't speak. "And if I don't go, Roma will take over."

She cleared her throat. "This must be so hard for you."

He sighed, and she pictured him rubbing his temples. "It's gut wrenching. I don't know what to do."

She forced herself to speak the words, wishing she could say something else entirely. "What does your heart tell you?"

She heard a grunt. "My heart aches over the thought of leaving. But..."

She held her breath. "But what?"

Royce moaned into the phone. "Something about it feels right. Now that I've had time to think about it, it makes sense."

"Why?" She wanted to be sure he was considering everything.

"I just think...I don't know." He sighed again, and she picked at her handkerchief. "I'm restless, Mom. I mean, what am I doing? Where exactly am I headed? I've never felt like I fit in. Because of who I am, I've never expected to share my life with anyone. At least not without keeping secrets."

"And you want that?"

He was quiet, and she knew he was thinking about it. "Yes. I do. And for the first time, I think I can have it."

The way he said it made her realize something. She straightened in her seat. "You met someone, didn't you?"

He chuckled. "Yes."

"Is it Jasper's friend?"

He made a snorting sound. "Surprisingly, yes. I'm still amazed by it. It happened so fast. I didn't even like her when I met her."

"It happens like that."

"Oh, man." He moaned.

"What?"

"I've been telling myself it wasn't serious."

"But it is, isn't it?"

"Jeez, Mom. What's happening to me?"

She could see him in her mind's eye, running a hand through his hair. She smiled softly. "You're falling in love."

"That's hard to believe."

"It's nice, isn't it?"

He made a quiet sigh. "More like completely insane."

"But it's a good insane."

He took another deep breath. "I can't believe it. How is it that everything is happening at once?"

She patted her face with her kerchief, but this time she wiped away a tear instead of sweat. "Probably because it's meant to be. She's here for a reason. If she didn't come, then you probably would have never considered leaving."

Another pause. "I don't want to leave you, Mom. Or Gilli and Eve." There was a slight quiver in his voice.

She steeled herself. "Sweetheart, listen to me." Realizing this was a moment where being a mother sucked, she braced herself and kept going.

"You have to listen to your gut. You could stay here with me and your sisters, but what for?"

"You're my family. I don't want to leave you alone."

"Your sisters can fend for themselves. Besides, Gilli and Eve are building their own lives. And I can't ask you to stay for me. I want you to do what you're meant to do."

"But that leaves you vulnerable. What if someone else like Galen comes looking?"

"How is that going to happen if you're in charge?"

He paused. "I didn't consider that."

"Perhaps you should. Maybe by going, you're ensuring our safety, not endangering it."

"There will always be a risk."

"That's life, honey. You can't protect us from everything. I could get hit by a bus tomorrow. What are you going to do? Kill the bus driver?"

"If I got my hands on him, I would."

"But what would that solve? I'd still be dead."

"That's why I should stay."

"What, so you can slay every bus driver that drives by the house? Don't be silly. I love you, son, but you need to stop thinking of everyone else. We're not your responsibility. Just because your father hasn't been here doesn't mean you need to take his place. And I'm not talking about being the High Child."

"What do you mean?"

"You know what I mean. You took over for your father. He wasn't here, so you became the man you wanted him to be. But you need to realize that you've accomplished that. You are that man. You've done everything you've set out to do. You're ready."

"I am?"

She put a hand on her chest. "Royce, you're the strongest, kindest, smartest man I know. Your father's always been so proud of you. He loves you very much, and he knows he hasn't been there for you. He understands how you feel. But don't let your anger and disappointment with him stop you."

"Stop me?"

"From following your destiny."

He spoke softly. "Gus said the same thing to me."

The face of her son's Native-American friend flashed in her mind. She'd met him on her last visit. "Gus is a smart man."

"You're a smart lady."

"I know, dear."

He cleared his throat. "I think I'm going to go with them."

Her chest ached, and she gripped her handkerchief. "I know that too."

She heard a soft whimper. "I'm gonna miss you, Mom."

Tears welled up. "You better come and visit."

"As often as I can."

She pressed her fingers against her mouth and bit back a sob. "When do you leave?"

He sniffed. "Tonight."

The ache in her chest sharpened. "So soon?"

"Jasper and Sarna can't stay any longer."

"You'll call your sisters?"

"That's next on my list."

She nodded and wiped her eyes. The pain coursing through her was almost too much to bear, but she knew it was his time to follow his calling. "You know how much I love you? How blessed I am to call you my son?"

She heard the hitch in his breath. "I know." He took a deep breath. "I love you too, Mom."

Tears streamed down her face. "You tell your father that I love and miss him. He better watch out for you."

Royce sniffed again. "I'm going to put him on the first plane out, other family be damned."

She laughed. "Drive safe. Or should I say fly?"

"I'll tell Jasper. He's the captain."

She blotted her wet cheeks. "And if anything changes, you know you always have a home here."

"I know, Mom." His voice shook. "I promise to come back."

"You better." More tears fell, and judging by the sounds she heard over the phone, she knew it was the same for him.

"I love you."

"I love you too."

· · · · ● · ● · · ·

Royce hung up the phone. Feeling emotionally wrecked, he swiped his fingers over his wet face and stared at the floor, feeling almost numb as his tears fell. Taking the time he needed to calm down and stop crying, he found a tissue and blew his nose. Then he took a deep breath and called his sisters.

He conferenced them in at the same time. Their conversation lasted close to an hour. They shed more tears, but Royce was again surprised at its outcome. Gilli and Eve had surmised over the years that if the opportunity appeared to visit their father's home planet, then Royce would be the obvious choice to go. Royce felt tremendous relief when they told him they supported whatever decision he made. Before the call ended, Gilli told Royce she would contact an attorney who would draw up some papers giving Gilli power of attorney while Royce was gone, allowing her to make decisions on his behalf.

They talked a few minutes more, shed additional tears, and Royce hung up. He blew his nose and wiped his eyes again. Taking a deep breath, he stood, walked to the window, and stared out.

A knock on the door sounded, but he barely heard it. The door opened, there were soft footsteps, and Sarna walked up beside him.

"You okay?" she asked.

He nodded, still looking out over the hospital parking lot. "How'd you find me?"

"Wasn't hard. I could feel you down here. I just followed the signal."

Royce remained quiet. "Where's Jasper?"

"They finally sent someone to take out his IV. The papers are signed. He's changed into the clothes we brought him. Now he's just waiting for a wheelchair to take him down to the lobby."

Royce nodded again.

"Did you talk to your family?"

"Yes."

She stood silently, and her worry was evident. He was sure his face was red and eyes were puffy. "And?"

"I told them I was leaving."

"What did they say?"

Suddenly, all his doubts fired at once. He sighed and turned away from the window. "What am I thinking?" He put a hand on the wall and hung his head. "Am I really doing this? Leaving this planet? Going to another one? Taking on a role I know nothing about in a place I've never been? It's crazy."

"It's not crazy."

"Leaving my family? Never seeing them again?"

Sarna took his hand. "Who said you would never see them again?"

His mouth dropped open. "Sarna, I'm leaving *the planet*. It's not exactly traveling cross country. And I'm going to a place where universal travel is banned. Where I'll likely be arrested the moment I step off the plane...or ship...or whatever you call it." He sighed. "And that's another thing. What about your language? I don't speak it. How am I supposed to communicate? Defend myself? Lead a country? And what happens to you and

Jasper? You could suffer the consequences for bringing me back. What if I can't stop that?" He raked his hand through his hair, sat in the chair, and studied the floor.

Sarna didn't say anything but walked over and squatted in front of him. She put her hand on his wrist. "First of all, you are not going to be arrested when you step off the ship. Jasper will know where to land. We have a story as to why we were gone. No one should even suspect that we left the planet." She squeezed his arm. "You will have time to acclimate before we introduce you to anyone. We'll keep you somewhere safe. And don't worry about communicating. Red-Lines are adept at learning languages. You will pick it up quickly. Plus, you'll have your own personal interpreter." She smiled. "If you'll have me." She tried to catch his eye. "When you feel like you're ready, we'll take you to see your father. He'll be thrilled to see you. You two can talk, work through whatever issues or decisions you need to. He'll likely try to talk you out of taking his place, but don't let him."

Royce looked up. He put his hand over hers.

"You can decide with him how you want to announce who you are and how you arrived. That will be the defining and risky moment. It will take time for people to understand what your existence means and the repercussions of you being the High Child. There will be Council members who will be openly angry and derisive, and Roma will be a powerful adversary."

"This is not making me feel better."

"But that's why you must go. Because you can handle all of that. By then, you will be more comfortable and better prepared to deal with those things." She raised up on her knees and held Royce's face with her hands. "You won't be alone. I promise."

He laced his fingers around her back and pulled her in. "And where will you be?" he asked. "What will happen to you because of your involvement? If they hurt you because of me, I'll—"

"Hey," she said. "Don't worry about me. There's no reason for anyone to suspect my involvement. If anyone's going to be suspected, it will be Jasper. But he is your brother, the son of the High Leader, and he can take care of himself."

"I don't want anyone hurt because of me."

Sarna shook her head. "You forget. You have a powerful ally. Your dad."

"And what about my family here? How can I be sure they'll be safe?"

Sarna dropped her hands down to his shoulders. "We don't even have to disclose their existence."

"Galen knew. We have to assume others do."

"You do more for your family by assuming your new role. By doing that, you keep them safe. Once you assume your position as High Leader, then harming your family gains them nothing. And if you open up the universal borders again, then what purpose does anyone have to hurt them? People will see there is nothing to fear. Besides, your mother is human. They won't touch her. And your sisters are Red-Lines, and from what you say, a formidable team."

His mother had come to the same conclusion, but that didn't make him feel better. "They shouldn't have to look over their shoulders, worried that someone will come for them."

"They're doing that now. The only reason to hurt them is to stop you from taking charge. Once you're in charge, then what is the point?"

"Revenge. Look what Galen tried to do."

She squeezed his arms. "The reason Galen came after you was to stop you from being discovered and to assure Roma's ascension to power. It wasn't revenge."

"How can you be sure?"

"Because it risks everything. Going after the High Leader's family is a death sentence. And keeping that a secret would be very difficult. The consequences would be swift and harsh. And I know Roma. She'll fight for power, but she would have no interest in hurting someone millions of miles away."

He hung his head and rested it on her shoulder. "You don't know that."

Her fingers moved into his hair, and she kissed his head. "I know one thing. One thing you keep forgetting."

He looked up. "What's that?"

"Remember? You'll be the High Leader. You'll have access to a variety of resources. If you want, send someone to watch out for them. You can come and visit. See for yourself that they're okay. We can open up communications again. You'll be able to stay in touch."

He widened his eyes. "You're sure about that?"

"Why not? We did it in the past. I'm sure we can get in touch with Sarah and John's Gray-Line community. They could help keep an eye on your family." She rubbed his cheek. "It will be okay. Your family will be safe."

Her words made sense. His shoulders came down, and he sighed. "Am I worrying too much?"

"No. You have legitimate concerns. But we can deal with them."

He clasped his fingers together. "You still want me to come? I can be a handful."

She smiled. "If you can put up with me, then I can put up with you."

Royce raised his hand and cupped the side of her face. His thumb slid over her cheek. "Will I still be able to eat a juicy hamburger?"

Her eyes narrowed. "Now that may be a problem. I said you'd be the High Leader, but even that position has its limitations."

"We'll see about that."

"I should warn you. I'll put up a good fight."

He chuckled, touched his forehead to hers, and closed his eyes. "You're going to stay with me?"

She nodded her head. "I'm not going anywhere. I'll be with you every step of the way. So much so that you're going to get sick of me."

Pulling back, he held her gaze. "Not likely. Although the hamburger thing may be a problem." He paused. He still felt uncertain, but her words helped. His stomach churned with anxiety, but some of the weight lifted. "Okay." He sighed. "I guess I'm going on this big adventure."

Her eyes lit up. "You're sure?"

He leaned in and gave her a kiss. "I'm sure. I can't follow my gut by staying here. I guess at some point, I just have to trust it."

"That's what John said," she said. "He's right. You've been unsettled for a while now, since your Shift. And I think now you know why." She glanced at the ceiling. "What was the phrase he used?"

"Trust destiny," said Royce. "It's been in my head since he said it. Guess it's time to listen."

She looked at him with soft eyes, and the warmth from her body traveled from her into him. Suddenly, his worry lifted, and he felt light. Now that he'd spoken to his family and decided, he relaxed, and the excitement he felt before returned.

"Then let's go get packed," she said. "I'm sure Jasper is about to wheel himself back to your place on his own."

They stood, and Royce took her hand. "It's you and me, right?" he asked. "We'll do this together?"

She smiled and raised on her toes to kiss him. "There's no place I'd rather be."

# Chapter Twenty-Five

ON THE CAR RIDE back to Royce's, Royce called Gus. He wanted to explain to his friend his impending absence and ask him to watch over his cabin. Gus agreed to stop by that night, before Royce left with Jasper and Sarna. He also made a mental note to check his email for Gilli's paperwork. He'd have to sign it electronically before he left.

Arriving at the house, Royce and Sarna got out of the truck and Jasper got behind the wheel. "I'll go prep the ship. I'll pick you two up later tonight, after dark. Be ready."

"We will," said Sarna.

"And you be careful," said Royce. "Pay attention to your surroundings. Don't let anyone knock you over the head again."

"Are you kidding?" said Jasper. "I'll be keeping an eye out this time."

"Wait a minute," said Sarna, grabbing Royce by the elbow. "What about RJ?"

"Who?" asked Jasper.

"Ah, hell," said Royce. "RJ." He'd been so caught up with his impending departure and his budding relationship with Sarna that RJ's plight had fallen to the wayside. How were they going to deal with the pink shoe?

"What's the problem?" asked Jasper.

"Jasper," said Sarna. "Do you know what happened to your shoe?"

"Shoe?" asked Jasper. "Sarna, I'm sitting in a running car, about to prep our ship to leave, and you're asking about a shoe?"

"Yes, I am. You were only wearing one shoe when they found you in the woods. Do you recall anything about taking it off, or having it taken off?"

"The sheriff asked me about that," said Jasper. "No. I don't remember anything about my shoe. But thankfully, I have a second pair. Can I go now?"

"Jasper," Royce said. "Sarna says you have some sort of camera on the ship. Can you use it to detect anyone coming around?"

"Yes, why?"

"Was it on the night you arrived?"

"Probably. It usually remains on for the first twenty-four hours. Then it drops into low-power mode."

"What's that?" asked Royce.

"The cameras are only on for the first twenty-four hours because that's the highest risk of discovery. If someone heard or saw something, they might come to investigate. After that, the cameras shut off and the motion sensors kick in. The cameras don't turn on unless a sensor is triggered."

"The sensor picks up on motion?"

"Yes."

"But what about animals? They're all over the place."

"They would have to be of a certain size to trigger the sensor. Birds and squirrels wouldn't trigger it, but deer or a bear probably would."

"We need to check the cameras," said Sarna.

"What for?" Jasper asked.

Sarna stood beside the driver's window. "The night we arrived. A woman was murdered in those woods near our landing site. We might have caught something."

"Since when are we crime solvers? We have got things to do if we want to get out of here tonight."

"Her shoe was also taken," said Sarna.

"There's a teenager," said Royce. "His name is RJ. Someone is trying to make it look like he killed her. The victim's shoe was in his trunk."

Jasper sighed. "Well then, I'd say mystery solved."

"He didn't do it, Jasper," said Sarna.

"How do you know?"

"Because he came by here after you left angry. He told Royce about the shoe. He was panicked. I could read him easily, and he was telling the truth. He never hurt anybody."

Jasper shook his head. "Am I missing something here? Why does this matter to us?"

"Because I took the shoe out of his trunk," said Royce. "It's in my shed."

Jasper's eyes narrowed. "You what? What did you do that for?"

"He's a child, Jasper," said Sarna. "He needs help."

"He's a teenager. There's a difference. Are you sure he's the telling the truth?"

Sarna cocked her head, and Royce could feel her shoot out a telepathic message to Jasper that was best not repeated out loud.

"Fine," said Jasper. "What do you want me to do?"

"Check the cameras. Look at the night we landed. See if you see anything that might tell us who killed that woman."

"You want me to watch cameras? I don't have time to do that."

Sarna raised a hand. "You don't have to sit and watch. Just set it up to alert you if something unusual occurs. Get the ship ready and let the computer do the work."

"I can't leave until we make sure RJ is okay," said Royce. "And I figure out what to do with that shoe."

"And what if we find nothing?" asked Jasper. "Then what?"

"Then I'll destroy the shoe. Throw it in the lake. At least I'll know it can't be used to incriminate RJ."

"You should look at the night you were attacked too," Sarna said. "Maybe it caught something."

"I don't know if my incident was close enough to the ship to trigger the sensor."

"It's still worth checking," said Sarna.

"I should call RJ before I leave," Royce said. "Let him know what's going on."

"You aren't going to tell him about us, are you?" asked Jasper. "About where you're going?"

Royce rolled his eyes. "Yes. I am going to tell him I'm leaving this planet with my alien half-brother to take over as High Leader on another planet. Our ship leaves in one hour." He stared dully at Jasper. "I'm sure he'll understand."

Jasper smirked. "You don't have to be a smart ass."

"Then don't ask dumb questions."

Sarna sighed. "You two are acting like brothers already."

"To be honest," said Royce, "I don't know what I'm going to tell him. Depends on if you discover anything on the camera. Can you contact us from the ship?"

Jasper thought about it. "I should be able to."

"You shouldn't have to tell him anything," said Sarna. "At least not about the shoe. Just tell him whatever you want to about leaving. Then assure him he doesn't have to worry. That you are looking into what happened that night. If Jasper discovers anything, then you need to notify the sheriff. Let RJ be just as surprised as anyone else."

"Can he keep his mouth shut about giving the shoe to you?" asked Jasper. "If he can't, then it's pointless."

"I can't worry about that," said Royce. "If it happens, then it happens. But if we catch the killer, then maybe it won't matter."

"Let's see what's on the cameras first," said Sarna. "The sheriff is looking for the man in the store we met that first day. The one looking for his sister."

Jasper tilted his head. "The guy who we saw in the woods? Why?"

"Because he thinks the woman in the picture may be the woman that was murdered," said Royce. He thought of Alice, knowing the woman in the picture was likely her, but didn't see the point in saying anything.

"That makes no sense."

"Regardless, if that man's on the footage, then we know," Sarna said. "But if we don't see anything, then let's drop the shoe in the lake and let the investigation take its course. And if it is this guy they think it is, then hopefully they'll find him and link him in some other way."

"And if he says he threw the shoe in RJ's trunk?"

"Then that still only implicates him," said Royce. "RJ may get into trouble for messing with the evidence, but at least it's not a murder wrap."

"It gets you into trouble, too, if he says he gave you the shoe," said Sarna.

"Again, it's not a murder wrap. And I'll be a million miles away, so it will be a little hard to find and question me."

"It's not ideal," said Sarna.

"Maybe not, but right now, I've got bigger fish to fry."

Sarna grimaced. "Really? You have to use that metaphor?"

Royce looked at Jasper. "You have fish on your planet?"

Jasper nodded. "As a matter of fact, we do."

"You ever had fried fish?"

"Royce..." said Sarna.

"Sounds tasty," said Jasper.

"It's delicious."

Sarna turned white. "You can go now, Jasper."

Jasper chuckled and put the car in reverse. "All right. I'll prep the ship and check the cameras. If I find anything, I'll let you know." He glanced at Royce. "Your friend is stopping by?"

"Gus?" said Royce. "Yes. Tonight. He should be gone by the time you get back, though."

"Wouldn't matter if he was," said Sarna. "He already knows about us."

"What?" Jasper stomped on the brake as the car began to move. He cocked an eyebrow at Royce.

"Never mind," said Royce. "I'll explain later."

"He's Native-American. Very sensitive. You'd probably like him," said Sarna.

Jasper opened his mouth to say something, but apparently changed his mind. Shaking his head, he backed out of the driveway and drove off, leaving Royce and Sarna behind.

Royce turned and faced his home. His eyes traveled over the wooden exterior, the brick chimney, paned windows, and paneled front door. He'd built it himself, and now the thought of leaving it behind put a lump in his throat. He had no idea when, or if, he would ever see it again.

Sarna leaned closed. "You'll be back one day."

He put his arm around her. "I hope so."

She squeezed his midsection. "Come on, let's get ready."

He nodded, and they walked into his cabin. Everything was in its place. The kitchen was tidy, the living room clean, and the breakfast table still had the morning local paper on it. Royce had not had time to read it that morning. He wondered when he'd ever read another morning paper. He picked it up and scanned the headline. The big news was about the impending retirement of the local president of the school district. At the bottom of the front page there was a small article with a title which read, "Still no leads in murder investigation."

Royce dropped the paper back on the table. He made a mental note to pack it. It would be some small tie to his home and his last day here.

Sarna squeezed his fingers. "You okay?"

Looking around, he sighed. "Yes. I'm okay. Just going to miss this place." Looking in the kitchen, he spotted the coffee machine his mother had given him and the framed picture of a bear Gus had taken on one of his walks. He had given it to Royce on Royce's birthday. On the counter was the blender he'd bought at a garage sale, and resting against it was an envelope. Royce didn't recognize it.

"Where's your suitcase?" asked Sarna. She let go of his hand and walked to a hall closet. "In here?"

Royce walked over and picked up the envelope. "R" was written in bold script on the front. He slid his finger under the flap and pulled out a piece of paper.

Sarna found a suitcase and pulled it out of the closet. "Is this what you want to use?"

Royce read the note and felt the color drain from his face. He read it again.

*Royce,*

*I need to see you.*

*A.*

"Royce?" asked Sarna. Holding the suitcase, she walked over to him and stopped. "What is it?"

Royce dropped the letter on the counter and stared at it. *Alice.* She was back. And she wanted to see him.

"Royce?" asked Sarna. "What's wrong?" She picked up the letter. When he didn't answer, she read it. "Who's A?"

Royce shut his eyes and made a soft groan. "Alice," he said softly. "Her name is Alice."

Sarna put the suitcase down. "Who's Alice?"

Royce opened his eyes. "A woman."

"I suspected as much. Who is she?"

Royce tried to gather his thoughts. Why was she back? What had happened? He shook his head. "I, uh...had a relationship with her."

Sarna stared at him and the letter. "This is the woman..."

"What?"

"This is the woman you were thinking about when you came home and found us in your house."

He cocked an eyebrow. "You knew that?"

Sarna put the letter down. "You were upset. It was hard to miss."

Royce nodded.

"What happened?"

Royce wasn't sure how to answer. "I—we—she…"

She watched him stammer. "You knew her before you ever met me. I'm not the jealous type. Just tell me."

Royce cleared his throat. "I met her a few days before you and Jasper showed up. I'd been injured. A snake bite and the bear attack."

"Your chest wounds?"

"Yes," said Royce. "She was staying in the cabin on the property next door. She found me, somehow helped me inside her house, and took care of me. She called Gus and the two of them nursed me back to health."

"Why didn't you go to a hospital?"

"Because of you and Jasper."

"What?"

"Gus had told me I had visitors coming. At the time, all I could think about was Galen. If I was in a hospital, then I was an easy target and easy to find, so I asked them not to bring me to the hospital. They complied."

"They obviously took good care of you."

"They did. Alice was a nurse once, so I was lucky."

Sarna nodded. "What happened then?"

He told her about Alice, how she was on the run and that he suspected the man in Tiny's store showing the woman's picture was her ex who was searching for her.

Sarna picked up the letter again. "Did she know he was close?"

"She knew she'd stayed at the cabin too long and that she needed to leave, but remained to care for me. Once I'd heard her story, I wanted to help, but she wouldn't let me." He looked away. "We found brief comfort with each other."

Sarna nodded, understanding his implication. "It sounds like you both needed it."

"We spent one night and day together, and then she disappeared. She left me a goodbye note." He hung his head. "I came back here that morning, angry, confused, and hurt. I half wanted to get in my car and find her, and I half wanted to forget I ever met her." He looked up. "And that's when I met you."

Sarna paused. "I always did have great timing."

Royce chuckled. "You could say that."

Sarna waved the letter. "And now she's back?"

Royce eyed the paper in Sarna's hand. "Apparently so."

Sarna faced him. "You want to go talk to her?"

That surprised him. "I don't know. How would you feel about it?"

She hesitated and set her jaw. "Do you love her?"

Royce shook his head. "No," he said. "I don't love her."

Her shoulders relaxed. "What would you say?"

He thought about it. "I have to admit. I'm curious about what happened. And if she's okay."

"And what are you going to tell her if she wants to rekindle the romance?"

Royce squared his shoulders. "I'm going to tell her that our brief encounter was exactly that. Brief and over. What we had was exactly what we needed at the time. Nothing more and nothing less."

"She'll be okay with that?"

"She strikes me as a logical woman. I think she feels the same way. And if she doesn't, then I'll explain how I'm already taken."

Sarna walked up closer. "You better."

Royce reached out and put his arms around her. "You sure about this? If you don't want me to go, I'll understand."

She hugged him back. "No. You should go. Talk to her. See what she wants. Just make sure she knows that you're going on a trip, and you won't be back for a very long time. Make sure you tell her that."

Royce smiled. "I thought you weren't the jealous type."

She ran her hand up his chest. "I'm making an exception in your case."

He touched his forehead to hers. "I won't be gone long."

"I'll start packing for you. I found your suitcase." She pulled back. "You want me to pack anything special?"

"Just my clothes and amenities. I can get the rest when I'm back."

She nodded. They stared at each other, and Royce's belly flipped as his body parts warmed. He smiled when he saw her face redden in response. He leaned down and kissed her. The soft kiss made his body heat rise, and he heard her breathing deepen. The kiss turned passionate, and he pulled her close. Before he lost control, though, he retreated, catching his breath. "I better go because if I don't, I'll never make it over there."

"I'll pack fast," she said, pushing back a stray hair. "Maybe we can have some alone time before Gus shows up." She pressed up against him.

He moaned. "I like that idea." He kissed her again before stepping back. "You hold that thought."

"I will." She held his hand, but then let it go as he walked away. "Come back soon."

"I will. Maybe if I'm lucky, you'll be naked when I return."

"Only if you're lucky." She smiled. "But I'll see what I can do."

He grinned. "That's one way to ensure I don't take too long."

Her eyes narrowed. "Then I'll be waiting in your bed, with open arms...wearing only a smile."

Hands to his chest, he winked at her, turned, and left.

# Chapter Twenty-Six

ROYCE WALKED THROUGH THE woods toward Old Man McDermott's cabin. The cabin looked forlorn through the trees, like the only ship at dock. He made a note of the time. The sun was dipping lower in the sky, and the trees cast their shadows against the forest floor. They had waited at the hospital for staff to take Jasper down to the lobby and they'd stopped to eat on the way back. Royce had to have one last hamburger before he left. But he realized that darkness was fast approaching, so he would need to keep this conversation short. The image of Sarna naked in his bed made him quicken his pace.

Approaching the home, he could see the small garage that sat just down from the rocky driveway at the front of the cabin. It was closed, but parked next to it was a brown four-door sedan. He stared at the vehicle and sighed. She was here.

Before stepping up onto the porch, he pulled out the small pouch of Spirit powder Gus had given him. Before he'd left the house that morning, he'd rubbed some on his skin, knowing he would have a lot on his mind before talking with his family. He'd put the pouch in his pocket. Now, as he considered what he would tell Alice, he used some more. A little clarity and calm right now couldn't hurt. Putting the pouch away, he took a deep breath, walked up to the front door, and knocked. It was quiet for several seconds, but then he heard soft footfalls and the doorknob turned. The door opened slightly, and Royce could see one eye peer at him through the crack. It was Alice.

"Alice," he asked. "You okay?"

She watched him for a moment. "It's just you?"

"Yes," he said. "It's just me."

After a pause, her face disappeared, and the door opened. She stood sideways to him, and he stepped inside. He looked around. The cabin looked the same as when he had left it. Clean and quiet. He turned toward her. "You all right?"

She shut the door facing away from him. Looking her over, he saw she wore another shapeless dress and her hair was back in its long braid. "Alice?"

Finally, she turned, and he saw her. She still wore the locket with the intersecting hearts around her neck, but it was the bruise on her cheek that caught his eye. It was purple, and her eye was swollen.

"Hi Royce," she said.

He stepped forward. "What happened?"

She touched her face. "It's nothing. I'm fine."

That made him angry. "Did he do this to you?"

She shook her head. "I don't want to talk about it. That's not why I asked you here."

"You don't want to talk about it?" Royce dropped his jaw. "What happened after you left? Where did you go?"

She walked past him and into the kitchen. "I'm sorry I left like that. I had to get out of here. I'd stayed too long. I knew he was close." She opened the refrigerator and stared inside. "I went up to the next town. Found a hotel."

"I wish you would have at least said goodbye." He waited, but she didn't answer him. "How'd you get the bruise?"

Continuing to stare at the near empty fridge, she said, "I had a lot to think about after I left." She closed the door, but didn't turn around. "After I got to the hotel, I sat there staring at an empty room. I thought about you and me. About all the running I've done. About Joey."

"Joey? Is that his name?"

She placed her palm against the refrigerator. "Does it matter?"

Royce didn't know if it did or not. "And?"

"And I'd decided I was fed up. I had to do something."

"What?"

She turned then. "I went to the county store and bought something, using the one credit card I have left with my name on it. Made sure the grocer got a good look at me. Told him where I was staying."

Royce narrowed his eyes. "Why would you do that?"

Her fingers curled into fists. "Because I was angry, tired, humiliated. I needed to do something, say something, throw something...hurt something."

At the word "hurt," Royce felt a chill move through him. "Alice...what happened?"

"I–I–" She wrung her hands together. "There was something you didn't know. Something I didn't tell you. When you were here."

His heart beat faster. "What's that?"

Her jaw clenched and expelled a deep breath. "I had a gun."

"You what?"

"I had a gun. I kept it hidden."

"Where did you get a gun?"

She shook out her hands and paced around the kitchen. "I bought it from a man who had several in his trunk. Said it couldn't be traced. I don't have a license. But he gave me a quick lesson."

Royce feared where this story was going. "Alice, what did you do?"

She kept pacing, but didn't say anything.

"Alice?"

She murmured. "I waited for him. In the hotel."

Royce swallowed. "Did he find you?"

She chewed a nail and nodded her head. "He showed up. Took about a day. I was packed and ready. I didn't exactly know what I was doing. I mean,

I didn't have a plan. I wanted to talk to him, but I also knew he would get angry. I counted on that."

"Alice..." said Royce. He hated to ask his next question. "Did you kill him?"

Her face furrowed, and she gripped the locket that hung from her neck. "I wanted to."

Royce stood like a cement block in the room. What was he going to do if she said yes? Turn her in? "But did you?"

She paused. "He knocked on the door. Or should I say pounded. I didn't answer because I knew it would piss him off. I wanted everyone to hear him make a scene. Finally, after I let him yell my name a few times, I opened the door. He was furious, slammed the door shut, and pushed me back against the wall. After calling me all the colorful names he has for me, he finally calmed down enough to step back. I stood there, letting him vent. I didn't say a word."

Royce held his breath. "What happened then?"

"He told me to get my things and get in the car. We were going home." She clasped her hands. "I told him 'no.' That's when he hit me."

"Hell..."

"I went down, of course, which is what I expected. I knew he would get violent. Which is why I put the gun under the bed. It was in easy reach."

Royce began to think that maybe shooting the bastard wasn't such a bad idea. "Did you pick it up?"

"I did," she said, nodding. "I picked it up and pointed it at him."

Royce didn't move. "What did he do?"

Alice smiled softly. "He laughed at me." She stared at the floor. "The bastard laughed at me." She looked up and Royce saw the tears in her eyes. "Can you believe it?"

Royce could feel the pain radiate from her. "Are you surprised? He's an asshole. Didn't believe you would do it."

"I know," said Alice. Her face went still and took on the look of a confused child. "Which is why I shot him."

Fear slammed into Royce's stomach. "God, Alice..."

She started to ramble then. "I saw him fly backward. He hit the wall, went down. I was shaking, crying. I was so angry, so angry at him for everything. He took everything away from me. I hate him, Royce. I hate him." Tears streamed down her face and her nose ran.

Royce grabbed a chair from the dining table and pulled it over. "Sit down."

She stared at the chair blankly and then sank into it. "I shot him," she said, almost mumbling. "I shot him."

Royce grabbed his own chair and sat across from her. He tried to find the right words. "Alice?" She wrung her hands, but wouldn't make eye contact. "Alice, take some deep breaths. Just relax." His words seemed to penetrate. She took a deep breath, let it out, and swiped her eyes. Royce saw the paper towels, stood, and retrieved one. He handed it to her. "Take this. Blow your nose."

She acted automatically and did as he asked. "I'm sorry," she whispered.

"It's okay," he said. "Take your time." She nodded, and he waited for her to collect herself before he asked the inevitable question. "Alice...did you kill him?"

She made an uncomfortable chuckle and sniffed. "At the time, I didn't know. I panicked. Grabbed my suitcase. He was on the floor moaning, not unconscious, but there was a lot of blood. I was shaking so hard, I almost dropped the gun, but I put it back in my purse, grabbed my suitcase, got in my car, and left. I didn't call anybody. Not an ambulance or the police. I just left. I drove for a while. I didn't know where to go. Who to talk to. I slept in my car last night. I was too scared to go anywhere."

"So you came back here?"

"It's still rented until the end of this week. I figured I could come here, collect my thoughts, figure out what to do next."

"What about Joey?"

She dabbed at her eyes with the towel. "I called around this morning to area hospitals. I finally found him. He's alive. I shot him in the shoulder."

Royce released a relieved breath. "What about the police? What did he tell them?"

"I have no idea. I don't know if they're looking for me or not. I don't know what Joey will do. Feed me to the wolves, or steer them in another direction." She pulled at the paper towel. "It doesn't matter, though. Because I'm going to turn myself in." She looked at him through watery eyes. "I'm going to tell them the truth."

Royce held her gaze. A flurry of emotion fluttered through him. He admired her courage and strength. "Is that what you want to do?"

She stood. "What else can I do? I can't keep running. At least this way, I can call him out in court. Tell everyone who he is. Maybe I'll go to jail, maybe I won't. But if I'm going to go to jail, everyone is damn sure going to know why, no matter what story he tells." She leaned against the sink and crossed her arms.

"When do you plan on doing this?" asked Royce.

"Today." Her face was tear-stained, but she was much calmer. "I want to do it before he gets out of the hospital, and before this bruise fades. And before all the hotel witnesses become too hard to find."

Royce stood and walked over to her. "What do you think he'll do? Will he come after you again?"

She shrugged. "I don't know, and I don't care. I'm tired of running." She paused. "I wasn't sure you'd still be here when I came back."

Royce remembered telling her about his plans to leave. "Something came up. I ended up staying."

"I debated whether to contact you. I hate to get you involved, but after what happened between us, I didn't know who else to go to." She reached out and touched his chest.

His body warmed at her touch and the sensation surprised him. He thought of Sarna. "Alice..."

She sniffed and wiped her nose. "I'm really hoping, if you still want to help, that you'll come with me when I turn myself in." Her hand moved over his shirt. "This whole thing is pretty terrifying. Having someone there, especially you, will make it bearable."

Guilt washed over him. The thought of her confronting her accuser in a courtroom, or anywhere else, without someone standing by her side, made him feel sick. "Listen." He put his hand over hers to stop her from moving her fingers. "I don't think this is a good idea."

She stilled. "What's not a good idea?"

He searched for the words. "Us...this."

Her gaze held his. "You mean this?" she asked, and moved closer, sliding her hand down his midsection. He sucked in a breath and froze. "What about this?" She slid her fingers lower.

He jumped back. "Don't."

Her face fell. "What is it? I thought..."

He clenched his jaw as he tried to figure out how to explain. "Listen, Alice. This is the last thing you need. How is it going to look if you have to tell the police you met up with your lover after shooting your husband? It doesn't look good."

Her eyes widened. "But that shouldn't matter. You weren't there. You didn't do anything."

"But in a case like this, appearance is everything. If it looks like you've slept with other men while you were on the run, then people will lose sympathy with you. They'll suspect you have other motives."

"What other motives?" she asked. "And what other men? There's only you."

"It doesn't matter. Any good attorney can twist it to make it look sordid and suspicious. The best thing you can do is leave me behind. Don't even tell them about me."

Her jaw slackened. "Is that what you want?"

He raised a hand. "I want you to be in the best possible position when you talk to the police. Right now, you're an abused wife on the run from her husband, who shot him in self-defense. You introduce me, then suddenly, you're a married woman with a lover. Then the story becomes about me. They'll wonder if we worked together to kill Joey."

She gripped the kitchen counter. "Is that what you think? That's ridiculous. There is nothing that connects you to anything. No one will suspect you."

"It's not me I'm worried about. It's you."

She opened her mouth to speak, but then stopped. After a brief hesitation, she spoke. "I think I understand."

"Understand? What do you understand?" asked Royce.

Her face was solemn and her shoulders drooped. "You don't want me anymore."

"Alice, please...that's not what I meant."

Her features hardened. "Yes. It is. Look at you. You won't come near me. You're scared. Aren't you? You think I'm going to say something? To implicate you?"

He held up a palm. "All I am saying is that the best thing for you is to call your family. Tell them where you are. Tell them what happened. Let them be the ones who stand beside you. Not me."

Her face softened, and she hugged herself. "But I don't want them. I want you. I thought you wanted me too." She paused and her features fell. "Or was that all a lie?"

Royce tried to settle himself. He didn't expect to be caught up in yet another police investigation, or to be dealing with a break-up. "I didn't lie. At the time, I was caught up in the moment. And caught up in you. I want you to be happy. I want you to find peace. I thought maybe I could help you find it. But the fact is, you don't need me. You never did. We had a moment of escape that we both needed. You said it yourself in your note. The timing wasn't right for us." He hesitated. "And it still isn't."

She stood there, unmoving, and Royce felt the acute discomfort of having to wait for her response. After a second, he saw her blink and her eyes start to shine. "I see," she said.

"I'm sorry."

"Please don't say that. In my experience, most don't mean it."

Royce tried to think of what else to say to appease her, but his mind was blank. He had not prepared himself for this conversation. For some reason, he'd expected to check in on her, see that she was okay, wish her well, and leave. Now he realized his mistake. Obviously, she'd expected something far different.

A tear slipped down her cheek, and she wiped it away. "It's my fault. I'm the one who is sorry. Sorry I ever got involved."

"I didn't mean to hurt you.

She pushed a loose tendril of hair off her face. "You're right about the timing. It's awful. I'm running from a nightmare husband. Someone I almost killed. My life is a train wreck. I don't blame you for wanting out."

The guilt overwhelmed him. "Please understand."

She sniffed. "Understand what?"

He stepped closer. "You're dealing with a lot. I know you're scared. You don't know what's next. But you need your friends and family right now. You and I barely know each other. I'm not the one who should stand beside you in a moment like this. Isn't there someone you can call? Your mom? A sibling? A best friend?"

She dabbed her red eyes with the towel. "I...yes, there is."

"I'm sure they're worried about you."

She nodded. "They are."

"Then call them. Let them know you're all right. Let them help."

She squeezed her shoulders. "I'm a mess. I'm sorry I'm bothering you with all of this. You must think I'm crazier than Joey."

Feeling a little relief that maybe she could reach out to someone, he stepped close and hugged her. "I do not think you're crazy. You've just been through so much. You're probably exhausted and on top of that, Joey is still out there. It's okay to wig out a little."

Her arms went around him, and she dropped her forehead into the crook of his neck. "I don't know what to do."

He rubbed her arms. "First, you need to settle down. Try and relax. You're as tense as a board."

"I wish I could."

"When's the last time you slept?"

She rested her cheek against his chest and almost chuckled. "I can't remember." She gripped his shirt and looked up. "Well, except for when I was with you." Her hands moved over his lower back, and she sighed. "I know you think it's a bad idea, but maybe you could help with my stress." She pressed against him. "Take my mind off my troubles."

Royce let her go and stepped back, bumping against the kitchen counter. "I know that may sound nice, but it's better if we don't."

She reached out to touch him, but backed up against the counter, Royce couldn't move away. She touched his arm. "You sure? You don't want just one more for the road?"

Before he could react, she stepped close and leaned in to kiss him, but he caught her hand as it traveled behind his neck. "You're a beautiful woman, Alice," he said, "but I can't."

She stopped and studied him, and then she moved back. Her brow furrowed. "Wait a minute..."

"What?"

She stared pointedly at him. "Is there someone else?"

He debated his answer. Was there any point in lying? He nodded. "Yes. There is."

She waited, but said nothing.

Standing there, Royce felt awful. He knew how it looked. "It's recent. It just happened."

"Uh huh." Alice turned and faced the wall. "I guess I was just a temporary distraction...from your girlfriend."

Royce groaned. The conversation was going from bad to worse. "It's not like that."

Alice whirled on him. "Isn't it? You lied to me. You never wanted me."

"That's not true."

She glared at him. "Everything you said to me. You said it because you knew I needed to hear it, is that it? To get me into bed? To take advantage of the poor, vulnerable, abused girl, who just needs a little loving to make her all better?"

Royce pushed off the counter. "That's ridiculous. That's not what happened between us."

"Then what did happen?" She walked into the living room and shoved the chair out of the way. "Explain it, please, because I'd like to know."

Royce's anger erupted. "You took me in when I was sick. You cared for me, fed me, bathed me. We talked. I told you things I didn't expect to. I liked you and you liked me. You have problems. I have problems. It was perfect for us to come together. But it didn't mean anything more than that. You know it didn't."

She threw out her hands. "What about your girlfriend? You think it meant something to her?"

"I didn't know her yet," Royce yelled it out before he could stop himself.

"You didn't know her yet?" Alice did the calculation in her head. "Royce, that was only four days ago. You're telling me you met and fell for this woman since I last saw you?"

Royce tried to rein in his frustration. If he was in Alice's shoes, he didn't know if he'd buy it either. He tried to catch his breath. "Yes. That is what I'm telling you."

She snorted. "Well, then, I hope she knows what she's getting herself into. A no-good, lying, cheating, say-whatever-he-has-to jerk. I should have stayed with Joey. I think I'd rather take a punch to the face than deal with a two-timing asshole like you." She stormed out the back door and slammed it behind her. The cabin rocked with the force.

Royce stood woodenly in the kitchen. He didn't know how their conversation had dissolved into such ugly turmoil so quickly. Standing there, he debated with himself. Should he leave now, go back to Sarna, and disappear into the cosmos tonight, with things as they were? His first thought was yes. It was better for him to let Alice face her own demons. He couldn't help her, even if he wanted to. And if she thought the worst about him, then he would have to live with that. But before he could move, another thought entered his mind. One where he realized why Alice would think the worst. Considering her history, she probably had reason to suspect all men. And Royce had given her plenty of reasons to think he was lying. He knew his story was improbable. He should at least attempt to apologize again and tell her goodbye. If she wanted to hate him after that, then he could deal with it.

Making up his mind, he followed Alice through the back door and into the backyard. "Alice. Wait." He walked out onto the patio and froze.

Alice stood there, just a few feet away from the porch steps, frozen and terror-stricken. Not ten feet away, standing amidst the trees, was a brown bear. Judging by its size and massive jaws, it was the same one that had attacked Royce. At Royce's appearance, the bear swiveled his head toward him. Opening its mouth, it grunted and pawed the ground.

Royce didn't breathe. His mind raced. "Alice," he spoke in a mere whisper. "Don't move."

Alice was complying. Her hands shook, but she stood rooted to her spot. The bear chuffed and continued to paw at the ground, as if debating which of them to eat first.

Royce scrambled to think. What was up with this bear? Did he hold some sort of grudge? He looked around, trying to find anything that might be used as a weapon. All he saw were flowerpots and a wooden rocking chair. Royce continued to scan the area until his gaze stopped on a shovel propped against the patio railing.

"Stay still," he said, as he slowly stepped sideways to grab the shovel. The bear watched him move, and then, opening his enormous jaws, stood on its back legs and bellowed into the air.

The noise filled the forest, bouncing off the walls of the cabin and the bark of the trees. Alice screamed. Holding the shovel, Royce watched everything unfold at once. He wasn't sure who moved first—Alice or the bear, but Royce saw Alice run for the house and the bear react. The animal's huge haunches flexed in pursuit. Royce knew that in two quick lunges, the bear would be on her. He raised the shovel. Running off the porch, he stepped between Alice and the animal, swinging and aiming for its head. Alice ran by him and then the bear was there. His huge paw swung out and hit the shovel as Royce drove it forward. There was a loud slapping sound, and the shovel flew out of Royce's hand. Royce heard Alice scream again, but there was little he could do. The bear swiped at him again, and Royce felt the impact. Knocked backward, his body slammed into a beam that supported the deck. His head cracked against the hard wood, pain flared in his back, and he had a split second to think of Sarna before everything went dark.

# Chapter Twenty-Seven

JASPER WORKED FURIOUSLY in the ship's cockpit. It was a small, but efficient space, with all the instrumentation and equipment needed to fly a small crew. He sat at the main console, staring at the screens and studying the data as it appeared on the monitors. He'd been running diagnostics, ensuring the ship was ready for the long trip back. He'd prepped the suspension tubes. The trip through space would be taxing and long and sleeping through most of it was required. He'd been careful to ensure Royce's tube was properly calibrated. Being half-human, Royce would feel the effects of a suspension sleep more so than he or Sarna. And he wanted to make it as comfortable as possible.

He looked out the front window, seeing only trees. The sun was coming down, and the light was fading quickly. He made a mental calculation in his head, and considering what he had left to do, he figured he'd be able to leave in about an hour. Then he could head back to Royce's. He flipped a few switches and read the computer monitors situated within the console. Everything was reading within the normal range.

He smiled to himself as he thought about what it would be like to show up with Royce on Eudora. The thought of walking his half-brother into a Council meeting while everyone stared and wondered who the stranger was made Jasper grin. The time for change had finally come. He thought of what his dad's reaction might be. When Jasper had first learned that his father had another family on another planet, he'd felt hurt and betrayed. It had taken him a while to see his dad's side of things. But time had softened the anger and given Jasper the opportunity to think. He'd begun to see the implications. Roma was no longer the High Child. That changed everything.

He pushed a few buttons and typed some keys. Another thirty minutes passed as he continued his checks. The computers splayed numbers across their screens and all results were in the green. Jasper nodded, pleased at the progress.

As he sat back and admired his view, a buzzing alarm sounded from an adjacent computer. Jasper frowned, swiveled in the pilot's chair, and viewed the screen. When he'd first arrived on the ship, he'd done what Sarna had asked. He'd pulled up the camera footage that the ship had captured since their stay. He didn't have the time to sit and study the screen, so he'd programmed the computer to alarm whenever a larger object passed through the footage. It had triggered twice when a large bird had flown in front of the lens, so he'd increased the size parameters. The video had been running since Jasper had been on the ship. It had already completed its review of their first day here. It had caught some teenagers walking through the campgrounds late at night, but nothing of a woman walking alone or any violent crime. Bypassing that footage, Jasper had brought up the video of the day of his assault.

He recalled little about what had happened that day. All he remembered was that he'd been walking through the woods, angry. Thoughts of failure and betrayal had consumed him. They'd come all this way to meet his brother, and he'd been gravely disappointed. He'd been debating what to do, but couldn't find any answers. He'd been thinking about going home. How would he confront those he'd promised that change would happen? What would he tell them? What would he tell his dad?

Stomping down the trail, he'd paid no attention to his surroundings. There'd been a flare of pain in his head, and that's all he'd remembered until he woke up in a hospital, with ugly tubes inside him and bizarre machines surrounding him.

Staring at the computer, he shut down the alarm and pulled up the footage that had triggered it. Pushing a button, he scanned through the frames quickly, expecting to see a large animal. It would be the most likely reason the alarm would sound. He didn't think his attack had been close enough to trigger the camera.

He caught movement and depressed the button to go back, slow down, and re-scan the footage. Going slowly, he waited for the object that had triggered the alarm. He watched closely and stopped when a figure entered the frame. It was distant and grainy. Adjusting the video, he zoomed in on a person walking through the trees. It was definitely not an animal. Jasper looked closer and magnified the image even more. The image was pixelated, but it was clear enough to make out a face.

Jasper stared, his eyes focusing on the figure. His mind raced. He checked the time stamp. It was around the time his attack had occurred. He sucked in a breath. How could it be? It wasn't possible.

His mind sharpening, the implications became acutely clear. Realizing the danger, he thought of Royce and Sarna. He pushed back from the computer, flipped open a panel, and punched some keys. He didn't have a cell phone, but his ship's computer could act like one. He quickly dialed Royce's cell number and listened as it rang three times and went to voicemail. Cursing, he hung up and rang Royce's house phone. It rang several times, but no one picked up. He tried both phones again, but with no luck.

Frustrated, he slammed his palm on the console and stood. He took one last look at the footage, shaking his head. He grabbed his jacket, and, as darkness descended outside, ran out of the cockpit.

· · · • • · • • · ·

A bird cried overhead, and the noise felt like a drill in his ear. Royce cracked his eyes open, but then quickly closed them as a sharp crease of pain flared but then subsided. He moaned under his breath and slowly noticed his surroundings. Based on the aches and numbness in his joints, he knew he was lying on the hard ground. A cool breeze made him shiver. The shrill in his ears gave way to the soft sounds of the wind blowing through trees. He opened his eyes again, but this time managed to keep them open. His vision was blurred, and he blinked several times. Finally, he made out the shapes of the forest. A long ago fallen tree branch lay in front of him. Royce stared at it and, as his vision cleared, watched a lizard scamper over the bark and disappear beneath a blanket of leaves.

He blinked again and tried to move. Pain shot down his back and into his legs. He went still for a moment until the discomfort eased. Moving slowly, he pushed himself up, trying to recall what had hit him. Based on how he felt, he knew it must have been big. He managed to get his upper body up and he sat that way for a moment. He studied the area. For a few seconds, he had no idea where he was. Nothing was familiar. But, as he shook his head, everything came back at once. Pain flared once more as he recalled Alice, their conversation, and the bear. Alice. He was lying outside the porch of McDermott's cabin.

He looked around, searching. Everything was quiet. There was no bear, and more disturbingly, no Alice. Fear swept through Royce when he imagined the bear carrying her off, kicking and screaming. The thought forced Royce to move. Despite his body's protests, he got his legs beneath him and pushed himself upright. He swayed, but grabbed the porch rail to support his weight. His head throbbed, and he touched the back of his head, expecting to feel wet, sticky blood, but felt only a large lump the size of an egg.

The bear's attack flashed in his mind. The animal's paw had come down and knocked Royce backward. He must have been thrown against the porch beams and knocked out. What had happened after that? Where was Alice?

He rubbed his forehead, not sure if he'd been out fifteen minutes or fifteen hours, but seeing the sun's position and the lengthening shadows, he didn't think he'd been out for long. But it would be dark soon. He knew Sarna would be worried, and he needed to get back, but he had to find Alice. He scanned the woods behind the cabin but saw no signs of any violent attack. There was no blood trail or any indication that she'd been taken by the bear. Royce could see the animal's tracks in the dirt, but didn't see any other footprints. He looked at the back door of the house. Had she gone inside? Recalling their difficult conversation, he considered that she may have left, leaving him to the bear, too angry to care if he became prey. Taking slow, careful steps to ensure his balance, he climbed the steps to the porch.

"Alice," he called. His voice sounded strained and weak. He cleared his throat. "Alice?"

Gaining strength despite his stiffness, he pulled open the back door and went inside the cabin. It was unchanged. It was quiet and empty, with no sign of her. "Hello?" he asked with a stronger voice. "Alice?"

He walked through the house, but no one was there. The likelihood that she had left him to fend for himself grew. It was not something he would have expected from her, but maybe it was more than she was prepared to handle, considering all she'd been through. He stepped outside to the front of the house, which was just as quiet as the back. There was nothing but trees and the narrow, pebbled driveway that led to the main road. No bear, and no Alice. He eyed the one-car garage. Her brown sedan was not there. He sighed, realizing she was gone. Likely for good. The woods were quiet as he replayed their last words of anger. Thinking back, he regretted how he'd handled it. He should have offered to help. But now she was gone and back on her own to face Joey.

Royce stood there, prepared to leave, when he eyed the garage. It was closed, but the door was partially lifted from below. Thinking back, he recalled when he'd approached the cabin earlier that the door had been closed. Or had it?

Knowing he had to get home, he figured he would take one last look to make sure Alice was gone. It was probably pointless, but if he was about to leave this planet, then he had to ensure he'd done everything to help before he left. He didn't want to live with regrets.

Taking his steps slowly, he walked toward the small barn-like structure. His vision blurred for a moment, and he stilled. Blinking, he waited until it passed, then continued to walk. When he reached the door, he stooped and grabbed the handle, and pulled the door the rest of the way up. It slid along the track with some creaks and groans. Surprised, Royce blinked again when he saw a car.

It was a small blue SUV with tinted windows. He hadn't expected to see another vehicle. Where had it come from? He knew it was not Old Man McDermott's. Did Alice have another car? Confused, he frowned and considered closing the door and walking away. He didn't know who the car belonged to and why it was here was none of his business. But something didn't feel right. He knew in some way, it had to be connected to Alice, so he stepped around to the driver's side.

He studied the SUV. Maybe she'd acquired another car since he'd last seen her. But then why did she still have the brown sedan? And if this was her car, then where was she? The questions bounced around his head. It didn't make sense. He swiveled and looked back around the front yard and surrounding woods. "Alice," he yelled.

No one answered.

He looked back at the SUV as another idea occurred to him. Joey. Had she taken Joey's car after she'd shot him? But then, how did she have two cars? That thought made him stop. She wouldn't have two cars, unless...

His mind searched for answers. Had Alice told him everything? The only reason there would be a second car would be if...

He grimaced as an idea took shape. The only thing that made sense was that Joey had found her and followed her here, and they'd left together in Alice's car. But Joey was supposed to be in the hospital. Or was he?

Staring at the car, he noted the tinted windows, and froze when he saw a red drop of liquid on the garage floor. Feeling the twist of fear curdle his stomach and wishing he could walk away and never look back, he stepped closer and crouched beside the car. Looking at the drop, he confirmed his suspicions. It was blood, and it was fresh.

# Chapter Twenty-Eight

STARING AT THE DROPLET, a large lump formed in Royce's throat. He looked at the closed car door and had the worst possible thought. Alice said she'd had a gun. What if Joey had been here, confronted and overpowered her...and left alone? He stood in stunned silence as the idea gained traction. He told himself that he was overreacting. His mind was jumping to the worst possible scenarios. If anything, Alice and Joey had left together.

His heart thumping, he rose from his crouch and stepped closer to the car. He prayed he was wrong, but he had to look. Swallowing hard, he peered through the tinted window. The light was murkier the farther he went in, but there was still enough sunlight to see.

A slumped form lay across the seat. The sight made Royce buckle over and grab his knees. "No," he said. "No, no, no." Dizziness made him sway, and he dropped to all fours. He couldn't breathe, and he forced himself to suck in some air. His mind tried to make sense of what he'd seen. Alice was dead. It couldn't be true. Joey had found and killed her.

Royce cursed himself. How could he have been so stupid? He should have offered to help her. She'd been all alone, and she'd asked him for help, and he'd said no. There were any number of things he could have done. He could have gotten her out of there. Taken her to the police as she'd asked. But he'd pushed her away and made her feel alienated. She'd been ready to face her fears, and Royce had focused more on his own needs instead of hers, and now she was dead.

Royce moaned and gripped his head. He sat that way for several minutes, dreading what he would have to do. He would have to call Rick. Make sure her family was found and notified. He'd tell Rick what had happened and make sure that her bastard ex was punished. He thought about Sarna. Their trip would have to be delayed. There was no way around it. Royce had to ensure that Alice's killer was found.

Pulling himself together, he got his feet back under him. A wave of nausea hit him, and he fought the urge to vomit. Finding his footing, he made himself straighten and look back toward the driver's car window. Peering inside again, he saw the slumped form, but this time, he paid more attention.

Cautiously, Royce used his shirt to open the driver's door. Leaning in, he dropped his jaw in shock when he got a better look at the body. There was no shapeless dress or long braid. It wasn't a woman. It was a man, wearing dirty jeans and a leather jacket. Royce saw the man's face. He had long, stringy blonde hair and stubble shadowed his jaw. The stranger's lifeless eyes stared back, and Royce, horrified at what he was seeing, wondered what the hell was going on.

After a second of thought, Royce stopped cold. *Joey.* Long, stringy hair and stubble. Royce recalled Sheriff Rick describing the man in town and Sarna's description of the drifter who'd stopped at her and Jasper's campsite. The man who'd been looking for a blonde woman. Royce glanced back down at the dead man. Studying the scene, he saw the blood spatter on the dash, the pool of blood on the seat, and a gun lying on the floor on the passenger side. Royce finally understood.

It was Alice's husband who was dead in Alice's garage.

Stepping back and careful not to disrupt the scene, Royce quickly closed the car door without touching it, then stepped outside and pulled the garage door down, removing the fingerprints from the door handle.

He stood outside, just staring. He rubbed a hand over his face. "What have you done, Alice?" he muttered to himself. "Hell."

He tried to collect his thoughts. What exactly was his role now? Did he somehow have an obligation to this woman who'd just killed her husband? How would it look if he called the sheriff?

He quickly concluded that the best thing would be to leave. Right now. If Alice was on the run, then it was up to her whether to turn herself in. Not Royce. The bastard Joey probably deserved what he got, anyway. If Royce hung around and reported it, then there would be numerous questions. He'd never be able to leave without looking guilty. No. There were too many unknowns. Better for him to head out tonight, and when they did find the body, he'd be long gone.

He jogged back into the woods, leaving the house and Alice behind him. His head ached, but he was too caught up in the events of the day to care. He couldn't help but think of Alice and wonder where she was. Whatever she had gotten herself into, she would have to figure it out for herself. Royce had his own future to consider, and he was ready to embrace it, with Sarna by his side.

His cabin came into clear view, and he ran up to the front door. Breathless, he opened it and ran inside. "Sarna?"

The house was quiet, and there was no sign of her. Where was she? He had been hoping she'd be waiting for him as she had promised. All he wanted to do was fall into her arms and hold her. The bedroom was empty, though. A suitcase lay on the bed with his clothes in it and another suitcase sat closed on the floor.

Something cold twisted and crept up his spine. He'd been gone longer than he'd planned, and he'd half expected her to be pacing at the door.

"Sarna," he shouted. He headed toward the back bedroom, but stopped when he glanced toward the kitchen. There was a smear of dark liquid on the countertop. His breath caught when he saw several round droplets of red on the floor. Blood.

His heart thumped hard against his chest, and he rushed past the counter and stopped cold. Sarna lay unmoving on the floor, partially on her side, her hand clasped over her stomach. Blood oozed from between her fingers, and it dripped and pooled onto the tile.

Royce couldn't move. He was in complete shock. A few seconds passed where all he could do was stare, and then he dropped beside her. "Sarna." He pushed the hair off her face. "Oh, God. Sarna."

The outside world felt muffled to him, as if he was under water. With trembling fingers, he felt for a pulse, praying she was alive. A whoosh of air escaped him when he felt her heart beating. He moved up closer to her. The blood on the kitchen floor soaked into the knees of his jeans. "Sarna." He cupped her head in his hand. "Sarna. Can you hear me?" She didn't move. "God, what happened?" he asked himself. He could barely think. Who would do this?

She was pale, but her eyelids fluttered. He grabbed for his cell phone with a shaky hand but couldn't find it. He'd put it in his back pocket before he'd left to talk to Alice. It must have fallen out when he'd been attacked by the bear. "Damn it," he yelled. He started to stand to get to his house phone.

"Royce..." The word was meek and labored.

Royce looked to see her peering at him through slitted eyes. "Sarna." He rubbed her cheek with his fingers. "What happened? Who did this?"

She opened her mouth to speak, but coughed instead. She grimaced.

Royce could feel her waning energy. "Don't talk. I'm going to get some help." He wanted to get up to access the phone, but her voice stopped him.

"I'm sorry," she said. A moan escaped her, and he felt her curl against him.

"Don't move, honey," he said. "Shhh. It's okay. I'll get help."

She raised one of her blood covered hands and gripped Royce's wrist. Her breathing was labored. "I...didn't know. I'm sorry."

Royce shook with terror. What was happening? Who would want to hurt her? "Please," he said with agony, "don't die." He tried to pull away, but she held on. "I need to get help."

She moaned again and her eyes clenched shut, but then relaxed. "No help for me," she said in a whisper.

Royce shook his head. "No. Don't say that."

She blinked up at him and a tear trickled from her eye. "I'm...sorry."

"No." He leaned closer and lifted her head to ensure she heard him. "You listen to me. We did not come this far for you to die. You hear me? We have a destiny. The two of us, together. You fight. You fight to survive. Don't you dare leave me. You promised, remember? You promised to be by my side. I can't do this without you." He was shaking so hard, his voice was quivering.

Despite her pain, she seemed to almost smile. "Yes, you can." She closed her eyes, but then opened them again. "You...have to." She grimaced and her fingers gripped his arm, but she spoke again. "It's...your destiny...not mine." Squeezing his wrist, the blood squished between her fingers.

Royce wanted to scream, but he whispered. "Damn it. Stop being so melodramatic." He looked at the house phone. "We're going to get you to the hos—" Then it occurred to him. He looked at Sarna's wrist. "Where are your pills?"

"Hospital...can't help me," she said, as Royce gripped her hand that held him and turned it over. He clicked the compartment on the blood-stained watch she wore, and it opened. He dumped the pills into his shaky hand. There were six of them.

"Open your mouth," he said.

"Royce..."

He ignored her and grabbed her jaw and dropped the pills onto her tongue. "Let them dissolve."

She closed her mouth and watched him with watery eyes. Another wave of pain made her moan.

"Easy," he said. "Jasper. I've got to find Jasper."

He moved to stand, but a whimper from Sarna made him drop back beside her. Despite her need for medical help, he didn't want to leave her.

Her eyes closed, and she wrapped her hand back around his wrist, and the blood continued to pool on the floor. Royce pulled open a drawer and pulled out several dishtowels. He moved her other hand away and pushed the towels against her stomach. "Stay with me, honey." When she didn't respond, he spoke again. "Sarna?"

Her eyes cracked open. She spoke so quietly, Royce had to lean to hear. "I should...I...."

"Sarna," he said. "I have to get to the phone."

"Not safe." She whispered as her eyes blinked once slowly and then closed. The fingers she had wrapped around his wrist went slack.

"No," said Royce. The sheer terror that gripped him almost made him scream. "Sarna...no."

He released the pressure on the towels and reached for her. He felt for her pulse again and almost sobbed in relief when he felt a weak throb in her neck. But he knew he didn't have much time. He pushed up with reluctance, hating to leave her. The movement jostled her hand that he had pushed away from her belly. Her fingers, now unclenched, revealed a shiny, blood-stained object within them. Seeing it, Royce reached to take it from her. As he pulled it from her grasp, a long gold chain uncoiled from her palm. It was covered in blood.

Trembling, he stared at it, unable to comprehend what he was seeing. It was a locket, and wiping away the sticky liquid, he saw the shape of two intersecting hearts.

· · · · · · · · · ·

Jasper took the turn into Royce's driveway at an accelerated rate. The tires spun on the gravel but gained traction as Jasper drove down to Royce's cabin and hit the brakes. The truck slid to a stop, and Jasper killed the engine and jumped out of the vehicle. He sprinted into the house.

"Royce. Sarna." He was breathing hard and sweating. "Where are you?" He glanced toward the bedroom.

"Jasper."

Jasper turned toward the kitchen and saw Royce kneeling on the ground. The kitchen counter partially blocked his view, but he could see Royce's hands. They were covered in blood. One was gripping the side of the sink, leaving bloody streaks, and the other was clutching what appeared to be a necklace. All Jasper could see was a long chain dangling from Royce's palm.

Jasper ran over to Royce. Rounding the corner, he saw the pool of blood and Sarna. He gasped. Royce appeared to be in shock. His face was pale, and he seemed frozen in place.

"What happened?" Jasper dropped next to Sarna. He felt her pulse and observed her injuries. The amount of blood she'd lost was critical. "Royce?" he asked again. "Are you okay?" Jasper grabbed him by the shoulder and shook him. That seemed to snap Royce back to attention.

"We've got to get her to a hospital," said Royce. "I'll call an ambulance." Shaking his head, he made himself move, and he pushed off the counter and stood on unstable legs.

Jasper's quick assessment of Sarna told him that a hospital would not save her. "Royce, stop. That won't help."

Royce whirled. He grabbed Jasper by his shirt and yanked on it. "She won't make it, Jasper. She needs help. I can't let her die."

Jasper grabbed his brother's fist, which was curled into his shirt. "How did this happen?"

Royce went whiter. "We can deal with that later. We have to help her."

Jasper tried to think. Looking down at Sarna, he noted her pale features and sunken skin. Her condition was critical. Royce's fists were still in his shirt, and he reached up and pulled them off. "Let me look at her."

Royce glanced at his hands as if surprised he was holding Jasper, and let go. Jasper leaned down to check on Sarna. He lifted the bloody towels and bit his lip. It was bad. He leaned over her and took her pulse. He eyed Royce.

"I gave her the pills in her watch," said Royce.

"How many?"

"Six," said Royce, trying to catch his breath. "There were six."

Jasper raised his own hand. A watch similar to Sarna's sat on his wrist. He opened a compartment, popped out four pills, and dropped them into Sarna's mouth. "Your friend," he said, turning to Royce, "the one who healed me. Where is she?"

Royce's face changed from terror to hope. His jaw dropped. "My God. Yes. Sarah. Why didn't I think of that? Sarah can help her." He stood and ran for the phone.

"How far away is she?" asked Jasper.

Royce picked up the phone and appeared to think. "Three hours."

Jasper shook his head. "That's too long. She won't survive."

Royce's jaw clenched. "You don't know that."

"Look at her Royce. I say we have an hour, tops."

Royce slammed the phone down. "Damn it." He ran his trembling and bloody fingers through his hair. "We have to do something, Jasper. Please. We have to save her." He looked lost and was so pale it looked as if all of his own blood had been drained. "Please." He returned to Sarna, kneeled next to her, repositioned the bloody towels, and applied pressure. "She can't die." He shook his head. "I won't let her die."

Jasper watched in helpless despair. He thought about what he'd discovered and considered his options. "We have to get her back to the ship."

Royce swiveled his head toward Jasper. "What?"

"The ship," said Jasper. "It's the only hope she has. If I can get her back to Eudora, they can treat her."

"But you said she had less than an hour."

"There are suspension tubes on board. If I can get her in one, then she'll be held in a suspended state until I can get her to people who can treat her. She won't get better, but she won't get worse either. It's her only chance."

"They can treat her on Eudora?" asked Royce. "In time?"

"Yes," said Jasper. "There are others like your friend Sarah. I'll radio ahead. Tell them we're coming."

"But then they'll know where you've been."

"We don't have a choice. Pick her up. We have to go now."

Royce didn't hesitate. He stooped low and got his hands and arms under her. He lifted her with ease as he stood. Jasper ran out to the car and opened the passenger side. Royce sat in the seat with Sarna cradled in his lap.

Jasper jumped into the driver's side and started the car. The tires spun and gripped and the truck shot backward. Jasper reversed and slammed the accelerator. The car lurched forward and climbed the driveway.

Jasper looked sideways at Royce. He held Sarna tightly, with her head cradled into his neck. "Royce," he said. "Do you know who did this?"

Royce didn't act like he heard.

"Royce?" asked Jasper.

"That bitch..."

"What? Who?"

Royce mumbled something.

Jasper took a curve, and the tires squealed. "Royce, I can't hear you."

"Alice," Royce yelled. "She did this. She came after Sarna. She must have been jealous. I didn't know. I didn't think..." His forehead came down to Sarna's. "I'm so sorry."

"Who's Alice?" asked Jasper.

Royce scowled. "What the hell does it matter?"

"Tell me who Alice is," Jasper said. He had to get Royce to explain what had happened.

Royce groaned. "She's a woman I slept with. It was recent. Just before you got here. I told her I was with someone else. I thought she'd left. She didn't. She came after Sarna." He squinted his eyes shut. "Damn it. How could I be so stupid?"

Jasper didn't let up. "How do you know it was her?"

"Because Sarna had something in her hand that belonged to Alice."

"What? What did she have?

"Shit," said Royce. "What does it matter? Just get us to the ship."

"We're almost there."

The sun had descended, and Jasper was glad the darkness would help conceal them. The last thing they needed was someone watching two men carrying a bloodied, unconscious woman through the woods. He drove the car faster down the road. Nearing the small parking lot that accessed the trail to the Shady Point campgrounds, Jasper slowed and parked in a secluded spot, well hidden from the road. He looked around but saw no one.

"Royce," he said before getting out of the car. "Tell me how you know it was her. How do you know it was Alice?"

Royce growled at him. "Damn it, Jasper. I found her necklace, okay?" He held up a hand that still had the chain dangling from it. He opened his fingers and Jasper saw the locket. "It was Alice's. She wore it all the time. Sarna must have ripped it off when Alice attacked her."

Jasper stared at the necklace. "Royce..."

But Royce was already halfway out the door. "Come on, Jasper. We have to move. Where do we go?"

Jasper hesitated, but then jumped out of the car. He double-checked again for anyone who could be nearby, but there were no cars and no people. "This way," he said.

· · · • · • · • · ·

They dashed across the road. Royce held Sarna close and followed Jasper into the woods. He paid little attention to where they were going. He trusted Jasper was keeping an eye out for anyone or anything suspicious. Royce didn't see or sense anything. He was blind to everything but Sarna and getting her to safety. They walked for several minutes, passed the campgrounds, and went deeper into the trees. It was getting dark in the woods, but the rising moon provided some illumination. Finally, they came to a small clearing.

Breathless, Jasper stopped, and so did Royce.

"Where are we?" asked Royce. "Where's your ship?"

Jasper raised his watch. He depressed a button and there was a soft hissing sound. A small, silver, tubular craft suddenly materialized in front of them. Its metallic sheen glinted in the moonlight. Royce stared in wide-eyed silence. The forest went quiet also, as if it too were amazed by what sat invisible within it.

Jasper approached the ship, and a small door dropped open. Jasper looked back. "Wait here." A narrow ramp slid down, and Jasper walked up and disappeared into the vehicle.

Royce held Sarna tightly and tried to keep her warm as the Earth's heat dissipated into the night. Slowly, the frogs began to croak again and the crickets chirped. He heard a soft moan and looked down to see Sarna's eyes were partially open. "Sarna?" She peered up at him. "Don't move. We're going to get you home. They'll take care of you." She moaned. "Shhh. Be still."

He heard footsteps on metal and saw Jasper walking down the ramp. Next to him was a padded table with no legs that moved beside him. With no means of support, it appeared to be floating. Jasper walked up to Royce. "Put her down on it."

Royce stared at the floating object. Jasper patted the cushioned surface. "Don't worry. It will support her."

Royce did as Jasper asked and laid Sarna down on the table. She whimpered, and he held her hand as a blanket emerged from the bottom of the device and traveled up and over her, covering her up to her neck. "Take her inside," said Jasper, and the floating bed moved on its own, traveling back up the ramp with Sarna in tow.

Royce started to follow.

"Royce, wait," said Jasper.

Royce startled and stopped. The device carrying Sarna disappeared into the ship. "What, Jasper? I need to be sure she's okay."

Jasper walked up to him. "The ship's computer will assess and treat her, then prep her for suspension. That will take a few minutes, then you can see her. But first you need to know something."

Royce fidgeted. "What's there to know? Some jealous girlfriend tries to kill the woman I..." He froze. "I'm responsible for this." He looked back at the empty ramp. "Some leader, huh?"

"This is not your fault."

Royce shook his head in frustration. "We don't have time to argue. Sarna doesn't have time." He walked toward the ship.

"Wait," said Jasper.

Royce grunted and threw out his hands. "Damn it, Jasper. What is it?"

"Show me that locket."

Royce held out the bloody necklace. "What for?"

"You need to see something."

Royce stared at the red-spattered chain. He thought of Alice. Things had happened so fast, he hadn't stopped to think. Where was she? He couldn't let her get away with what she'd done. But what could he do? Report a crime when he was about to leave the planet? And what about him? He'd left without seeing Gus or signing the power of attorney over to Gillian. He'd even left his suitcase behind. Royce rubbed his face. What the hell was he doing? Could he leave like this? But if he didn't, Sarna would not survive.

"Royce…"

Jasper's voice startled him, and he felt all his strain and tension burst out of him. "What is your problem? Why do you give a shit, anyway? You just want to make me feel worse?"

Jasper grasped his hand and pulled the necklace out of it. "Exactly the opposite." He gripped the sticky locket and popped the lid open. "This is what I'm trying to tell you."

Looking inside the small compartment, Royce's eyes widened in stunned silence. He moved closer to look. He eyed Jasper in confusion.

"It's exactly what you think it is," said Jasper.

Royce stared again. Inside the locket were several tiny white pills.

# Chapter Twenty-Nine

ROYCE BLINKED. "Is that?"

"Yes," said Jasper.

Royce tried to focus. "But...but that would mean..."

"Yes, it would."

Royce shook his head. "She's one of you?"

Jasper nodded. "She's one of us. She's a Red-Line."

"What?" Royce looked again at the white pills, as if they might evaporate at any moment. "I don't understand."

"Her name is Desde. Not Alice." Jasper waited, but Royce didn't know what to say. "Is she pretty, with blue eyes and long blonde hair?"

Mute, Royce nodded.

"She's from Eudora. I saw her on the ship's cameras. She was walking through the forest the night of my attack. She is the one who knocked me out and almost killed me. Maybe wanted to kill me."

Royce shook his head again. "But, I don't understand. Why is she here? What does she want?"

Jasper closed the locket. "Desde is the daughter of a former Council member. He died last year in an accident. He was a good man, but easily swayed and manipulated by his wife, Melda. Melda is," he paused, "an unpleasant woman. She enjoyed the privileges that came with being a Councilman's wife. But with her husband dead, those privileges disappeared. Desde's father was not a smart man. He'd made no arrangements concerning his death, and there were no extra funds to support his wife and child. Melda and Desde had to move out of their nice home. Friends disappeared, and the invitations dried up."

Royce squeezed his eyes shut and opened them. His head was throbbing. "But that doesn't explain why Alice, or Desde, is here."

"Yes, it does. Desde is like her mother. Cunning and manipulative. She liked the prestige of being a Councilman's daughter. When that disappeared, she and her mother must have plotted a way to get it back."

"But what does that have to do with me?"

"You're the High Child, Royce. Think about it."

Royce's mind was too clouded to think. All he wanted to do was get Sarna to safety, but he had to know what was going on. "I don't understand. How would she even know that? I thought it was a secret."

Jasper stared at the ship, thinking. "My guess is Melda. That woman has her hands and ears everywhere. I wouldn't be the least bit surprised if Galen said something to her. There were suspicions that the two of them were too friendly, perhaps even having an affair. It would be like him to connive with someone else."

Royce clenched his fingers. "What are you saying, Jasper?"

Jasper hesitated. "Desde knows who you are. What better way to regain the graces of the Council than to show up pregnant with the High Child's baby?"

Royce dropped his jaw. "Pregnant?"

Jasper nodded. "She would be carrying the next High Child."

Royce stared open-mouthed. "Pregnant?"

"Yes, Royce," said Jasper. "Pregnant."

Royce thought back. "But she said..."

"I would consider anything she said to be lies. All lies. She got you in a state where you felt vulnerable, Binded with you, and..."

"Wait. What? Binded with me?" asked Royce. "I didn't Bind with her."

"Did you sleep with her?"

"Yes, but..."

"Were you together for at least twenty-four hours?"

Royce thought about it. "Yes."

"Did you have feelings for her? Did you care for her?"

Royce wanted to slink into the ground. "Yes. At the time, I did."

"Then I've got news for you," said Jasper. "You Binded with her. Or she Binded with you. And a Binding typically results in pregnancy."

Royce remembered his time with Alice and recoiled. "But I didn't say I was Binding with her."

"You don't have to," said Jasper. "It's the female who's got the control in these situations. And it's not about the words so much, it's the feelings."

Royce opened his mouth, but nothing came out.

Jasper bobbed his head toward the ship. "That's why she came after Sarna."

That snapped Royce back to attention. "Why would she come after her?"

"Because, the forty-eight to seventy-two hours after a Binding are critical to the health of the baby, and sometimes the mother. Any sort of disruption or dishevel in energy can lead to a miscarriage. Desde had to be sure her pregnancy didn't end."

"But she left," said Royce, "after our time together. She left. Wouldn't that be a disruption?"

"I suspect she didn't go far. Distance can be a factor too. She may have told you she was gone, but she probably didn't stray." He grunted. "That's probably why she came after me. She realized I was here and probably surmised why. She knew I would recognize her, and she couldn't take the risk of being discovered."

Royce thought about the timeline. "But after the forty-eight hours, why not go home? Why did she stay?"

Jasper shrugged. "She may have been preparing to leave, but my presence probably alerted her. After taking care of me, she must have gotten curious.

If she returned to watch you, then she would have seen Sarna. Then she knew she had a problem."

"But why?" asked Royce. "What did Sarna do?"

The side of Jasper's mouth raised. "Are you kidding?"

"No, I'm not," said Royce.

"The two of you. You were attracted to each other. You took the time I needed to recuperate to...as you said...get to know each other better."

"So?"

"So there's no bigger threat to a Binding pregnancy than another woman showing up. Especially if the father falls for that woman. If the flow of energy is disrupted from father to mother, then the pregnancy will end."

Royce gripped his forehead. "My God."

"Desde knew if you Binded with Sarna, then she would likely miscarry. Her sole plan is to go back to Eudora and tell everyone that she's carrying your child. Sarna's arrival threatened that."

"But who would believe her?" asked Royce. "Why would anyone trust that she's carrying my child if they don't even know I exist?"

A wolf howled in the distance. The sun was down and the nocturnal creatures were stirring. "It would be shocking at first, but Melda is smart. She knows our father. Knows he would not deny his grandchild, or you. If it came out, he would not deny your existence. It would ruin him politically. But the Council would not be able to ignore who you are or who your child is. Roma would take over and one day, your child would take his or her place as High Leader. But until then, the Council would be forced to take care of Desde, and thus Melda too. They would return to the stature and lifestyle to which they'd become accustomed. That's been their plan all along."

Royce was stunned. He recalled the day he'd met Alice. He'd never had an inkling of warning. All that time she'd been playing him, using him, to get what she'd wanted. And when it was threatened, she'd come after Sarna. He thought of Sarna, lying injured in the ship, and cursed himself.

"There's no point in doing that," said Jasper, picking up on Royce's thoughts. "There's no way you could have known. Desde is a powerful female Red-Line. Cloaking her thoughts and intentions comes easily to her. She's learned it from her mother."

Royce considered something. "But Sarna and I didn't Bind."

Jasper stared at him.

"We didn't," said Royce. "We told each other..."

"It's not about words, Royce."

Royce stared at the ship. He swallowed. He knew Jasper was right. "Then is she? Is Sarna pregnant?" He looked back at Jasper.

Jasper's face fell. "She may have been, if your Binding was complete, but after this? It's unlikely." He sighed. "It would be hard to sustain a pregnancy after this."

Royce nodded numbly. A swell of emotion overcame him, and he pushed it back. "You're saying Desde is still pregnant with my child?"

"Since she came after Sarna, she must be," said Jasper. He held up the necklace. "But not for long."

Royce stared at the locket. "What do you mean?"

"Like I said, this is a delicate time for her. She may still be pregnant, but the harshness of this environment is just as difficult for her as it is for us. Without these pills, she will probably lose the baby. Maybe even get sick herself."

"What if she has more on her ship?"

"Considering how long she's already been here, I'd say her supply is running low. These pills are scarce. Even Sarna and I have a limited amount. And pregnancy would only up the required dosage." He stared at the locket. "No. I'm sure Miss Desde is a little panicked right now, wondering where her pills are." He smiled.

An image of Alice...or Desde...frantic and desperate, appeared in Royce's mind. He saw her searching, wondering what had happened to her necklace. But then he realized what she would do. In his mind, he saw her face twisting as understanding dawned. She would return to his cabin, looking for the locket. And then...

A cold flicker of fear sliced through Royce. "I have to go back."

Jasper's smile evaporated. "What? No, you don't. We have to leave."

"I can't," said Royce. He stared at the ship. "I have to go back."

"Royce..."

Royce pulled the necklace out of Jasper's hand. "She'll come back Jasper."

"So what?" asked Jasper. "She'll come back to an empty house. You'll be gone. She'll have lost. Her pregnancy will end. She may not even get home alive."

Royce's skin prickled. "That's the point, Jasper. Gus is coming over. He'll run right into her. She'll be angry. Pissed." He stopped as he thought about it, the images growing more gruesome in his head. "She'll kill him."

"You don't know that," said Jasper.

"Yes. I do." He thought of his family. "And it won't stop there. She'll want revenge. She'll want to hurt me, take from me, the way I took from her."

"But you didn't take anything from her," said Jasper, his voice rising.

"She won't see it like that. She knows how to strike back. If she can do what she did to Sarna to save herself, then she is certainly capable of hurting Gus. Or Gillian. Or Eve." He squeezed the locket in his hand. "I have to go back."

Jasper groaned. "Royce, you don't know if that will stop her."

Royce held his brother's gaze, willing him to understand. "It will. I know what she wants." He held up the necklace. "She wants this. And I'm going to give it to her."

"After her attack on Sarna, she may not even be pregnant anymore. And if that's the case, it won't matter."

Royce stilled. "If she isn't, then all the more reason to find her and stop her before she gets to my place and finds Gus. Or worse, goes after my sisters."

Jasper shook his head. "I doubt she'll live long enough to hurt your family."

"You can't be sure of that. If she's determined, she'll find a way."

The moonlight shone on Jasper's paling face. "Royce. Listen. We can't stay. I have to get Sarna back. I can't suspend her until we get into space. We have to go now."

Royce went cold, but he knew what he had to do. "Then you have to go without me."

Jasper's face dropped. "We may not have another chance like this again."

Royce nodded, feeling his chest constrict. So much was happening that he didn't have the luxury of time to explain his thoughts and emotions. He did his best to muster how he felt and send it to Jasper energetically. Jasper's posture softened. "I know," said Royce. "I'm sorry. But I cannot leave my family at the mercy of Desde's rage. I won't do it."

Jasper started to speak, but no words came. He shut his mouth and clenched his jaw.

"Tell Dad I'm sorry. If things were different..." He paused and his throat wanted to close. "If you get a chance to return..."

Jasper closed his eyes tightly and then opened them. "I can't promise that. Once they realized what we've done...and if Roma takes over, she'll do everything in her power to keep us on Eudora and you here. Especially if Desde returns pregnant."

Royce understood. The swell of emotion grew. "I understand. But I won't sacrifice Sarna by making you stay, and neither would you." He waited as Jasper studied the ground. "There will be another chance. At some point, you will return. One day."

Jasper met his gaze. "You're sure about this? What if we call the sheriff? Have him check on Gus?"

Royce shook his head. "Won't work. Sarna would hurt him too. She won't stop until she gets what she wants. Her baby, or revenge."

Jasper groaned. "Can you call Gus? Stop him from going? You could call your sisters? Tell them what's happening?"

"There's a saying," said Royce. "'Hell hath no fury than that of a woman scorned.'" Jasper pursed his lips. "Even if I could reach them, it wouldn't matter. If I left Earth, Desde would spend her few remaining days here going after everyone I hold dear. She'll make me pay."

"Or she might just hop on her ship and go home."

"You think she'd go back to a planet with no baby, with me there to tell everyone what she did?"

Jasper stood stony in the dark. "Shit."

Royce almost smiled. "You're getting better with our language."

Jasper threw his hands on his hips. "How about damn it, fuck, and hell? I think that covers how I feel right now."

Royce agreed. He felt like a child who'd just been told there would be no presents for Christmas. "Me too Jasper. Me too." He glanced at the ship, feeling the weight of what he had to do next. "I need to see Sarna."

Jasper rubbed his temples. "Up the ramp, to the left."

Royce wished he could say something positive, but nothing came to mind. He turned toward the ship and walked up the short, metallic entryway. His footsteps made soft clangs as he walked onto the small craft. It was narrow inside and sparse. He entered a small circular room with two metal chairs and a table attached to the floor. A quick glimpse to the right appeared to show the bridge or cockpit. Royce didn't know what to call it. But he could see a window, a convoluted instrument panel, and a pilot's chair. He looked to his left and saw a short corridor. Various items that looked like tools were secured to the walls. He headed down and found himself in a small room with three tubular beds. Each with a panel above it. They looked like three clear, round caskets, with comfortable bedding inside each. Sarna was in one of them.

A blanket covered her, and she looked almost serene. The blood that had been smeared on her face from Royce's fingers had been cleaned off. He walked up and sat beside her. Reaching beneath the covers, he took her hand.

The motion alerted her, and her eyes parted slightly. She blinked a few times. "Hey," she whispered.

Royce leaned lower to hear and talk to her. "Hey, yourself."

Taking a deep breath, her face scrunched in pain. "You okay?"

He brushed a strand of her hair. "I don't think either of us is doing too great."

She squeezed his fingers. "I'm sorry." Her eyes welled up. "I didn't..." She moaned and shifted in the bed. Her eyes widened. "It's...her. Be...careful."

"Easy," said Royce. "Take it easy." He stroked her cheek. "I know. Don't worry."

"She...she..." The brief flare of energy waned, and she settled back.

Wanting to scream, Royce stayed calm and didn't let his face reveal his anger. "Relax. I'm safe. It's you I'm worried about."

She let out a slow breath and mumbled. She blinked heavy lids. "The ship...wanted to give me pain killers..."

He grimaced. "You should take them. I don't want you to hurt." He rubbed his thumb over her jaw and thought of the stone he wore. He instantly reached for it and pulled it off. "Here." He carefully placed it over her head and slid the stone beneath her shirt. "You wear this. It will help protect you."

"No," she said meekly. "It's from your dad."

"You can return it. After you're well." He took her hand again and touched her face. "Now rest."

She blinked again as she tried to stay conscious. "Wanted to talk...see you..."

Royce spoke over the lump in his throat. "You've seen enough of me. Stop being so stubborn."

She made a soft grunt. "I'll never...be able...to see enough of you."

Royce felt tears well, and he sucked in a shaky breath. "Me too," he said. "I dream of waking up next to you every day." He took in her soft brown eyes and pale lips. The thought of Alice hurting her almost made it hard to speak. "I'm so sorry, Sarna. I didn't know."

She made a quiet moan. "Not your fault." Her voice was so quiet Royce could barely hear her.

Royce wished he could take the minutes he needed to explain, but he knew she didn't have the time and neither did he.

"Sarna..."

"I lied to you," she said.

He raised a brow. "What?"

She gently nodded. "I..." Her eyes drifted shut.

"Sarna..." Royce leaned lower. "Sarna, please..." He shook with sadness and fear. He wanted so desperately to talk to her in their last remaining moments together, but knew she didn't have the strength. "I can't..." He couldn't stand to tell her he was staying behind.

She opened her eyes in a show of strength, as if she also fought to spend as much time with him as she could. "I Binded with you." The words came out in a rush and a tear slid down the side of her face.

He blinked back his own tears, and he swallowed hard. "I know, baby. I know." He leaned forward and touched his forehead to hers. "I Binded with you too." He paused to collect himself. "The moment you started bitching about eating meat."

She made a small noise, as if she were laughing. "I'm not giving up...on you. One day you'll crave...apples and nuts."

Royce smiled and lifted his head. Another tear spilled from her eye, and he wiped it away with a trembling finger. He cleared his throat. "No matter what happens, Sarna, I want you to know that I love you, and I always will."

Her eyes began to drift, and he knew she was fighting to stay awake. A small breath escaped her. "I love you too, Royce Fletcher," she said. "Forever."

One of his own tears fell, and he watched her lids closed. A fierce pain ripped through him and, out of sheer terror, he felt her wrist. A weak but steady pulse beat there, but he knew Jasper had to get her away and into suspension fast.

Wiping at his eyes, he pulled himself together. "Jasper," he yelled. He stood and sent out a silent goodbye, let go of her hand, and put it back under the covers.

Jasper appeared at the room's entrance.

"You have to go," said Royce, standing. "Now."

Jasper stood quietly as Royce walked up to him. "You're sure about this?"

Royce didn't take the time to think. "I am." He stepped around Jasper and headed toward the exit.

"Royce..."

Royce reached the edge of the ramp leading down to the ground. "I'm not changing my mind. I can't leave with you."

Jasper walked up to him. "You don't know that Desde will do any of this."

Royce turned. "Yes, I do. I can feel it. I have to assume that she's still carrying the baby. Now that I know who she is, I can see her for what she is. Conniving and cruel. She won't stop until her pregnancy is secure. I have to make sure she leaves this planet."

"How are you going to do that?"

"I'll give her what she wants. The locket. Once she has that, she has no reason to stay, and no reason to hurt me or my family."

"You want her to carry your child?"

Royce gripped at a piece of metal on the craft. "There's nothing I can do about that right now. I'll have to leave that up to fate. But what I can do is protect the ones I love."

"But what about Sarna? You love her too."

Royce's stomach churned. "I do. Very much." He let go of the metal and clasped Jasper's upper arm. "But I'm counting on you to take care of her. To keep her alive. I need you to do that for me." He squeezed his brother's shoulder. "And if Desde makes it back to your planet, pregnant or not, you'll still have to protect Sarna." Jasper's eyes rounded. "Please."

Jasper looked almost as desperate as Royce felt. After a few seconds, he finally spoke. "You know I will."

"Thank you." Royce waited, knowing what else he wanted to say. "I'm glad you came here, Jasper. I know I was a pain in the ass, but I'm glad I met you."

Jasper's face remained unchanged, but a quiver in his clenched jaw told Royce everything.

"Tell Dad," Royce paused. He wasn't sure what to tell him. "Tell him his Earth family misses him. And we love him."

Jasper nodded, his own jaw clenched. "There's something you need to know."

Royce couldn't imagine there was more. "What?"

Jasper swallowed. "It's Dad. There's another reason his reign is threatened."

Royce felt a cold lump in his chest. He didn't know how much more he could take. "What's that?"

"I didn't want to tell you before. I didn't want it to sound like I was manipulating you."

The lump grew. "What is it?"

Jasper bit his lip before he spoke. "Dad's sick. We don't know what it is. He's been getting weaker over the last few months. No one's been able to help or figure out what the problem is. He's been trying to hide it, but the Council suspects something is wrong. It's why we fear a vote will come soon to end his rule."

Royce stood like a dead tree. Dealing with losing Sarna was bad enough, but this was excruciating. The tears threatened to come again, and he forced out his next words. "Why didn't you tell me this sooner?"

"You know how it would have looked. I tell you Dad is sick, and then ask you to leave with us? It puts you in a terrible position. I wanted you to come because it was your choice to do so. Not because of guilt."

Royce felt his throat swell. He stared at the ground. "Okay." It was all he could say.

"I'm sorry. I hate to have to tell you this way."

Royce could only nod. A few seconds passed, and he raised his head. He took a deep breath and released it, but the weight on his chest remained. "I wish..."

"You wish what?"

He forced out the words. "I could be there."

Jasper nodded, his face wooden. "Me too."

Royce said the only thing he could think of. "Take care of him. Tell him if things were different..." He couldn't continue. After a few seconds, the pressure eased. "Just tell him I love him."

Jasper spoke softly, his own voice shaky. "I will." The words sounded stunted. "Royce..."

"What?"

Jasper's shoulders dropped. "I was a pain in the ass, too."

Royce half-smiled. "I know."

"Please be careful. Desde is dangerous."

Royce stiffened. He directed his mind back to his current situation. It was the only way for him to think straight. "I can be dangerous, too. Especially in the mood I'm in."

"She can sense things, so cloak yourself."

Royce thought about his encounter with the bear. "She'll be lucky if she can see me standing in front of her."

Jasper paused and cleared his throat. "If you can get her off the planet, then you should be safe. She won't be able to return. These ships only carry so much fuel. And she won't have enough pills. She'll have to go home. And if she does that, baby or no baby, I'll make sure she never finds a way off the planet again."

Royce grunted. "I'd appreciate that."

"You have my word."

"Thank you."

Jasper nodded. "I hope one day..."

Royce could see a glint of shine in his eyes. Royce knew what he wanted to say. That one day they would see each other again. "Me too Jasper. Me too."

Jasper held out a hand, and Royce took it. They shook. Before they could part, though, Royce pulled Jasper in and wrapped his free hand around him. He spoke into his ear. "You be careful."

Jasper went still for a moment, but then Royce felt Jasper's arm on his back. "You too, brother," he said in return.

The swell of emotion Royce had been trying to control suddenly reached tidal wave proportions, and Royce pulled back. Jasper turned quickly, as if feeling the same thing, and Royce watched him walk into the front of the ship. Royce let out a deep breath, took a last look around, turned, and walked down the ramp.

As soon as his feet hit the Earth, the ramp lifted. A soft, wooshing sound emanated from the craft, and the nearby trees and blades of grass shook. Slowly, but almost silently, the ship lifted. Royce felt the rush of air in his face diminish as the narrow vehicle rose higher and higher in the night sky. Then, as fast as the blink of an eye, there was a brief popping sound, the air vibrated, and then it was gone.

Royce stared at the stars. The trees swayed and the frogs and crickets resumed their croaks and chirps. Staring upward, the emotions of loss, regret, and anger overcame him. Royce sank to his knees. He thought of his father and wondered if he would ever see him again. He thought of Alice and how she'd manipulated and lied to him. And he thought of Sarna and how he'd grown to love her strong opinions, their disagreements, and her beautiful face. But now, she and Jasper were gone, and Alice was still here, threatening everything he held dear, while at the same time, taking from him the one woman he loved.

Royce sank back on his heels, stared up at the moon, and summoning all of his pent-up anguish, fear, and fury, bent his head back and bellowed.

# Chapter Thirty

GUS PULLED INTO ROYCE's driveway and parked. He didn't see Royce's car, but figured his friend would return soon. He opened his truck door and stepped out. It was a beautiful night, and he took a moment to admire the glittering stars and crescent moon. Mother Earth was showing off tonight, he thought.

Normally, he would have walked to Royce's cabin on a night like this. His home was only a couple of miles away, but he'd already had a busy day helping to track a neighbor's lost horse. It had been spooked by a snake and galloped away. The neighbor's daughter was distraught, and her parents had called Gus. Most of the people who lived in the area knew about Gus and his tracking skills. It had taken a couple of hours, but Gus had followed the animal to the lake, where he'd found the skittish horse drinking water.

Now standing outside Royce's cabin, he thought about why he was here. Royce had told him he'd made a decision, and he needed to see Gus. Gus suspected he knew the answer. He also suspected it involved Royce's two visitors. He leaned back against his truck, still staring up at the sky. He was going to miss his friend.

After a moment, he pushed off the truck and headed for the house. He didn't wear a watch, but he had a good inner clock. He would wait inside until his friend arrived. Walking up to the cabin, he stopped at the threshold. The front door was open. Something tingled through him. Starman would not leave his door open if he wasn't home.

He took a moment to connect with his surroundings. He felt for anything out of place. Perhaps someone else was here? The house was dark and silent, but it didn't take a medicine man to know something was amiss. Gus walked up to the doorway. He peered inside but saw no one and nothing. "Royce?" he called. There was only quiet.

He took a step inside, reached around to the wall, and flipped on the lights. The interior illuminated. Gus saw the small living area, the breakfast table, the kitchen... He stopped at the kitchen. There were bloody handprints on the sink and countertop. Leaning to get a better view, he saw blood smeared on the tile. Moving farther into the house and past the kitchen counter, he sucked in a breath at what he saw. A large pool of blood. All over the floor.

"Great Spirit," he said. He looked around. "Royce?" he asked again. There was no answer. He spied the phone on the wall. His mind raced to pull up the sheriff's number from memory.

Careful not to touch anything, he walked over and grabbed the phone. Recalling the number, he dialed, but heard no dial tone. He tried again with no success. Hanging up, he groaned, but remembered the cell phone in his car. Gus had reluctantly embraced technology over the years. He still preferred the old ways of someone calling his house phone, or dropping by if they wanted to reach him. Although he had a cell, he used it mainly for emergencies, and he figured this situation fit the bill. Turning to exit, he stopped when he saw a woman standing at the entry.

Gus opened his mouth to ask for help, but something about her made shivers pop out on his skin. The shivers turned to icy chills when he recognized her.

Gus stepped back as she strolled into the house. "Hello, Gus," she said. She closed the door behind her. "Waiting for someone?"

Gus didn't know what to say. Alice stood in front of him, but this was not the same woman he'd met a few days earlier.

"I'm waiting too," she said. She scanned the room and her eyes stopped at the blood-smeared, but empty, kitchen. She smiled and crossed her arms. "Why don't we wait together?"

· · · · · · · · · ·

Several seconds passed as Royce's scream reverberated through the trees. Breathing hard, he sat numb, wondering what in the hell had happened over this past week. How he had gone from a quiet existence into a living hell?

Shaking his head, he didn't ponder for long. The thought of Desde going to his place, looking for the locket, and finding Gus instead spurred him into action. He jumped up and headed back into the forest. He ran fast down the trail and passed the campgrounds, but spotting a small stream, he stopped and dropped beside it. Sarna's blood covered him. It was on his hands, jeans, and Desde's locket. And his shirt was red with it after he'd carried her through the woods. He wanted it off. All of it. The thought of confronting Alice, or Desde, while stained with it, sickened him.

He cleaned the necklace, his skin, and did his best to rinse the sticky liquid from his clothing. It was dark, but the moon was out, and he felt confident he'd removed most of it, although his shirt was stained pink. His clothes wet, he shivered in the night air, but he didn't care. It would help to keep him focused.

The blood removed, he sat back. But even though his clothes were clean, he was still a mess. His mind was in disarray, and his emotions were in turmoil. He had to calm down, or he would be no good to anyone. Taking slow, deep breaths, he tried to settle himself. He had to think clearly in order to deal with Desde. Still holding the locket, he dropped it into his pocket and felt something bulky. Feeling for the other object, he found it and pulled out the pouch containing Gus's Spirit powder. Staring at it, he figured now was a good time to use some. He opened the pouch and poured a healthy amount into his palms and rubbed it over his neck and shoulders.

The powder seemed to help. Sitting against a tree, his mind cleared and some of the tension in his neck and back eased. Even his head throbbed less. Resting his elbows on his knees, Royce tried to quiet his mind.

He put the pouch back in his pocket. Thinking of Sarna, his turmoil returned. He had to relax and let the powder kick in. He took several more breaths, but his doubts surfaced and worries grew. He thought of his family, and a vivid memory returned of his dad telling him that solutions didn't come from asking the question but from realizing you already knew the answer. As a child, Royce was never sure what that meant, but now he decided to go with it. He went still and trusted he already knew what to do.

He didn't know if it was Gus's magic potion, or the quiet of the moment, but an idea took shape. He thought about it and decided. It was crystal clear. He knew what he had to do to deal with Desde.

A few minutes later, he stood, feeling centered and determined, and headed back through the trees. The parking lot was close, but before Royce could access the trail back to the car, he froze. The light of a bobbing flashlight flickered through the forest. Avoiding the beam, he ducked back behind a tree.

Cursing, he leaned forward and peered out to see who was walking along the trail. Despite the darkness, Royce could make out a hat and uniform. Royce squinted to see who it was, and as the light of the flashlight illuminated the woods, Royce recognized the figure. It was Aaron Carsons, the sheriff's deputy.

Royce swiveled back behind the tree and held his breath. Damn it, he thought. What was Aaron doing out here? He knew the answer, though. Rick was sending patrols through the woods. Since Jasper's attack and the woman's murder had occurred in similar areas, the sheriff didn't want to take any chances. Few people had been venturing out to this area since the attacks, but Royce knew the sheriff was vigilant and the area's residents would expect it.

After a few moments, Royce glanced back around the tree. The flashlight was still visible, but no longer moving. Royce could see through the woods that Aaron had stopped walking and was sitting on a long dead fallen tree trunk. Royce caught the delicate tendrils of a wispy haze drifting through the air. It was smoke. Aaron was smoking.

Royce ducked back. He hadn't known Aaron was a smoker. He cursed that now was the time he had to find out. His mind flipped through an array of ideas. Should he walk out of the woods? Say "Hi," and head to the car? No, he thought. Not an option. His clothes were soaked and stained pink. And his car likely had blood in it. He did not need to draw attention to himself. Not a good idea.

He could wait Aaron out. Stay where he was until Aaron left. He discarded that theory. Aaron didn't look to be in any hurry. And Royce couldn't afford to wait.

He could attempt to sneak away, but he knew that wouldn't work. The woods were quiet, and the sound of his footsteps as he traversed the canopy of leaves and roots on the ground would travel. Aaron would hear it and come looking. That wouldn't work either.

What the hell was he going to do?

Another idea popped into his head. He mulled it over, considering its practicality. Could he do it? Royce recalled his last attempt with the bear. He'd cloaked himself and the bear had walked right by him. The animal had suspected Royce's presence, but it was a bear—an animal who made the woods his home, who survived every day by following his instincts. This was just Aaron Carsons. A man whose only instincts were to buy beer on Friday night.

Royce knew it was his best option. He had to try. If he was able to cloak his physical presence, he could walk right by Aaron. The only problem would be the noise of his footfalls, but Royce figured that might work to his advantage.

Royce leaned back against the tree. Taking deep breaths, he attempted to silence all thoughts. It wasn't easy. Images of Alice, Sarna, Jasper, his sisters, his dad, and Gus plagued him. But he kept at it. Slowly, the images dissipated, and all that was left was a blank slate, much like the night sky on a cloudy night. He let everything fall away, until there was nothing left but him, standing in silent emptiness. The noises of the forest drifted into a muffled background. Everything stilled, and when he felt ready, he imagined in his mind a large blanket, or cloak, dropping over him. It settled over his head and shoulders, passed his torso and lower body, and finally over his legs. He stood that way for a moment, feeling the blanket pressed against him, and seeing himself disappear from all earthly eyes. When his skin tingled and went almost numb, Royce knew it was time.

He opened his eyes. He'd never done this while moving. He would need to remain in this active meditative state until he could get past Aaron and return to his truck. It would be a challenge, but he was well motivated. Feeling cloaked, but not exactly sure he was, he peered around the tree. Aaron was still sitting on the trunk.

It was now or never. He stepped out from his hiding space. For a moment, a well of panic emerged when he imagined Aaron turning and seeing him. He figured if that happened, then he'd have to talk his way out of it. He didn't know what he would say, but he'd deal with it.

He took one step. The area was covered in dead leaves. There was a small crunch. Royce waited, but Aaron didn't react. Royce kept moving, going slowly, and trying to stay as quiet as possible. He knew if he stayed on the trail, then it would be a quieter path, but it would take him right past Aaron. If he strayed off the path, then he would be easily heard. He chose the trail. If he was cloaked, then walking past Aaron wouldn't matter.

He took several more steps as the wisps of smoke grew closer. Nearing the trunk where Aaron sat, he could make out the deputy more clearly. He was puffing on a cigarette and looking at his phone. The light illuminated Aaron's face in the darkness of the woods. As Royce neared, Aaron put his phone in his pocket and mumbled something. Royce thought it sounded like *this sucks*.

Royce stepped closer and heard the snap of a twig as his foot came down. He froze. Aaron picked up the flashlight and swiveled toward the sound. The light bobbed, and Royce braced himself. He would learn now if he was indeed cloaked. Aaron flashed the beam over the trees, crossed Royce's torso, and moved it into the clearing next to him, then swiveled back again. Aaron never stopped on Royce. Royce released an anxious, silent breath. The deputy couldn't see him. The flashlight moved again, but after a second, Aaron put it down. "Damn squirrels," Aaron said. His voice shook slightly.

Royce kept going. Maintaining his mental focus, he walked past Aaron, but the trail became rockier as he continued. A stone crunched beneath his foot, and he went still again as Aaron stubbed out his cigarette and stood. The flashlight swiveled. The beam swiped over Royce, but with no reaction from Aaron.

"Who's there?" asked Aaron. The flashlight whipped through the woods. Aaron took a few steps forward but stopped, narrowly missing Royce.

Royce didn't breathe. He stood stock still and maintained his calm state. He had to stay cool. Aaron bobbed the flashlight in a wide circle, but seeing nothing, he backed up to the log and stood there, studying the area.

Royce wondered what to do. At this point, if he kept walking, every footstep would be heard, and that might alert Aaron enough to call on his radio and alert the cavalry. Royce didn't need that. He needed to effectively get Aaron out of his way without worrying about additional law enforcement. He also needed to get to his truck and drive away without Aaron hearing the engine, running out to the road, and recognizing Royce's truck.

Royce considered his options and finally settled on one. He didn't think it was the best idea, but decided it would work as well as any other. And the deputy would eventually recover. Or at least Royce hoped he would. Not wasting any time, Royce turned toward Aaron, and taking two long strides, which were easily heard, walked right up to the man and said loudly, "Boo."

The effect was instantaneous. Aaron flailed his arms, dropped the flashlight, and shrieked. The pitch was high enough to scare off any animals within a three-mile radius. The deputy tripped on a root, fell backward, and scurried back on his butt, anxious to get away from whatever had spoken to him. It was exactly what Royce had planned for.

Royce watched with a little amusement as Aaron gained his footing and scampered deeper into the woods, still flailing and yelling, "Get away from me! Get away from me!"

Within seconds, Royce couldn't see him anymore, although he could still hear him.

He took advantage of the situation and sprinted down the trail. Making it to the parking lot, he ran across it to the hidden spot where Japer had parked. Seeing the police cruiser at the head of the trail, he hoped Aaron had not bothered to survey the area before entering the woods. Stopping at his driver's door, he closed his eyes and lifted the veil that cloaked him. The last thing he needed was for someone to see a moving car with no driver. He jumped into his truck and started the engine. Punching the accelerator, he backed out and drove out of the lot.

# Chapter Thirty-One

ROYCE DROVE DOWN HIS driveway and saw Gus's red two-door, beat up truck. He slowed down and parked next to it. Killing the engine, he looked around. The lights were on in his house, but Royce did not see his friend. Royce knew that if Gus had walked into his home and seen the blood, he would call for help. Royce had wondered what he would have done if he got to his cabin, only to see a driveway full of circling, flashing lights? He didn't know.

Now that he was here and there were no police cars, he had to consider the other option. Gus was here, and so was Alice. He felt around his jacket pocket and pulled out the necklace. Staring at it, he remembered Sarna, bloody and in pain, lying on his kitchen floor. Remembering that fueled him, and he stepped out, slamming the door behind him. He made no effort to be quiet. Putting the necklace back in his pocket, he walked up to the door and opened it.

The first thing he saw was Gus sitting on the couch. When the door opened, he and Royce made eye contact. Neither spoke as Royce walked in and shut the door with a bang. He walked into the living room.

"Hello, Royce." Royce swiveled to look behind him. She was sitting at the breakfast table. "How are you?"

Royce didn't answer. He was too dumbstruck. He gazed at the woman he knew as Alice. The shapeless dress and long braid were gone. As he stared, she stood. She wore fitted dark jeans; high heeled, sleek, black leather boots; and a fitted, collared black shirt. It was unbuttoned enough to show some cleavage. But the most striking feature was her hair. Undone, it fell down her back in layered, riotous blonde waves. He remembered when he'd seen it out of the braid, but it had been tamer then. Her eyes flashed at him, and he picked up on her irritation and anger. He also noted that the bruise on her face had faded to a grayish yellow, even though it had been black and blue that afternoon.

"Hello, Alice," he said, squaring his shoulders. "Or do you prefer Desde?"

The side of her mouth quirked up. "Desde, of course. Alice is so...Earth."

He wanted to scream at her. "Nice outfit."

She looked down. "You like it? It's more my style."

He willed himself to stay cool. "What happened to the bruise?"

She touched her cheek. "Oh, this?" She rubbed it. "Luckily, Red-Lines heal quickly."

He set his jaw, and his anger grew. "You and I need to talk."

She crossed her arms. "Indeed, we do."

He glanced at Gus, who sat quietly on the couch. "Why don't you go home, Gus?"

Gus rose. "Would love to."

The silver picture frame with the photo of Royce, his sisters, and mother flew off the mantel and hit Gus on the forehead. He fell back onto the couch.

"I don't think so," said Desde.

Royce saw blood seep through Gus's fingers. "Damn it." He moved to the sink, ignoring the smears of red on the floor and counter, wet a towel, and brought it to Gus. He looked at his friend's injury, but the damage was minor.

"I'm okay," said Gus, holding the cloth to his head.

"Stay put," said Royce.

"Don't think I have a choice."

Royce straightened and faced Desde. "What do you want?"

She sneered at him. "You know what I want."

He thought of the necklace in his pocket. "You'll leave after I give it to you?"

"I can't get off this planet fast enough."

He was ready to give it to her, but he needed to know a few things. "Before you ride off into the sunset, I'd like to know how long you've been planning this."

She laughed. "This?" She threw out a hand. "You and me?" She rested her hand on her belly. "Not long. After my father died."

"That's right," said Royce, nodding his head. "I heard. Dear ole' Dad died, and Desde suddenly wasn't so popular anymore."

She glared at him. "You've obviously talked to Jasper, but he's just as big a fool as you. Neither of you have any idea what you're talking about."

Royce felt the calm he'd tried to maintain begin to uncoil. "I know enough to see that you think you deserve to be treated like some kind of princess. When you're really just the ugly stepsister."

Her face was flat, but he saw her pale. "That's where you're wrong. Ugly stepsisters never win." She stepped closer. "But I have every intention of going home with exactly what I want." She patted her belly. "And leaving you exactly as I found you. Sad, pathetic, and lonely."

Royce didn't respond.

She studied her nails. "When I first got here, I wasn't sure what to expect." She grimaced and looked up. "What is the big deal about Earth? It's a terrible place. So much violence. You all seem to solve all your problems by hurting yourselves or others."

"You fit right in."

She ignored him. "It did work to my advantage." She walked through the house. "When I got here, I wasn't sure how to set up our initial meeting." She stopped at his bedroom door. "I had to find a way to entice you quickly. I didn't feel like taking the time to woo you." She glanced inside the room.

"But then I figured you're a man. How hard could it be? Earth men want sex like Earth women want beauty. Give him the means and it's easy."

Royce shifted. "You were Alice then. Not...this."

She smiled. "Alice...poor sweet Alice." She sighed. "Sad she had to die."

Royce frowned. "Was there an Alice?"

She leaned back against the doorframe of his bedroom. "Yes. Of course."

Royce's mind worked. Then he understood. "The woman in the woods."

She nodded. "I met her on my second day here." She pushed off the wall and walked toward the fireplace mantel. "I came early to watch you. Get my bearings. Learn more about this place, the town, the people." She made a face. "How you and your friend here live out in these woods is a mystery to me."

Gus sat forward. "The Earth shows her magic to those who appreciate it."

She swiveled to face him. "The Earth's magic is nothing more than an illusion. Just like your medicine man bag. It has no more power than this." She touched the fireplace poker with her fingers.

"Depends on who's holding the poker," said Royce.

She grinned. "That's where you're wrong, Royce. If you understood, then you'd realize that you don't need the poker at all."

He clenched his fists. "What happened to Alice?"

Her eyes narrowed. "As I was saying, I met her my second day. I'd been watching you, debating about how and when to approach you. I was in the woods, near some campgrounds and hiking trails, not far from my ship, when she walked up to me and started talking." She stared off. "We chatted like two girlfriends and then later agreed to meet again." Desde rested her hand on the mantel. "She was a lonely, troubled woman. I could sense her need to unburden herself. We met again the next day, back in the woods. She didn't want to be seen in public. I soon found out why."

Curious, Royce couldn't help but ask. "Why?"

Desde turned away from the mantel. "She was running from her husband. He was abusive. She told me the story that I told you. He was searching for her, and she was on the run. She told me everything. I didn't particularly care until she told me where she was staying."

Royce swallowed. He thought of Old Man McDermott's house.

"Right next door to you," said Desde. "I couldn't believe it. She even looked like me, except she wore those horrible dresses. She told me she hid from men. She didn't want the attention. That's when I knew."

"Knew what?"

She glanced at Gus, who didn't speak. "What I would do to get to you." She looked back at Royce with a smirk.

"You had to kill her?"

She made a snorting noise. "I didn't have a choice. I couldn't well become her if she was still alive. She was perfect. The best way to meet you." She stepped up to the couch and touched the fabric. "My mother told me a way would be shown, and she was right. I walked right into Alice's life. Became the sad, solitary, abused creature. I moved into the cabin, wore her clothes, took her name. I had to ensure no one came looking, so I disposed of her identification. I didn't want the police to come sniffing around. It would take some time for them to figure out who she was." She smiled. "I even gave them a clue as to who might have done it. I know how Earth people love a good murder mystery."

"What do you mean?" asked Royce.

She laughed and her eyes gleamed. "The shoe, Royce. The shoe."

Royce recalled the pink sneaker in his shed.

"I had her meet me early. At dawn. It would be quiet then. I told her we'd go for a walk. Take our mind off our worries. She did. The woods weren't quiet, though. Some kids had partied the night before at the park. They staggered out early, before Alice arrived, but one car was left. I had to hope that no one stumbled upon us. I didn't need anybody seeing her with me. Luckily, we walked alone. And as soon as I had the chance, I took a rock and hit her." She stared off, recalling the event. "It was easy. As soon as she was down, I took anything that would identify her, and then I saw her pink sneakers."

Royce forced himself to take a steady breath.

"I took one off. On the way out, I stopped at the car in the lot. I recognized it. It belonged to the sheriff's boy. I'd seen him driving around before when I'd surveyed the town. He liked to play his music loud. His car was unlocked. I opened the trunk and threw the sneaker in. It was perfect. If anyone came snooping around, I could throw them off the scent with one phone call."

Royce thought of RJ. "You'd let a harmless teenager be accused of murder?"

"Nobody's harmless," she said. "He's not innocent of stupidity."

Royce didn't see the point of arguing.

"So, after she was out of the way, all I needed to do was get your attention. I made sure you saw me, but I stayed mysterious. I didn't want to look obvious. Then the perfect opportunity showed itself. You were on the property. That bear came sniffing around. I just had to point him in the right direction. That was simple. For some reason, I think he holds a grudge against you."

Royce thought back to that day in the woods.

"I didn't plan on the snake though," she said. "You really are a bit of a klutz, aren't you?" He didn't answer, and she smiled. "Once you were suitably disabled, I got you into the house and became the trauma nurse Alice, taking care of her patient. I wasn't sure about that snake bite, though. Thankfully, Gus came through for us. I didn't want to take you to the hospital. I needed to keep you close." She walked up beside Royce. "So we could get to know each other."

He almost stepped back. The thought of their time together and her betrayal made him shudder.

"I had to admit, when I planned this, I was worried about getting here and finding you...unsuitable." She looked him up and down. "But I got lucky." She grinned. "You look like your father." She tipped her head. "I wonder if he would be as pleasurable in bed?"

Royce felt sick. How could he have been fooled by this woman?

She stepped up closer, and he smelled her perfume. He wondered if it was Alice's perfume.

She leaned against him. "If you're interested, we could enjoy each other one more time before I leave."

He gritted his teeth. "I think I'll pass."

She trailed her fingers down his arm. "You're sure? As I recall, you liked it when I touched your—"

He stepped back. "Get away from me."

She laughed. "Touchy, touchy." She looked at Gus, who sat quietly on the couch, his head no longer bleeding. "Bet you'd like to watch, wouldn't you?"

Gus's expression didn't change.

"So you got what you wanted from me," said Royce, his gut churning. "Why didn't you leave?"

She rubbed her stomach. "Yes. I got what I wanted. It worked beautifully. We spent a lovely twenty-four hours together. All I needed to do was make sure I got through the next seventy-two with no disruptions or energy fluctuations. I know you'd thought I'd left, but I wasn't far. I had to stay close. I went back to the ship, made sure I took my medicine. I had to stay in peak condition. I couldn't let this toxic place affect my pregnancy." She released a satisfied sigh. "I am carrying the High Child, after all."

"You're sure?" asked Royce. "How do you know you're pregnant?"

She patted her belly. "Because I can feel it. The child's energy is there. Growing inside me. In fact, I think it's a girl."

Royce wanted to moan, but he clenched his jaw instead.

"Your daughter, Royce." She smiled again. "I think I'll call her Es-merelda, after my mother."

Royce's heart thumped against his chest. "You don't deserve her."

She dropped her hand to her hip. "Don't I? I planned everything to get to this point. My mother and I knew the moment we realized you existed we could be more than just the wife and daughter of a pathetic Councilman. We could be the mother and grandmother of the next High Child."

Royce wasn't sure he heard right. "You planned this when your father was still alive?"

She frowned as if Royce had asked her if she was pretty. "Of course. We started plotting as soon as your uncle Galen told my mother. They'd been having an affair at the time. People were already whisper-ing about it. It wasn't long after that my poor dad had his accident."

"Your father?" asked Royce. Shock rippled through him. "You...did you kill your father?"

"You killed your uncle."

Royce dropped his jaw. "How do you know that?"

"He told my mother what he was going to do, what he wanted to do, with you and your sisters. They argued. It was the last thing we wanted. At least not until I got to you first. But we couldn't stop him. When he left, we knew our plans would be ruined. He would destroy our chance to find you. But he never came back."

Royce recalled Galen's death. He felt no remorse. "No, he didn't."

She ticked up a brow. "I figured he'd met an untimely demise. And he did, didn't he? It was just a guess, but I assumed it was at your hand, and probably your sisters, too. You're the only ones who would have had the ability. Am I right?"

"He deserved what he got."

"I don't disagree." She crossed her arms. "So mother and I moved forward. She used her connections to get me a ship and the pills. Made up an excuse for my absence. And here we are."

He grunted. "Lucky me."

"You're the High Child. The father of our baby. I'd say you're very lucky."

"If I could change it, I would. I don't want to be the father of our child."

She grinned. "Don't worry. You won't be. She'll know nothing about you, except what I tell her."

Royce pushed back the desire to grab Desde by the throat.

"That's why I panicked when I saw Jasper in the woods. I didn't know if he'd followed me, or if he'd seen me. I didn't know who he was with. I suppose, looking back, I should have bided my time. Watched and waited. If I had, he and Sarna would be gone, and so would I. But what is your saying?" She thought about it. "Something about eyesight?"

"Hindsight is twenty-twenty," said Gus.

"Yes, that," said Desde. "I overreacted. Hit him on the head too. Only he didn't die. Sadly."

"What is the matter with you? Aren't Eudorans supposed to be peaceful?"

"The boring ones are," she said. She leaned toward him. "But I'm not boring."

He narrowed his eyes. "No, you're not."

"I'd hoped that was it. All I needed was another day or two to be sure my pregnancy could be sustained. And then I learned Sarna was here." Her face dropped. "That was a problem."

Even though Royce knew the answer, he still had to ask. "Why?"

She glared, and her eyes darkened. "You know why. Because you're so damned weak. Another woman shows up and you pant after her just like you panted after me. You're so predictable."

"Alice..."

"It's Desde." She straightened the cuffs on her shirt. "I watched you that night."

"What night?" asked Royce.

"The night on the porch." Her eyes furrowed. "Your 'connection' moment. So touching."

"You were out there?"

"Who do you think scared the bird? I had to try and stop your pathetic lust from ruining everything. I thought I had succeeded." She gripped the countertop. "But no. She got her claws into you. I can't blame her, though. She's smart. Probably wanted the same thing I did."

He straightened. "That is not what Sarna wanted."

"Wasn't it? She tried to Bind with you, didn't she?"

He stepped forward. "She didn't expect anything. She didn't want to Bind."

Desde pointed at him, and Royce felt a force emit from her and push him backward. "Stop lying to me. You two plotted together. She and Jasper were going to take you back, parade you in front of the Council, make you the next High Leader, all while Sarna flaunted her pregnancy."

"That's not true."

"Then you're lying to yourself and she fooled you, too. That's exactly what she planned."

"You're wrong."

"Think whatever you want. But I wasn't going to let that happen. She wasn't going to win. I had to get rid of her, take her baby away, and save mine. And the last thing I want or need is for you to go to Eudora."

"Why? Because I would tell everyone about the witch you are?"

Her brows lifted. "Everyone knows by now that I'm a witch. No. If they knew I was carrying your child, the Council would make us honor the Binding between us. We would be forced to live as a couple. You would be High Leader, of course, which has its perks, but I would be forced to live as your partner." Her face squinted as if she'd eaten something sour.

"I can't do that. I look forward to getting back home, having this baby, finding someone to take care of it, and then having some fun."

Royce felt the bile rise in the back of his throat. "You're a real catch."

"No." She stepped forward. "You were the catch, but I'm throwing you back like all the others. You served a purpose, nothing more." She trailed her eyes over him. "You were one of the better fish, though. More like a barracuda."

Royce wanted to throw something. "And you're a shark. You destroy everything in your path and leave nothing behind. I'm surprised your eyes didn't roll back in your head when I met you."

"Oh, they did." She smirked. "You just didn't notice."

He had to admit she was right. "Now we know where we stand. You want to go, and I want you to leave. Seems we're finally on the same page."

"I want to leave all right. But that bitch took something from me...and I need it back."

"Your pills?"

"You know about the pills?" She grunted. "She told you, didn't she? Probably took them from me because she wanted to destroy my baby."

"You tried to kill her."

"That's your fault. That was a last resort."

Royce went cold. "You go after Sarna and it's my fault?"

"I gave you the chance to save her. You didn't take it."

"What are you talking about?"

"This afternoon. The note I left you. You came to see me."

Royce scowled. "I came to talk to you. To check on you. To make sure you were okay."

"Oh, you're such the hero."

Royce's skin grew hot, and he was sure his face was red. "But all you wanted was to get me out of the house so you could come after Sarna."

She flicked out her hand. "That's where you're wrong. I invited you over to give you the chance to save her. I gave you a choice. I told you my sob story. Asked you to help me. But you said no. You chose Sarna. If you'd said yes, if you'd helped me, then I would have known our Binding was intact. But you didn't, thus my pregnancy was threatened. I had to get rid of her." Her face relaxed as if she spoke about vacation plans. "I had to distract you, then. I planned to run outside, have you follow me, and then incapacitate you, but I ran into that damn bear." She shook her head. "That worked fine, though. I have some sway with animals. And I knew when the bear saw you, it would make him angry. And, of course, you rushed in to save me. It worked perfectly. I just had to make sure the bear didn't kill you."

Royce stood stunned. "Because I chose not to help you, you attacked Sarna."

"You gave me no choice. Your Binding with her was intact. Mine was not. I had to act fast. As soon as you were out cold, I headed over here." She cocked her head. "You should have seen her face when she answered the door. I was the last person she expected to see."

Royce shut his eyes.

"It wasn't personal, Royce. Just business. She was going to take what I had. I couldn't let that happen."

The guilt twisted his insides. He couldn't speak.

"Oh, and by the way, there's a dead man in Alice's garage."

Royce opened his eyes, remembering. "I saw him. Did you kill him too?"

Desde grunted. "He showed up out of nowhere. Said he was Alice's husband." She laughed. "Can you believe that? That idiot found her...or me. He must have traced the car. I knew he was in town, searching, but I'd thought he'd left."

"So you never met up with him in a hotel?"

"No," she chuckled. "I made that up. He showed up this morning before you came over. Knocked on the door. Of course, he realized I wasn't Alice. Started screaming at me, demanding to know where she was. I tried to put him off, but he was insistent. Then he hit me."

Royce gritted his teeth.

She touched her skin around her eye with the yellowish tint. "I was stunned. No one has ever hit me before. The bruise had its advantages, though. It got your attention and made my story more believable. But once that happened, he was a," she looked at Gus, "what's another one of your more colorful terms?" He shook his head, and she tapped her chin. "Dead man walking. That's it. Perfect analogy."

"You shot him?"

She grunted, as if becoming bored with the story. "He had a gun. He pulled it on me. Wanted me to get in his car with him. Said he was going to take me to the authorities. Find out what I did with Alice. I let him take me outside. Acted all frightened and scared. But as soon as I was in the car, I pulled the gun right out of his hand." She grinned as she thought back. "His face was perfect. All 'shock and awe.'" She looked almost serene. "Then I shot him."

Royce dropped his head. "Hell..."

"Thankfully, most of the blood didn't get on me. I mean, I was expecting you to arrive at any time. So I left him in the garage."

"And when did I arrive?"

"About an hour later. Gave me enough time to clean up. And the bruise to turn nice and purple."

Royce berated himself for playing right into her hands.

"Don't feel too badly." She stepped close. "I'm very good at getting what I want." When he didn't answer, she asked, "Tell me. Is Sarna dead?"

The urge to throw up returned. He hated this woman. "No, she isn't."

"I see." He felt her energy probe him. "They left, didn't they?" she asked. "Jasper took her home. To save her. And you stayed here."

Royce didn't answer.

"How loyal of you."

He still didn't speak.

"You have the necklace?"

He looked at his friend. "You'll leave Gus alone?"

She chuckled. "That's why you came back, isn't it? To save Gus." She glanced at the man sitting on the couch. "You're lucky, Gus. He was right. You'd be dead now if he'd left."

"I don't fear death," said Gus.

"You would have." She looked back with a stony expression. "You know what I'm capable of. You know what I want. You threaten any of that, and I won't stop until I take everything you love." She walked over to the back door and opened it. She picked up a plastic bag, carried it inside, and dropped it on the couch.

Royce looked at the clear bag. He could see clearly what was inside. It was a pink tennis shoe and a gray sneaker. It was the match to Jasper's missing shoe. "You test me, and I'll throw you to the wolves." She touched the bag. "I considered taking this to Eve's place. She lives in the city, right?"

Royce tensed.

"Yes," she said. "I know where she lives. If you hadn't returned, I would have had enough time to find her, hide this in her home, and make a phone call. It wouldn't have taken them long to figure out her connection to you."

Royce imagined giving her another black eye. Maybe a broken nose, too.

"You may have been gone, but she likely would have taken the brunt of the investigation." She raised a brow. "I could have thrown in some of Alice's clothing, too. That definitely would have at least made her look like an accessory, don't you think?"

Without thinking, Royce summoned all his energy and sent a vicious, energetic wave toward Desde, intent on knocking her through the wall. Before it could reach her, though, it hit an invisible barrier, and like a trampoline, it bounced back toward Royce. The force hit him in the chest and threw him backward. His feet came off the ground, and he hit the wall behind him with a thud. Sliding down, he put his hand on his chest as the air left him.

Desde cackled. "Don't be stupid. I'm much better at this than you are."

Gus swiveled on the couch. "You okay, Starman?"

Royce groaned, but got his feet under him. "I'm okay." He pushed up and stood. He took a shaky breath. "I give you what you want, and you'll leave?"

"I'll be out of here within the hour. I can't take this place anymore. I never liked being here. All I want is the pills."

He almost snarled at her. "I'm surprised Momma didn't secure an infinite supply."

She scoffed. "She supplied plenty. But I've been on this planet longer than I planned. And I'm highly sensitive. I need those pills to make sure my pregnancy survives the journey home. I have a few left. That will get me only so far, though." She rubbed her belly. "Things are delicate right now. Any more energetic disruption could jeopardize our daughter. And that encounter with Sarna didn't help."

"You should have left her alone."

Her eyes narrowed. "I don't want to talk about her anymore." She took a step closer. "Now give me the pills."

Royce eyed her, wishing he could do anything but give her what she wanted, but he had no choice. He reached into his pocket and pulled out the necklace.

She took it instantly and opened it, eyeing the tiny white discs inside. Satisfied, she snapped the locket shut and put it around her neck. "Well, I'm feeling better now. How about you?"

Royce shook his head. "I don't ever want to see you again."

She grinned. "I think for once that I won't disappoint you." She looked back at Gus. "Nice to have met you, Gus."

Gus didn't speak as Desde sidled up next to Royce. "I'll remember our time together with fondness."

"I'll try to forget it."

"Hmm," she said. "You'll try, but you won't succeed."

He grimaced. "Don't you have a ship to catch?"

She laughed softly. "Yes. As a matter of fact, I do." She stepped away from Royce and walked toward the door. "I can't wait to tell Mom she's going to be a grandmother." She glanced back at the two men. "And tell your father I'm carrying his grandbaby."

Royce summoned all his strength to stop himself from drop kicking her out of the house. "Get out of here."

"I'll send him your love."

Royce didn't speak as she walked out the door. He stepped up to the entryway and watched her disappear into the woods. He figured she must have parked her car, or Alice's, somewhere nearby. Gus came up beside him, holding the bloody rag.

After a few quiet moments, he spoke. "You okay, Starman?"

Royce watched the woods, although Desde was no longer in sight. "You're the one with the head wound."

Gus paused. "But you're the one with the heart wound."

Satisfied she was gone, Royce closed the door. Exhausted and emotional, he walked to the couch and sat.

Gus sat beside him. "Thank you."

Royce leaned forward and put his head in his hand. "For what?"

"For coming back."

Royce grunted. "I wouldn't let her hurt you."

"I could have handled her."

Royce rubbed his head. "You sure about that?"

"She's from your planet?"

Royce sighed. "It's a long story, Gus."

Gus nodded. "The blood. It's Sarna's?

Royce felt like he had fifty-pound sandbags on his shoulders. "Yes."

"But she's still alive?"

"I hope so." Thinking of her, he felt his throat swell.

Gus put his hand on Royce's shoulder. He sat quietly for a few moments. "Is it true what Alice...or whoever she is...said? Is she carrying your baby?"

Royce wanted to sink into the couch. "Desde? Yes. For now."

"For now?"

Royce lifted his head. His eyelids were as heavy as rocks.

Gus eyed him. "What are you up to, Starman? What did you do?"

Royce stared blankly at the wall. "I figure we have an hour. Maybe two."

Gus leaned forward. "Until what?"

"To make sure she's gone."

"Why wouldn't she be? Why would she come back?"

"She is. She won't."

"Then why do we have an hour or two?"

Royce groaned. "Because," he raised a hand and pulled the pouch of Gus's Spirit powder from his pocket, "by then she'll be in space, and then it will be too late."

"Too late for what?"

"For her to do anything when she realizes I poisoned her pills."

Gus stared at the pouch and then at Royce. "You didn't."

"I did."

Gus's mouth dropped open. "You sprinkled the powder on her pills?"

"I doused them in it. Not long after she takes them, she'll feel the effects. If what she says is true, and if your powder truly is a purging agent, then her pregnancy will end. Everything she planned for will be gone. She'll go home with nothing."

Gus dropped his hand back to the couch. "What if she comes back?" asked Gus. "For revenge."

Royce massaged his shoulders. They were so tight they were numb. "She can't. She wouldn't survive the trip. Not enough fuel and not enough good pills to keep her alive. Plus, she'll be sick as a dog."

Gus sat quietly. The house was silent as they both contemplated the day's tumultuous events. "Is this what you wanted?"

Royce sat still, not knowing the answer anymore. He glanced at his friend, feeling almost too tired to speak. "She did it to me, so I did it to her."

Gus didn't reply but watched as Royce stood, walked into the kitchen, flipped on the sink, and began to clean Sarna's blood off his countertop.

A few seconds passed, and Gus stood, too. He dropped his bloody cloth on the coffee table, walked to the pantry, found the mop, and helped.

# Chapter Thirty-Two

TWO DAYS LATER, SHERIFF Rick Henderson stood in Royce's driveway. RJ leaned against a nearby tree, and Royce and Gus watched the police activity at Old Man McDermott's cabin next door. Even from a distance, they could see patrol cars parked in the driveway, and Royce could see they had the garage open.

"It's hard to believe," said the sheriff.

"What is, sheriff?" asked Gus.

"That all this happened in our small town." He looked at Royce. "And culminated in your neighbor's house."

"Yes. It is," said Royce.

They all continued to watch the police walk around the property. Yellow tape was going up around the garage.

"What do you think happened over there, sheriff?" Gus asked, glancing at Royce, who looked away.

The sheriff gripped his belt buckle. "Near as we can tell, that man who was snooping around town, the one your friends ran into," he pointed at Royce, "his wife was the woman in the woods. We finally identified her. She's Alice Montgomery. Been missing since last year. Her family says she's been on the run. Husband's abusive." He paused. "Apparently, she came out here to hide. She was renting McDermott's cabin. Her husband must have caught up with her. Killed her in the woods."

"Poor woman," said Gus. "Never had a chance."

"How do you know he did it?" asked Royce, still staring at the trees.

"Found her pink shoe. In his car." He sighed. "Must be a fetish thing. I've seen it with city folk."

Royce glanced at RJ. RJ's head popped up, and his face froze. Royce looked away.

"He had your friend's...rather brother's, shoe too."

"Jasper?" asked Royce.

"Yes. I don't understand why he went after him, though." The sheriff grunted. "His attack was in the same area. Maybe our killer thought Jasper saw something, or knew something."

"Maybe," said Gus.

"He still around?" asked the sheriff. "We may need to talk to him."

"No," said Royce. "They left a couple of days ago."

"You know where?"

Royce shook his head. "No idea. Nowhere close."

"I'll call his mom, I guess, if I need to. Nice woman."

Royce didn't respond, and the group stood in silence as they watched the police activity.

"There's still something I don't understand," said Rick.

"What's that?" asked Royce.

"That woman. At the cabin," he said to Royce. "You remember seeing her?"

"When?" asked Royce. He studied the ground.

"That day we found Alice Montgomery in the woods. I brought RJ over. We saw a woman in the distance. On the porch."

Royce stared off. "Vaguely."

"She must have been staying or visiting with Alice. A friend of hers, I suspect. You ever meet her?"

Royce maintained his somber expression. "I've never met any of McDermott's guests, or their friends."

"Strange. I wonder who she was."

"There's no telling, sheriff," said Gus. "Maybe she was staying with Alice, and when Alice didn't come home, she left."

"I hope the husband didn't come after her too," said Royce. "Why else would he be at the cabin if his wife was already dead?" He continued to watch through the trees as a white van with the word *Coroner* printed in block letters on its side joined the fray on McDermott's property.

"Well," said Rick, "if he killed his wife, and then went after Jasper, then he probably was on a spree. The blonde woman we saw may have become a target if she was helping Alice." He sighed. "I hope we don't find her body in the woods, too."

"Yeah," said Royce. He scratched at the dirt with his boot. "That would be a tragedy."

"Maybe she's the one who made the anonymous phone call," Gus said. "The one that told you about the body in the garage."

"No," said Rick. "That was a male caller."

"Hmm," said Royce. "Strange."

"Maybe she'll turn up, eventually," Gus said.

"Or maybe she won't," Royce said, glancing at Gus.

The four of them continued to watch the commotion. Even though the trees obscured the view, it was pretty clear what was happening.

"I need to get back to work," Rick said. "I just wanted to come by and see if you saw or heard anything."

"Not a thing, sheriff," said Royce.

"You ready, RJ?" Rick asked.

RJ pushed off the tree and walked over. "Sure." He stared at Royce.

"We heard you're leaving town," said Rick. "RJ wanted to tell you goodbye." Rick patted his son's shoulder. "Soon as we're done here, I've got to take you home and get back to the crime scene. I need to check in on Aaron, too."

Royce swiveled his head. "What's up with Aaron?"

The sheriff shrugged. "Heck if I can figure it out. Came back spooked the other night from surveilling the woods. Said he saw a ghost or something. Hasn't slept since. Can you believe that?"

"Really?" asked Gus. He chuckled. "The woods hold secrets. Maybe he stumbled into one."

"Or he stumbled into too many beers," said the sheriff. "That's my theory." He checked his watch. "He better get over it, though. I need his help today."

"I'm sure he'll be fine," Royce said. "Probably heard an animal or something." He tipped his head at RJ, who stood by the sheriff's car. "Hey, RJ." The teen straightened. "Before you leave, walk with me for a second." Royce looked at the sheriff. "We'll be right back."

"No problem," said Rick. "So Gus," Royce heard the sheriff say, "you got any theories about our murderer? Why would he choose to go to McDermott's and shoot himself in the garage?"

Royce heard Gus answer. "Why does anyone do anything, sheriff?"

Royce stepped away from the driveway, and RJ followed. When they were out of earshot, Royce stopped next to a willowy tree. RJ stood next to him and waited. Royce couldn't tell if the teen looked happy or sad. His eyes held a flat look.

"Listen," said Royce. "I don't want you to worry about the shoe. No one will ever know it was in your trunk."

RJ hesitated. "Did you put it in that guy's car?"

Royce shook his head. "It's not important. The less you know about this, the better. Just know that the man in the garage...he is the bad guy."

RJ opened his mouth to speak, but stopped.

"What is it?" asked Royce. "If you have any doubts, then now is the time to express them."

RJ swallowed. "How do I know?"

"Know what?"

RJ hemmed and hawed.

"Spit it out. Speak now or forever hold your peace."

RJ bit his lip, but finally answered. "How do I know you didn't do it?"

Royce almost chuckled, but stopped himself because RJ looked like he was about to puke. He leaned against the tree. "I suppose that's a valid concern. But all I can tell you is that I didn't. I didn't hurt that woman in the woods. I didn't put the shoe in your trunk. And I didn't hurt that man next door." He kept an eye on RJ, who looked worried. "Do you think I did it?"

RJ stared at the ground. After a few seconds, he looked up. "No."

"Then you would be correct."

"But I think you know who did. And that's why you're leaving."

That froze Royce to his spot. The kid was smarter than he looked. Royce pushed off the tree and squatted low. He picked up a long piece of grass and ran it through his fingers. "That may be true, RJ, but that has nothing to do with you."

"Then why don't you tell my dad? Let him go after whoever did this. So you don't have to leave."

Royce smiled sadly. "Believe me. If I could, I would. But it's not that simple."

RJ shoved his hands in his pockets. "Why do adults always say that?"

Royce wondered about that. "I don't know."

"Where are you going to go?"

Royce held the grass between his fingers. "I don't know that either." He sighed. "I just need to leave. To get lost for a while."

RJ nodded. "Are you going to go look for the person who really did this? The person who hurt you?"

Royce dropped his jaw. "You're a pretty smart kid, but no. I'm not."

"I'm not a kid."

Royce sighed. "You're right. You're not a kid. Which is why I'm going to ask you for a big favor. I need you to keep everything that happened between you and me to yourself."

RJ paused. "What if I don't?"

Royce played with the grass. "It's your choice. I can't stop you from telling your dad about the shoe. But if you want to tell him, then do it now. You wait, then it only casts more suspicion on both of us."

RJ dug his hands deeper into his pockets and the two sat in silence. "I won't tell him. And I know you would never hurt anyone. You helped me when I needed it, so I'll help you too. I owe you."

Royce smiled fondly. "Thanks. I appreciate it." He dropped the grass and stood. He looked down at the teenager. "I want you to know that I think you're a good kid...sorry...person. I see a lot of potential in you. Your father does too, so try not to give him too much grief."

RJ shifted on his feet. "Okay."

"He loves you. It's just that...sometimes dads have a hard time expressing that."

RJ nodded. "Yeah."

"Good." Royce patted RJ on the back and turned toward the driveway.

"You ever coming back?" asked RJ.

Royce stopped. He stared out over his property and realized he wasn't prepared for the question. "I don't know. I guess that just depends."

"On what?"

Royce released a deep breath. He thought of all that had occurred over the past week. "Me."

They exchanged a look, and Royce felt an unexpected lump of sadness well up inside him. "Your dad's waiting."

"Yeah. Okay."

They walked back to the driveway, and RJ hopped into the front seat of his father's patrol car.

Rick stepped up with an outstretched hand. "Good luck, Royce, with wherever you're headed."

Royce shook his hand. "Thanks, Rick."

"How can we get in touch with you, in case we need to...you know..." He nodded toward the crime scene where more yellow tape was going up.

"I'll be in touch with Gus. Just let him know if you need to reach me."

"Will do." He let go of Royce's hand and tipped his hat at Gus. "See ya, Gus."

"Sheriff."

Rick got in his car and started up the engine and drove away with RJ.

As the police vehicle disappeared, the two men stood quietly on the driveway. The only sounds were of the murmured voices of the distant crime scene workers and the birds in the trees. Royce watched the activity.

"You think they'll find anything?" asked Royce.

Gus shrugged. "We cleaned it well. I doubt it."

"Don't you think they'll wonder why there are no fingerprints?"

Gus fiddled with the feather that hung from his neck. "Maybe, but hopefully they'll just think that whoever was there last kept a clean house. Either way, there's no reason for them to suspect you."

Royce nodded. He patted his front pocket and felt his cell phone. They'd found it in the dirt beside the porch at McDermott's cabin. "Thanks for your help, Gus. I didn't mean for you to get mixed up in this."

"Don't forget. My fingerprints were over there, too."

"Yeah, I know."

They continued to quietly observe the events at the neighboring cabin.

"You got your stuff?" asked Gus.

Royce turned away. No matter what they found next door, he knew there was nothing more he could do. "In the truck already."

Gus grunted. "You got your toothbrush?"

"Yes."

"Comb?"

"Sure."

"Shoes?"

"Got 'em."

"Good."

Gus faced him. "You're sure about this?"

"I am," said Royce. "You don't mind watching the place?"

"No. Not at all. What about your family?"

"What about them?"

"They know what you're doing?"

"I told them."

"What did they say?"

"Nothing to say, Gus." He hung his head. "I need to get out of here. After everything...I need to get my head together."

Gus grunted. A gust of wind blew, and Gus pushed his hair off his face. "I get it. You need to walk."

Royce crossed his arms. "Exactly. A walk. Like you do."

Gus's eyes softened. "I always take my walks in the woods. I believe nature has a way of soothing our pain."

Royce chuckled. "I brought my camping gear."

"Sleeping bag?"

Royce smiled. "Yes."

"Canteen?"

Royce nodded.

"Toilet paper?"

"Of course."

"Good."

They stood that way, unsure of what to say next.

"You be careful, Starman."

That well of emotion that Royce had felt with RJ returned. "I will."

"Don't hide from any bears."

"I won't." Royce reached into his pocket. "Here." He held out his house keys.

Gus took them. "I don't plan on keeping these forever."

Royce headed for his truck, and Gus followed. "I know." Royce opened the door.

"Before you go," said Gus, "tell me your intentions for your walk."

"My what?"

"Every walk needs an intention. A goal. Something you plan to accomplish or learn or find." He rested his hands on the car door. "You should know that before you leave."

Royce slid into his seat and pulled out his car key. He stared out the windshield. "I just want to shut everything out."

"That's only temporary. What then?"

Royce gripped the steering wheel. "Then I want to silence this gnawing guilt."

Gus nodded. "And after that?"

Royce sighed. He thought that was enough, but then he realized there was more. "I want to prepare."

Gus squinted. "Prepare for what?"

Royce swallowed and stared at his friend. An array of conflicting emotions fluttered through him. "For when she comes back." Royce pulled the car door shut and started the engine.

Gus spoke through the open window. "Which one?"

Royce tipped his head at Gus, but said nothing. He backed his truck out and, waving, drove away, leaving his friend and his home behind him.

## What Happens Next?

Get ready for Eve's story next in *Spark* . She's on the run from the mob with a mysterious stranger. Can she trust the man she's falling for with her life, or will his secrets expose her and her family?

Enjoy an excerpt below.

## Want more from J. T. Bishop?

Sign up for her newsletter at jtbishopauthor.com to get the short story, *Red-Line: Prelude to The Shift,* plus a novella, missing scenes, excerpts, future books, and fun promos for free.

## How did it all begin with the Red-Lines?

Discover the *Red-Line Trilogy*, which started the Red-Line story. Sarah Randolph holds the key to the survival of a secret community. But first she must survive her "Shift." Her protector, John Ramsey, is assigned to keep her alive, but falling for her was never in his plans. When a powerful adversary reveals himself and his intentions for Sarah, her unique destiny may be their only hope.

The Red-Line Trilogy includes *Red-Line: The Shift, Red-Line: Mirrors,* and *Red-Line: Trust Destiny*. A boxed set is available, too!

## What's next after the Fletcher Family Saga?

Do you like detective mystery thrillers with a touch of the paranormal? Then check out the *Family or Foe* saga featuring Detectives Daniels and Remalla. A killer with strange abilities is on the loose and he's targeting the family he believes wronged him. Can Daniels and Remalla catch him before he seeks his revenge and kills them all?

## Detectives Daniels and Remalla get their own series.

After *The Family or Foe Saga*, the two charismatic and affable detectives battle psychopaths, unexplained evil and unsolved cases. In *Haunted River*, book one in the series, the ghost of a woman haunts a small town where she lived and died. When a second woman's body turns up twenty-five years later, Daniels and Remalla become suspects, and the next targets.

Or pick up the omnibus *Shadows and Secrets*, which contains *Haunted River*, *Of Breath and Blood*, and *Of Body and Bone* (books one through three) of the paranormal thriller series.

# A Note from J.T.

I LOVE TO HEAR from my readers about their experiences with my books, and I'd love to know what you thought about *High Child*. Royce's story was fun to write because he's a such great character. Who wouldn't want a brother like Royce? Kind, protective, but tough when needed, and someone who will give you his whole heart when he's ready to share it. I enjoyed telling his love story with Sarna. But will they get together again? Will Royce ever claim his title as High Child? Well, you'll just have to keep reading to find out. (Authors can be kind, but tough, too.)

Next up is Eve, who's got a slew of problems of her own. She's not looking for love, but it just might find her anyway. It's not going to be easy, though and she'll have to learn to trust her gut, and her heart.

And if you've read the Red-Line trilogy, then expect to see more of the Ramseys in *Spark* and in book four, *Forged Lines*. Both they and the Fletchers will learn they'll have to depend on each other to survive.

Reviews are a huge plus and big help for a writer, and potential readers. I would love it if you could please take a couple of minutes to leave a review for *High Child*. And if you'd like, please leave a few comments, too.

As always, thank you for your time and readership. It is deeply valued and appreciated.

Now, on to the next book!

# About the Author

Award-winning author, J.T. Bishop, is a writer of mystery thrillers with a paranormal edge. Growing up, she read Stephen King, Mary Higgins Clark, and Dean Koontz, devoured every episode of the X-files and watched plenty of TV shows with great partnerships that leave you wanting more. She loves tangled relationships, unexpected twists and turns, heart-stopping love stories and the complications that come with all the above. Throw in a little supernatural fun and she's hooked. Her evil plan is to hook you, too.

She's the author of The Red-Line Trilogy and its sister series, The Fletcher Family Saga, which features touches of urban fantasy, light sci-fi, and paranormal romance. She's also happily writing mystery thrillers featuring two charismatic detectives who may occasionally encounter a supernatural villain or two, and a crossover series which follows the exploits of a gifted, but troubled, paranormal PI and his spunky sister.

All the above keeps her busy, but in her spare time, she loves good movies, tasty food, an unfortunate sugar addiction, and traveling.

# Books in Chronological Order

Although recommended but not required, in case you prefer to read in order...

*Red-Line: Prelude to The Shift, a short story (subscribers only)*
*Red-Line: The Shift*
*Red-Line: Mirrors*
*Red-Line: Trust Destiny*
*Curse Breaker*
*High Child*
*Spark*
*Forged Lines*
\*\*

*The Girl and the Gunshot, a novella (subscribers only)*
*A Hamburger Christmas, a novella*
*The Magic of Murder, a novella (subscribers only)*
*First Cut*
*Second Slice*
*Third Blow*
*Fourth Strike*
*Murder Unveiled*
*Haunted River*
*Of Breath and Blood*
*Lost Souls*

*Of Body and Bone*
*Lost Dreams*
*Of Mind and Madness*
*Lost Chances*
*Of Power and Pain*
*Lost Hope*
*Of Love and Loss*
*Lost Lives*
*Dominion*
*Lost Time*
*Illusions*
*Lost Love*
*Vendetta*
*Black Bird*

# Acknowledgements

As USUAL, THERE ARE many to thank for helping me with this journey. To my family and friends, and there are many of you - your love and support makes all the difference. There are no books without you. You keep me going when I'm tired, you celebrate with me in my successes, and you cheer me on when I doubt myself. None of this is possible without you. I can't wait to see what happens next and to enjoy it with all of you.

To my editor and cover designer, Amie McCracken – your work ethic puts mine to shame. Thank you for helping me make this book beautiful.

And to those who've crossed over but still stand beside me. Thank you for all your whispers of encouragement. I hear you and I thank you.

# Enjoy an excerpt of book three in The Fletcher Family Saga, Spark

EVE FLETCHER WALKED INTO Benny's Juke Joint. The usually crowded bar was quiet, and the stage from which she sang her ballads was dark. The crimson curtains were pulled back in their usual place. Benny never closed them. The smell of stale cigarettes still hung in the air. It seemed to have permeated the walls after years of puffing patrons had come and gone. The chairs hung upside down on tables and the floor was clean, but Eve pictured the spilled drinks, dirty napkins and cigarette stubs that would litter the ground a mere three hours from now. The bar and lounge would be humming with customers, and she would be thirty minutes into her first set. The crowd would be boisterous, but respectful. The rowdy ones wouldn't come out until her second set, after the haze of several rounds of drinks and whatever fashionable drug people were trying these days settled in. By the second set, inhibitions were lost, and Benny posted bouncers at the sides of the stage to keep the loons at bay. Crazy as it was, it was that set that Eve enjoyed the most. There was something about the energy of the crowd during that time that gave her a thrill. Or it was the element of risk. She always sang better then, too.

She headed backstage toward her dressing room. The hall was quiet. She'd agreed to come early to practice. Although she knew the songs well, her most recent piano man, Richie, had asked for the time. They worked well together but there were still some areas that needed polishing. She glanced at her watch. Richie would be there in fifteen minutes.

Walking down the hall, she flipped a switch and illuminated the small corridor. A drawer slammed nearby and she jumped. She walked across the hall to Benny's office. "Benny?" she asked, heading toward the door. "Is that you?"

Eve pushed the door open to reveal a small, cramped work area. One window with partially opened blinds allowed enough light for her to see the wooden desk piled with folders, books and papers. A laptop sat precariously on top of the mound. The room had a small window, dark paneled walls and the only picture displayed was a black and white photo of a young man and woman. The woman wore a wedding dress and held a small bouquet. The man wore a tux and had his arm around her.

Benny sat in the desk chair. His thinning gray hair, narrow frame, striped pants and orange shirt gave him the appearance of a retiree on a golf course in Florida. "Spark?" he asked when she walked in. He pushed his glasses up on his nose. "What are you doing here so early?"

"Hey, Benny," said Eve, walking into the small space. "I'm practicing with Richie. I could ask you the same question. Why are you here?" She looked over his clothes. "Shouldn't you be playing golf?"

"Aaah, I hate that game." He opened another drawer and closed it again. "I had business crap to deal with." He eyed her outfit. "You look beautiful, as usual."

Eve glanced down at her slim jeans, red low cut blouse and red heels. "This?" she asked. "I just threw this on."

"Babe, you could wear a pillow case and look good." He glanced at the picture on the wall. "You remind me of my Maggie." He made a sign of the cross. "God bless her."

Eve looked at the framed photo. "She was more beautiful than me."

Benny smiled. "Not by much."

Eve eyed his desk. "When are you going to clean this so called desk of yours?"

"This?" He waved a hand. "I know exactly where everything is. If I cleaned it, I'd be lost." He dug through some papers and pulled out a folder.

"You okay?" she asked.

Benny stopped rifling. "Sure, babe. Why wouldn't I be?"

A blur of orange jumped out from behind the desk and Eve startled. "Jeez," she said, holding her hand to her chest. Benny's cat sauntered to the worn brown couch that sat against the wall. "Louie, you scared me."

Louie made himself comfortable on the sofa and Eve walked up to pet him. Holding her hand on the animal's head, she stilled for a moment, then she turned and faced Benny. "What's going on?"

Benny looked at her as of she'd asked him why he was wearing shoes. "Wrong?" He placed the folder on his cluttered desk. "Nothing's wrong."

"Something's going on."

Benny narrowed his eyes. "You and that spidey sense of yours. It never ceases to amaze me."

"I've known you a long time Benny. I can tell when you're stressed."

"You've known me three years. But my own kid doesn't get me like you do. How is that possible?"

"Vince is an idiot."

Benny chuckled. "So why'd you date him?"

She shrugged. "I had a less discriminating filter at the time."

"Not anymore you don't."

"Things change."

He raised a brow. "What about your latest? Jerry is it?"

She tilted her head. "Yes."

"He's an idiot."

"You're changing the subject."

"You're the one that brought up idiots."

Eve scratched Louie's ears. "He's not an idiot. He owns Barwells."

"A retail store?" Benny waved a hand. "Big deal. He's a suit. He's worse than an idiot. He's boring. You don't belong with a suit."

Eve sighed. This was not the first time they'd had this conversation. "Who do I belong with then?"

Benny hesitated, and Eve waited. "Somebody who makes you laugh."

"I laugh."

"Not near enough. And not with him."

Eve stopped petting Louie. "How did we go from talking about you to my love life?"

"Because I'm boring too. Don't worry about me kid. Just take care of yourself. You understand? If something happens to me, stay out of it."

Eve stiffened. "What would happen to you?"

"Nothing. Forget I said anything."

"No. What is it? What's wrong?"

Benny sighed and tapped on his desk. "I've owned this place for years. Problems are second nature to me. I've dealt with robbers, liars and thieves my whole life. And I've always managed to survive. This is no different."

Eve crossed her arms and studied him. She had her suspicions, but she'd never voiced them. "Does this have to do with the mob?"

Benny winced. He pushed up from his seat and walked around the desk. "Listen, Spark. You and I are close. You're my best singer and you draw the biggest crowds." He reached out and took her hand. "I love you like my own. You're a daughter to me. You know that?"

Eve squeezed his fingers. "I know that. You're like a father to me."

He nodded. "Despite that, if there's one thing I need you to do, it's to stay out of this part of my life."

"Benny—"

He held up a finger. "Don't argue with me. Don't mention that word again. You know nothing. You see nothing. And don't you ever get mixed up with my boy Vinny again. You got that?"

His anger surprised her. She'd never seen him like this. "What's Vinny got to do with the mob?"

Benny shook his head. "Stay out of it. It's not your business."

"But—"

Benny waved his hand. "End of discussion." He walked back to his desk. "Don't you have to meet with Richie?"

His tone told her everything. "I don't want anything to happen to you."

He sat. "Nothing's going to happen to me." He rubbed his eyes. "I think you're just picking up on my fatigue. That's all it is."

She knew it was more. "Sure." She fiddled with the edge of his desk.

"You like Richie?" he asked.

"What?"

"The new guy. The piano man. He working out?"

She tried to focus. "I like him. We just need to get our timing down."

"He likes you, too. He's got that puppy dog look in his eyes."

She rolled her eyes. "He's got a girlfriend."

"So what? You have that effect. That sparkle. Men can't take their eyes off of you."

"You're exaggerating."

"What about that new guy? The bartender. Adam, is it? I see him watching you."

"Adam?"

"Yes. Good looking guy. Been here what? Two months now?"

"I know who he is."

"Well?"

"Well, what?"

"You like him?"

"I'm seeing Jerry."

Benny laughed. "Babe, that's never stopped you before."

She almost argued with him, but realized it was pointless. "He's cute, but he barely speaks to me."

"The kid's tongue-tied around you. I've seen him with the patrons, though. He's good with the customers. They like him."

She picked up a paper from Benny's desk. "Good for him."

Benny took the paper out of her hand. "You should talk to him. Make an effort. Help him open up. Be approachable. Besides, if you two got together, you'd be Adam and Eve. Sounds destined to me."

She cocked her head. "What are you doing? Matchmaking?"

He smiled. "You forget. I know you, Spark. You need someone who brightens the stage, not dims the lights."

"And you think Adam is the man for me? You barely know him."

He leaned forward on his seat. "You're not the only one with a good sense of people."

She couldn't deny that. She glanced at the clock on the wall. "I should go. Richie will be waiting."

"Knock 'em dead tonight, kid."

"I always do." She turned to walk away.

"Hey."

Reaching the threshold, she looked back. "What?"

"Thanks for checking in on me. I appreciate it."

She nodded. "You're welcome."

He paused. "You're my sparkler, kid. Have been since I've known you." She smiled. "And one day I want you to meet your own sparkler. Someone who lights you up." He glanced at the wall. "Like me and my Maggie."

A lump welled in her throat. "I love you, Benny."

He winked at her. "I love you too, kid." He sat back in his seat and grabbed the folder. Eve saw and felt his gruffness return. "So go teach Richie who's boss."

She laughed softly. "I will."

www.ingramcontent.com/pod-product-compliance
Lightning Source LLC
Chambersburg PA
CBHW021433240626
47153CB00001B/140